Lord
of Swords

ANN LAWRENCE

Lord of Swords

Published by Ann Lawrence
http://www.annlawrence.com

Cover Art by Croco Designs
Interior Formatting by Author E.M.S.

ISBN: 098983851X
ISBN-13: 978-0-9898385-1-1

Printed in the United States of America

DEDICATION

In memory of my sister Helen who loved to read.

ACKNOWLEDGMENTS

No one writes in isolation. All authors have their elves behind the scenes who encourage and help them get the book off to the publisher. So, thank you to Nan Jacobs, Lena Pinto, Sally Stotter, and Terri Brisbin. I must say I would still be *talking* about this book if they hadn't kicked my butt. I also want to thank the many readers who keep in touch with me. You're the reason I write. My husband always deserves a thank you for being there to pick up the slack . . . and there's always a ton of slack when I'm writing!

In the spring of 1143, England enjoys a moment of peace as a civil war rages between King Stephen and his cousin, the Empress Maude, who vie for the English throne. Their war has torn apart not only the country, but also families.

ONE

Joia drew her mare to a halt and looked across the moonlit moor at the great stones. They stood in a circle like old women sharing secrets around a fire.

She wanted to know their secrets.

In the sky, a full moon blazed, eclipsing the stars. Ahead of her lay the moor and the stones—mystery and magic. Behind her, the forest was dark, only the roadbed visible like a pale finger pointing toward the castle. She tethered her mare behind a tangled deadfall and finished her journey to the stones on foot. It would soon be midnight.

She crossed a small ditch and climbed a low embankment to where the stones stood in silent splendor. Only the wind and the whisper of her hem on the grass disturbed the night.

Before she entered the circle, she ran her hand over the lichen-covered surface of the tallest stone that stood her height and half again as much. Did druids still come here to practice their ancient rites? As she looked to the moon, she wondered if she might finally discover the answer.

She took a deep breath and stepped into the circle. Here within the embrace of the stones, silence lay thick enough to touch. She turned from the unnatural quiet of the circle and walked the perimeter of standing stones, ones she called the Sentinels for they seemed to watch over the moor.

Movement at the edge of her line of vision made her turn. A touch of annoyance flicked like a whip. Her maid, Edith, was

1

climbing the embankment. Edith ran to Joia, her skirts held high at her knees, her blonde braids bouncing on her shoulders.

"My lady, are you mad?" Edith asked. "What are you doing here?"

"What are *you* doing here?" Joia continued her journey about the henge.

"Did you think I would let you come to such a place alone?"

Joia bit her tongue on the wish Edith had done just that and walked on. "Where is your horse?" she asked.

"She's with your mount, my lady." Edith dogged her steps about the circle. "Your father will have our heads."

"Lower your voice, Edith."

Edith wrung her hands. "Can we not return to the hall? It will soon be too dark to see our way home," she continued in a whisper. "Your father's in such a temper. He's searching everywhere for you."

"Come, Edith, you exaggerate. *If* my father notices I'm gone, he'll not forfeit a night in his mistress's bed to hunt me down." Joia swept her hands out to encompass the stones and the open moor. "Have you not noticed the moon? Druids worship on a night such as this."

Edith glanced about. She shivered. "This is what you want here? Druids?"

"Aye, Edith, just druids." Joia turned her back on her maid.

"Come, my lady, we must go."

"And I must have this moment." Eight years ago she'd left Stonewold as a bride. Six months ago she'd returned a widow. It was the first time since her return that the moon and the weather had cooperated in such complete harmony.

"My lady—"

"If you cannot be silent, get back to the keep or wait with the horses, for I have no need of one who won't obey." Joia ignored Edith's muttered curses. It was as close to silence as one could expect from the girl.

Joia returned to her contemplation of the stones. Did those who still harbored superstitions of the old gods make sacrifices here? Her throat dried. Her pulse fluttered.

Was it anticipation or fear?

Across the circle, aligned with a gap in the stones that could only mark an entrance, lay a wide stone on its side. The ancient stone could not have fallen to its present position, and she imagined it placed just so as an altar. She also imagined a maiden stretched across its flat expanse, her breast bared to the moon, a blade descending . . .

Edith touched Joia's shoulder. She swallowed a scream as she was jerked from her imaginings.

"My lady." Edith pointed.

Joia looked across the moor that lay like a stretch of silver cloth cast over a bed. It appeared deserted, but then Joia saw what Edith had.

A man walked across the heath. Joia's excitement returned in a rush. A druid? Or the spirit of one long past? She remembered the tales her mother oft told of King Arthur and his men who many said had used this circle. Did the great king's spirit walk at midnight?

The man's long shadow followed him as he strode toward the stone circle. Surely druids walked slowly, heads bent in reverent prayer. She imagined they did not carry heavy packs on their backs either. She sighed. Naught but a simple traveler.

"A giant," Edith said by Joia's ear.

As the stranger approached the entrance stones, Joia drew Edith behind one of the Sentinels.

The man did as Joia had, stood and contemplated the empty circle for several long moments. He couldn't see them where they crouched in the inky shadows, but still, Joia found herself holding her breath. He crossed the surrounding ditch and bank and walked to the altar. He dropped his pack on the ground and removed his mantle, draping it over the stone.

Midnight was upon them. He will ruin everything, Joia thought. No druidical band would practice their rites with this man desecrating their place.

The man pulled off his tunic. And his shirt. Beside her, Edith hissed in a breath and dug her sharp elbow into Joia's side. Joia could only stare as the man methodically stripped to his braies.

"King of the faeries, my lady," Edith whispered.

He cannot be both a giant *and* the king of the faeries, Joia wanted to say. Instead, she signaled her maid to remain where she was. Joia flitted to the next stone. Her new vantage point allowed her an unimpeded view of the stranger. Even surrounded by the huge stones, Joia could see he was much taller than her husband—may he rest in peace—and might rival the castle smith for breadth of shoulder. The moonlight silvered the stranger's body and cast shadows, delineating the muscles of his chest and arms.

A flush heated Joia's face. Indeed a king, she thought when he turned his head to look at the moon. Her heart thudded. He might be one of the emperors depicted on a Roman coin, or perhaps this was Arthur come back to life.

What brought this man here and why now? He *would* ruin everything. She scanned the hills for approaching druids, but the rolling heathland lay stark and empty.

The man undid his pack, revealing a row of weapons. Moonlight gleamed on the steel of his blades. He took up a sword, then another.

He walked to the center of the stone circle and extended his arms out to the side. He bent his head. It was a reverent pose. Was he part of a religious ceremony? Was he here to make a sacrifice? Where was his victim?

Then he moved.

Yet, moved was too humble a word for what he did. He turned and twisted, swept his blades through the night air. Slowly. In unsettling silence. No wind hissed on his blades, no sound whispered from the dry grass beneath his feet.

Was he real?

She squeezed her eyes closed and then opened them again. He was still there.

The steel of the man's blades flashed as he performed his midnight dance. His body was as honed as his weapons. As sweat slicked his skin, his braies clung to the long lines of his flanks.

Joia melted into the stone, entranced. Heat twisted through her insides with each turn of his blades. She had seen her father's and her husband's men practice in much this same way and yet, here, bathed in moonlight, without a partner to parry his moves, his swords an extension of his arms, she felt she witnessed magic.

The man fell still. Joia let out a long breath. He returned to the altar stone and exchanged one long sword for a short one, and began his sword dance again. He smote invisible foes from left and right. He moved with fluid grace, and Joia felt a strange sensation burn low in her belly.

Edith sighed.

The man froze.

Joia dropped to her knees in the shadows. The man stood as still as one of the stones for an interminable time, then shrugged, and returned to his array of weapons. Joia darted back to Edith. Silently, she pointed at Edith and then in the direction of their horses. Edith shook her head and turned away with an expression Joia knew well. She tapped Edith's arm and jabbed her finger with more vehemence toward the horses. Edith's mouth opened in a wide O.

Suddenly, Joia was snatched off her feet. Edith screamed. Joia couldn't scream, her breath trapped in her chest by the arm about her middle. The man dragged her across the circle toward the altar.

She struggled, scraping at his hand and forearm with her nails, but his grip was a band of iron. He shoved her against the altar stone and held her in place with the one hand. The other held his sword.

"Who are you?" he asked, his voice as hard as the body pressed against her.

Edith leapt on the man's back. He shook her off like a horse does an annoying fly.

He turned his sword in Edith's direction. She dropped to her knees. "Nay, I beg you, don't harm my lady."

The man gave a short laugh. Joia jerked her knee up,

contacting his hip, just missing her target. He grunted but didn't relinquish his grip.

"I have a mind to slay you both—" He broke off and Joia heard what he had.

Horses.

The man pulled Joia in front of his body. He did it so quickly, she had no opportunity to escape his grasp.

"You coward, using me as a shield," she managed to gasp out. She clawed his hands.

He bent his head. His breath was warm against her cheek as he said, "You are far too scrawny to offer much protection . . . but any is better than none."

The air filled with the sound of horses but here, within the henge, the hoofbeats were muffled—unearthly—the sound of spirit horses, though the horses that swept into the circle of stones, as invaders flooding through castle gates, were all too real.

Joia cringed when her father drew his horse to a halt. Although shadowed by a Sentinel, she could see the anger on his face. Even his wind-blown hair, streaked with gray, looked angry. His men ranged themselves behind him.

A look of contempt replaced the anger on his face. "You shame me, daughter," her father said in a cold voice.

Edith whimpered. Joia struggled for release. To her surprise, the man gave it instantly. She collected her dignity, tugged her skirt straight, and faced her father. "There is a full moon—"

"So, you have a lover," her father interrupted.

The man stepped to her side. Moonlight flashed off his sword. Suddenly, Joia felt the man was less a threat and more a source of protection.

"He is not my lover," she said simply.

"Then what do you here? You shamed me before everyone when you left the hall, and where do I find you? Here, behaving like a common light-skirt." His last words were shouted.

"The moon is full. I thought druids might come." Her words trailed off at a derisive snort from her father.

"Lies." His gaze shifted to the man who stood at her side, his sword still held at the ready. Sweat prickled across Joia's skin. The man *was* half naked, *had* been holding her. His black hair was wild from his exertions, his expression as harsh and cold as her father's.

Her father turned to his men. "Kill him."

Three men leapt from their horses and drew their swords.

"Papa! Stop! I do *not* know this man." She might have spoken to the moon.

The man thrust her into Edith's embrace. Bile rose in Joia's throat as her father's men stalked forward. The man stood by the altar, alone, soon to be sacrificed. Then, with blinding speed, he snatched up another sword and attacked.

It was over in a heartbeat.

The three men lay on the ground, bleeding, one senseless. The strange silence in the stone circle thickened. The air felt as heavy as if a pair of hands had been clapped over her ears.

Joia shook Edith off and ran to one of the injured guards. He whimpered as she pressed a hand to his bleeding arm, and she thanked God he was not dead. She used the man's dagger to cut a wide strip from her hem.

"You fools. Kill him," her father cried.

Edith shrieked. The rest of the guards—seven in all, climbed from their horses. They were not so quick to close on the stranger. Instead, they circled him. The man moved with them, his swords gleaming.

Joia crouched over the wounded man, bound his bloody arm, then crawled to the next guard. He, too, was bleeding from his sword arm.

She could not prevent a cry as the men met in a clash of weapons. She forced herself to remain in place as another guard fell inches from her. The swordsman smashed the hilt of his sword to a man's brow, and he dropped like a stone.

"Stop this," she cried to her father. "I beg of you, stop it."

Her father ignored her. Steel rang on steel. She leapt up, ran to her father, and clutched at the hem of his mantle. "Stop this now!" Each clash of metal was a jolt to her body.

Men might die for her foolish whim to come to this holy place.

Her father swore. He jerked his mantle from her hand. "Enough," he bellowed.

Immediately, the fighting ceased. The stranger stood in the center of the circle. Two of her father's men held him at bay. Or was it he who held them at bay? The other guards were scattered, clutching wounds, crawling or stumbling toward their horses now her father had called a halt. She felt as if she were an hourglass and all her strength had drained away.

Her father dismounted. There was a tang of blood in the air she could almost taste on her lips. With shaky legs, she went to one of the wounded, cut more strips from her hem and ordered a guard who cravenly scurried toward the horses to apply pressure to the man's leg wound.

"I have never seen such work. Who are you?" her father, hands on hips, demanded of the stranger.

"Guy of Chelten," the man said. His gaze flicked from the guards to her father.

Her father spat on the ground. "Chelten, that turncoat. One day he's for King Stephen, the next for Empress Maude. Our king should cut off his balls. I routed Chelten and Maude's bastard brother, Gloucester, but eight weeks ago on the banks of the Tavest." Her father swept out his arm in the general direction of the river. "You are bold to come this way. I hang spies."

"I'm seeking service with one of the king's *faithful* barons now Chelten is renegade, nothing more."

Her father examined the man from head to toe. "And how come you to be naked with my daughter?"

"Papa—"

The man turned to her. A jolt ran through her where she knelt. He made no move toward her, but still she felt transfixed by his gaze, by eyes pale as river agates in the moonlight. It was an order, that look. She fell silent.

He turned back to her father. "I've been walking for most of the day and simply felt a need to test my strength with the swords before I bedded down over there." He pointed to the altar. "I thought myself alone. It seems your daughter was hiding and *watching*."

The man spat the last word as if it were a crime worthy of hanging.

A flush of embarrassment brought heat to her face. "Papa, let me explain."

"Silence." Her father's voice cracked like a whip. "I'll hear no more from you." He surveyed his men. "I've never seen such utter ineptitude. Cannot ten men take one?"

The midnight swordsman shrugged. The motion rippled along his arms and chest. "Not when I am the one."

"Why did you not kill them?"

"The king needs fighting men, not dead ones."

Her father nodded, then stalked to where she knelt and gripped her arm and hauled her to her feet. "Let Edith see to these fools whilst you explain yourself."

The swordsman lifted a brow. He seemed as interested in her answer as her father.

"I was simply examining this . . . place."

"Again, I ask you, were you running to this man?" Her father shook her.

The swordsman answered for her. "I know this woman not. She invades my privacy. She's an unseemly wench."

Joia gasped at the frost in his tone. One of her father's men snickered.

Her father turned to the guards. "Take her."

Guy de Maci wiped his blades, then drew on his clothing, aware of each man, adjusting his own position as they shifted and moved around him. He was especially aware of their lord who stood with arms crossed on his chest, anger flowing off him like water over rocks.

"Where is your horse?" the lord asked.

"I have none," he said with barely concealed impatience. Had he not just said he'd been walking all day?

"You could not have walked here from Chelten."

Guy shrugged. "I made most of my journey in a cart with a company of merchants." It wasn't quite a lie. He had ridden most of the way in a cart, but from Winchester not Chelten, but this man didn't need to know that.

The lord slapped a hand down on Guy's weapons. "Again, I ask who has your loyalty?"

"The king, of course." Guy dislodged the man's hand by lifting his roll of weapons. "But as I said, I hope for a position on the morrow with one of the king's *loyal* barons."

The man set a foot on Guy's pack. "The lord of Stonewold Castle has no need of more warriors."

Guy looked at the wounded men. "Indeed?" He'd done his best to disable them, not kill them, but only two would be of use in the next few weeks.

"I have men enough to replace them."

This was Walter Fortranne, lord of Stonewold Manor, the very man Guy sought, but if this lord had no need of men, Guy's plans were ruined. "Then I will seek a position elsewhere."

"Nay." Walter reached out and placed a hand on his arm. Three jeweled rings graced the man's fingers, fat as sausages. "I have need of one such as you. Name your price."

"For doing what?" Guy asked, but continued to pack his weapons.

"I need a personal guard. One who can be counted on to do what you have just done here."

"Fend off a few men? Ill-trained ones at that?" Guy put a sneer in his tone.

"Aye. Just that. I need a personal guard for my child."

Guy looked across the stone circle in the direction the woman had been taken and felt a punch of desire. *Jesu.* The thought of having charge of such a woman sent the heat directly to his manhood.

He quickly sought something to say that would not result in a mace to his head. "It would serve you better to hire someone to teach her manners."

Walter threw back his head and laughed. "Oh, aye, she needs a good lesson, I grant you, but 'tis not Joia who needs guarding. 'Tis my son, Crispin."

Joia.

Relief mingled with disappointment that it was not the woman who needed guarding. Yet, was this not just what he needed? Serving as a guard to this lord's son would give him entrée to Stonewold Castle, as well as to every corner of its environs. It had been one of Guy's worries—how to breach the fortress that was Stonewold. Guy bowed to the lord of Stonewold Castle. "I would be honored to guard your son."

"You'll not find guarding my son as easy as taking down my men."

Guy heard the annoyance behind the lord's words. "Is he as troublesome as his sister?" Guy kept his tone light.

"Nay. 'Tis just—" Walter broke off until his men were out of earshot. "There have been a few accidents. Young boys are always having accidents, but my steward . . . he thinks it might be more. As does my wife."

Guy watched the man shake off his thoughts.

"Just see my son safe." Lord Walter stepped onto the hands of a waiting guard and mounted his horse. "And train him to do what you do." He nodded to the wounded, and then turned his horse and called back over his shoulder. "I'll send a cart for these fools. Ride with them."

Guy waited patiently for the cart to arrive, the wounded to be loaded, their horses tethered, and for the party to move off. The men made no effort to make room for him in the cart or offer him a mount, but it suited him to be left alone at last.

He stood in the stone circle and looked at the bright moon now sinking into the treetops. As he stared at the moon, he mused on the woman who'd hidden here and watched him. All the sensations that had assailed him when he'd snatched her into his arms flooded back. Anger followed by amusement. *And then that inconvenient desire.*

"What ails me?" he asked of the silent stones.

He shook off his thoughts. If he didn't hurry, he'd lose the light. He took a dagger and cut the turf at the base of the large flat stone that lay on its side. After scooping out sufficient dirt, he opened his leather pack and drew out his grandfather's sword. It was finely made and adorned with a sapphire in the hilt. With regret he rolled it up in its oiled leather wrap and buried it, for it was not the weapon of a lowly man-at-arms. He scattered the excess dirt, fitted the turf in place, examined his work, and tamped down the grassy squares with his boot.

He took one final look at the ancient circle. Why had Lady Joia come to this place alone with only her maid? He didn't believe in Lady Joia's druids any more than her father did.

Guy shouldered his pack and began the long walk for Stonewold Castle. He passed a gibbet and inspected the bodies. Were these spies of the Empress Maude's? Despite their rotting flesh, Guy could tell one thing about them, they were not his son, Alan. It was for his son that Guy had come to Stonewold.

Finally, the towers of the massive square keep came into view. Guy found his mind not on his personal mission there, but instead on the woman. He saw her in his mind's eye as she'd appeared, confronting him, her hair loose down her back, a spill of liquid moonlight. A beauty.

Her gown, chopped short in the front from her efforts on behalf of the wounded, had swirled about her slender calves and ankles as she'd been dragged away, squirming in a soldier's arms. They'd been muddy legs, though very fine ones indeed. Guy frowned. She was as unruly as her hair, running about in a stone circle at midnight.

There was nothing worse than an undisciplined woman.

TWO

Two soldiers pushed Joia through the crowded hall of gaping men and women and toward the great hearth. Despite the dozens of people in the hall, only one man sat at the high table.

Martin Hursley, one of her father's three knights, was tall, fair, and comely, four years older than she at a score and ten. Martin, who'd recently acquired the neighboring manor upon his father's death, and who could never let an opportunity for touching her pass, rose as she approached. Without so much as a bow in her direction, he stalked off, his men tripping over their feet to keep up with him.

The hall was still arranged for eating. Joia assumed her foray to the stone circle and her father's pursuit had kept these folk in their places. At this hour after midnight, the tables should be dismantled and those who slept in the hall should be snoring on their pallets. She felt a pang of remorse that these people had been kept from their beds by her caprice.

Her mother huddled in a corner with her advisor, Father Ilbert, whilst her women sat in a stern row before the hearth, eyes downcast, although one woman, Avis, had a small smile hovering on her lips. Joia's spirits wilted at the sight of that smile. It boded ill.

Joia stood facing the hearth, hands clasped before her for what felt like hours. She saw the physician rushing off and assumed he went to tend the wounded. Still, she waited.

Only the rustle of clothing and the occasional murmur or whisper told her the hall behind her remained as crowded as if 'twere noon. A crash of the hall door heralded her father's entrance. He came and stood before her, his face flushed with anger, but his voice was low, extending no farther than where she stood.

"Pleased I am that Martin's gone. I'd not want him further shamed."

"Martin?" *What had Martin to do with her?* But her father raised a hand for silence before she said more.

"Henceforth, you'll be confined to a chamber in the south tower. I have ordered your belongings carried there." He turned to her mother. "Lady Blanche." But the priest scurried forward instead of her mother.

"Beg his mercy, child," Father Ilbert said softly, but her father's next words showed he'd heard the priest's whispered suggestion.

"The only mercy here will be for your maid," her father said. "I shall not punish the girl if 'tis true she was only trying to persuade you back to the keep."

Joia nodded, then started back when her father held out his hand. The wide belt he used to punish recalcitrant servants uncoiled from his fist. She understood her banishment to the tower room, had been sent there often as a girl, and had expected to be consigned there for several days before being forgiven, but this, the belt, this she did not understand.

"You have torn my patience, shamed me, daughter," her father said, this time in a deep, carrying voice.

"I don't understand how a ride to the stone circle warrants a whipping." She nodded to the belt in his hand. Sweat broke on her skin. She forced herself to stand still.

"You do not? Are you really so stupid? I planned to announce your betrothal to Martin tonight."

Joia gasped.

"Aye, but *you* were not here to share in the joyous occasion, were you?" Her father's voice rose, and a vein throbbed at his temple.

Joia pressed her hands to her stomach to still the nausea there. She pitched her voice to a whisper. "I will *not* wed Martin

Hursley. I've refused him three times, and he agreed not to ask me again."

"Oh, you'll marry Martin, daughter. This time he asked *me*, and I have given my consent. You'll do as bid, and let this be a sample of what you'll have in return if you don't."

He snapped his fingers, and Father Ilbert put a hand on her shoulder, but not to comfort. Joia's mind was in turmoil. She wanted to run but instead dropped to her knees. *Betrothed to Martin*. The very thought made the bile rise in her throat.

Joia shook off the priest's hand when he made to shift her hair off her shoulders. She set her jaw and squeezed her eyes shut. As a child, she'd had but to beg and grovel to stay her father's hand. She was not a child. She remained silent.

Guy curled his fingers into fists and watched the lord of Stonewold Castle whip his daughter. Every crack of the belt seemed to echo through the hall. Guy had never understood how whipping a servant—or a wayward daughter—resulted in obedience. If it had been him, he'd be plotting with deep resentment against Lord Walter with every stroke.

"Why did he not lock her up and feed her bread and water for a week?" Guy took a step forward, but Owen, Walter's steward and Guy's escort, put a hand on his arm.

"Don't think to interfere. Most believe she deserves all that and more. She shamed us all when she ran off tonight."

"He lays it on too heavy." Guy clenched his fist on the hilt of his dagger.

Owen, his balding head spotted with age, shrugged. "Don't question our lord's decisions, and if you interfere, you will join her."

Guy heard sympathy for the young woman in the old man's voice that belied his hard words.

"Be still," Owen continued. "See. 'Tis done."

The steward was right. The baron dropped his hand and barked an order. The women from the dais hurried forward to help Joia to her feet, but she jerked away from them, and although Guy could see her steps were unsteady, she held her head high as she walked to the south tower of the keep. She disappeared into the deep arch of the steps.

The hall stirred. Men and women rose, gabbling about the matter, heads together. Servants rushed to dismantle tables and push benches aside.

Guy shifted his shoulders, tense with displeasure. Two of Walter's soldiers passed close by as the many who slept in places other than the great hall made their way to their beds. Guy caught their words as they passed.

"I'd have enjoyed the spectacle more if Hursley had stayed and wielded the belt," said one. "He'd have stripped her."

His companion grinned. "Aye, but I wager he'll be back ere the fortnight is out. She's a tasty morsel."

Guy looked at his escort. "Is he right? Will this Hursley be back for her?"

"'Tis said Sir Martin much covets our Joia, but I warn you, don't be drawn into any wagers on her. If the baron hears such a thing you could lose your position."

Guy frowned over the events of the evening: the skirmish in the stone circle, the beauty on her knees being whipped. Who was this suitor she'd run from? At least he now knew why she'd been in the circle. He'd likely interrupted her flight and for that she would not thank him.

He kept his hand on his dagger hilt as he followed Owen's path to the fore of the hall where the baron paced. "Would the morrow not be a better time to meet Lord Walter's son?" Guy asked.

His escort shrugged. They reached the dais and bowed to the baron. "My lord. You wished to see this man?"

Walter cast his belt aside. It fell with a dull thud on the wooden floor near Guy's boots. The baron bellowed as if to call someone from the neighboring village. "Crispin!"

From a smoky corner of the hall came a small boy of about eight or nine. He stalked forward, a miniature of his father, too wide at the waist, his chin in the air. Guy saw little of the sister in the boy's round face.

Walter set his hand on his son's fair, curly hair. "This is Guy, my boy." Walter shoved his son forward.

The boy ignored Guy, yawned, and rubbed his eyes. His tunic was spotted with food.

"My heir, Edmund, was killed at the Battle of Tavest. Now, Crispin will have Stonewold. You serve me best, Guy, if you keep my son safe."

"I will do my best, my lord." Guy bowed.

"Owen, add Guy to the rolls."

With those few words, the baron dismissed Guy and the boy, disappearing through a door behind a tapestry flanking the hearth, where Guy assumed lay the lord's bedchamber, the warmest place in the keep. As the boy yawned, Owen explained that Guy was to sleep in the hall and take his meals when the boy did.

A woman Owen indicated was Lord Walter's wife approached. Guy saw some of the daughter in the woman's face, but her languid manner indicated she had none of the spirit of her daughter. Although Owen introduced Guy to Lady Blanche, she did not acknowledge him, but took the child away with but a nod to Owen.

"Do not let the lad order you about." Owen hesitated and bit his lip. "My lord may not think as I do on one point; our Crispin may be in very real danger."

"Lord Walter mentioned accidents," Guy said.

"Ah, mayhap he is coming to see things my way. Aye a few accidents. Since the Battle of Tavest, since our Edmund died." The old man pursed his lips, glanced about, and lowered his voice. "Crispin ofttimes sleeps in the woman's solar with Lady Blanche. It were there one of the accidents happened . . . or close by there. He fell down the steps. Now boys fall down, but he swore someone pushed him. Most think 'tis all nonsense, but . . .

well . . . ." The old man spread his hands. "He has also twice sickened who is never sick."

Guy had no answer. His own sons were oft covered in bruises from falls and fights amongst themselves. He imagined they had likely eaten much they should not as well. But he kept silent as he knew not this place and the people in it and who might wish the child ill.

"It may just be fancy, but keep it in mind as we are all fond of the boy. As we were of Edmund." He cleared his throat. "Now, as to weapons practice—once a day, Guy, but when the lad chooses."

Guy acknowledged the man's orders with only a curt nod. It mattered not what duties Owen assigned as Guy did not intend to linger at Stonewold one moment longer than needed.

A few days. Mayhap a sennight at most. Only as long as it took to find his own son, Alan, who had disappeared during the same battle in which Lord Walter had lost his heir.

Disappeared.

Alan may be only ten and five, a squire of little account in the tally of the value of men, but still he had weapons and a horse. Very fine weapons, with their family motto, *A priori*, or *What Comes Before*, etched on each piece to remind Alan of their family's service to the English throne since William the Bastard.

But those words had not meant enough. The thought brought pain and disappointment in equal measure to Guy as he settled himself for sleep with the other men and women in the hall.

The Earl of Chelten had reasons enough to switch sides in this war over the English throne. Had King Stephen not ceded several of the earl's French manors to the Empress Maude in an appeasement effort? Guy understood the earl's rage. And when the earl had switched allegiance, most of his knights, squires, pages, and servants had gone as well, including Sir Edward de Mille, to whom Guy had fostered Alan that he might be trained as a knight.

Alan had followed Sir Edward whilst Guy's family had chosen to remain with the king. De Macis had borne arms for King

Stephen's family more than four generations ere the Earl of Chelten had claimed their service.

But Alan's choosing of Sir Edward, one of Chelten's closest cronies, over his family was something Guy couldn't understand. Guy shook off the thoughts he knew would not ease him into sleep. He'd learned long ago to leash his emotions and bide his time.

Guy found a place against the wall and wrapped his mantle about him. Tired as he was, still, he surveyed his surroundings. Stonewold's keep was little different from many others he had visited over the years with its four square towers facing to each point of the compass. It stood on a high promontory in an embracing bend of the Tavest River.

The hall soared two stories, galleried on the south and east sides. A fine tapestry, likely Flemish, flanked the hearth. Swords of ancestors decorated the walls—none so fine as the sword he'd buried.

The rushes were sour and needed replacing. He could almost taste their foulness. Or was it just his mood that was foul?

Sure he would never sleep in the few hours left before the sun rose, Guy rolled to his back and stared up at the soot-blackened beams overhead thinking of Lord Walter. His men had fought a bloody battle at Tavest against the Empress Maude's bastard brother, the Earl of Gloucester and his new friend, the Earl of Chelten. Walter may have routed the earls, but the victory must be a bitter one for Walter.

The Battle of Tavest was almost eight weeks past and the cold and miserable conditions that had likely killed its share of the wounded were now past as well, the air balmy, the land greening again with hope. Walter had used the time of truce after the battle to ransom the defeated forces back to the earls Gloucester and Chelten.

But no ransom demand had come for Alan. Instead, Guy received a short missive from Chelten, himself, saying Alan had disappeared and was not numbered among either the living or the dead. A boy, nay, a *man*, of Alan's size and stature didn't just disappear.

As Guy studied the blackened beams he admitted to himself that Alan was not far wrong if he feared disinheritance. When Guy had determined he must take this time of truce, the time of the Easter court, and go to Stonewold, Guy's father had said, 'Let that traitorous boy rot in hell, and if you go after him, rot there with him.'"

The words had been shouted at Guy as he'd prepared his weapons. To Guy's father, Chelten—and Alan—were traitors.

Guy rubbed his eyes. They were gritty with lack of sleep trying to reconcile his son's actions. But when he found Alan, Guy intended to make no recriminations. He would see his son freed. What Alan did after that was his choice.

Guy noticed two men who lay a few feet away were still gabbling about Lady Joia's punishment. They appeared to be servants. Guy cleared his throat and joined their conversation by asking, "Why did Lord Walter not put Lady Joia in the dungeon? Or are there still prisoners there?"

The closest, the older of the two men, shrugged. "Lord Walter might put 'er in the dungeon, but Sir Martin wouldna want 'er damaged. He's a fine young cock to service that hen." The men snickered.

Guy bit back a retort on their disrespect of their lady. "So . . . you still have prisoners in the dungeon?"

"Oh, aye. A few," the younger man said, scratching his greasy beard. "They's always some that's in the dungeon—thieves, cutthroats, and the like."

"But surely, not all the men from Tavest have been ransomed yet?"

The older man leaned near, his breath redolent of rotting teeth, and whispered, "Oh, they's dozens still 'ere. Lord Walter wanted to 'ang em all, 'e did, fer our Edmund's death. Burned 'im, they did. Seemed they might a skinned 'im first. Lord Walter almost went mad wiv grief."

The other man closed his eyes and yawned. "There were so many o' the Empress Maude's men, they were everwhere, but a few o' 'em Lord Walter kept special in the towers. Thought they might know who kilt our Edmund. I'd a skinned 'em, I would. And then burned 'em as well."

"Nay, the ones as could not pay are in the dungeons not the towers. He's starvin' 'em. Canna pay, canna eat. What a sum Lord Walter's taken. Wealthy 'e is now." The two men began to argue over how rich Lord Walter was.

Guy wished he could have simply stood before Lord Walter and demanded his son, one father to another, but rumors of treachery and spying twined through England like a snake in ivy, knotting loyalties and twisting others. Guy could not risk being accused as a spy for Chelten. But it chafed at Guy, this deception. He prided himself on his honor. It was his family's honor that held them to King Stephen rather than follow Chelten's whims.

Guy knew he must see these remaining men of Maude's whether in the towers or in the dungeons. Luckily, the many rituals of the Easter season would give Guy time to look about ere he was missed at court.

Then Guy froze. Was that a rat he heard scuttling through the rushes? He shivered and looked about for an empty bench that he might be off the floor. He hated rats. No empty benches beckoned, but he edged his pallet away from the wall and drew his mantle tightly about his body. He cursed rats. He cursed the Earl of Chelten. He cursed King Stephen and the Empress. He cursed whoever was moaning and coupling under a mantle but a few feet away.

Nay, he finally admitted to himself it was not rats nor the moaning that kept him awake. The words of the men chilled him. The flaying of a man was torture. Had Lord Edmund been tortured before he'd been killed? And had Walter tortured Maude's men in revenge?

Guy understood Lord Walter's need to punish those responsible for his son's death. He also understood Walter's grief for his heir, but Guy refused to grieve. His son must be alive. He'd feel it in his bones, would he not, if Alan were dead?

The men's words ran through Guy's mind like rats through the dungeons below. If Walter had tortured or starved Alan, Guy knew what he must do.

First, free his son. Then . . . vengeance.

THREE

Joia waited until after morning chapel before descending to confront her father. She paused before leaving the shelter of the tower steps to catch her breath as a hot pain pulsed her back.

Her father scowled when she approached his table, but did not protest when she sat at his side. His face was puffy from the few hours of sleep. Her mother's place was vacant, Joia was sure, as her mother hadn't the fortitude to withstand the storm Joia intended to foment in her father. Her mother might cower in the solar, but Joia would not.

"A word, Papa, if I may," she said when he'd finished tossing bones to his dogs. "I want to apologize for my behavior," Joia began. Her father's face softened and he smiled. "But had I known you planned to betroth me to Martin, I'd have fled to the Convent of St. Mary and sought sanctuary there. You'll have need to beat me a thousand times ere I'll wed Martin Hursley. Better you kill me than wed me to that beast."

Her father's face suffused a deep red. "You shame me with such a challenge."

"No one can hear me, Papa. 'Tis your choice to act upon my words if you will."

Some of the color subsided from his cheeks. He raised his tankard and drank deeply of his ale. He thumped the empty tankard on the table and a boy rushed forward to fill it.

"You don't understand who you are," her father said.

"Chattel for you to sell to whomever has the most to offer?" She couldn't keep the bitterness from her voice. Her back burned with a fiery pain, but she wouldn't allow him to see how he'd injured her. Nay, the pain in her back could not equal that in her heart.

Her father's fingers curled into a fist. She braced herself for a blow. When he relaxed his hand, his voice was weary. "You don't understand your place. Marriage is for land and power. Martin now has both. Would you have Crispin treated as Edmund was? Would you have the child taken, murdered, his body burned, desecrated? Crispin needs a strong alliance behind him when I'm gone. Martin will stand in Edmund's place and hold Stonewold for Crispin if you wed him."

Joia bowed her head and offered a prayer for Edmund. She had nightmares about his soul drifting somewhere, unshriven. "Edmund died in honorable battle."

"His body was burned like a heretic's. Never shall a son of mine be so humiliated again. 'Tis why I've hired yon man, and why you *will* wed Martin Hursley—if he'll still have you."

Joia looked across the hall. Beside Crispin sat the midnight swordsman. He was not as tall here, in the hall, as he had been in the stone circle, where his long shadow had made him a giant. Still, only Tom, the smith, might be taller, and hair she thought black during the night now proved streaked with shades of brown like skeins of silk tangled together. A deep line between the swordsman's dark brows gave him a look of displeasure even in repose.

Had he watched her punishment? Shame heated her cheeks. A small gasp of dismay escaped her lips.

"What did you say?" her father asked.

Joia shook her head. She clutched her hands together in prayer before speaking. "I don't understand why that man is here."

"That man appears to be a master of the sword, so I've secured his services to guard Crispin and teach him as I should have Edmund. I never exerted myself for Edmund, and I'll not make that mistake with Crispin. He shall know the way of every weapon as well as how many sacks of grain are in my storehouses. Edmund went into battle ill-prepared, and I can see that now, by God. But you know, as well as I do, another way to protect Crispin is to give him a strong brother-by-marriage to stand in Edmund's place until Crispin's a man. You *will* marry Martin."

"There must be some other man who could wed me——"

Her father's hand shot out and snatched her wrist, jerked her toward him. "I'm sure many will wed you, you're comely enough, but what will it get *me*? Had you not gone off adventuring we would have celebrated not only your betrothal, but also the lands the king has granted Martin for his valor at Tavest.

"Martin now has a fine property on the Solent, and your alliance with him will give me access to the sea. How many men can do as much for me? We suit each other well, Martin and I. And I thank God your useless husband died when he did. Now, Martin and I can use your quarry."

Joia forced herself to remain calm. "Robin pleased you well enough when you chose him. And my widow's portion is mine." But Joia knew her words were empty. The quarry was hers, and the income from it, but only as long as she remained unwed.

Her father dropped her hand. She rubbed her wrist.

"Nonsense. With Martin's land and your stone, I shall build a castle to rival Porchester in Portsmouth. Now, let's speak no more of husbands. Spend your time in the chapel, on your knees, praying naught happens to Crispin as it did to Edmund."

"Papa, please hear me. Martin will treat me as badly as he treated his wife."

"Isabel died of a chill. You have only to keep your place by the hearth, and you'll have nothing to fear."

Joia bit back a sharp retort at her father's callous dismissal of Martin's hapless wife.

"And to ensure you have not the resources to make a foray to St. Mary's Convent or elsewhere, your mother has given your coffers to Martin for safekeeping."

Joia stared at her father. Her jewelry. Her coins. How would she ever escape this wretched coil with naught of value to her name? "I'll not be sold into slavery to Martin Hursley."

"Get away," her father roared and jumped to his feet. His face went almost purple with anger.

The hall fell silent. A log dropped in the hearth in a burst of sparks and a billow of smoke. Joia rose shakily to her feet. She felt every eye like the touch of many hands. With slow steps she walked away from the table. She stumbled on the dais step, going down on one knee. The room shifted, spun, then righted itself. A man took her elbow, helped her to her feet. The midnight swordsman. A murmur rose, running the room like the tide over sand.

"Come, my lady," he said. He turned her toward the tower steps. Toward safety.

Every wound on her back felt wet and sticky. Her skin was fever hot. "I pray you would return to your seat. I need no assistance."

No man or woman moved. Their gazes were not on them, she saw, as she turned and faced her escort. Nay, everyone watched her father, waiting for the ax to fall on this man who dared take her arm.

The hall was suddenly icy cold.

"You cannot climb these steps." He slid his hand up to encircle her upper arm. His hand was so large, his fingertips met. A row of red furrows ran from the back of his hand up into his sleeve. She remembered placing them there. His face shimmered. A roar filled her ears.

Guy watched the color run from Joia's face. He spared a glance toward her father who flicked his hand out in a dismissive gesture and called for music. A thin boy, no more than ten and three, ran forward and sat near the baron's feet. The boy opened his mouth and sang, his voice as clear and beautiful as an angel in God's choir.

Joia sagged against Guy. He had no choice but to hoist her into his arms. She weighed as little as a half-empty sack of grain as he carried her up the steps. He told himself he didn't enjoy carrying disobedient daughters whipped by their fathers, but in truth her white face and the sheen of sweat on her lip made him want to tear Lord Walter apart. Guy had never punished his daughter in such a manner, and she oft tormented him with words and deeds.

As Guy mounted the steps to the first landing, opposite the gallery, he nudged open a door with his boot to see naught but a storeroom filled with pallets. He continued up the next round of the steps and admitted ruefully his motives for helping Lady Joia were not so pure. After all, he'd wanted to examine the towers and here he was within but hours of his coming to Stonewold.

At the third turning he saw Lady Joia's maid seated on a bench. She jumped up, exclaiming in shock, and threw open the door behind her as he neared. He noted Lady Joia's chamber was directly across from an open door. He spared the space a glance and saw it was the woman's solar.

The solar, a large airy room directly over the hall, would be where Lady Blanche's women slept and where they likely escaped the men below. He saw two women at a table, stitching in the sunlight. It was also where Lady Joia would spend her time when behaving herself, and also one place he need not explore for his son.

"Come," the maid ordered, tilting her head to Lady Joia's prison cell. "Set her on the bed."

Guy examined the well lighted chamber, noted an arrow loop that admitted the morning sun but also a chilly wind. A cushioned stool sat beneath the loop. He swung back to the large bed, one worthy of the heir who'd likely inhabited this space. Hung with heavy blue woolen drapes now tied back, the bed was piled with linens and furs. Stools encircled a table, each with an embroidered cushion that Guy doubted were the heir's. Guy noted unicorns and faeries in multicolored hues. Clean rushes gave off the scent of lavender as his boots crushed them underfoot. It might have been the heir's bedchamber, but it had been transformed into a fragrant bower for a lady—a fanciful lady. It suddenly occurred to him that such a fanciful woman might, indeed, seek druids in the moonlight.

He saw no bar on the door. Did Lord Walter not think his daughter capable of another midnight adventure? Guy thought any woman bold enough—or foolish enough—to visit a stone circle alone at night needed not only a bar on her door but a shackle on her ankle.

Guy carefully placed Joia on her side, then rolled her onto her belly. Flecks of red stained the back of her ivory gown. Anger coursed through him, but he must hold it in check. It was the baron who governed his fate, not this woman. Yet, before he turned away, he touched her forehead wondering if she was fevered. Wounds festered quick enough left untended, but her skin was cool.

"Guy?" the maid said behind him.

He jerked his hand away, hoping the maid had not seen him touch her lady. As he reached the door, the maid darted around him and stood in the arched entrance, blocking his way. "Guy? Your name is Guy, is it not? Guy of Sussex?" she asked.

Why correct her? It would be an advantage if he and Chelten could be separated in these people's minds. "Aye?"

"I'm Edith," the woman said, offering him a winsome smile.

Joia stirred and moaned but Edith appeared not to hear. She beckoned for him to bend to her height. She rose on tiptoe and set her lips by his ear, her hand on his chest.

"I reckon you need a friend here. I'll look for you in the stables if you've a mind for some company this night," she said, her words a whisper. She ran her hand from his chest to his belt and stroked her fingers along it.

"Tend to your mistress." He pulled from her grasp.

Edith smiled and put her hands behind her back. She thrust out her bosom. "You'll not be sorry. I could tell you a few secrets, show you how to get on here, if you like."

"I'm flattered, miss, but I prefer to shop the market, so to speak, before making a purchase." He instantly regretted the words. This maid might know something of Alan. He smiled at the maid to soften his words.

He looked her over. If Guy did not know her for a servant, he might mistake her for the mistress as she was garbed in a gown of uncommon color, a yellow as rich as those of the flowers of Provence, trimmed with ivory stitching. Her head cloth matched it for fineness. Perhaps a cast off from her mistress? The bodice was taut over the maid's large breasts, but he looked instead to the maid's mistress who lay just a few feet away. She held more allure.

He'd not yet succeeded in banishing the feel of Lady Joia's lithe body as she'd struggled in his grip the night before.

Joia murmured some inarticulate words. Her fingers curled into a fist. "Have you aught for her pain?"

Edith waved a negligent hand. "Oh, aye. I'll see to her. Remember, if you need a soft pillow this night, I'll be in the stable." She tapped his chest. "But not for long."

"Perhaps we'll meet there if I'm not attending Crispin."

The maid simpered and headed for Joia. He took his opportunity to leave, closing the door behind him. He waited a moment to be sure no one climbed the steps then quickly took the next round of stairs that led upward. He paused at a closed doorway near the opening to the ramparts. He eased it open to see only ranks of bows, quivers, and barrels of arrows for archers. He also heard the sound of a sentry's footsteps pacing close by—too close.

He'd lingered long enough, so he returned to the hall. There was some wary shifting away from him when he resumed his seat by Crispin who sat a few tables away from the dais.

"Guy, come hither." The baron stood with his hands on his hips. The hall fell as silent as a tomb. The angelic singer slipped away.

"My lord." Guy bowed.

"You are bold." It was not necessary for the baron to say where that boldness lay. "I could dismiss you for such

29

effrontery."

"It is my understanding you wish your daughter to wed Martin Hursley."

"Be plain."

"I was simply preventing damage to your valuable property."

Walter stared at Guy. His hands fell from his hips. "Damage indeed. You don't know my daughter. You'll likely find a dagger in your back if you don't keep your distance."

"More likely she'll rip me with her sharp tongue when she awakes."

The baron burst into laughter and set a hand on Guy's shoulder. "I like you, Guy, though I have always thought a Kentish man dour."

Conversation burst around them when the baron thumped the table and called for the missing minstrel. So, Guy thought, there would be no punishment for his presumption of touching the daughter. And he was now miles away from Chelten in Kent as far as the baron was concerned.

Crispin was gorging himself on a small mountain of honey cakes. No wonder the boy was as wide as he was high. Guy picked up the tray of cakes and handed it off to a passing servant.

"I'm not done!" the boy cried. "How dare you." He puffed out his chest. His face grew as red as his father's.

"Warriors should only eat honey cakes on the third saint day of the month."

Crispin stared at Guy, mouth open, chin glistening with honey. "Only the third saint day?" he whispered.

"Aye," Guy said. "But . . . if you can pry my fingers open, you may eat them *every* saint day."

Whilst Crispin tugged and struggled with sticky fingers to open Guy's fist, Guy asked the child the names of those who took their ease in the hall. The boy was a fount of information on who was who, who was honest, who was not, who treated him badly, or had a kind word. Guy learned the names of Lady Blanche's women and felt a moment of sadness when the child blithely named one, Avis, as his father's mistress.

As the boy rattled off the latest gossip of the keep, Guy saw Edith stroll through the hall, a sweet smile for each man she passed. Guy thought of her offer. Could he wheedle any information about Alan from the pretty wench without having to lift her skirts?

Edith charmed her way through the men who loitered about, batting her eyelashes. Her blue eyes, however, held no comparison to her lady's. Lady Joia's eyes reminded him of the sapphire in the hilt of his grandfather's sword. It was a valuable piece given to Guy when he'd been knighted. Guy hoped it would be enough to secure Alan's freedom.

Edith wandered Guy's way and as she passed, she dragged a fingertip across his shoulders. He felt no ripple of desire. The maid was simply not to his taste. He much preferred a sharp wit to an easy smile. If the prey offered no challenge, there was no thrill in the hunt.

A vision floated through his head of Lady Joia, her skirts swirling high on her legs. Heat rose on his face. He forced himself to banish the lady from his thoughts.

FOUR

Joia woke, the taste of one of Edith's foul potions in her
mouth. When she tried to rise, she discovered the fire in her back
had gone to be replaced by a tight, dull pain. It was matched
only by the one in her head.

She saw her mother stitching by the arrow loop, catching the
morning sun on her work. Joia knew instantly why her mother
was here, and it had naught to do with keeping her wayward
daughter company. Her father must be entertaining Avis in their
bedchamber. This quiet space was certainly a less humiliating
place to wait for her husband to finish with his mistress than the
hall below or in the solar with her other women who would be all
pitying and sly glances.

Joia sat up and threw back the furs.

Edith hastened to the bedside. "Now, stay where you are or
you'll dislodge your wraps, and I'll not have you ruining my fine
work."

"Have I slept long?" Joia passed a hand over her face.

"A full day since you fainted in the hall. I gave you something
to help you sleep."

Heat ran over Joia's cheeks. How shameful. To have fainted
in front of the man hired to turn Crispin into a killer.

Edith danced around the chamber, folding a gown into Joia's
coffer.

"Why are you so blithe this morning?" Joia asked.

Edith put her finger to her lips and nodded toward Lady
Blanche as she slipped onto the bed by Joia's side. Edith propped
her head on her hand, her face inches from Joia's. "My lady,

32

why do you not wed Sir Martin?" she whispered. "He's comely and well situated. 'Tis said he dines on swan at every meal."

"He eats no better than you do." Joia pitched her voice as low as Edith's so her mother couldn't hear. "If I wed Martin, I'll soon find myself sitting as my mother does this morn, waiting for him to finish with one of his mistresses. 'Tis said poor Isabel died for his neglect."

"She was delicate, took a chill. You'll not suffer her fate, strong as an ox, you are."

Joia frowned at the unflattering comparison. "Perhaps not, but Martin's so much like my father, I have only to look at Mama to see my fate." Joia studied the gold ring on her finger, set like a flower, each petal a tiny cabochon of amber. Her husband, Robin's, gift. Her father gave her mother similar finery whenever she ventured a complaint. The gifts usually stitched her mother's lips closed for a few months. "I shall wither and die with such a man till 'tis only my clothing that holds me upright."

Another, unwelcome thought made her look again at the ring. Her mother had taken her jewelry, her coins. Only one of her chests remained, and it held only clothing. The chests with her jewels, her coins, a book, and a satchel containing her Roman treasures, including a short sword she thought might be Crispin's one day, were gone.

She realized this little token on her finger was all she had of her husband now. Martin had the rest. She knew the man would spend the pennies quick enough and hold the book in no esteem, might even have the sword melted down. She valued the Roman coins as they'd been collected at her husband's side and, as such, were more precious than the jewelry.

A heaviness filled her. What if Martin burned the book? It had been a gift from Edmund, a collection of verses he'd composed and bound for her.

Edith shifted and sighed beside her.

"Speak, Edith. You have some secret, and you need to get it out before you burst."

Edith's voice dropped to an even lower whisper. "I spent last night in total bliss."

"Who was it? Tom, the smith?" Joia asked.

Edith placed a finger to her lips. "Nay."

A few moments of silence passed, and Joia watched Edith's face as she tried to decide what to tell her mistress. Edith's smooth cheeks were touched with rose. Her hair, fair and silky, was plaited and wrapped in a crown about her head and covered with a gauzy veil. The embroidered circlet that held it in place was as blue as Edith's azure eyes. She was lovely and always in bliss.

"The man from the stone circle. The faerie king."

Joia stared at her maid. Something as hot as the pain of her whipping flared in Joia's middle. "I-I don't understand."

"He's called Guy." Edith rolled to her back, her words as soft as the dust motes floating in the air. "I bid him meet me at the stable if he'd a mind to and he did. All those lovely muscles. He has a cock on him the length of my forearm."

Joia closed her eyes and tried to imagine such a thing whilst Edith whispered on about the man's stamina, the beauty of his body, his hands, his mouth.

"Enough. And such a size would render the act impossible," Joia said with a hiss.

"Well . . . mayhap it were more the size of *your* forearm." Edith giggled.

Joia could not help smiling back. They began to laugh. When they drew Lady Blanche's gaze, they choked off their amusement lest they be called upon to share it.

"Could you fetch me some watered wine?" Joia asked in a normal tone to shift the direction of the conversation.

Edith gently smoothed her fingers along Joia's cheek. "You're cold as a winter wind, my lady. I'll bring you some mutton broth instead."

Lady Blanche rose, casting aside her stitchery. "Would not hot fig broth with a touch of sage be better?"

The two women left debating their choice of remedy for chills. Joia sat up and muttered a curse. She couldn't even command a drink without it was someone else's choice. Was it the drink that angered her? Or Martin and her pennies?

But when Joia knelt on her mother's abandoned seat and peered from the arrow loop in the direction of St. Mary's convent—and the stone circle for that matter—it was the man named Guy she saw in her imagination, turning in the moonlight, his body ivory and black shadows, his blades flashing.

The vision caused an unholy heat in her middle, but the thought that he'd lain with Edith the first time she'd crooked her finger made him common, no different—or better—than Tom, the smith. Men took what they wanted without heed to anything beyond a pretty face and a willing smile. Nay, Martin would want her if she had a wart on her nose and black teeth. Was her father not bargaining the rule of Stonewold for Martin's access to the Solent?

Joia bitterly chastised herself for not realizing how much Martin coveted her . . . or her quarries. How was a woman to know what a man really wanted?

Joia thought of her husband, Robin, dead for a nearly a year. She'd not wanted to wed him, either, as he'd been one of her father's friends with sons her age.

If only Robin were alive. She'd not be confined to the tower, although she might grow to like Edmund's private space. Nay, she'd be ankle deep in the slick mud of the stream behind Robin's manor house, hunting Roman coins, or she might be sitting by him as he ran his manor, consulting on matters small and large. He'd listen and consider her ideas with a deference her father had never accorded a woman. Would she ever know such respect—or freedom—again?

Resentment flared through her that she could be so easily promised to another man's bed on her father's whim. Unbidden, her thoughts turned again to her maid. Edith slept where she willed. On a pallet in the hall or on straw in the stable. With a blacksmith if she liked. Or a faerie king. The knife edge of jealousy turned. Joia pressed her fingertips to her eyes and groaned. She must leave. Now. Before her father forced the betrothal.

She couldn't return to her husband's manor in Canterbury. The stepson who'd inherited had summarily packed her off home—or his wife had. Her father's sister had died this past Michaelmas. Her mother's family in Lyon were all dead now as well. She could think of no one who might take her in—and keep her—if her father or Martin pursued her.

It must be St. Mary's Convent. A thought thrown out in anger now proved her only option. Joia sighed. "I shall make a most wretched nun."

Her shoulders slumped. A convent such as St. Mary's would want a great sum to accept a woman running from her father, and with her treasures gone, she had naught to bribe the nuns.

She must find a poor priory with a desperate prioress who would be glad of what little she could offer. If she could somehow prevent the wedding, she could offer the earnings of her quarry. The sins of concealing a recalcitrant daughter would pale in comparison to those returns. Aye, a suitably poor prioress would be happy to hide her. Unhappily, Joia also realized she'd need ready coin to pay her way to that faraway priory. After that, the quarry profits would sustain her and the pauperish nuns she could envision awaiting her largess.

Joia grieved for her coins, her jewelry, Edmund's book. She needed a plan for the restoration of her wealth, and plans did not come to laggards. She must rise and pretend all was well. Mayhap some scheme would present itself.

She threw open her chest and groaned as her back protested. As she rooted through the layers of neatly folded gowns, she saw just what she wanted to match her mood—a linen gown the color of dung, decorated at hem and sleeve with twists of faded black braid. It was travel-stained and a bit short in the sleeve.

"The market," she said aloud, discarding her night robe. With Easter but a few days away, a market was being held all week long. "I shall purchase something costly and have it tallied on my father, and thus recoup my losses."

"My lady!" Edith burst in, a jug smelling of hot mutton fat in her hands. "What are you thinking? You look like a mud hen. Sir Martin will not approve."

Joia smoothed her hand over the ugly brown gown. She knew the mud hen—or coot as it was often called—was not only known for its drab plumage, but also for its rapid flight.

Joia smiled. "Then I'm perfect!"

FIVE

Guy walked through the marketplace at Crispin's side, but paid little heed to the boy's prattling conversation. The morning was bright, the air still and unusually warm for the start of April. There were even a few bluebells blooming amongst the greening trees.

Stonewold's market rivaled ones Guy had seen in large towns. The air was filled with the scents of spices and roasting meats and the sounds of men calling their wares. He saw stalls for fabric, gloves, leather goods, oysters and ale, and a woodworker whose small figures were very fine.

Guy kept an eye out for one particular man as Crispin examined a row of tiny carved animals. Tink, a stableman, was one of Guy's most trusted servants. Guy had sent Tink to Stonewold to quietly seek Alan. A week later Tink had sent word that Guy must come himself as he could do naught. But his man had also urged secrecy.

The old man found Guy when the child moved to the far reaches of the market. Whilst the boy watched the village children pitch stones at a pile of rotting fruit, Guy leaned on a crumbling stone wall. Tink ambled over and boosted himself up on the wall to be close to Guy's ear. The stableman wore a dirty tunic. One toe peeked through the end of his shoe. Guy dug in his purse and pressed a few coins into Tink's hand. "You look like a beggar."

Tink tucked the coins into his purse. "No one pays me any mind like this, but I'll take the pennies. Yer in a fine position wiv the care o' the little lord."

Guy frowned as Crispin backed away from a larger boy who berated him for getting too close to their game. "I stumbled into this situation quite by accident. Now, what news do you have for me?"

"Spies is everwhere. Did ye see the ones in the gibbet? They simply crossed the Tavest at night, and Walter strung 'em up as spies."

"I presented myself simply as Guy of Chelten, a man without a lord now the earl is renegade, so cease worrying about me." Guy looked his man over. Tink's cheeks flared a red as fiery as his faded hair must once have been. "What is it?" Guy felt a thump of discomfort in his chest.

"I fear ye made this journey in vain, 'e may not be 'ere."

Guy stared at the old man. "He must be here."

"I found no hint o' him in the gossip. Not at the castle. Nor the tavern."

Guy paced a few steps, then forced himself to lean on the wall. "I cannot accept that. He must be here." Tink touched his arm, but Guy wanted no sympathy and shook him off. "Alan must be here. The hostages from Tavest were brought *here*." Guy felt his anger rising.

"They says as most o' those from Tavest were ransomed. 'Tis said Walter will spend it all on a wedding feast, one fit fer a king."

"I care not what he's spending the money on. And most is not *all*."

"Whoever is left . . . they dint seem to suit our boy, and they're soon to be sent to one o' Walter's manors in the Welsh marches, no longer free men, save them what died."

Guy searched Tink's face. "Is that it? Are you afraid to tell me Alan is dead?"

Tink shook his head. "Ye've known me all yer life. I would no' lie about such a matter. I'd 'ave told ye the instant I saw ye."

"I must see the castle records. Surely they tallied all the weaponry, the horses, saddles, every link of mail?" He realized his voice had risen. He took a steadying breath. "I must get a look at the records and see these remaining men."

Tink touched his arm. "Are ye not forgetting the child there?"

Guy looked over at Crispin. The boy had given him a reason to enter Stonewold, but he also couldn't be left alone. "The steward thinks someone is trying to harm the child. Have you heard aught I should know?"

Tink shrugged. "Only what old Owen says, falls and such. Likely Lady Blanche feeds it, seeing evil in everthin' after what were done to Edmund."

"If you need anything, Tink, or if you want to leave, just say the word. Everyone, my father, my brothers, they're all at Winchester for the Easter court." He paced, his eyes on Crispin. "I wish I knew why Alan chose to remain with Chelten and serve the Empress."

"Alan always said up when someone else said down."

"Are you saying I should not have been surprised? Was it simple defiance of me?"

"Who knows what Alan thought?" Tink said. "Mayhap it were simply a squire's loyalty to Sir Edward who wouldna gainsay Chelten if ye 'eld a 'ot iron to 'is feet."

Crispin retreated to crouch in the shadows of an old chestnut tree, watching the game. Guy realized that Crispin reminded him of Alan. He, too, had stood on the outskirts and observed, been reluctant to join without a prodding.

"I may not be able to take Alan home, but I can find him, determine a ransom, and see it paid. After that . . . Alan will have to find his own way."

"What will ye use to pay for our lad?"

"My grandfather's sword."

Tink leapt off the wall. "Ye never! Ye love that sword!"

"It is only metal and—"

"It were the old man's. 'E would roast yer cockles if 'e were alive!"

"He also set great store by Alan. Do you remember how he carried the boy everywhere on his shoulder?" Guy looked away, blinking at the sudden bright light of the sun as it came from behind a cloud. His throat felt tight. He wouldn't give in to this grief that seemed to rise and choke him at the worst moments.

Tink was silent for a time, then he said, "Sorry I am I failed ye."

Guy put his hand on Tink's shoulder. "You did the right thing sending for me."

"But the king might miss ye."

"The rituals of Easter will keep Stephen well occupied. He'll not notice I'm missing."

Tink spoke the words Guy could not. "If Alan is dead, what will ye do?"

"Kill whoever took him . . . be it Lord Walter or another."

"Kill one of Stephen's barons? Yer mad."

The words stood between them as if living things. Was he mad? To abandon his place at court for a son who had, in his own way, abandoned him?

"Tink, I'd not be here, nor have sent you here had not Alan disappeared. Alan knows the rule. If I taught him nothing of loyalty, still I taught him that one always sends word. Always. Ergo, he cannot. And if he isn't dead, he's imprisoned *somewhere*." Tink acknowledged the truth of what Guy said with a nod. "Keep an ear out for gossip and we'll meet on the morrow, at the stables."

Guy drew Crispin from his contemplation of the village boys. Did the child have no friends? Not every child they met in the market was of low birth. Several were garbed well and had servants attending them.

"You didn't like the game?" he asked Crispin.

The boy shrugged. "'Tis stupid."

"Throwing stones is a useful skill."

"I see no purpose to it."

"It trains the eye and the hand to work together. If I had no dagger or sword, a stone would make a fine weapon. A warrior must learn to use whatever is to hand, whether a rock or a blade."

As they headed toward the bustle of the market, Crispin

looked back over his shoulder at the boys. Guy welcomed the chance to walk off some of his frustration. What had at first appeared a simple matter—find his son—now looked more complicated. He did not suffer complications well. He much preferred a simple battle of blades.

Crispin chattered about how angry his father was with Joia. She was a thorn. A thorn from a rose perhaps, but a thorn nonetheless.

Crispin's step quickened as they approached the open grounds of the market. They entered a long path flanked on both sides by stalls with fronts that folded down to form counters for displaying wares. The path was crowded, but the first person Guy saw as they strolled the stalls was the thorn herself.

Heat coursed through him as he examined her from her graceful neck and shoulders to her slim waist and hips. Her gown was the color of a dark honey sauce his father's cook poured over pears. The lady was as appealing as that honey sauce, and he suspected her taste would be as sweet.

Her hair, dressed in one long plait coiled at the nape of her neck, no longer gleamed silver as it had in the moonlight. Here, lit by the sun, it was burnished gold, worthy of a jeweled circlet to hold her linen head covering in place. He realized her gown was too short in the hem and sleeve. Did she know how alluring the snug fit was?

She held a basket and bickered good-naturedly with a merchant. Her manner told Guy she was likely mended from her lashing. He imagined again the feel of her body against his and frowned. He understood why Martin Hursley wanted her. Though lissom, she was still well-rounded. He imagined she smelled of flowers.

"Guy. Heed me." Crispin tugged on his tunic.

Guy forced his attention from Joia to the boy. "I don't heed whining. Warriors don't whine."

The boy pouted and crossed his arms on his chest. "You are impertinent. I'll have you whipped."

Guy ruffled Crispin's curly hair. "I can move quicker than a whip."

The boy's eyes opened wide. "Can you? Now? Can you do it now?"

Guy looked over Crispin's shoulder and said, "A puppy."

Crispin whirled around, and Guy took one quick stride behind the baker's stall.

"Guy. Guy. Where are you?" Crispin called and then burst into giggles when Guy stepped back.

"You tricked me."

"Indeed." Guy followed the boy who skipped to catch up with his sister. She had moved to a stall arrayed with blades. She reached for an eating dagger whose silver hilt had been fashioned to resemble the head and neck of a swan, but as she leaned in, she grimaced and quickly withdrew her hand. Perhaps she was not so healed as he'd thought.

"May I?" he asked, plucking the small dagger from the board and offering it to her. He was right. She smelled as fragrant as a flower garden.

"Thank you," she said, but did not meet his gaze. The icy lakes of his northern home could not be more cold than her manner.

Her voice was equally cold as she spoke. "Which blade here is the best?"

She might as easily have been speaking to the grizzled old man who commanded the stall, but Guy knew she addressed him. "I could not say," he answered.

She turned now to fully face him. If he were closer, the ice she radiated would fill the air between them with snow.

"Nay? Are you not a man of weapons? And yet, you cannot say which of these is the best dagger?"

Crispin tugged on his sister's skirt. "Edith said Guy is lord of the *sword*, not of the dagger."

"Did she indeed?" Joia's brows lifted. Her fine blue eyes swept him head to toe, returning to linger somewhere around his belt.

He felt his cheeks flush. Crispin's remark flustered him. Why was Edith bandying his name about?

"So, my *lord*," Joia said. "Why is it a man of your . . . abilities cannot judge these blades?"

"If I may explain." Guy leaned a shoulder against the stall with what he hoped was an air of indifference. He swept a hand out to the array of daggers. "Do you mean best for you? Best for me? Best of the table for workmanship? Best of the table for killing? Or for skewering a pear from a tray of fruit?"

She kept her eyes on his face. "Oh, definitely killing."

Guy plucked a blade from the long board that served as a counter. He glanced at it for a moment, set it down, hefted another. He examined the whole row and then chose the second one he'd handled. "This one."

She frowned. "An ugly thing." She stroked the hilt wrapped in strips of leather. "Why?"

"'Tis the most balanced blade. It would fit well in your small hand, and it wouldn't take much effort for you to thrust it home."

"Ah." She weighed it in her hand as he'd done. "I'll take it. And a belt for its sheath. I'll wear it now."

The merchant took the blade, but Guy stayed his hand. "My lady. You used the word ugly, and that's what this is. Ugly. This blade is for naught but killing. Make no mistake that there is any other use for this dagger. If you truly intend killing someone, wear it with my blessing, but if you're indulging a whim, set it aside for this one." He placed the swan eating dagger in her hand. The hilt was silver, the eyes and bill chased in gold. "And skewer your pears with grace."

She bit her lower lip and slid the little swan dagger in and out of its highly-decorated, leather sheath. Guy tried not to think of another kind of blade—or other sheaths.

"Which knife costs the most of all these?" she asked the merchant.

"The one you hold. 'Tis almost as valuable as one of those saddles yonder."

"Saddles?"

She swung about and stared across the way at two Spanish saddles displayed by a leather merchant. They were crafted by a master and likely worth ten of the little dagger no matter the merchant's claim.

"I shall have this knife and that saddle. Nay. Both saddles. My father's steward will pay what you ask. Could you see to the business for me, kind sir? And ask the steward to hide them well." She leaned down and spoke in a conspiratorial manner by the merchant's ear. "They are gifts—surprises."

Guy rolled his eyes as she batted her lashes much as Edith had done. Women were shameless. The little man ran across the path to do her bidding with his fellow merchant.

"I hope your father's coffers are full," Guy said to Crispin as they followed Joia from the stall and made their way once again through the crowds.

"Papa has more silver than someone named Croesus."

"Does he indeed?" Guy would gladly add his jeweled sword to that hoard if only to have his son back.

"'Tis quite boring to follow my sister." Crispin nibbled on his thumbnail. His hands were a disgrace. Did his gnawed nails reveal an unhappy boy who hid behind a haughty facade? Alan had bitten his nails.

"Must I remind you that a warrior's task is to protect the women of his manor?"

"My sister can protect herself." Crispin spoke with irritation, but he puffed out his chest and stalked like a small soldier in his sister's path.

"Will she wed Hursley?" Guy wanted to snatch the words back into his mouth, for Joia whipped around in a swing of heavy skirts and stumbled into Crispin. The boy went down. Guy snatched the boy up by the back of his tunic and set him on his feet.

Joia stared at Guy.

Cold? This woman was *not* cold. How could he have been so wrong? It was hot anger he saw in her eyes. He conjured an image of her kneeling on a bed draped only in her golden hair, a single large sapphire—like the one in his sword—dangling between her lush breasts, this same heat in her gaze. His body clenched with desire.

"I forbid you to make me an object of gossip, Guy of Chelten. Keep your place."

Guy felt all the weight of her anger. He bowed deeply. "Forgive me, my lady, I forgot myself."

"Do it again and I'll speak to my father about you."

He inclined his head. They said nothing for a moment but watched Crispin wander to a stall piled with bread.

Joia quivered with anger. "I've had enough of those who would sport with my fate. If you are like the rest of my father's men, you've wagered a fine sum on me and Hursley. How I hate you all."

She put a hand to her head, then swayed as if buffeted by the wind and dropped her basket. He plucked it off the ground. She licked her full lips. Guy felt a surge of lust so powerful, his fingers closed on the handle in a spasm of movement he could not control.

"Are you ill, my lady?" Guy asked.

Joia's back was in flames. Had she a fever? Her body felt cauldron-hot. "Nay. Nay. I cannot . . . that is . . . this wagering. It is everywhere. It plagues me." She waved her hand to encompass the stalls.

"I am my own man, and I've wagered nothing." Guy offered her the basket.

His eyes, so oddly pale, examined her in a way that made her insides churn. She remembered that Edith had bedded this man. A sudden vision of him in the stone circle, half-naked, made her stomach muscles quiver.

A thought kindled along with the heat in her middle as they stood in uncomfortable silence. Martin might not want her if she were like Edith . . . wanton.

She gripped the basket tightly and looked about at those who wandered the marketplace. There was Owen, likely tending to her purchases. Mayhap she did not need to replace her treasures. If Martin rejected her, her father might be angry for a time, but some other worthy would surely want her—eventually.

Joia thought of Edith . . . of Martin. She turned to Guy, examined his face. He had high cheekbones, eyes that might be light gray, or palest blue, or even in moonlight, silver. His skin was burnished by the sun.

The wind tugged at her hair. He smoothed a tress from her brow.

"Do not touch me." The words were out before she could cut them off.

He bowed. "As you wish."

"Just so." She licked her lips.

His gaze settled on her mouth. Her insides felt liquid.

He smiled.

She dropped the basket, threw her arms around his neck, and crushed her lips to his.

His body went rigid. He pushed her away, his fingers digging into her arms. He stared at her, anger radiating like heat from his body. In the tick of one moment, he'd changed from a smiling, enthralling man, to a warrior who might draw his sword and kill. He jerked his hands away as if he'd burned his palms.

He strode away and disappeared between two stalls.

She looked about. Men and women wandered, haggled, bought and sold, but not one betrayed any interest in her or what she'd done. Only Owen watched as he stood by the leather merchants, likely seeing to her saddles. Owen gave her a bow and mimed the sealing of his lips.

How was she to convince Martin she was wanton if no one paid her any heed?

She took a deep breath and smoothed her gown. Her skin felt hot, her stomach twisted in painful knots. She began the long walk back to the keep. She stopped to pick a few early bluebells that struggled to lift their heads above the long grass. A jangle of harness made her look up. So, the gossip was right. Martin had returned.

He sat on his horse, blocking the drawbridge, four of his men ranged at his sides. He gave her a curt nod before turning his horse and trotting under the stone arch.

But her thoughts were not of Martin or the coil that was her life as she knelt among the bluebells. She lifted one to her nose, drawing in its sweet scent. Nay, she thought of only one thing, one man. She thought of Guy, a man who had so readily lain in Edith's arms, but had stood like a stone in hers.

He'd not kissed her back.

SIX

The soldiers' quarters were against the castle wall, close enough to be at hand, but far enough to remind those who slept there where they stood in the hierarchy of Stonewold. The distance chafed at Martin Hursley as he paced the area curtained off for his use. He waited impatiently for Baldric, one of Walter's other knights, to report that they were alone. When the man finally pulled aside the curtain, Martin could hardly contain himself. "This is a damnable mess you have gotten me into, and every day it grows worse."

Baldric shrugged and sat on a stool by Martin's bed. He began to hone the edge of his ax. "I acted as I saw fit."

"Aye. As *you* saw fit. Had you consulted me, I'd have told you this was madness. Now, what shall I do? She says she'll not have me. She *ran* away!"

"Walter said she wasn't running away, but simply looking for druids. Walter said she's a bit touched in the head."

"Druids?" Martin stared at Baldric.

"He whipped her. That should do it."

"Walter and you are *both* touched in the head if you think a simple whipping will change her mind. I've known Joia since childhood. She's one of the most stubborn women in Christendom."

Baldric shrugged.

"What shall I do now?" he repeated. "She *must* marry me or all my plans are for naught!"

Baldric looked up. "How many times must I tell you to simply say we have Edmund, and if she does not wed you, we'll kill

49

him."

Martin shrank from Baldric's answer. It was the same answer each time he asked the question. He and Edmund had grown up together as friends, and he could not be responsible for Edmund's death. Martin said what he always said. "I cannot kill him."

"But I can. 'Tis the matter of a moment. He'll simply suffer the fate of all inconvenient men in a time of war." Baldric went back to sharpening his blade.

Martin watched Baldric's hands. Indeed, he could snap a man in two with his bare hands and not regret it, but Baldric had not grown up on Father Ilbert's horrifying tales of hell. Nay, Baldric may have been trained as a knight in Walter's household, but he'd not been privileged enough to have lessons with Edmund.

Those lessons of Father Ilbert's chilled Martin. Surely the cold-blooded killing of a friend warranted the most wretched part of hell. "There must be another way to persuade her. And the next time you have a plan, share it with me."

Baldric smiled, but didn't look up. "And the next time you decide to wed, allow me to pick your bride."

Martin flung himself onto his bed. The mattress was lumpy, the coverings damp. "I'm going to build my castle on the Solent twice the size of Stonewold. I'll use every stone in her quarry if I have to."

"You need the wedding first." Baldric tested his blade with his thumb.

"Aye, and King Stephen *will* come to our wedding. He'll never insult so loyal a man as Walter, not now when another baron has deserted him. And we both know there will be that one perfect moment at the revels when one of Stephen's men will turn aside, or have too much wine. It is then I shall strike."

Baldric continued his work, the only sound in the deserted building the hiss of his stone on the blade. "When you've handed Stephen over to Maude, she'll be so grateful, she'll make you a baron."

"An earl, friend. I want to be an earl. One to equal Gloucester, that bastard." Martin could see Maude now in all her regal glory, stepping off her ship onto *his* land on the Solent. She would reward him as he presented to her not only a port in England but also the man who had usurped her crown. "The war will end."

"Songs will be sung," Baldric said.

"Aye. Songs will be sung. I'll have single-handedly ended a war. You shall have Fairoaks."

"I'm grateful, and 'tis what I want more than anything, but that's why I took Edmund. Joia will not wed you without a threat."

Martin flung his arm over his eyes to blot out the light and Baldric's words. "Not yet. No threats yet."

"It's been weeks. How much longer will you wait? Father Ilbert said he might die of a fever and be useless if you wait much longer."

"You said he was well." Martin leapt off the bed. "And Ilbert simply grows tired of waiting for his bishopric. Tell him if Edmund dies, his ambitions go with him."

Baldric shrugged. "Still. It's been weeks. You could have done it all within a day of the battle had you used a threat. You could have secured Joia and taken over Stonewold."

Martin bit his lip. He sought to avoid the truth of Baldric's words. "And what of the other one? Is he still alive?"

"Aye. Imagine one of Maude's men coming to the defense of one of Stephen's. A fool."

"But a wealthy fool, you said."

"Aye, he claims a grandfather as well situated as Walter. I need somewhere to sell his weapons."

"Put them in the armory. What's one more sword? And why bother with such matters?"

"They are too notable for the armory, and I, too, wish some of the spoils of war, my friend. Mayhap I'll keep them in the crypt and sell the weapons back to his wealthy grandfather when this is over."

Martin grunted. He cared not what Baldric did with the spoils or the man. "Keep the weapons hidden until the wedding, then do as you please. If you need funds, my purse is always open to you."

Martin lay down again and closed his eyes. No matter what Baldric said, Martin knew that after the wedding and after he'd put the Empress on England's throne, he'd still be wed to Joia. He'd wanted her when he was a boy of ten and four. He still wanted her, and not as a prisoner or one who bent to him from threats. He wanted her willing. Aye, after Isabel, he wanted a willing wife in his bed.

Baldric shook Martin's arm, waking him from his reverie. "Remember, 'tis said the king will leave Winchester after the Easter court. Will he come to a wedding here if he hies himself off to some distant place like Shrewsbury or York? He's close at hand *now*, but a few days' ride away."

"Aye. That's all I need. A few days. A few more days to convince her, and if I cannot . . . then I'll try it your way."

SEVEN

Edmund Fortranne scratched his chin and then his legs, rattling the chains that held him pinioned to the wall behind him. Fleas, he imagined, though he couldn't see them in the blackness of his prison. The floor was cold, strewn with sour straw. He'd been stripped of his mantle and boots, so he felt every errant twist of cold air that filtered beneath the heavy wooden door. It was also as quiet as a tomb, allowing him to hear every rat that scuttled past. His nose had long ago learned to ignore the stench of the slops bucket.

A line of light appeared beneath his prison door, and a few minutes later, he heard the sound of the bar being lifted. In the doorway stood Father Ilbert. He held a stub of candle in one hand and a sack that experience told Edmund contained bread and cheese, and if lucky, a skin of wine.

"How is he?" Father Ilbert asked.

Edmund had heard naught but snores from his fellow prisoner in the last few hours, but the young man was silent now, so must be awake. "Likely dead for the little you feed us."

Edmund had given up asking the priest why he was imprisoned. He worried his lack of caring might be a sign that he'd soon die.

Father Ilbert dropped the food sack on the floor and advanced a cautious foot closer than usual, but never those final few feet to bring him close enough to overpower. The chains were very short.

The priest cleared his throat. "I've been asked, by he who keeps you here . . . that is . . . he wants you to write to Lady Joia and tell her you'll die if she does not do as he asks."

Edmund sat up. This was the first time any demand had been made of him. It was a strange demand. He'd expected to be ransomed. Why else keep him alive?

"Joia? What is it this man wants her to do? He's a coward by-the-by not to do his own asking, and you're an equal coward to serve someone who'll not own his deeds!"

The priest backed toward the door. "Will you do as bid? Write to Joia?"

Edmund struggled to lean forward and look the priest in the face by the feeble candleglow. "Father, you almost raised me, you taught me to read and write. How can you do this to me?"

The priest bowed his head, but said nothing.

"Tell me why I'm here and what you want of Joia, and mayhap I shall do as you ask."

After many moments of silence, the priest said, "I beg you to do as you're asked."

"I'll not write to Joia unless you tell me what is wanted of her. And you must name our captor."

The priest clasped his hands and muttered a prayer.

"Come, Father." Edmund swept out his hand, his chains rattling on the stone floor. "Who do you fear? I shall certainly not tell a soul whom you name."

Father Ilbert looked up at last from his folded hands. "If yon man dies, it will be on you." The priest turned, left them, shutting the door, and plunging them back into a false, black night.

"I'm sorry. I couldn't do as he asked," Edmund said into the heavy silence.

"I learned long ago, from my father, that if you act against your better judgement, you may not pay for it now, but you *will* pay for it later."

"Aye, Alan, your father's right," Edmund leaned his head against the cold stone.

His companion, on any other day, was his enemy, but Edmund owed this enemy his life. Edmund had few memories of the battle at Tavest. He did know, however, that Alan had saved his life. For Alan's efforts, he'd been captured and wounded, although not seriously.

Edmund asked the same question he'd been asking since their capture. "I wish I knew who attacked us, who holds us, and why."

"He was just another armored man covered in blood, albeit one of Stephen's. One moment I was expecting you—and the man—to take me prisoner, and the next, he was attacking you. But we know something new today."

"Aye. We've assumed we were wanted for ransom's sake and now, we find 'tis something else all together."

"What can this man want of your sister?"

"I must think about it. She has only her widow's portion, a paltry quarry, so it cannot be that. She holds little sway over my father, although if asked to beg some outrageous amount for me, she would do it, but I cannot imagine my father not paying whatever was asked, if applied to directly. Nay, I need to think."

At Alan's stifled groan, Edmund asked himself what they wanted of Joia. He asked himself how long it would be before he gave in and wrote as bidden. He wondered how long it took to starve.

EIGHT

"Ah, there you are." Father Ilbert snatched at Crispin's tunic. "You were overlong at your lessons today," the priest said to Guy. "He should be with the steward. Come, my boy."

Guy smiled at the woeful expression on Crispin's face as he handed over his wooden sword and was hauled away by the priest.

Guy surveyed the lower bailey with its many buildings for workers, masons, carpenters, a poultry house, along with sheep and geese pens. He walked in the priest's wake through a gate separating the lower bailey from the upper grounds. Here were the men's quarters, the stables, the bake house, the laundry. The priest pulled Crispin up the stairs to the keep that stood on the highest point of the fortress's grounds and looked down on the sluggish waters of the Tavest River.

Guy crossed to the yard used for weapons practice where he saw Tink on a bench, his feet resting on Guy's pack of weapons. It was two days after Easter, the sixth of April, and still, Guy felt he was no closer to finding Alan. The only tangible fact he'd learned was that there were still fourteen men to be either ransomed or sent as serfs to Walter's manor on the Welsh marches. He needed to see those men.

Tink nodded as Guy approached and sat by his side. The old man tipped his head as he did so, speaking in a whisper. "There's word in the tavern that two or so o' the Tavest men were seen in the village."

"What would they be doing there?"

Tink shrugged. "Assisting the bakers and miller. The castle

56

canna keep up wiv the many as need feeding. Shall I see who they is?"

"Nay. I'll do it."

"And I learned where Walter keeps the castle records. Under Owen's bed."

Guy sighed. "I saw some chests when Crispin had a lesson there."

"Well, only 'e and Lord Walter 'ave the keys to them chests. Owen's key's under 'is mattress."

"Good work." Guy wondered how he could carve out time to look in the chests when Owen was not about? Mayhap on the pretext of teaching Crispin the cost of armament. For Guy thought that if he were caught in Owen's bedchamber, which was in the men's quarters though the old man had long ago hung up his sword, it might be construed as spying.

Guy sat by Tink's side for a few moments, seething with frustration that his time was not his own. "Thank you for watching my weapons. It must be a burden." He shook off Tink's protests. "Each day I've thought, 'I'll find Alan today,' or at least some sign he was here."

"Ye'll find 'im," Tink said into the simmering silence.

"Of course." Guy cleared his throat and changed the subject. "I hate to admit it, Tink, but the child exhausts me."

Tink grinned.

"You may smile, but he never stops talking."

Tink's smile widened.

"He sleeps with Lady Blanche, and if she stays in the hall, he stays with her. That woman never sleeps, so I don't either. As I attend nearly every lesson with the boy, I've searched less than half of Stonewold, and I've failed to see even one cell or prisoner. I've done no better than you."

"What are ye saying?"

Guy scrubbed his face with his hands. "I don't really know. Crispin slipped his lesson yesterday when Owen fell asleep."

"Ye dint stay fer the lesson?"

Guy shook his head. "I used the time to look in the armory. If

Alan's weapons are there, well, I might confront Walter directly, but there were far too many weapons for such a quick look."

"And?" Tink prompted when Guy fell silent.

"If I'm to believe the accidents to Crispin were no accident, then I should never let the boy out of my sight."

"Something happened?"

"He thought to see the men at the quintain. Climbed the moat dam." They both looked toward the field where men practiced battle tactics on horseback. "He managed to fall in a pile of manure instead of the moat."

"Ah. I wish I'da seen that."

"Be thankful you couldn't smell him. But he says he was pushed. If he's telling the truth, this is his second push."

"I don't see 'ow 'e could be pushed wivout someone would see it."

"Crispin says he climbed the dam from a wagon piled with barrels. If he could do it, so could another. He has a way of looking at his toes and biting his lips when he's lying—which is often. He looked me in the eye as he told me his tale."

"I know ye'd never forgive yerself if somethin' happened to 'im."

Guy nodded; he felt the weight of the task he'd taken on without thinking of the consequences surrounding it. "I need trustworthy men to guard him when I leave. Can you search out the names of a few men I might enlist? I'll ask Lord Walter for their help, and then when I'm gone, I'll not feel I'm abandoning the child."

"I'll think on it. There must be some o' Edmund's men about. They may serve."

"Think quickly as I'm here almost a sennight as it is," Guy said, but to Tink's back as the man scurried into the stables. Guy needed sleep. He must commandeer a tower room for Crispin this day.

Guy flexed his neck and shoulders. He was stiffening up with inactivity. He pulled off his tunic and linen shirt and threw them over the bench. He opened his pack and with a reverence he always felt when handling fine steel, he honed his blades. But as he examined the edge on his dagger, Guy knew it was more than Crispin's safety that kept him awake at night. He spent far too much time thinking of Lady Joia's kiss. He'd waited all that day and the next—and the next—for Lord Walter's retribution for that kiss. Guy shook off the twisted circumstances that had him, within hours of his arrival, accused as Joia's lover, and then kissed in truth by her.

The last thing he needed was a woman on his mind, Lady Joia in particular. But setting the kiss aside seemed nigh impossible. Mayhap sweat might clear his head. He went through an orderly set of motions he'd learned almost two decades before from a master in Germany. His lessons had been both in conventional and unconventional methods of fighting that required he know as much of wrestling and barehanded fighting as of blades.

He much preferred the short sword and longer dagger, preferring to come in close and deal with an opponent quickly. It had taken all his self-control not to kill Walter's men in the stone circle, but Guy knew he couldn't be involved in any questionable killings with Stephen so dependent on Walter's allegiance now the Earl of Chelten was renegade.

The king may have a reputation for easy forgiveness, but his present anger with Chelten might cast doubts on Guy's actions, his loyalty, and that of his father and brothers.

Guy mulled these thoughts over as he tested himself. Many of his practice movements were meant to loosen the muscles and retain the strength required to lift the heavier, longer swords. Each muscle was honed and forced to its limits. Halfway through his routine, Crispin careened across the yard and into the circle of his reach. With an oath, he swept his blades from Crispin's path.

"Come, come." The boy threw his arms around Guy's thigh, heedless of the great danger he'd placed himself in. He was shaking, tugging on Guy to follow him. Guy heeded the boy's urgent entreaty and saw immediately why the child was near breathless with fear.

In the bailey, a circle of men had formed about the baron's minstrel, Eudo. Only gifted with half the wits of his fellow man, yet Eudo had been compensated by God with a voice like a nightingale, a talent that made him as valuable, Guy had heard, to Lord Walter as his mistress. The youth stood in the center of the ring of men, shaking and weeping, his hose and braies about his ankles.

Guy forged a path through the men with but the threat of the two long daggers he held. Martin Hursley stood in the circle with a hand on his hip, a negligent smile curling his lips as he watched the sport.

"Eudo," Guy said gently. "You may go now."

The boy, shaking like a willow buffeted in a gale, struggled to pull up his braies. Tears made clean tracks on his dirty cheeks. He clutched his clothing at his waist, turned, and ran through the path Guy had carved in the crowd. Guy kept his eyes on both Hursley and another man with an ax named Baldric. The man, Guy knew from Crispin, was not only one of Walter's knights, but also the brother of Walter's mistress.

"What sin did the boy commit he needed such a public chastisement?" Guy asked.

Hursley laughed. "He was merely sport for a few idle men. He came to no harm, although methinks he'll not sit at ease for a few days."

The surrounding men laughed.

"There is pain and there is pain," Guy said.

Baldric ran his thumb along the blade of his ax. Hursley shook his head. "You appear a man of weapons, Guy, but your words are weak."

Guy smiled. "Shall we test my weakness?"

NINE

"Joia. Come. Come. Guy's killing Martin." Crispin tugged at her skirts.

"Sweet heaven!" Joia ran through the laundry and out into the bailey, Crispin at her heels.

"Baldric pulled Eudo's hose down and kicked him. Then Martin kicked him. Then Baldric kicked him."

Joia swore and lifted her skirts higher. She ran toward the throng of people gathering as they always did whenever amusement promised—be it the torment of a minstrel or the whipping of their mistress.

"Eudo," she called, shoving a fat baker aside and bursting into the open space. She stumbled back.

Guy faced Martin and Baldric. They came at the swordsman, Martin with a sword and Baldric with a huge ax. Guy had only two daggers. Long ones, but still, what match could they be against a sword and ax?

The ax whistled as it whipped through the air.

Joia clasped her hands and prayed aloud.

It was the midnight dance she watched, though the sun shone brightly overhead. Guy moved with ease, not as if his life were in danger. There was a smile on his face. It wasn't an expression of joy or kindness. It was a smile of confidence in his ability to triumph.

If she were Martin and Baldric, she'd turn and run.

Guy's curiously pale eyes were deep in shadow under his dark brows. Martin and Baldric circled and made quick ventures near him, then retreated. Guy made no forward moves, just parried their quick efforts. After the demonstration in the stone circle, she didn't understand why he didn't attack. A shiver of fear ran down her spine.

Martin and Baldric danced about in front of Guy. Martin's men chanted insults on Guy's peasant ancestors; Baldric's called Guy's mother a beggar, his sister a whore.

Joia knew this wasn't sport for women's eyes or ears, but she couldn't retreat. It was less the magnificence of Guy's half-naked form than the seduction of Martin's fall that held her. She quickly crossed herself for such a thought, but surely, if Guy chose to do so, he could lay both men out in moments.

Martin and Baldric closed on the swordsman. They raised their weapons in concert, but Guy ducked under the ax, swiping his blade across Baldric's chest. Martin's sword passed within inches of Guy's arm. As Baldric bent over his chest, Guy kicked him in the head.

Baldric crashed to the dirt, blood blooming across his tunic. Guy kicked Baldric's ax aside and faced Martin over his friend.

The crowd fell silent.

Martin frowned and tipped his blade. He raised a hand palm out to Guy and knelt by Baldric. Out of duty, Joia knelt by the man as well. Guy remained where he was, his daggers pointed at the ground, but still ready. The crowd burst into a babble of sound behind her.

"We cannot tend him here." She tore back the rent in Baldric's tunic and examined the gaping edges of his wound. It would require many stitches, but she thought him suffering more from the kick to the head. So, the swordsman didn't need his blades to render a man unfit for duty.

"Will he die?" Crispin asked, crouching near her.

Father Ilbert pulled the boy away and hustled him off ere she could answer.

"You there," she called to two of her father's men. "Carry this man to the physician." The men stepped forward and grasped Baldric by his ankles and wrists and dragged him off.

Martin touched her hand. "Thank you for your care of him.

He has oft proved a fine friend. Anything you can do, I pray you will try."

Joia didn't acknowledge him, just stood up and went to Guy. His body was running with sweat. It dripped down his face and arms, trickled in the valley of his muscled chest. She stepped into the V of his outstretched arms, the daggers still ready for the kill. She dropped into a curtsy as deep as she might make to the king. "On Eudo's behalf, I thank you."

He lowered one blade. The other, he raised in silent salute.

A shiver ran down her body. It felt as if someone had taken ice and drawn it down her back in a single stroke. She thought of what it would be like to reach out and touch his skin, slick with sweat . . .

What would it be like to be Edith and follow the swordsman somewhere private, to lift her skirt, and offer herself up to his pleasure?

Or hers?

He turned and walked away. The crowd parted and then closed behind him.

TEN

Guy washed in the back of the stables, away from the men who wanted to pick apart every move he'd made or taunt him for not killing Baldric, a favorite of no one.

He donned his shirt and tunic and belted on his dagger. As he wandered about, he inspected the stables from one stall to another. He examined the saddles and bridles in search of anything that might indicate Alan had lost his trappings to Lord Walter.

Finally, Guy abandoned the effort, one he was sure Tink had done much better already. In truth, the grooms were as annoying as Walter's soldiers. Although they could talk of little else but the fight, they cared only about the wagers they could make over whether Baldric would survive the day. Guy refrained from saying the man would only die if the physician were completely incompetent.

If Guy wanted a man dead, he was dead. Did none of these people understand that if you brought an ax to a fight you intended to kill your opponent, and so, must expect to die yourself? If Joia had not appeared, the fight might have ended differently, but her presence reminded him that one of the men was as good as her betrothed. It wouldn't be politic to kill either of Walter's knights, betrothed to Joia or not. Guy reminded himself he was here to find his son, not get involved in petty squabbles.

As he listened to the gossiping grooms he also realized he'd drawn far too much attention to himself. What if he was recognized? Since leaving the Earl of Chelten, Guy had served as part of King Stephen's guard. Although Guy had never seen Lord Walter or his men at court, yet he knew he had a certain reputation. Guy shook off the thought. Who here at Stonewold would know him simply by the way he fought? He was worrying about nothing.

He should worry more about Joia and his body's reaction to her each time she got within a sword's length of him. He'd come close to dropping his blades and hauling her into a dark corner and ravishing her. Just thinking of her beneath him made him hard. He needed to find Alan and leave.

Guy still wished he could simply march up to Walter and demand his son. Yet, Guy knew he couldn't do it. Had Walter not just this morning been ranting that spies for Maude were caught in Portsmouth? Had he not ranted every night, whilst in his cups, about the death of his son, vowing to draw and quarter those responsible?

Guy looked up at the towers. Nay, he couldn't take the chance for Alan's sake.

He must use this time free of his duties to Crispin. He walked through the bailey and over the drawbridge. He followed the ribbon of well-groomed road into the village. The village meandered along the base of the castle, looking both prosperous and sorry at the same time. The bake house and brewhouse were busy. He idled a moment with the baker, learning he was oft given prisoners to aid him, but the men sounded too old to be Alan.

A miller made use of Walter's dam for grinding his grain, and although Guy said nothing to the miller, two men, shackled at the ankle and heaving sacks of grain onto carts were happy to answer his questions. They were mercenaries of the Empress Maude's husband, the Count d'Anjou. When asked, they knew little of the earls of Gloucester and Chelten's men with whom they'd fought at the Battle of Tavest. They'd be ransomed by the Count and return to fight wherever he might need them next. They thought there might be a few young lads amongst the others still awaiting ransom, but shook their heads and shrugged when Guy described Alan.

A few moments later, Guy left the mill, seething with frustration, continuing on through the village. The air held the softness one found only in spring, but fields, now greening with new crops, also showed the wanton trampling so common when soldiers moved about the countryside. He walked past a row of daub and wattle cottages and headed toward the village church, St. Cedric's. A priest ran from the church, lifting his hand in greeting to Guy, and Guy realized it was Father Ilbert. The man must do double-duty here in the village.

St. Cedric's was ancient, much older than the castle, with decorations scored into the plaster walls that spoke of Saxon origins. The windows were oiled skins and in good repair. He imagined Lord Walter or his lady saw to its care and someone had spent a great sum of money here as the roof looked new.

Guy wandered with what he hoped was an aimless manner to an observer, examining the abandoned cots, greeting and speaking to villagers, asking after strangers and thieves as if to add to his store of knowledge in protecting Crispin. None had aught to say about the ransomed soldiers or those not so fortunate. They also feared spies or, worse, a siege. A siege meant starvation. There seemed naught to Stonewold's village but earnest folk intent on their lives.

His mind drifted to Lady Joia, the fragrant scent of her—some flower or herb. His body responded as it had in the yard. He swore aloud. He must not think of her, nor think of the way her gaze had moved over him, inspecting him. It meant only one thing—trouble.

He noticed a shuffling sound from beyond a tangle of hawthorne. He'd been aware for the last few minutes of someone following him, keeping to the wooded edge of the village. Too light for a man.

Lady Joia?

He sighed. In truth, no matter how she smelled or inspected him, there was not one reason on God's earth that such a woman would follow him.

He thought again of her kiss. He was sure she'd acted on impulse, but why? He could still feel the softness of her lips, feel the press of her breasts against him. His body had hardened immediately to her embrace, but he regretted how harshly he'd shoved her away that day in the market. She'd looked stricken, and had she told her father it was *he* who'd embraced her, he'd have been in grave trouble.

Yet, she'd not acted as if aught were wrong between them after seeing to Baldric's care. Her obeisance had shocked him. It was a slap at Hursley.

Guy veered into the woods, wandering a narrow path he assumed the villagers used when foraging. Here, too, he saw signs of the passage of soldiers, and thought it likely Lord Walter's men had come this way to meet the earls of Gloucester and Chelten.

Walter had done well at Tavest, surrounding the Empress's men, the fighting lasting less than a day. Or rather Walter's son, Edmund, along with Hursley and Baldric, had done well. Walter no longer rode into battle, merely drafted the plans for younger men to follow.

A twig snapped behind him. Close. A rustling sound followed. Guy circled back to the road that led toward the castle. He heard furtive feet on dry leaves. He whipped around and snatched at the air, and grasped . . . nothing.

Crispin had flung himself backwards and lay laughing in a pile of vines. "Was that not magnificent? I did as you told me this morning. I made not one sound. I *evaded*. I was not *taken*."

Guy reached over and scooped the boy up and set him on his shoulders. "You did exceptionally well." He would take up the matter of the noisy steps later. Why dampen the boy's enthusiasm? "You're supposed to be with Owen. Your father might cut off my arm for letting you wander alone."

The boy's arms tightened about Guy's neck. "He'll never know, as Owen fell asleep over my lessons again. I used every shadow, Guy, I was a mouse. Are you not proud of me?"

A lump formed in Guy's throat that this child had only a

guard's favor to care about. Guy thought of his other sons, Alan's brothers, well thought of, well cared for. "Did I not tell you that honey cakes were dependent upon seeing the lessons through?"

Crispin sighed. "Aye, but I wanted to show you my new bedchamber. Papa said I should have a place of my own now I'm the heir."

Guy felt a sense of relief that he'd not have to beg a space after all.

"Why are you so far from the keep?" The child did not wait upon an answer. "I know. You were *evading*."

"What would I evade?" Guy smiled at the child's reiteration of a word new to him from their morning lessons, but if Crispin was going to *evade* his lessons, then Guy realized he must spend every moment with the child, further limiting his search for Alan.

"You were evading Edith. I saw her following you."

Guy frowned. That damned woman. "How far did she follow?"

"All the way to the baker's."

Guy swore under his breath, but not at Edith's interest, but his own lack of notice. Had the woman overheard any of his questions to the baker?

"Guy, can you tell me what Edith does in the smithy?"

Guy felt the heat rise on his neck. 'Twas said the blacksmith was well satisfied with the maid's attentions. "Why, she was just on an errand."

"Polishing his sword, do you mean? Papa says he's polishing his sword when he's tupping Avis. Would you like Edith to polish your sword?"

Guy almost dropped the boy. "I need no one to polish my sword."

"Edith would—"

"Enough of sword polishing."

The boy wrapped an arm around Guy's neck and huffed with dissatisfaction. "Is that not *evasion*? I shall ask Joia then, for she knows everything."

Guy's fingers closed involuntarily on the boy's fat leg and the child yelped. "You'll not ask your sister such a thing. 'Tis a man's business, and no one likes others talking about them behind hands. So cease gossiping and repeating gossip."

Guy hoped the matter was closed. They passed through the market where villagers made obeisance to Crispin.

"My father said 'tis not tittle-tattle if the words spoken are truth. So if Edith polishes swords, to speak of it is not wrong."

How to contradict the boy's father without offending?

Crispin combed his fingers through Guy's hair. "If Edith's not to your liking, there are whores enough for you." Before Guy could stem the flow of the boy's words, he said, "If you've no coin for a whore, Guy, I could give it to you. Whenever Papa wants me to go away, he gives me a penny. I hide them in an old chamber pot."

A deep sadness filled Guy. He thought of his younger sons, Albert and Adam, both safely and happily fostered with one of King Stephen's barons. "That's good of you, but I've no need of your pennies."

A string of carts lumbered up the road toward the castle drawbridge. Crispin wiggled from Guy's grip. "Why did you not kill Martin and Baldric? Everyone asks."

Guy gritted his teeth and forced a smile. "There are many lessons to learn about fighting. You have to survey the fighting ground—I was hemmed in by the crowd, all innocents. You must remember that when you attack, if you fail, you die, but most importantly, I think your father would not have been best pleased had I killed his knights. I tried to keep them happy with a bit of a challenge and yet, not really hurt them."

"I saw Baldric's wound and it was this big." The child spread his arms a distance far more that the breadth of Baldric's chest. Guy imagined the man would be cut in two before nightfall if Crispin was doing the telling. They reached the roadway to the castle gates.

"We stood here and kissed my brother good journey when he rode off to Tavest. Joia planted violets for him, so we don't forget him." The child pointed to a place where early violets grew in a circle about a white stone placed, Guy now saw, deliberately amid the flowers. "I heard her weeping for him. They were good friends."

"Was he your friend as well?"

"He teased me." Crispin took Guy's hand. "He was always reading. Papa said such nonsense ruined him."

Guy laughed aloud. His own father said a man was ruined if he could *not* read.

A party of riders crossed the castle drawbridge.

"Joia," Crispin called.

Guy held the boy with one hand and smoothed his wind-blown hair lest the sister think him ill-cared for, but he pulled away and dashed toward the riders.

Joia was flanked by Hursley and his men. She smiled when she saw her brother, and Guy felt as if the sun had come from behind a cloud.

He must get some sleep, or he'd be composing verses to her next.

She drew her mare from the group. When she reached her brother, she dismounted. Her skirt caught on her saddle, and Guy glimpsed her long, shapely legs in blue hose before she whipped her hem free.

She scooped the boy into her arms and kissed him soundly. Guy couldn't hear what she said, but Hursley and his men rode toward the marketplace with ill-concealed annoyance. Her cheeks were pink as she chatted with Crispin. Guy sincerely hoped the boy was not discussing sword polishing.

Guy bowed. She ignored him and knelt by the flowers in the wet grass, hands clasped. Whilst she prayed, Crispin scrambled up on a pile of rock. He jumped up and down and feigned slaying an army of men.

Joia finally crossed herself and stood, brushing off the front of her mantle. "He has taken to imitating you at every turn."

"Indeed?" He felt completely at sea, knew not what to say or how to act with her. He tried to keep his gaze on the child and his sword play.

She stepped between the child and him so he had to look at her. She worried the cuff of her glove. It was of the finest leather, dyed to match her green gown. Both her underdress and the long, loose tunic over it were a deep green, decorated with embroidered vines that entwined in an endless circle about her hem and sleeves, but he thought it might be the blue of her hose that lingered in his mind.

A line appeared between her brows. She gnawed her lip. "This latest fall of Crispin's, it worries me. Can you keep my brother safe?"

"I shall do my best, my lady."

She turned her gaze on her brother. "Please be patient with him. He's been indulged and can be demanding, but there's no bad in him."

Guy bowed to her. "I find it so myself, although I've known him only a short while."

"Papa said I may have my own bedchamber," Crispin said, coming to dance about before them.

She captured the boy, tossing her reins to Guy to free her hands. "See you sleep there and cease running about in the hall. I fear for you."

"Guy will sleep with me."

Guy watched color flood her cheeks as she met his gaze over the boy's head. "Will he? Then you'll be safe, my sweet. Quite safe."

ELEVEN

From the corner of their dank cell, Edmund heard Alan stir.

"Edmund?" Alan whispered. "What time is it?"

"Just before dawn."

"How do you know?"

"I'm marking the church bell." Edmund was only partly lying. He was marking the bell, but thought he might have lost count days ago. It could just as easily be midnight. "Did you eat the bread?"

"Aye. Can you write what the priest asks?"

Could he? Edmund had to admit he didn't know. He supposed he would make the decision when he saw Father Ilbert again. Mayhap the man would finally tell him the why of their imprisonment. Frustration filled him to almost choking. "I cannot believe my father has not found us. We're under his nose. I knew where we were the moment I heard St. Cedric's bell."

Edmund tried to shift without chafing his wrists any worse than they were already.

Alan sighed. "I wonder if anyone is searching for me."

"Of course they are."

"I no longer think my life worth so much—"

"It is to whoever stripped you of your weapons, took your horse, and left you here with me," Edmund interrupted. They'd been over this so many times. Alan had bragged of his family's importance. It had likely saved his life.

"But who would pay for me? My grandfather would lock his gates and starve rather than change his allegiance. He's a man who'd never go back on his word. Ever. My father either."

Edmund didn't like the lethargic sound of Alan's voice. If one didn't have hope, one didn't survive. "'Gird up your loins . . . and hope to the end,'" he said. "I believe that's Biblical, although I cannot remember more or who said it." He felt a moment of sadness that Father Ilbert would know.

"My grandfather quotes the Saints, but only when he's trying to point out my sins."

"And you think your grandfather does not care what becomes of you simply because you chose Maude over Stephen?"

"'Tis not a simple matter, Edmund, it makes me a traitor."

"Stephen has seen turnabout in his barons so often, one young squire will be as naught to him."

"My father will not care what the king thinks. *He* will only think of the dishonor I've placed on the de Maci name."

Edmund lay in silence save for the drip of water somewhere nearby. If only it were closer, they might, at least, have something to drink. Father Ilbert had not left them a wine skin this time. Edmund's throat felt scratchy, but he wasn't so sure it was from thirst.

"I didn't think for myself. Sir Edward left with Chelten and so did I. One day on the road, and I knew I should have gone to my father. It's not as if I cared that the Empress rules," Alan said into the silence. "Though I still think it was wrong of Stephen to steal her crown."

Edmund heard Alan tossing about, his chains betraying his anxieties.

"If only the old king could have made his bastard, Robert of Gloucester, his heir. How much easier it would be for everyone to accept."

"Aye," Edmund agreed. "If the old king had sired another legitimate son, there would not be this war between his daughter and his nephew." The death of the old king's son by drowning had precipitated the civil war. "The barons may have sworn to have Maude as King Henry's heir whilst he was alive, but once dead, well, she's a woman, and men don't want to be ruled by a woman." Edmund scratched his chin and wondered if he'd ever be clean again.

"My father never doubts his choices." His voice sounded distant and tired.

Alan needed hope, but Edmund wondered if writing to Joia would simply hasten their end, some nefarious plot accomplished.

Alan turned the subject. "Tell me again, Edmund, why you weren't fostered out."

"My father holds no baron in high enough esteem. He considered his man, Sir Godric, an able warrior to see to my training."

"And why are you not wed?"

Edmund answered patiently. "I was betrothed, but she died of a fever last spring. I never met her and, in truth, my father was not so happy with her dowry. He believes that if I distinguish myself, King Stephen will grant me a better match." Edmund didn't say he hadn't the skills to distinguish himself, had proved that quite blatantly by his capture. "Enough of women. It does me no good to think of them whilst here. Tell me more of your father."

"My father? My father's perfect. He never makes mistakes."

"Would that I could meet this paragon, but I believe 'tis easy to have high ideals when you have great wealth. Think of all your father stands to inherit when your grandfather dies."

"Nay, my father will get naught as I have three uncles older. That's why my grandfather originally sent him to Germany to learn all manner of weaponry there. If a man has certain skills, he can always make his way. My father can kill with any weapon and just as quickly without them, too."

"I hear admiration in your voice."

"Oh, one cannot help but admire his prowess, but he paid little heed to me or my brothers save seeing our lessons were complete and that we obeyed our mother. I've two brothers, Adam and Albert, who are eight and nine. My mother died birthing Adam. My sister, Adela, who's a year older than I, looks much like her, else, I think, I might not really remember her after all these years."

"My brother Crispin's your Albert's age." They'd told each other these same stories over and over as if they were old men reminiscing on past battles around a fire.

"Adela hates my father."

"Why?"

"He wanted to betroth her to Geoffrey, a nephew of the Earl of Surrey."

"A fine match surely?"

"Aye, but she wants to choose her own husband. Can you imagine such madness?"

Edmund grinned at the wonder in Alan's voice. The boy had much to learn of women it seemed. "Women ever want their way be it a tavern wench or a princess."

"Knowing Adela as I do, she'll never forgive my father if he succeeds in making the match for her."

"Your Adela and my sister, Joia, have much in common. Joia was furious when my father betrothed her to Robin de Tille. She sulked for weeks, but I believe she was happy with him in the end, so we cannot understand why she refused one of my father's knights, Martin Hursley. We grew up together as Martin was fostered to my father. Martin and Joia would be a fine match, but she'll not have him.

"I don't understand why Martin's not searching for me as well." Edmund never voiced aloud the words that always followed these thoughts. *They must all believe me dead.*

"Mayhap Joia's enamored of someone else."

"She claims there's not a man alive worth shackling herself to."

"I ask as my Adela loves one of my father's squires."

"Is the regard mutual?" Edmund heard the jangle of chains and imagined Alan's shrug.

"It matters not. My father won't permit the marriage. The man has naught to offer in lands or goods."

"Joia thinks Martin ill-treated his first wife."

"Did he?"

"What is ill-treatment? Ignoring her? Swiving any woman who lifted her skirt? She was a whining little thing. He paid her little heed." Edmund laughed. "Joia would carve out Martin's stones if he behaved to her that way."

They men lay in silence a few more moments. "I wonder if the king will come to Stonewold for Beltane once this war is over," Edmund said. "King Henry oft did, and Stephen accompanied him a time or two. If we are freed by then, I could meet your father."

Alan's next words were whispered. "*Jesu.* He would learn I was a prisoner here. He'll think me a fool to have been imprisoned like this."

"Watch who you call a fool. I'm here, too."

"Forgive me. I intended no insult."

The silence stretched, and Edmund was wondering if Alan had fallen asleep when his voice came in a near whisper from the dark.

"I pray I am dead before Beltane, Edmund. 'Twould be preferable to facing my father."

Guy woke with the dawn. He'd slept poorly on the hard pallet set across Crispin's door, and he'd spent the night boiling inside that he'd not been able to search for Alan within the keep. Nay, Guy thought, he should not lie to himself. Lying was for cowards. His frustration was real, but it wasn't the only reason for his anger with himself. He'd dreamt of Lady Joia, woken hard with want for her.

He opened the door and brought in a bucket of water placed there by a servant, then scrubbed in the cold water to banish his thoughts.

Something scurried along the corridor beyond the door. A rat? Was his son being harried by rats even now in the dungeons below? No matter what transpired, Guy knew he must contrive to see the rest of the castle ere the sun set again. Someone thumped on the door and called out that Lord Walter wished to see his son at chapel. Guy shook Crispin awake. "Your father wants you at chapel. Move smartly."

When the service was over, Guy placed Crispin before his father. The man merely pushed the child aside and beckoned Joia forward from where she stood in the shadows behind his chair. "'Tis you I want, swordsman. At every turn I see my daughter, a daughter I banished to the tower, and yet, as Martin points out, she's in the keep, the bailey, the bake house. The village even——"

"Papa!"

"Silence," Walter snapped at her. "She behaves as if she's not under punishment. I could put a bar on her door, or *you* could guard her and see she does not stray."

Joia gasped.

Guy wanted to swear aloud. Guarding one person curtailed his movements, two would make him a virtual prisoner in this musty pile of stones, not to mention cause him more sleepless nights filled with arousing dreams.

"I'm not sure I can do justice to both tasks, my lord. I had thought to ask for a few men to aid me with Crispin. He's slippery as an eel. I blame myself for this fall he took."

"Nay, Guy," Crispin said, but Walter silenced him with a look.

He studied Guy, his arms crossed on his chest. "*I* don't blame you, but still, it worries me. As long as you can guarantee the men you pick are not the author of these attempts on my Cris, you may have whomever you like."

Walter's words gave Guy hope that if he could muster a few men for Crispin, he could muster a few men for the lady, yet his frustration knotted and twisted inside him. "I had thought to choose from Edmund's men. I shall test their skills and then submit their names to you."

"Excellent idea. Ask Father Ilbert's opinion as well. Now watch the girl."

"Papa—"

Walter rounded on his daughter. "If you don't submit to my wishes, I'll not simply bar your door, I'll put you in the dungeon, and I warrant you'll not relish the other residents. If you simply marry Martin, none of this would be necessary."

"I merely wished to say, Papa, that I've thought on this matter of the wedding and must beg some time to accustom myself to the idea. I ask only that. Time."

Walter patted her arm. "And you shall have it. A few days only, mind you. Shall I tell Martin?"

Guy watched alarm cross her face, but she quickly masked it. "Nay, Papa, he'll bedevil me with his attentions. I want peace to reconcile myself. Please, Papa, Edmund is only gone these past few weeks. May I have until the harvest is in?"

"Harvest?" Walter stared at her. "Nay. You have until Beltane. Not one moment longer."

Guy thought he could hear Joia's teeth click shut on a retort.

"The king is grateful for our service *now*. I want him here for the wedding lest he forget his gratitude later." Walter turned to Guy. "Pick your men."

Guy bowed. Walter tossed a coin in his direction. He missed it. It lay between his feet. Joia bent to pick it up at the same time as he. Their heads met with a crack.

She reeled back, hand to her brow. "Your head's as hard as Tom's anvil."

Guy ignored her muttered comment and held out his hand for the coin. She dropped the penny into his outstretched palm.

"I don't need a gaoler, Papa."

"Call him whatever you wish, daughter, but have him you will. I'll not be shamed again by you or any other within my domain! Return for the noon meal, Guy, I'll be finished with Cris by then. Both of you be gone."

Guy watched Joia survey the hall. He sensed her anger and frustration was as strong as his. He also sensed her perfume. Her skin was smooth, the color of rich cream. He imagined the taste of her skin would be as sweet as the taste of her mouth. He shook his head.

He soon *would* be composing verse in her honor.

She looked long at the women on the dais and turned to him. "What shall we do? I imagine you'd prefer not to hold my embroidery silks."

What shall we do, he thought? Find a hidden, dark corner. I'll lift your skirt. I'll bury myself . . . Guy thrust the thoughts aside before they spilled from his lips, and he found himself hanging in a gibbet at the crossroads. "Mayhap a tour of the castle, my lady. I'd know more of this place if I'm to guard your brother—or find him when he runs away from me."

She laughed. "A tour you shall have, then. Where shall we start?"

This was his chance, and he must take it. "The north tower?"

She led him across the hall to the stairs, and he followed her up. Her gown, the one he liked that reminded him of honey sauce, clung to her hips. He watched them sway as she preceded him up the tower steps. He was going to have another uncomfortable night.

Joia flung open doors as they climbed. There were three chambers, similar to those in the south tower, along with another entrance to the solar on this side. From the ramparts they entered the western tower. There was a gallery that wrapped to the southern tower and allowed one to look down upon the hall. They stood there a moment and watched the servants at their tasks, then examined another two chambers, empty, Lady Joia explained, to accommodate visitors.

Guy wished Lord Walter had chosen one of these for Crispin—far from Joia.

The last chamber before the ramparts held more weaponry. Guy started at the right hand side of the chamber and inspected every lance, bow, and mace. None were Alan's weapons.

"What are you looking for?"

"I'm simply inspecting the weapons."

"Do they meet with your approval?"

He heard the amusement in her voice. "They're passable. A

few are unacceptably dull."

"I'll speak to the armorer, if you like."

"I'll see to it myself." He needed more time to be sure Alan's weapons were not in the armory.

Joia stood near the arrow loop that allowed in a dull gray light along with a brisk wind. It fluttered the edges of her head covering, tugged a few strands of her hair loose to tease her cheeks. Her nipples pressed boldly against her gown. He forced his gaze from her to the center stand of lances. "Lady Joia, I would make a request of you."

She rubbed her upper arms which only served to rattle his composure. Her slender form drew him as Edith's more lush one did not.

"What do you want? I cannot imagine you are in need of more coins . . . not with those boots."

Joia watched Guy look down at his boots, a frown on his face.

"They were a gift from my lord," he said.

"Hmm. As you say. More like a gift from your lord's wife. Or mayhap *your* wife."

He lifted his dark brows. "I'm not sure I understand you. What would you have a man such as I wear? The pig keeper's sabots?" The man feinted a sword thrust, pretended to trip, and caught himself inches from her. For a brief moment she felt as if she were frozen in place, held by something intangible, unable to blink or breathe. He was so very close, but she fought the urge to make a fool of herself once again and kiss him.

She smiled instead. "I take your point." Before she could stop herself she asked, "Do you have a wife?"

"I had a wife. She died eight years ago."

"I'm sorry."

He inclined his head.

She'd *not* ask if he had a mistress who gave him boots. "Now, what is it you wanted to ask me?"

"I feel I'm at a disadvantage in seeing to Crispin's safety."

"How? I've never seen a man more able." She instantly wanted to call back the words. She felt the heat on her cheeks. What was she doing bandying words with this man? Ever since the madness of kissing him in the market, she'd been blushing and tripping over her words as if she were a novice just freed from a convent.

He was damned annoying with his strange pale eyes always inspecting and examining, from these weapons to her breasts. Robin would have said the man was like a boil on the rump of opportunity—his favorite phrase for inconvenient people who took him from his few hours of pleasure. The boil would now be keeping her from her pleasure—hunting a way to escape marriage.

But that was not the pleasure she had in mind when looking at the shape of his hard, arrogant mouth. What had he been saying? "Would you repeat that?"

He tipped his head and considered her in silence, then said. "I don't doubt my ability to fight for Crispin—and your—safety, but I also don't like knowing so little of this place. I thank you for this tour, but I need to see more than these towers. A good warrior must know the terrain on which he does battle."

"Would you prefer it if Edith showed you about?" More ill-chosen words spoken in haste.

This time his cheeks flushed. "Whatever pleases *you*, my lady."

She feigned the examination of a rank of bows. What would please her was to snap her fingers and find herself in a convent safe from marriage. She'd asked for time, now she'd only until Beltane. Well, she'd not be here at Beltane.

Guy had donned the stiff, haughty look he'd worn in the marketplace. She hastily sought something to say else she might begin to babble.

"Do you know aught of embroidery? Can you ply a needle as well as a sword?" She turned and left the weapons room, throwing her words over her shoulder at the man.

"I can stitch a wound."

She stopped at the foot of the steps, and he bumped into her, though he hastily stepped back, but not before she felt the whole of his body against her. I shall tell Edith that she's an idiot, Joia thought. Why would she seek the bed of such a man? He was as comfortable as a stone wall. Who would want to embrace stone? With a sigh she remembered her dear Robin. He'd been too infirm to do much more than embrace her, but he'd made a soft and loving pillow on cold nights. Would that he'd lived longer and saved her from this fate.

"Have you stitched up many wounds?"

"Enough. A few of my own as well."

"I warrant you did the one on your brow."

"I did. My first effort. I should've left it to one more skilled."

She tried not to look into his eyes, lest he read her mind. Instead, she examined the thick, ropy scar on his temple. "Who did that to you?"

"My brother."

"Ah. So, you have a brother."

"Brothers. Once a wife. I have a mother and a father. Now, my lady. Could we see below?"

"Or shall we ride over the fields? The woods?"

"I need to see below. For Crispin's sake."

She thought he was about to say more, but he remained silent and swept out a hand that she might lead him. The thought of riding out with him, riding into the darkness and privacy of the woods heated her blood.

What would Martin say to her riding with this man? A man who could slice him in two without breaking his stride as he almost had Baldric? She wondered as did the castle folk why Guy had stayed his hand.

She sighed. If he wanted to see more, she would show him more, dungeons included, although she hated the dark and noisome place. As she led him down to the lower levels, she gave him the history of the castle. "Stonewold is quite new, built only in 1070, but my father is far from satisfied with its situation as the river has too many fords to bring any vessels of size here. 'Tis one of the reasons my father's so enamored of Sir Martin. He has property on the Solent now."

"Does he?"

Was Guy listening? She was chattering like a magpie and couldn't stop. "We have lands both here, along the Welsh marches, and in Lyon, through my mother. Our wine is very fine. If you would light our way?"

He obeyed, taking a torch from a wall bracket. Why did the simplest of actions seem so enticing when he did them? Was it the way the muscles of his arms moved against his sleeve or the intense concentration he seemed to lend to every action. She realized she was staring . . . and he had noticed. His dark brows were once again lifted in arrogant disdain. Tiny flames flickered in the centers of his eyes.

She was sure he was remembering her ill-advised kiss. Was it arrogance—or worse—was it contempt he felt? She placed a hand on her middle and with him following at a respectful distance, she showed him to the storerooms. Mice scurried along the edge of the wall, sent running by the sound of their footsteps.

"Here is our wine." She pointed to an arched opening that was filled with barrels. "Along here, you'll find the usual stores of fruit, grain, and one of our two wells. I suppose you should step in there." She pointed.

He lifted the torch and peered at the laden rows of shelves. "Why?"

"As Crispin's guard, you should know where we keep the last of the pears. He cannot live without them." She giggled. Guy grinned and she felt a welcome lessening of the tension between them.

"Indeed. He'll be completely unmanageable if we run out."

She smiled back and led him to the final chamber holding several benches. In the center of the floor was a large trap door.

"What is this, my lady?"

She wrinkled her nose. Could he not guess by the stink

emanating from beneath them? "Cells for prisoners. Did you know my father held the men who were captured at Tavest?"

"What happened to them? Were they hanged?"

He stood there with his legs spread, one hand on the hilt of a long dagger. He radiated anger again.

"No one was hanged. They were ransomed."

"And none were kept here to be tortured?"

"Tortured?" She watched his face. His jaw was clenched, his eyes boring into hers, no longer pale, but black shadows in his face. Her stomach clenched. They were alone here in the depths of the castle. He was close enough that she could feel the heat of his body. Or was it just the torch? She suddenly felt she wasn't safe with him. Some strong emotion had him in its grip. It came off him in almost tangible waves.

Joia took a step back. "My father would never damage a man who might prove of value to his overlord."

"And if the person had little value, or might know who killed your brother and desecrated his body?"

An image came to her mind, the charred remains of her brother. She felt suddenly ill and faint, and put her hand on the table to steady herself. "My father questioned many about my brother, but I swear to you, torture was not used on any man. Even if they'd no one to ransom them, my father has need of able men on the Welsh border. There were very few without claim."

Why was it important what this man thought? She swallowed hard. "Do you not approve of ransom?"

He shrugged, and with the motion, his attitude changed from one of taut emotion to one of casual indifference. "'Tis the way of things. I want to see the dungeons."

"You'll find no torture victims there. They're simply men who deal in petty crime."

"And those who cannot pay their ransom."

She shook her head. "Nay, those men, and any who have not *yet* paid their ransom, are in the gatehouse cells."

"My lady?" A stocky man walked toward them from the

shadows, carrying his own torch. "How may I serve you?" He bowed to her and then to Guy.

Joia thought it interesting the respect other men gave this man though he was but a simple man-at-arms. "We wish to see the dungeons and the prisoners, Ivo."

Ivo pulled a key from his tunic. "I was just about to relieve the guard below." The man unlocked the trap door and flung it back. Noxious odors billowed out, causing her to stagger back and cover her nose and mouth with her hand.

"Stay here, my lady," Guy said. She nodded and watched him descend the ladder leading below. Ivo followed him, pulling the trap closed.

She ran quickly toward the wine storeroom. It was airy and cool there. She gulped the fresher air, sure the stink from the dungeons would cling to her skin and hair. She leaned against the wall and closed her eyes.

A few moments later, Guy touched her shoulder. "Are you well, my lady?"

"Why did you want to see the cells?"

He shrugged. "I want to see everything."

"The privies? My bedchamber? Everything?"

"I've seen the privies and your bedchamber."

Joia remembered he'd carried her there after her whipping. Would that he might carry her there again. *She must be feverish.*

"Indeed. What did you think of my bedchamber? How does it compare to the accommodations below?"

He smiled. The torch he held smoked, banishing some of the remaining smell of the cells. "They're far less commodious, warmer, however, without an arrow loop to bring in the winds. And they lack the lavender you strew about."

"Anything else?" She couldn't help smiling back.

"No faeries on pillows."

"You're very observant. No torture victims either?"

His smile dimmed a bit, but his tone was still light. "Not even a sign of a whipping."

All the shame she'd felt at the public punishment flooded

through her. She led him quickly up to the ramparts. Clouds boiled in a sky almost purple in color. Wind whipped her skirts. Two guards walked the narrow way connecting the towers.

She propped her arms on the cold stone and looked out over the fields that flowed out from the castle walls like skirts about a woman's feet. The village was like the trim, a lacy edge to the grassy skirts.

"Thank you for showing me over the castle. I feel better able to defend your brother, now."

"And me? Don't think my father wishes you to *protect* me. You're for me as one of those who serve in the dungeons." She heard the bitterness in her voice but couldn't curb it.

"I know you don't want or like to be guarded, but you must acknowledge that you didn't stay where I asked when we were below. You don't heed orders very well."

"Orders? And who are you to order me?"

She thought he was about to make a sharp retort, but instead, he bowed and stood as stiffly before her as if he were one of the sentinel stones in the circle.

"Forgive me, my lady, my words were ill-chosen. I would like to see the gatehouse now."

"As you wish."

He was overwhelming this close. How old was he? Two and thirty? Five and thirty? What ill fortune had befallen him that he must look to the care of a child and accept the pennies contemptuously tossed his way?

Lord Walter called for Joia to take Crispin with them as they crossed the hall. Guy relaxed and thought he couldn't be more pleased. The child would distract the lady whilst *he* looked over the prisoners in the gatehouse. He must remember that if he really wanted to know what went on at Stonewold, it was Lady Joia he must ask. Crispin danced around them as they headed toward the castle gates. Guy couldn't help smiling at the boy's boundless energy, then he frowned. He'd entangled himself as surely as a fly in a spider's web with this child.

A commotion at the gates made Crispin grip his hand and Joia's skirt. The portcullis was lowering at the approach of a small cavalcade of men.

"Mummers?" Crispin asked.

"Mayhap," Joia said.

Guy knew one didn't lower the portcullis for jugglers and dancers. Guy could not hear what was said between the visitors and the guards, but a man ran down the wall steps and past where they stood.

"What is it, Guy?" Joia placed her hand on his sleeve and drew Crispin closer.

"I'll find out. Stay here." He gave her a sharp look and repeated the order, then headed toward the gates. He called up to the soldier on the wall walk. "Who goes?"

The man leaned over. "Some poor fool's father's come to claim 'im. We await Lord Walter."

Guy went to the portcullis and looked out at a covered cart and mud-splattered men—men who bristled with weapons.

"Guy," Lord Walter called as he rode toward the gates, Father Ilbert trailing behind, bumping along on an elderly palfrey.

"Just the man I need." Walter dismounted and snapped his fingers, and Father Ilbert placed a roll of vellum in his hand. "Here's a list of what I want for the lad. Fetch him will you, Father?" Father Ilbert muttered something under his breath but followed a soldier to a door cut into the castle wall.

Guy unrolled the list Walter had thrust into his hand.

"The good father will read it for you when he returns. Tally the goods for me, will you?" Walter rubbed his hands together. "This is almost the last of them."

"How many more are to be ransomed?" Guy asked, ignoring the list, careful not to appear to understand it lest it weigh against him somehow with Walter who Crispin said couldn't read.

"Two more men. And seven to be sent to the Welsh marches. They can work the sheep there."

Tink had said as much. Guy read the hostage's name. Hubert de Lorien. Guy knew that Hubert de Lorien's father served the Count d'Anjou, the husband of Empress Maude. This party was far from their home in France, hence their weary, travel-stained appearance.

The priest, accompanied by two soldiers, led a young man of about a score or so to where they stood. The man's face was fairly clean, although he'd not been shaved in his weeks of captivity. He was garbed in a dirty tunic and torn chausses. He blinked at the sun in his eyes as he stood apathetically before Lord Walter.

"Father, read the list for Guy. Be sure it's all there or this pup goes back inside." Walter slapped de Lorien on the back and laughed.

The priest followed Guy through a small gate in the portcullis. He ignored the civilities between the priest and the leader of the de Lorien party, headed to the back of the cart, and climbed up as one of de Lorien's men threw aside the covering that protected the ransom.

Father Ilbert chanted through the list, whilst Guy sorted the goods: four bolts of silk, six finely tanned skins, four barrels of wine, seven rounds of cheese, two casks containing an assortment of jewelry. Guy imagined the bare necks and fingers of Hubert de Lorien's mother and sisters. It was a rich taking, but Guy imagined the de Loriens might be beggared as the paper had said the family chose not to ransom de Lorien's horse. Destriers were worth a fortune.

Guy compared this haul to his sword. The sword was worth more than most of what was in de Lorien's cart, but would it be enough if he found Alan?

When the counting was complete, Guy took the reins. He awaited the raising of the portcullis, then drove the cart in. None of the de Lorien party moved from the road.

As the cart crossed into the castle grounds, Walter gave de

Lorien a push toward the gate. It was a humiliating leave-taking, Guy thought, as the man joined his fellows in the road, mounting a horse for the journey back to France. As a groom took Guy's place on the cart, Crispin climbed onto the back.

"Leave Crispin to me," Lord Walter said. "Father Ilbert and I'll show him how to tally the king's share of this fine ransom."

Guy stood torn. Calculating the king's share would put Guy near the records, but being left without his charge might gain him the gatehouse cells. He remained where he was as the portcullis creaked down again. Magpies, disturbed by the commotion, returned to settle near the gates. The guards resumed their pacing of the castle walls.

"A humbling matter." Lady Joia echoed his own thoughts.

"My lady, the gatehouse? We were interrupted." He hoped she'd not balk at seeing the cells.

"If we must." She sighed and wistfully watched a few men in bright colors tumbling over each other, practicing for the Beltane revels, Guy was sure. He must act now or lose the opportunity ere she suggested joining those gathering about the performers, so he marched toward the door of the gatehouse. But as they stepped inside, his mind filled with an image of Joia tumbling about, her legs in the blue hose.

He needed a bucket of cold water to pour over his head—icy cold water.

The man who stood guard, Hugh by name, snapped alert from where he leaned against a table on which lay de Lorien's shackles. "How may I serve you, my lady?"

Guy ran the manacles through his hands. Was Alan chained within these formidable walls?

"Guy wishes to see the gatehouse."

"Of course, my lady." The guard lifted a ring of keys from the wall along with a torch.

"Might I remain here, Guy?" Joia met his gaze. "Not much could happen to me if I sit here." Her tone was frosty as she sat on a stool and arranged her skirts primly about her feet.

Had she sensed his thoughts on blue hose? "I'll not be long, my lady."

He followed the guard. "Are there many prisoners left?"

"A few, but none so well off as de Lorien. He were a fine fellow. He could tell a tale, he could. Bawdy ones." The soldier laughed and Guy smiled, but he felt a tension in his shoulders that he revealed too much by asking to see these men without Lord Walter's permission. But Guy knew that in battle, one should never hesitate to take an opening whenever it presented itself.

Hugh led Guy along a narrow passage within the gatehouse. He smelled the stink of slop buckets and mold, but it was less noxious here than below the hall as there was more air moving through the passages.

The guard showed Guy the two remaining men to be ransomed who greeted the guard as if he were an old friend. They looked Guy over with curiosity. They were men older than he, and were also mercenaries of the Empress Maude's husband. They were the men who sometimes helped at the village ovens, housed rather well in rooms meant for guards who might be assigned to sleep in this space. They were shackled by only one ankle, could move about readily enough, and had stools, tables and braziers. Alan's description meant nothing to them.

"What of the men Walter cannot ransom?" Guy asked of the guard.

Hugh shrugged. "Soon for the Marches, they are." He lifted his torch, and they climbed a circular stair. Hugh unlocked a door.

This chamber had once been used for storing weapons. Now it was stripped so the ten men who huddled around a single brazier could be held prisoner in one place, convenient for guarding and feeding. They were shackled to each other and the wall. They turned defeated eyes in his direction and made no move when Guy entered and inspected them. These men didn't banter words with the guard. Their attitude was sullen and silent.

Guy searched their faces for his son. His throat felt tight again as he realized Alan was not among them. Three were much younger than Alan, four much older. They were likely servants not valuable enough to their lord or knight to be worth the cost of return. Guy turned to the guard. "May I talk with these men a moment?"

The guard hesitated. "I should be at my post."

"You can leave me here. I'll lock the room when I'm finished."

The guard handed Guy the keys. The man fired another torch, thrust it in a bracket by the cell door, and walked away, whistling.

Guy shook his head. If this were his castle, Hugh would lose his position. It mattered not that Guy had been accompanied to the gatehouse by Joia; Hugh had just given keys to a man who'd been at Stonewold less than a month of days.

Guy knew not how long Joia's patience would last so set to his task. "Are any of you from the house of Sir Edward, one of the Earl of Chelten's knights?"

One of the youngest raised his hand. He was little more than a child.

"Are there any others of Sir Edward's house here?"

The boy shrugged. When he spoke his voice sounded rusty. "Just me. I were a groom."

"What of Sir Edward's squires?"

"He 'ad six."

"What became of them?"

Again a shrug lifted the boy's thin shoulders. "I saw only one after the battle. 'E were dead."

"Who?" Guy asked sharply.

"Ralph, a nephew of Sir Edward. Saw Sir Edward weeping o'er the man."

Guy drew in a breath. "The others. What became of them?"

"Never saw. We were routed. It were a slaughter. We surrendered quick enough, we did, at Sir Edward's orders. He might a gone o'er to the Empress wiv Chelten, but our Sir Edward isna fool."

"Still, I want to know what happened to his squires, one

named Alan in particular. Did you know him?"

"Nay, but Sir Edward will 'ave ransomed them as lived," the boy said as if Guy were an idiot.

"What's your name?" Guy intended to see this boy freed before they were sent to tend sheep near the Welsh border.

"Piers." He slid along the floor on his heels and hands and leaned his back against the wall. He closed eyes as if he'd lost interest in Guy and his questions.

Guy locked the door and returned to where Joia waited. She was leaning on the door jamb looking out at the crowd gathered by the tumblers. He admired the long line of her back, the swell of her hips. With a sigh, Guy returned the keys to Hugh who asked him why he wanted to see the prisoners.

"I simply wanted to assess the methods here for young Crispin's sake."

"There's a lad," the guard said. "Loves a run on the ramparts, he does."

Guy passed Joia, and although he felt her eyes were on him as tangibly as if she touched him, he went to the portcullis. He hooked his fingers on the metal grill and looked down the empty road, in the direction de Lorien's party had gone. It was time to go. He had but to search the castle records of the battle, and then he was finished here.

TWELVE

Guy left Joia with her father and Crispin in the hall. He could feel the weight of her annoyance to be deposited there as she picked up her embroidery and stabbed the cloth with her needle, but he had to see Tink.

Tink was in the stables, grooming a gray gelding. Guy joined him, picking up a brush. Tink ordered a nearby groom to fetch a fresh bucket of water. When they were alone Guy said, "I have seen over the keep. Alan's not there. And I need men, Tink, now. Lord Walter has asked me to see to Joia as well as Crispin." Guy frowned at Tink's wide smile. "If I'm to leave in good conscience, I need to be sure there are worthy men to guard the child."

Tink's grin faded. "Aye. I understand, and I 'ave a few names for ye. They were Edmund's men and dint offer themselves to either Sir Martin or Sir Baldric. All are good lads. There's brothers, Peter and Elwin. And Ivo, a good Saxon boy, and the two Rogers, not the one wid the mark on 'is cheek, mind ye— and Colwerd."

Guy helped Tink with two more horses. When the grooms climbed to the loft overhead to gather hay, Tink tugged on Guy's sleeve and put his head close. "I 'eard in the alehouse that two o' Gloucester's men tried to cross the Tavest last night. It were thought they were going to watch the road. Hursley and his men routed 'em, but dint catch 'em."

Guy frowned. Watching the road helped estimate the size of the castle garrison and how well supplied it might be. Guy imagined being trapped at Stonewold by a seige.

"Be prepared to leave in a day or two at the most, Tink. Or

go now if you can find a merchant traveling to Winchester," Guy said and headed back to the keep.

The thick mist was lifting but a fine drizzle had begun to fall. Joia looked up as he approached and stabbed her needle into the cloth again as if it were he she poked. Guy couldn't help grinning, but passed where she sat beside her mother and approached Walter at the high table, maps spread out before him. Hursley stood at his side, whilst Crispin teased the hounds by the hearth.

"See, this is the perfect place to build," Walter said to Hursley, thumping the map with his finger. "I'm sure the king will agree."

Guy thought the king would be extremely pleased to have such a defense on the Solent and after Joia's wedding Hursley would have her quarry to build it.

"There's a deep stream here," Hursley said. "Sizable boats can easily navigate from there."

"You've a fine road here and a good ford just past the stone circle. It would be a simple matter to place another road—" Walter broke off when he noticed Guy. "You need something?"

"My lord, I've chosen a few men to serve as guards for Crispin. I seek only your opinion of them and Father Ilbert's, of course." He named the men.

"Excellent choices, our Edmund's men."

Hursley propped his hip on the table. "Use my new squire, Harald Redbeard, as well. He served Edmund and his skills need some work."

Guy bowed his acquiescence.

Walter returned to the maps. "Take Cris. He'll fetch the men for you."

Crispin tumbled off the dais with one of the dogs. Guy gripped him by the back of his tunic and hauled him to his feet. "Come, we have men to gather and train, you and I."

And as the child ran a few steps ahead, Guy again felt the uncanny sensation of Lady Joia's gaze upon him.

THIRTEEN

For the third day in a row, Guy met Edmund's men in the practice yard. They donned helms and hauberks in a timbered building that leaned a little drunkenly against the castle wall. The building housed the pages and those servants who cleaned and repaired armor for the men of Lord Walter's keep. Walter had freed Guy to train the men, consigning Joia to Old Owen and a pair of Hursley's men. Guy was thankful he had not the charge of her, but her glaring displeasure washed over him at every meal.

Guy found himself teaching the men as much as testing them. Crispin crouched nearby, imitating every move the men made.

Despite the light drizzle, Edith strolled into the yard, and then settled on a bench and watched. Others gathered, both men and women. Each day, several more of the men asked if they could join the effort and learn what Guy was teaching. He took them on. They might not prove able as Crispin's guards, but it bothered Guy that these men who served King Stephen through Walter were so ill-trained.

Guy mentally dismissed two of his original eight men. One was an excellent man, but not able to use the sword well in both hands as he was missing several fingers. The second man's attention constantly slid to the women. Distraction was deadly.

Guy liked several of the men who'd joined in as they learned quickly. He would still need to consider whether these other men would plot against the boy. He'd ask Father Ilbert and Tink's opinion of them later. He rejected three of his new students for Crispin's sake. They, and the man named Harald, were

Hursley's men. Guy was determined Crispin not weigh on his conscience when he left Stonewold, and he needed to leave as soon as possible. But as he watched the men move through a simple offensive technique they should know, he realized it would take more than a few days for some of these men to correct years of indifferent drilling.

Guy glanced over at Lord Walter's oldest knight, a grizzled warrior, Sir Godric, who had this charge. The man was sitting on a bench, dozing, chin on his chest, indifferent to Guy's teachings. Guy had expected some resistance to usurping this man's duties, but now realized he should also be looking for someone to hone these soldiers' skills after he left.

Joia walked the crowded market stalls with Owen. She felt a sense of relief and loss. Relief she'd not been under Guy's scrutiny for three days—a scrutiny that caused strange waves of heat to flush through her—and loss of his silent presence that protected her from Martin who watched her as if she were a morsel to devour.

At least with Owen's company she might buy as many valuables as possible and see their costs tallied on her father. Whether Owen believed in the many gifts Joia claimed to be stowing away mattered not as long as he remained silent. It mattered only that there were spices and silks and hides she could sell. And she gained a perverse pleasure in seeing Martin's men carrying her many purchases.

After a few hours Owen appeared exhausted, leaning heavily on her arm as they made their way back to the keep. A crowd of men and women were gathered about the practice yard. A frisson of fear ran through her, remembering how Martin and Baldric had taunted Eudo and challenged Guy.

"What's happening?" she asked Owen.

He shrugged. "'Tis simply Crispin's guard training a few

men."

She strained to see past a pair of women she knew from the laundry. "I don't see how training a few guards warrants such a crowd."

Old Owen smiled. "With the truce, the men have naught else to do with their time."

Joia kissed Owen on the forehead and left him at the men's quarters. When Martin's men lingered, she spoke sharply to them. "Take those to Owen. I'll not have the rain ruining my purchases." They hastened away to her great satisfaction. She edged through a small gap in the throng.

There were at least two dozen men within the embrace of the crowd, but she saw only one—Guy.

All, save him, wore helms and hauberks. The men listened intently to something he said and then paired to perform a maneuver Joia thought looked shockingly deadly.

Edith saw her. "My lady, come and sit by me."

Joia wanted to say she'd no interest in men and their games, but then reconsidered. The crowd ensured she could watch the swordsman without appearing to take too much interest in him. She sat at Edith's side.

Watching Guy caused the place between her thighs to throb with heat. And what were the small shivers of sensation that streaked through her if she lay at night and imagined a different ending to the hapless kiss in the marketplace?

Edith poked Joia in the side. "Is he not handsome?"

Heat rushed up Joia's cheeks. Had Edith read her mind? She feigned a yawn. "Not so very."

Edith poked her again. "Not *Guy*. That one over there. With the red hair. I believe his name is Harald. He just asked if he might learn that kicking thing Guy did to down Baldric. Right in the head he got him, remember?"

Joia hoped her cheeks were not as red as the man's hair. "Aye, quite handsome," she said, but Edith was no longer listening.

As they watched the men, Joia decided she should remember

some of what Guy was teaching for use against Martin one day if he should try to force her to the altar. She particularly liked the maneuver that put a man on one knee allowing a blade to cut his hamstrings. That would ensure Martin could not run after her as she fled.

The drizzle intensified, but no one paid it any heed. Joia and Edith remained in place as well, sheltered as they were beneath the long overhang of the thatched roof. And where were Martin and Baldric? They weren't among the spectators.

Crispin threw himself into Joia's arms, nearly toppling her off the bench.

"Have you learned much, my love?" He was damp and smelly.

"Aye, but I don't understand why Guy harps on thinking. 'Thinking is one's most potent weapon,' he says. Thinking makes my head hurt. Did you see how well he can kick a man in his bollocks and then cut his throat?"

"Crispin! You're speaking to your sister," Edith admonished.

Joia grinned and kissed Crispin's head. "I know what bollocks are, Edith."

Crispin's cheeks were red. She smoothed his hair off his brow. "You're too hot. You overdo. Go to the hall and see Mama."

"Nay. Guy does not stop, so I will not." Before she could prevent it, Crispin had run to join the men, but the lessons seemed over for the day, the men moving off to where several serving maids stood in the building's doorway, offering bread and ale along with simpers and smiles.

"I'll fetch the lad," Edith said. She lifted her hem and jumped puddles, joining the other women, paying no heed to Crispin but taking a jug and smiling sweetly for the men . . . or one red-haired man in particular.

Joia knew she should go to the hall, but watching Guy and the men was bewitching. It held her transfixed as if someone had nailed her to the bench. Sweat or rain soaked the men equally. Their shirts clung to their bodies now they'd pulled off their hauberks and gambesons.

But it was only Guy she saw. He'd tested the men at a grueling pace, taught what she knew were skills never learned here in her father's yard. Guy used the hilt of his sword as much as the blade, his fists, elbows, and feet as if they too were weapons, and if Crispin was correct—his head.

And what of the deference these men showed him? They treated him with more respect than they showed Sir Godric, who was laughing and drinking with the serving girls.

Who was this man from Chelten?

Her insides clenched in one of those strange, uncanny sensations when Guy abruptly turned from the soldiers and faced her. Could he read her thoughts? He threw his mantle over his shoulder and headed her way. It was his hands she watched as he came near, raking back his wet hair.

She wanted to know those hands. *I am run mad.*

"It rains, my lady," he said. "Should you not be in the hall?"

Joia rose. "I never noticed," she lied.

Mist had become hard pellets, splashing around them, filling the air with an angry hiss. He took his mantle and draped it around her shoulders and lifted the hood. She was swamped in the yards of cloth, enclosed in the scent of him.

"I'll pick six or eight men from these to help me watch over Crispin. I would value your opinion of them."

"I'll be happy to offer it."

He kept his hands on the mantle, gathering the woolen cloth close at her throat. She could feel the heat radiating from his body.

"And who, my lady, will I find to watch over you? You who appear here alone, among so many with weapons?" His voice was low as if he confided a secret.

She studied his face, the fine lines about his eyes, the furrow between his brows, the shadow of beard on his jaw. "Are you angry?"

He tipped his head, his fingers flexing on the cloth at her throat. "I have no right to anger." He dropped his hands.

The rain had molded his shirt and tunic to his body. Heat

shimmered through her. 'Tis naught but simple desire, she told herself. But somehow, there was nothing simple about this man. She sought for the thread of their conversation. "If you give me the men's names, I'll let you know my opinion . . . this evening? Is that soon enough? Shall I come to Crispin's chamber?"

Color flared on his high cheekbones. He bowed. "Only if it please you, my lady." He walked away.

Why had she offered to see him in such a private place? Would he think she wanted him to seduce her?

Did she want to be seduced?

As he rejoined the soldiers, she thought with regret of the years in the convent, never knowing what it was to lie in a man's arms and give way to passion. Nay, she lied to herself. The regret would be not lying in *this* man's arms and feeling his strong hands on her.

She would go to Guy after the evening meal, but in the hall, with many surrounding them, that she might not be tempted by him.

FOURTEEN

Edith kept to the shadows lest any who might tattle to Lady Joia might see her. Thankfully, the sky was thick with clouds and shadows were plentiful. She peeked in the smithy, and then darted past the lighted door. Tom still worked his bellows, stripped to the waist, his muscles gleaming with sweat, though 'twas near midnight. He did remind her of Guy. She tossed the thought aside as she reached the armory, a timber building against the castle wall and just past the sheep pens. It looked dark from without.

She cringed as the hinges squealed. She headed deep into the armory, past ranks of lances, walls of swords. She followed the beckoning glow from what she knew was a small flame in a dish of oil. She stepped into the final chamber, one redolent of metal and leather. Harald, once one of Edmund's squires, now Hursley's, sat at a bench, wrapping a dagger hilt in strips of fine leather. He laid the task aside and stood up.

Edith leapt into his arms. She kissed him hard. "You'll need to oil that door," she said.

"Aye. I'll do it on the morrow when everyone has gone. How fares my precious flower?"

"Dewy."

They giggled. Edith stripped from her over gown, leaving on her shift of linen. It had been Lady Blanche's and was finely embroidered. Edith knew it made her appear of better birth than she was. It mattered much what Harald thought. He must never know her mother had been a laundress and her father a thief.

Harald also stripped, but he was not so modest, and as she sat on the floor, arms about her knees, she admired his body. He was tall and lean, red of hair and covered in freckles from forehead to toe. He was also full of jests. She'd never met a man who made her laugh so much.

When Harald was finally naked, she rose to her knees and knelt before him. "Shall I oil your hinges, my love?" she whispered.

His skin was smooth and warm. He tasted of heat and sweat from his daily exertions. It made her drunk.

He pulled away. "Enough of that. Now show me that beautiful rump." He tickled her waist, and at the same time, pulled up her shift. She giggled and went down on her hands and knees. She gasped as he gripped her buttocks and thrust himself home. She could feel every inch of him inside her.

"I saw you talking to Guy in the yard," Harald said, caressing her hips, pausing to catch his breath.

Edith looked over her shoulder. "Like as not his cock's bigger than yours. You know what they say about the size of a man's feet." Harald slapped her bottom. "Or mayhap not," she gasped.

Harald eased out and then slowly back in again. "You're always trying to make me jealous."

Edith pulled away from him. She grinned at the disappointed expression on his face. "I'm just wanting a bit more comfort." She made a bed of their clothing and spread her legs for him. "Jealous are you?"

He stretched himself over her, let her guide him in. "Aye. You might leave me for a man with bigger feet."

She threw her arms around his neck, tightly hugging him to her breasts. "Never. I love you." Then she couldn't speak for many long moments. Harald hammered away at her, making sure she understood whose cock she entertained. She gripped his shoulders and dug her nails into his skin. She settled her mouth on his throat and sucked, making sure, in return, that any woman who might desire him, knew he was not free. Her need smoldered, then burst into flames, and she cried aloud as she found her end. A moment later, he spilled his seed.

She lay a few moments beneath his heavy weight, then pushed him away. "What if my lady will not wed Sir Martin? I'll die without you."

"We'll think of something, Edith. I love you, too." He stroked his hand over her breast.

"She wants to go to a convent with nuns—"

"That's where one usually finds nuns. Now, cease worrying. Mayhap you should just tell her about us." He cupped her face and kissed her gently.

Edith shook her head. "She'd think I was spying for Sir Martin, and then she'd never tell me her business. Let us wait a while longer. I'll keep pretending I like Tom or Guy."

"Tom turns every wench's head."

"Don't be jealous, sweetling. I just want to throw her off the scent."

He nuzzled her neck. "Watching you trifle with them makes me hurt."

"My lady would be dogging my steps, watching me every time I went near you. This way, she thinks I'm with someone, but she doesn't know who."

"Still. It hurts."

"If I cared for another man, would I take your cock in my mouth, like this?"

Guy stood in the shadows of the armory and wondered how he was going to leave without being heard or seen. He'd entered the armory to search one last time for Alan's weapons, bringing only one of the tallow candles from the hall.

He'd suggested to Lady Blanche that Joia help Crispin compose a song for the king's visit and left them all happily employed, giving him nary a glance as he'd slipped away. When he'd heard the whispering, he'd frozen where he was, his back against the door to the room where Edith and a man, whose face he could not see, lay entwined. To his chagrin, he found it hard *not* to eavesdrop when he heard his name. When the couple's whispering again turned to gasps and cries of passion, he made his escape, the weapons still not well inspected.

Across the bailey, the keep towers were dark. Fires lighted the ramparts, and he could see the guards stationed there. He would need to return again and still must see the battle records. He drew his mantle close, kept his head down, and headed for the hall.

"Sleep well, Tom," called one of the grooms he knew from helping Tink.

"Guy," he corrected.

A guard let him into the keep without question. Joia ignored him, writing what Guy assumed was the verse Crispin and she had composed together. On the dais, Crispin lay in a sprawled heap over a rebec, his head on his mother's lap. When Lady Blanche saw Guy, she gave him a kindly nod and stroked her son's brow.

Guy bowed, and then hoisted the child into his arms and carried him up to his bedchamber. He laid Crispin in the furs, pulled off his shoes, and covered him.

He stood at the arrow loop and let the cool air bathe his face. He felt unaccountably hot. Did he have a fever? Aye, but not the kind that any physician could cure. He blamed Edith's words to her lover. Never had a woman put her mouth on his . . . nay, Guy refused to imagine such a thing lest it was not Edith in his dreams who bent over him.

FIFTEEN

Guy left Crispin, and two men he'd trained, the Rogers, with the priest. He sat on a bench by Joia and rolled his head on his neck, trying to relieve the discomfort of a night spent on a lumpy pallet with mice—or he hoped it was mice, not rats—scampering up and down the steps inches from the door. He would *not* think about the painful cockstand that plagued his night, the result, he was sure, of his excursion to the armory.

Joia sat alone on the dais stitching on a fanciful tapestry of faeries dancing around a satyr. The subject matter shocked him. But he felt like a satyr, himself, with all the thoughts and images of Joia rattling around in his head. He crossed his arms and distracted himself from the lady by contriving routines that might test Walter's men, but as the time passed, Guy chafed at every moment of idleness. He wanted to read Owen's records. He wanted to leave Stonewold.

He *needed* to leave Stonewold.

He must also be grateful for a conversation he'd overheard between Lord Walter and a messenger. It seemed the king was being kept busy with visiting nobles. He knew the men in question, and they would surely keep the king occupied for at least another sennight, so occupied he might not notice the loss of one soldier amongst the many who served him.

"You need not stare at me like a fox with a hen in sight," Joia said.

He stiffened, unaware he'd been staring. "I'm doing my duty."

She tossed the stitchery aside. "I wish to ride. 'Tis a fine day, and we've had precious few of those."

He sighed and met her gaze. He'd prefer to inspect records. Mayhap she could be persuaded to visit Owen's quarters instead. "It will rain."

"Nonsense."

Edith ran up and handed him Joia's mantle before running off. Joia lifted her brows, and he realized he was standing like an idiot with her mantle held out in his hands as if it might bite. He settled the fine blue mantle trimmed with rabbit on her and resisted running his hands over her shoulders to know the woman underneath.

Her gown was as blue as the summer sky but was worn and darned. It looked as if it might be a servant's not a lady's, and yet, he found it oddly appealing. He wondered if she wore the blue hose today.

He shook off thoughts of blue hose "I'm not your maid."

Joia ignored him but her tone was a brisk command. "Come."

"We should assemble a company of men for protection."

"I shall ask my father if it's necessary."

Joia disappeared behind the tapestry, but returned a moment later, her cheeks scarlet.

"Papa is incommoded and wishes we go without escort." If possible, the red of her cheeks grew deeper.

With his mistress, Guy thought. "Your father said that? Those words?"

"Are you questioning me?" Her tone was icy, her expression haughty.

"I would never question you." He bowed deeply and stood aside. She swept past him and from the hall. Guy wanted to shake her. He found it unlikely her father had said aught to her. Guy hesitated only a moment, thought of seeking Walter's permission himself, but imagined the ire of the man if interrupted whilst in the saddle. And if alone with Joia, Guy thought, he might have a chance to ask about the records.

Guy trailed her to the stable. Tink held her bridle as she

mounted her chestnut mare. It was regally draped in Walter's colors of green and white. Guy chose a gray road horse.

"Where ye off to?" Tink asked.

"Naught but a simple ride. Crispin's with Father Ilbert and the Rogers, but I'm uncomfortable going alone with the lady."

"Ye can ask after Alan if yer alone wiv 'er."

Guy sighed. In truth, most of Walter's men were in the practice yard and challenging Joia over a party of guards would draw not only her wrath, but the attention of everyone around them.

Joia's mare danced and backed, plunging about, tossing her head, but Guy noticed she merely smiled at the horse's antics. His mount stood in mannerly disdain of the mare's behavior.

Tink grinned. "'Er Flora could give any mount 'ere a fine challenge in a race."

"She seems able to handle the beast." Moments later, he was swearing beneath his breath. She may have proceeded at a dainty pace through the bailey, but she seemed determined to lose him, weaving among the folk coming and going on their business, preventing him getting close enough to be what he was meant to be—her guard.

And then, she was gone, launching her horse into a gallop on the open road. The green and white trappings streamed out behind the horse as she flew along, only slowing when they reached the Tavest. It was sluggish, brown with mud, flowing slowly south.

"We cannot ford this," he snapped.

"I don't intend to." She slid off her mount and tethered the beast with a quick loop of the reins on a nearby hawthorn. She pulled her bulky saddle pack off and headed for the river bank.

He tethered his gray away from the mare lest they make trouble together.

"What do you intend?" he asked when Joia dumped out her pack. She flung an array of objects across the grass: a net, a ladle, hearth tongs, a horse brush.

It was quite obvious she had no intention of riding on this fine day. This river had been her object, her saddle packs arranged ere she'd asked him to accompany her.

She stripped her mantle, and to his utter amazement, she kicked off her leather shoes. She wore no blue hose under her gown. She wore no hose at all. Guy felt the heat flare up his face. She tucked her hem up into her girdle as a laundress might and splashed into the shallows of the river. The heat within him flared to a conflagration.

Damnation.

He tried, and failed, to look anywhere but at her legs. They were meant to be wrapped around a man's waist. He had another cockstand to plague him. He pulled his mantle closed.

"Are you mad? The water must be freezing. You'll catch your death!" he shouted, stalking down the bank toward her. His boots sank in the sticky mud. He swore, backing up to drier ground, staring down at his boots in disgust.

She choked back a laugh. "I'm not mad. And one becomes quickly accustomed to the cold water. If you're so fastidious, Guy, stay where you are." She waved the ladle and net in his direction, dismissing him.

He leashed thoughts of ravishing her, strived for something to say that would not get him dismissed—or worse tossed in the dungeons. He wanted to demand she climb out of the river and behave with some decorum. He wanted to snatch her out himself. He fumed and paced as she inspected some mud she'd swished through a net.

"Are you catching eels?" he finally asked. He'd used just such a small net when out with the elvers as a child, but the ladle puzzled him.

"Nay, I'm searching for coins." She looked up with a wide smile. "There was a Roman encampment here seven hundred years ago."

Her cheeks were bright with color. He forced himself to keep his gaze assiduously on her face. He would *not* look at her taut nipples or her bare calves, the water lapping around them. He would not allow her to see the evidence of his reaction to her.

Her words penetrated his haze of lust. "Coins? You're searching for coins? That's surely the last thing I expected you to say."

She poured mud from her ladle into the net. She swished the net about in the shallows, mewled in disappointment when all she had were a few pebbles. He watched her methodically work her way along the bank, scooping, swishing, and frowning.

He dogged her path along the bank, keeping well away from the water.

"You don't need to stay within arm's reach of me. What could happen to us here?"

But she smiled as she said it, and he thought she didn't really mind his company. Somehow the idea pleased him. "Much could happen."

Her gaze ran over him like a hand on his skin. "I've seen quite well that you can take care of whatever arises."

"If an archer were to place himself across the river, in those trees," he pointed to an impenetrable stand of English oak on the farther bank, "he could pick me off, or you. My sword on this side of the river is useless against an able archer on that side. Dead is dead."

"Those woods?" She sheltered her eyes with her hand and stared toward the forest. He bit his tongue on a comment that forests held more than faeries.

"I come here often, but have never given it a thought, that someone might watch me."

He had to further clamp his tongue on remarks that *any* man would watch such a beautiful woman. "I suppose the night we met at the stone circle you didn't consider that thieves or worse might have . . . captured you."

"Thieves are a lazy lot, Guy, they like their sleep, or so 'tis said."

"Ill-conceived nonsense."

The look she gave him could have frozen the river about her bare legs. "I'm not stupid. I know how to use my dagger, although *you* discouraged me from purchasing the perfect blade for killing thieves."

He rolled his eyes. "I could have raped and killed you, *and* held Edith off with one hand."

She stared at him, swinging the ladle, dripping water down her skirt. Something passed between them as if a summer lightning strike had enveloped them both. He saw the same heat in her gaze he felt within himself. He was heartily glad she was out of reach and hoped she kept her gaze on his face.

"I dispute that," she finally said.

He looked down at his muddy boots, toed a clump of cress, breaking the invisible tether between them. "Which? The fact you risked your life and Edith's, or that I could have killed you?"

"You don't understand." Water stained her gown. She had mud on her cheek. She used the back of her hand to stroke away tendrils of hair that had escaped her long plait, leaving mud on her brow as well. "I have to escape here. I cannot wed Sir Martin."

"Then I don't understand what you are doing playing in the water. You should be nagging your father to free you of your betrothal. I find nagging ends when one grants the nagger the wish."

"Nagging will never change Papa's mind. He wants access to the Solent, and Martin will provide it. Can you keep a secret?"

She stared at him so intently, he thought he might spill all *his* secrets if she asked for them. "A secret? Only if you promise it won't endanger Crispin."

She waved her ladle to encompass the river. "I'm collecting. My husband introduced me to the art. One can find fascinating—and very valuable—things from ancient people if one looks. I had quite a nice collection of Roman coins and some very fine jewelry, but alas, my husband's son didn't allow me to bring but a few pieces with me." She returned to her scooping and straining. "He thought 'twas part of his father's things and so forbade it. He failed to understand that I'd found them myself. I had a lovely silver chalice. I hope to find some coins here as Robin and I did four summers ago. When I have enough of them, I'm going to a poor priory somewhere that will value my paltry offerings."

A priory? "You intend to become a nun?"

Water now soaked her skirt so it clung to her thighs. He burst into laughter.

She looked up and sent him another icy look. Guy calculated that look had kept men at arm's distance for years. "You have but to borrow from Crispin if 'tis coins you need."

She tipped her head. "Crispin?" More water dribbled from her ladle to dampen her gown. "Who'd have thought?"

She scooped more mud. "In addition," she said, looking up at him, "there's a small burial barrow I'd like to explore, and 'tis said there are graves in the stone circle. All may hold treasure. Treasure will pay my way to a priory. Do you know any poor priories?" She waved her ladle around.

Graves? Explore? The stone circle? What if she dug up his sword? The sword would easily pay her way into a priory—poor or not. It might not keep her there if Walter hunted her down, however. He fumbled about for some excuse that would keep her from *exploring* the stone circle. "One should not disturb the dead."

She cocked her head. "Do you believe the dead walk?"

"Nonsense, but would you want someone disturbing Edmund's bones?"

A stricken look replaced her small smile. He instantly regretted selecting Edmund as an example. "Forgive me, my lady, I didn't choose my words very well."

She ducked her head. "I understand. Don't beg forgiveness for giving your opinion." She poured a ladle of mud into her sieve and shook it back and forth, her breasts swinging in time to her movements. He lost all sense of what she was saying, drawing his mantle closed again.

"Are you listening, Guy?"

"Forgive me." He tried to look attentive.

"I asked you about one of the lessons you were teaching the men. Edith and I much admired it. The one you used on Baldric."

"I understand Baldric is faring well."

"Aye. Avis and Edith see to him, but I don't understand why you didn't simply kill them. I imagine they'd have killed you, given the chance."

Guy followed as she began to retrace her explorations, going over the same ground a second time. She bent over, her damp gown clinging to her buttocks. He took a steadying breath and counted the many ways he knew to down a man without killing him. When he reached ten, he had himself back under control.

"Crispin asked me the same question. You must realize that if you take a weapon to a fight, you do intend to kill someone—no matter what you might later claim. But the best way of handling two men if you are one is to let them exhaust themselves and their amusement. When they grow weary of toying with their victim, they'll grow careless, as did Sir Baldric."

Joia nodded. "Crispin said you were using strategy, but Edith said you were just wary of my father."

"Wariness *is* a strategy," he snapped. Let Edith keep her opinions to herself, he thought, but then Joia smiled up at him and he forgot his rancor. The smile lit her face, her eyes, her whole being. Her eyes were very blue, her hair now in complete disarray, the plait unraveling over her shoulder. She looked like a water nymph, happy with the water lapping her legs, drenching her gown.

The memory of what Edith had done to Hursley's man enflamed Guy for he could imagine this woman, garbed as she was, giving herself up to passion. The thought that it could never be with him cooled his ardor as nothing else had. She was a woman of worth, he a man with naught but his sword. And his only sword of worth was buried in the stone circle.

He cleared his throat. "My lady, I have something to ask you."

She went very still, the ladle dangling from her fingers. "You sound very grave."

He squelched through the mud and crouched so he was eye-level with her. "It is nothing to concern you. I just want to know about the prisoners from Tavest."

Joia stared a him a moment. "The prisoners? The ones you visited? What of them, Guy?"

He should take her into his confidence, tell her the truth of why he was at Stonewold, but as he opened his mouth, he found the words wouldn't come. "There were a few who cannot pay a ransom. Do you see to them?"

"Do you think me negligent of their care?" Her voice frosted over.

"Nay, my lady. I'm simply curious."

She tipped her head. "I've seen them as has my mother. We treated a few wounds, made sure Father Ilbert sees to their spiritual needs. I wrote for two who wanted their families to know they were well and that they would be——"

"Sent as serfs to the Welsh marches?" he finished for her. "Are they needed at home, do you think?"

"I wouldn't know. I fear . . . I never asked."

She bent to her task, and he saw his question had raised the color on her cheeks. He thought Joia more of the world of the forests and faeries she stitched on her pillows than of the treachery of castles and kings. "It is possible that by sending the men away, their families may starve."

"You exaggerate."

"And you don't understand what ransom and not being able to pay a ransom means."

"You're angry."

He shrugged. "Did you see every prisoner who came here from the battle? Not just those in the gatehouse? Any young men of say, ten and five or so among them?"

"Aye, but why do you ask?"

"It is an age when young men are oft needed at home." It was not quite a lie, Alan was missed if not needed.

"You make me feel negligent." Her shoulders slumped. "But the young ones, of that age were ransomed, so *are* home. Do you think the amount they paid might beggar them?"

He looked down at his hands. He wouldn't soften the matter of ransom for her. "It is as likely a family will starve after paying a high ransom as it is that they will starve because their son is sent to the Marches. One hopes that after a ransom is paid the man will resume his place, his tasks, his wages, but who can say what a family may pay and not feel it come winter?"

She bit her lips as Crispin ofttimes did. "My father will use the ransoms for my wedding. I'm ashamed, Guy."

"It was not my intention——"

She held up her hand to stay his words. "No apologies. I'll not have it."

"I'd like to somehow redeem one of those still in the gatehouse. His name is Piers. Could you ask your father a price for him?"

Her eyes met his and for a moment she was silent, biting her lower lip. "Consider the boy paid for."

"I can pay his way."

"You need not; I'll see to it myself."

Her color was high, but she moved away, sifting mud, but in a listless manner as if she'd lost all interest in the effort. He wondered if the high color on her cheeks meant that she'd not thought that by sending the men as serfs to her father's lands in the Welsh marches, her father might cause a family to starve. She finally came back to where he stood and tossed her ladle and net onto the bank.

He picked up her tools and grimaced. One would need to get very muddy to rinse them enough to put in her pack.

"I must find a way to escape from here. I asked but one thing of my father and that was time. My father makes plans without any consideration for my feelings. Did you know my father sent a messenger out this morn to formally invite the king for the Beltane Feast? 'Tis really my wedding the king will come for, and I have yet to agree to wed Martin."

"The king?" Guy froze, one boot in the water, one on drier ground. One moment he was contemplating the thought he must be gone ere the king arrived, and the next, he was falling.

Joia yelped and reached for him. Her face was the last thing he saw before he went under.

The icy water stole his breath. His mantle wrapped about him like seaweed. He floundered, fought the cloth, fought his heavy sword. He hit the bottom, mud enveloping him.

Then Joia gripped his arm, hauling him up. He managed to thrust off the mantle's cloying tentacles and break the surface, spewing water and mud.

She helped him to the bank, but when they reached it, his boots sank in the mud, and he wheeled his arms to remain upright, knocking her over. He watched the water close over her head. He grabbed for her, but missed. She surfaced and ignoring his hand, struggled toward the bank. She stood there, water swirling about her waist, her gown plastered to her body.

He felt as naked as she looked. He scooped her into his arms, slogged up the muddy bank, and dropped her on the grass.

"Mon Dieu. You'll catch your death." He quickly stripped the green and white trappings from Flora, soothing the beast as she danced about, complicating the effort.

Joia sat on her heels, her arms about her waist. It did nothing to conceal the shape of her.

"What of you?" she asked, teeth chattering, when he made to wrap her in her mantle and the yards of green and white cloth.

He ignored the question. Her hair was in a twisted mass over one shoulder. It dripped on her gown. He gathered her hair in his hand and squeezed it out.

Before he knew it, she had her arms around his neck, her hands in his hair. Her eyes were wide and so blue they might be sapphires indeed. Desire hammered him. She was but a breath away.

She pressed her lips to his. All sense fled at their touch.

He plundered her mouth. She tasted of honey. He felt like a starving man who'd been given food. He tangled his tongue with hers. He pulled the mantle and cloth aside and spread his hands over her back to pull her even closer. He moaned as she arched against his manhood. She gripped his hair and did it again, but it was she who moaned this time.

The sound caused sense to flood through him, to quench the

fire she stoked with her shifting hips.

He coiled her hair around his fist and pulled her head back. "My lady." Her eyes fluttered open. She licked her lips. "Forgive me, I don't know what possessed me." He abruptly wrapped her in the voluminous folds of cloth.

She looked like a small bundle of laundry.

"I'll forgive you, Guy, but you can no longer claim the high ground." She struggled to her feet. "What are we going to do?"

"Get back to the castle and somehow explain ourselves without being given the lash." But as he spoke, he wasn't sure she spoke of making excuses for their wet clothing.

"Your boots are ruined," she said, hugging the green and white cloth, symbol of her father, around her.

"Pray my sword is not." He dried it and its sheath on the edge of his horse's blanket. His boots were likely ruined and the sword sheath as well. He stomped to the bank to retrieve and clean her tools, deliberately wading into the water to his waist in hopes the cold water might temper his ardor.

Something very familiar in shape lay in the bottom of the scoop. He did as he'd seen her do, he dumped the muddy contents into the net and swished it. In the bottom of the net lay a coin. It was dull, but recognizable. He grinned and after gathering the clean tools, he headed to where she stood. "I'm a collector. I have my first coin." He opened his hand.

She threw off the horse trappings and snatched the coin from his palm. "Oh. 'Tis only one of King Stephen's. Very new. His minting is poor, though. See, not well struck at all. He demands no excellence of his moneyers. Still, a penny is a penny."

Her next action sent his blood straight back to his groin. She polished the small treasure on her breast, blew on it, and then polished it again. When she looked up, her face muddy, her hair snarled ropes, he thought he'd never seen a woman so desirable.

She stared at him a moment. Heat shimmered like a living thing between them. "May I have it?" she whispered.

You may have whatever you desire of me, he thought, but aloud he said, "You'll have to trade for it." He plucked the coin from her fingertips.

A moment later, she threw her arms around his neck, and placed her lips on his, then just as quickly stepped away, her cheeks red. "Is that sufficient? A kiss?"

"I was hoping for new boots." He tried to speak lightly, but his voice felt hoarse. He must get away now, or he'd take her back into his arms. He walked to her mare and saddled the animal, putting his back to her lest she see how aroused he was.

She followed. "I want that coin."

He looked over his shoulder at her. She held out her hand. She watched him intently as he donned his gloves and then tucked the coin inside.

"What the devil." She stamped her foot. "We had a bargain."

"Nay, you made a bargain, but I never agreed to it. And 'twas a poor bargain."

Her cheeks flushed. "You didn't enjoy the kiss?"

He wasn't sure whether her high color resulted from her gaze which swept over his groin or his words. "Kiss? My lady, you know naught of kissing." The words were out before he could stop them.

"And yet you wouldn't kiss me, but would Edith."

He tossed her into the saddle. "I've never kissed Edith. Who told you such a thing?"

"Edith regaled me with tales of your time together."

Guy stared up at her. Why the devil was Edith lying? To shield her real lover whom she met in the armory? "I've had naught to do with Edith."

Why did he protest? Why was it important that Joia understand there was nothing between him and her maid? He sacrificed his sword belt to lash the yards of green and white cloth about Joia in a way that would not impede her riding, yet would keep her somewhat warm. The very act caused him to touch her too often, too intimately. He saw as much discomfort on her face as he feared was on his.

"I hate liars," she finally said.

It rankled him. He made every effort to be truthful. He might omit some facts, but he'd not lied to this woman. He mounted and touched his spurs to the horse's sides, leaving her at the river bank. He heard the sound of her hoofbeats behind him.

"We cannot just ride in like this," she said drawing to his side as they approached the castle. "There will be endless questions."

"Better to just have it done with. No amount of time will restore your gown or my tunic. Let them gossip. Simply tell the truth."

"Aye, Papa," she said. "Yon guard fell in the river, and I had need to jump in and rescue him."

He dragged on the reins, halting his mount. "What did you say?"

"I said the simple truth."

"*Mon Dieu.*" He contemplated the heavens. Despite the bright sunshine, he shivered. His hands were icy cold.

"Or, we could strike a new bargain."

He lifted a brow.

"I shall say *I* fell into the river and *you* saved me."

"What do you want?" He spat out the last word.

"I want that coin." She held out her hand and snapped her fingers.

No woman had ever snapped her fingers at him. He rode his mount in a circle and thought of the taunts in the yard when word trickled from grooms to men-at-arms that he'd been rescued from drowning by this very annoying woman. "You may have the coin."

"Excellent." Her sneering expression turned to a sunny smile.

He dropped the coin into her palm. "You will say you fell in and I pulled you out?" He would not be lying . . . she would.

"Agreed." She did as he had, she tucked the coin inside her glove.

They rode in silence through the castle gates and to the stable, ignoring the avid interest of those who went about their business there. Tink rushed forward to take Guy's reins as he stepped down from his horse and went to Joia. He waved off the grooms and encircled her waist, swinging her to the ground. He undid his sword belt, rearranged her draperies to allow her to walk, then followed her to the hall, his sheathed sword in his hand.

His body was cold to the core. He felt sticky and his feet hurt from so long in wet boots. His thighs *chafed*, damn it.

But Joia walked to where her father and Hursley sat as if she were garbed in velvet and fur. She curtsied, undid the sword belt, and let the horse trappings cascade to the floor. Her gown clung to her, delineating every curve.

Hursley stared at her. Guy felt an unreasonable desire to smash his fist into the man's leering face.

"Guy and I've had a misfortune," Joia said. "I was examining a coin I found on the river bank and fell in. Praise God, Guy was able to save me. I owe him my life. I hope you'll reward him with all speed as he has ruined his boots in the effort and most likely his weaponry." She handed the sword belt to him, curtsied to the men on the dais, whose mouths were open like two fish on a platter, and left them, disappearing up the steps to her chamber, consigning Guy to his fate.

Walter and Hursley stared at him. Hursley held up a hand when Walter would have spoken.

"What the devil! She fell in the river? When she's wed to me, she'll behave with more decorum. She's been allowed to run wild," he said. He rose and stood over Walter. "I'll see she acts according to her station. I'll not allow such utter madness to reign in my house."

Walter shot to his feet. "Madness? 'Tis her husband's doing. He allowed her to run wild, not I. You'll simply make her see reason. I'm sure she'll be biddable once you're wed, and I'll have my wife speak to her, shall I? We owe much to this man. Remember, there'll be no wedding if the girl is dead."

Hursley looked Guy up and down and grunted, then dipped into his purse, withdrew a coin, and tossed it to Guy. "If she should suggest such madness again, you have my permission to stripe her back with yon belt. Beat her bloody if you like." He threw himself into his seat and called for ale.

Guy restrained himself from stepping up onto the dais and beating Hursley bloody. He gripped his belt and the buckle bit into his palm.

A silver buckle, chased with twining leaves.

He coiled the belt around the buckle, hiding it from view. He'd thought of burying his grandfather's sword, had dressed plainly, borrowed spurs from one of the king's grooms. His boots had caught Joia's attention, and she'd pointed them out to these two men. Had they been paying more attention, they might wonder why he also had a belt buckle, albeit a tarnished buckle, worth more than any worn by Hursley.

As he turned to go, the knight spoke to his back. "Just do not mark her face."

Guy headed for the south tower, following the wet footprints of Lady Joia. He wondered why a man so in love had ordered his betrothed a beating rather than a hot bath.

Sixteen

Guy stripped in Crispin's small chamber. He stood by the brazier, hands out, but it did naught to warm him. He'd nothing dry to put on. Crispin had run off to find a shirt to cover his nakedness until the laundresses tended the muddy clothing. As Guy paced, he thought he should have traded the coin for a look at the Tavest records. Why had it mattered whether anyone thought he'd been rescued by a woman?

Pride. He had too damned much of it.

"Crispin, give these to—"

He turned. Joia stood in the doorway, a bundle of clothing in her arms. Her eyes dropped to his groin. He plucked his muddy shirt from the floor and held it before him, his cock swelling under her scrutiny. "Crispin's not here, my lady."

Her mouth was open, but at least she'd raised her eyes to his face. "I-I, that is, I-I—" She thrust out the bundle in her arms.

He bowed and stepped forward and took the clothing with one hand, whilst concealing his tumescence with the dirty shirt.

She backed through the doorway, two bright flags of color on her cheeks.

He dropped the soiled garment.

"Guy?"

"*Sweet Jesu,*" he said, diving for the shirt again, but this time, she didn't enter.

"I'll send you water and soap. You're very muddy." She giggled.

"I fell in a *river,*" he shouted.

He heard the swish of her skirts on the stone floor as she

121

retreated. "I warrant she's not only *not* been well kissed, but also not well bedded. She looked at me as if she were seeing a cock for the first time." He shook his head.

Guy calculated the number of arrows that might be needed by the Stonewold archers if Gloucester besieged the castle and tamed himself in the process, and just in time as Crispin, a linen shirt gripped in rather grubby hands, was delivered by his mother. *She* hardly looked at him as she directed two serving boys who bore a deep basin of steaming water along with a pot of fragrant sage-scented soap and a drying cloth.

Guy saw what Joia might look like if she had another score of years on her and lived with a man such as he father. Deep lines radiated from Lady Blanche's blue eyes. Her hair, haphazardly contained within a silken net had none of Joia's gloss. If Joia's hair was burnished gold, Lady Blanche's was withered leaves. Guy knew Joia would likewise wither in a life tethered to such as Hursley.

But Guy also knew that if Joia asked his opinion, he'd tell her the match was a good one from a father's point of view. Hursley was capable of serving in Edmund's place, protecting Stonewold for Crispin. What did it matter a daughter's happiness when weighed against holding such a place as Stonewold, not only for the boy, but also for the king?

As Guy washed away the river mud, he thought of his daughter, unhappy with his choice of husband for her. Was Adela's unhappiness much different from Joia's? He blanched thinking of what Adela might be plotting whilst he was here at Stonewold. Was she digging up coins in a river to run off as well?

He scrubbed his face. Nay, Adela didn't have the boldness of Lady Joia. *Yet.*

As he dried himself, Guy thought the difference betwixt himself and Lord Walter was simple. Whilst Walter wanted the best for Stonewold and would beat his daughter to have it, Guy wanted only what was best for Adela. And there lay the difference betwixt a landed lord and a man with naught but his sword.

What had he to offer any woman?

It was a bleak thought. Even if Hursley didn't exist, Guy could never reach so high. Yet, he wanted Joia, and recognized that the heated emotion that had gripped him in the hall was jealousy.

The hot water did little to warm him. He still shivered when he went to the hall for the evening meal. At least his duties put him close to the great hearth. He grinned and tossed off a few jests with several men who made ribald comments on his wet exploits of the day, then took his seat where he could see both Crispin and Joia. The child leaned on his mother who alternately talked to her ladies and fed the boy morsels from her trencher. It was something one would do for a child of three or four. Guy knew if he had the true rearing of the child, he would put a stop to it.

Edith sat beside Guy. He'd watched her carefully since entering the hall, but saw no one man the woman favored over another. She simpered about the men as if sampling from a banquet table. Guy knew he could never allow a woman he wanted to tease and flatter so many as Edith did.

Edith placed a hand on his thigh. He sighed and plucked her hand off ere it traveled higher.

She edged closer still. "My lady wishes to know if you suffered any ill effects from saving her life."

"Tell yon lady I'm cold to the bone, have surely taken a chill, and will need the physician ere the sun rises, and likely the priest by noon on the morrow." He folded his arms on his chest and glared toward where Joia sat, watching them.

Edith pressed her palms together in prayer. "Nay."

"Aye. Tell her."

Edith bit her lip. She did as bid, and he watched the swing of her hips as she worked her way to the high table. She whispered in Joia's ear. Joia raised a brow, her gaze on him. She shrugged, shook her head, and spoke without looking at the wench. Edith curtsied and then darted back to his side.

"My lady says she'll pray for your soul when you are dead."

Guy threw back his head and laughed. Edith stared at him, puzzled, but he ignored her. He bowed his head to Joia.

Crispin came down to where Guy sat and climbed onto the bench beside him. "Guy, you're shivering."

"Are you finished playing the babe?"

"Babe?"

"Aye. Men don't eat from their mother's hand."

"But she has honeyed pears and almonds."

"Eat pease not honey." Then Guy shushed Crispin. Joia and her father stood before the hall, his arm draped over a young man who oft accompanied Eudo on the rebec.

"Our good man Godric has composed a song in honor of Sir Martin." Walter held up his hands for silence as Hursley's men stomped and whistled their approval. Hursley leaned back in his chair and grinned. "My daughter," Walter said, pulling Joia to where Eudo and Godric stood.

She looked vastly unhappy, her hands knotted before her. Eudo began the song and she joined in the refrain, her voice sweet and clear. She, also, Guy thought, could entertain a king. Guy recognized the style of song, sung after battles, the victor's name and circumstances changed to suit the audience. At last, Joia stepped down from the dais when Walter called for Eudo to sing another song.

Joia came and sat on the bench, pulling Crispin onto her lap. "Are you bothering our guard?" She kissed the child's brow.

"I'm not bothering Guy, but he's cold." The child poked Guy's chest with the tip of his finger. "Feel him."

The damnable heat shimmered between them again.

Joia examined Guy over the child's head. "Fetch him one of Edmund's heavy mantles."

When the boy had gone, Joia turned slightly away from Guy and clapped with the crowd to the beat of the music. "My father has forbidden me the river."

"As he should."

"Actually Martin forbids it. He said he ordered you to beat me if I lead you into such a dire circumstance again."

Guy glanced about to locate Hursley and his men to be sure none could hear what he had to say. Hursley had moved along the high table and now spoke to Avis. She stroked the knight's sleeve. Hursley seemed oblivious of the entertainment but a few feet from him and sung in his honor. Avis drew Hursley away from the table. Was there something between the two beyond caring for the injured Baldric? Avis stood very close to Hursley, her hand on his arm. It suggested intimacy.

Guy picked up the rhythm of the song and clapped with the crowd, giving Joia his shoulder as she had him.

"Would you? Beat me?" There was tart impatience in her voice.

"It would be my duty."

She leapt to her feet. He watched her push through the singing folk as she left the hall. He shook his head. Had she heard nothing he'd said by the river? She would, and could, go where she pleased, whether 'twas safe or not. The guard held the door for her as she stormed out.

He remained in his seat, wrought with indecision. He was her guard as he was Crispin's. One searched for a mantle, whilst the other was fuming and running who knew where.

Damnable woman.

The fire at the hearth roared, but still, he felt cold. When Crispin returned with his brother Edmund's mantle, a fine garment of heavy brown wool, reminding Guy most uncomfortably of the color of the muddy river, he took the child's hand and led him from the keep. The sky was clear, the stars a cascade of diamond-like ornamentation overhead. He'd been very wrong about the rain.

They wandered across the torch-lit bailey, past the kitchen to the smith, no angry Joia in sight. At the forge, Guy asked Crispin to introduce him to Tom.

"How may I help you?" the man asked, setting aside a destrier's shoe. Tom was stripped to the waist, sweating by his forge. A small boy crouched nearby to work the bellows, a child, who by his coloring, was likely the smith's son.

Tom was close to Guy in height, but heavier of muscle, with a pelt of black hair on his chest. His hair was black as well, his eyes a light blue, and Guy accepted that there was a small resemblance between them.

Crispin hunkered down by the smith's son and asked him if he might work the bellows. The two children chattered like old friends.

"Can you fashion a buckle for this belt?" Guy drew off his belt, laying the sword and sheath aside. "I think this might be ruined."

Tom turned the buckle about in a hand almost as large as the shoe he'd been fashioning. He looked up at Guy. "What do you really want? There's naught I can see wrong with this."

"Can you do it? The buckle?" Guy ignored the man's question.

They exchanged silent stares. Guy sensed he was being weighed and measured by the man and was relieved when he said, "Of course. I could do it for you on the morrow."

Guy drew a dagger from his boot and sliced off the silver buckle, dropping the leather belt into the smith's hand and picking up his sheathed sword. "Make it plain."

Tom nodded. "Would you like me to melt that down?"

Guy remembered how his father had given him the buckle at Alan's birth. He rubbed his thumb over the engraving and thought of Joia and her search for coins. He remembered that Lady Blanche had decorative buttons trimming her sleeves. "Aye, melt it. And do you make buttons?"

Tom tipped his head to a row of iron molds propped on a ledge. Guy looked them over and selected one that might appeal to a fanciful lady, though 'twas flowers not faeries on the mold.

He set the mold on the bench. I'll fetch them when I get the buckle."

Guy wrapped the belt about the sheath of his sword. "Come, Crispin, help me find your sister." They walked through the torchlit bailey

"I really like Little Tom. He lets me help."

"Glad I am you treated the boy well. When you are lord here, he'll remember and offer you respect."

They found Joia pacing in the garden behind the chapel.

Guy took Crispin into the chapel, its vaulted ceiling in deep shadow as it was lighted only by a brace of candles on the altar and a row of devotional ones guttering on a ledge before the Virgin. Guy opened the door that led to the priest's quarters. The man was not within. Guy noted the luxurious accommodations provided to Father Ilbert. He had a trio of rooms: a stark, bare antechamber with benches for penitents, another chamber with a bed to rival that of Lord Walter, and a final space with a table and comfortable, cushioned chairs where Guy imagined Lord Walter or Lady Blanche consulted the man.

Guy dropped a bar over the door from the priest's quarters to the bailey, and led Crispin to a *prie dieu* in the chapel. "Crispin, I want you to pray for your brother's soul. Don't move until I come for you. If you move, there shall be no honey and almonds for a month of days."

The child hastily bowed his head and began to mutter. The candles gilded his curls. The boy did not remind Guy of his son, Albert, who was of an age, but instead, of Alan. He, too, had hair as fair and curly as this child's.

Joia ignored Guy when he joined her in the garden, stalking away from him toward a pair of flowering pear trees that would eventually bear the fruit Crispin so prized. The garden was surrounded by walls.

Pebbly paths were laid out in a neat grid with beds of herbs and other plants, though most were in their early spring form, their small tender heads barely above the soil, whilst others had wintered over, protected by wooden frames gone now that the danger of frost was past. Guy imagined the kitchen workers or the priest wandering this peaceful space, tending the herbs and vegetables.

The spring planting was one reason many were grateful for was this temporary cessation of hostilities between Stephen and Maude. It provided time to plant or else no matter whether noble or peasant, hundreds would starve this coming winter. It was another constraint on Guy's search for Alan. Once the planting was done someone, somewhere, would agitate to break the peace. If the king hadn't noticed Guy's absence by now, he'd notice it then. Guy needed no imagination to know how angry King Stephen would be with a knight who wandered about the country looking for his errant son. Nay, a knight who'd abandoned his duties, son or no son.

The scents in the confined space were heady—rosemary, sage, others Guy couldn't name. He caught the scent of Joia's bedchamber as he strolled along a path.

The garden allowed ample space for Joia to stalk about and fume. He went to the darkest corner, farthest from the chapel lest Crispin decide to listen at the garden door. Guy placed his sword aside, and sat on a long wooden bench, stretching his legs out in front of him after tucking his boot knife into the sheath that held his long dagger. He knew that eventually Joia would need to confront him. The child would not be long content to pray, so he hoped it was sooner rather than later.

She made one round of the garden before standing before him. "I hate you. And Martin. And all men." She paced in front of him. "Beat me? I will beat you back."

"That, I might enjoy."

His words brought her to a halt before him. "Enjoy? You mock me."

"Do you really think I'd do such a thing? Beat you simply because some man orders it? You don't know me."

Her voice dropped to almost a whisper. "I don't know you at all."

"I answered as I did to rouse your anger."

"Why do you want me angry?"

Her hair covering, a gauzy lavender, held with twist of lavender cord, hid the silk of her hair. He remembered wringing it out. He wanted to handle it as he imagined it was now, dry and burnished from brushing. "As I told you by the river, you're too contemptuous of the danger you might be in. Your brother is dead. A war is on despite the truce, and despite what you choose to think, you're a valuable commodity. You need to learn caution."

"Commodity!"

He went on as if she hadn't spoken. "Your father assigned me as your guard. A guard is supposed to be *with* his charge."

"Who says I'm safe with you?"

"Indeed."

She tipped her head and looked him over, then shrugged as if dismissing him. "If Edith does not fear you, why should I?"

"Edith. I don't want to hear one more word of Edith."

He jumped up and gripped her shoulders. He grazed her lips with his. Her lips parted. He slid his tongue in and gently caressed the silkiness of her. Then he jammed the hilt of his boot knife against her side. She froze. He abruptly stepped away.

"If I'd wished, I could have slid this blade between your ribs whilst you kissed me. Trust no one."

She licked her lips. Her eyes stayed on his, though he held his dagger drawn. He ignored the sear of sensation that burned his groin and slid the dagger back into his boot. "A mantle can conceal many a weapon." *And how much I want you.* "Never let any man get so close."

"You kissed me again."

Aye, he wanted to say, aye, I kissed you again because I cannot resist you.

"You needed kissing. You are woefully deficient in the skill."

Her fingers closed on his sleeve. "Have you kissed so many women, you can pass judgement on such a thing?"

"I've kissed *enough* women to know you have either kissed *no* men, or very few indeed."

"Have you many mistresses?"

"Many?" He stared at her.

"For kissing."

What had he started? "One such as I cannot afford to keep a mistress."

Joia looked up at the sky. "Only the ancient ones, those who course the sky, can see us."

He raised his eyebrows in question.

She pointed up. "Hercules. Perseus. Do you not know your star tales? Only they can see us."

"I know who Hercules and Perseus are. What do you mean?"

"I mean that no one can see us here should you choose to tutor me in the art of kissing." She gripped the edges of his mantle and lifted her face. Her eyes were closed, her lips pursed. It was an invitation he couldn't refuse.

He took her into his arms. He kissed her hard this time, urging her lips to open, thrusting his tongue into her mouth, imitating what he wanted if they were naked. He pressed his cock against her, making sure she understood what a kiss could arouse. She made small breathy sounds in her throat.

He pulled his mouth away, moving his lips over her forehead, then her eyelids, kissed her cheeks, whispered his breath on her brows, her temples. As he drew his lips slowly along her cheek and back to her mouth, he cupped her breast.

She clamped her hand over his, though she didn't push him away. Instead, she came even closer. He caressed her breast. It fit perfectly in his hand. He groaned as her nipple pebbled against his palm. Desire hammered him, his heart beating as if the smith stood nearby and struck his anvil.

Guy skimmed his thumb again and again across her hard nipple. In answer, she shifted her hips against him. Did she know what she wrought? Or was she innocent in other ways as well?

She moaned softly, her breath sighing into his mouth. He took her hand and pressed her palm to the turgid length of him. Had he ever been this hard before? This in need? He burned to have her, sensations roiling through him as she stroked her hand down him to his stones.

He thrust her away.

"*That*, my lady, is kissing. It arouses a man, makes him want to lift your skirts, do more than kiss."

She clasped her hands on her breasts. "I understand. I trespassed quite badly when I kissed you the first time, did I not?"

"Aye, but the worst of it—" he broke off before he spoke the truth and told her that consequences be damned, he wanted her in his bed.

"The worst of it?" she prodded.

"The worst is that you might have enraged your father to kill me, or some other hapless man you used to make Hursley jealous. You and Crispin never think before you act."

"May I ask you a question?" She looked stricken in the meager light from the chapel torches. He badly wanted to take her back into his arms, not just to taste her mouth again, but to smooth away her unhappiness. He shrugged assent and kept his distance.

"Was I so bereft of skill?"

"Aye, most unskilled, but don't mistake me, my lady, a man would desire you all the more. And it's what's under your skirt that's of interest to most men. Kissing is merely the honey on the cake."

"I see. Are you interested in what's beneath my skirt?"

"*Mon Dieu,*" he muttered. How could she ask such a question after touching him so intimately? "I'm but a man. If you offered yourself," he aimed for a lighter tone, "I would take you only if I thought I would live through the night, my manhood intact."

A weak smile formed on her lips—lips that looked puffy from a thorough kissing.

He sighed. "Any man of worth, if he were honest, would appreciate that you are not skilled. It means you are also," he'd almost said not well *used* but bit back the words, "innocent in other ways."

"I am not innocent. I'm a widow." She lifted her chin. Even in shadow, he saw that passion still clouded her eyes.

He took a step toward the chapel. "Still. A man wants to believe in chastity and ignorance." How had be gotten involved in such a conversation? He'd rather stitch his own wounds than talk of such matters. He floundered for another subject, *any* other subject. "Have you thought on the men who might guard

Crispin?"

He felt her draw on a cloak of hauteur, but as they walked side by side to the chapel, her arm brushed his. Was it deliberate? How close she was? But as she gave Guy her opinion on the men, he thought it likely only his own desires that made much of the simple touch. Mayhap if he could afford a mistress, he'd have better control of himself around this woman. He tried to concentrate on her assessment of the men.

"You agree quite well with Owen, but not Father Ilbert." They stood at the chapel door, a constraint now between them that Guy thought might not, and should not, be broken.

"What did Father Ilbert think?" she asked as Guy drew open the door.

"He thought I should pick only men in Hursley's service as he'll soon be your husband."

She stiffened and for a moment, Guy thought she might have something to say, but she remained silent. Crispin sat on the *prie dieu*, prayers abandoned, picking at a rent in his hose.

"My knees are sore. My head hurts. I think I need some honeyed almonds or mayhap a bun."

Guy swept the boy onto his shoulders and gestured for Joia to precede them. She waited patiently as he sent a page for the two Rogers. She did not say a word either when he consigned her to them. He watched her enter the hall, then took Crispin to the bake house.

It was very warm there, despite the fact the fires had been damped down at this late hour. Great hooks with pots hung over the fires for making stews. Outside, Guy heard the bleat of a kid, the snuffling of pigs in their pens. Somewhere, geese entered the conversation. All meals for the morrow.

He met the cooks and watched the boy charm some buns dripping with honey for himself and Guy. They ended the evening, sitting cross-legged in the boy's chamber, licking their fingers and yawning.

When Crispin was asleep, Guy settled on his pallet. Again, sleep eluded him. He considered climbing the stairs to Joia's chamber. The chamber would be warm and fragrant as it had been the last time he visited. Only tonight . . . tonight she was skilled at kissing.

SEVENTEEN

Joia sat on a stool and closed her eyes, enjoying the rhythmic pass of the brush as Edith tended her hair.

"I thought I would take a turn about the chapel garden, my lady, then make my bed in the solar."

"Please do. I've no more need of you." As she spoke, Joia blanched that Edith might have seen her kissing Guy. The thought of being caught in such a position did naught to dampen the heat that twisted through her belly.

Guy lay on his pallet, cold on the outside but flaming on the inside. His body ached for release. As the hours passed, his dreams alternated between those of his son imprisoned in a rat-infested cell, honey cakes just out of reach and those of a naked Joia climbing astride his hips, moonlight gilding her breasts as she rode him.

Joia's aching body kept sleep at bay. She turned on her side and drew up her knees. Guy's kiss haunted her—and the touch of his hand on her breast. Never had she felt such sensations coursing through her. Even now, lying sleeplessly and thinking of him, she felt her body heating and her insides growing liquid.

She remembered how his hard phallus felt against her palm and the quick pulses that had wracked her core as she'd stroked over him. That hardness meant he wanted her, wanted to be inside her.

Her throat constricted. These sensations swirling through her, raising this hot, heaviness between her thighs, must be what sent Edith to seek a lover.

Guy lay only a few steps below. Joia wondered if she could go to him and learn real passion.

If she wed Martin, he'd touch her, come inside her. She turned onto her back and rubbed her face. She could *not* wed Martin. She couldn't lie beneath him, have him grunting over her as she'd seen other men do in the hall. One could not live in a castle filled with men and women, whether Robin's castle or her father's and not know what they did when night fell.

Robin had rarely visited her bed and in the last three years, as he'd grown ill, he'd only wanted her comfort, not her body.

Joia admitted she'd never before felt as she did around Guy. Just looking at his hands made her uncomfortable. They were strong and calloused. They'd also been demanding when he drew her hand to his manhood. She pummeled her pillows. At least she knew Edith hadn't touched Guy, or she'd know the man was *not* the size of either of their forearms.

That thought made Joia smile up at the beams overhead. She threw out her arms, kicking off the bedcovers as heat filled her. She craved that hard length of him, the ache between her thighs becoming a nearly painful throb at the thought of him filling her.

He didn't have a mistress.

Was she wanton if she lost control of her desire to kiss him? She'd not pulled her hand away as he guided her caress of him. If she were completely truthful, she *craved* his mouth, and his touch.

She must get away from Martin.

She rubbed her nipples with the flat of her palms and tallied up the expenses of an escort to a priory. Six men. Six horses. Bribes for innkeepers to remain silent about her party.

If she sold her goods in Portsmouth, she would pass the stone circle.

Her mind conjured Guy in the moonlight, half-naked, then shifted to what she'd seen when taking him clean linen. That vision was emblazoned on her mind.

The long line of his back. The muscles of his shoulders. His flanks.

Joia leapt from the bed, eased her door open, and peeked down the night-dark steps. The hall below and even the ramparts above were silent save for the hiss of wind on stone. She pressed an ear to the solar door but heard only snoring. She tiptoed down the steps, keeping one hand on the wall to find her way, and groped about for Crispin's door. Was it barred?

She lifted the latch and eased it open but a few inches, then slipped in. The room was in complete darkness save for a wick burning in a dish of oil by Crispin's head. He was an indistinguishable lump in the shadows. She let her eyes accustom themselves to the inky night, relieved that Crispin always slept so soundly. The chamber smelled of the pallets she knew had been stored here and Crispin, who resisted most efforts to bathe him.

The room also held the scent of Guy—weapons, oiled leather, and something that was just him. She knelt by his pallet that lay just inside the door. He slept on his back, one arm behind his head, his shirt unlaced at his throat, a fur covering him from waist to foot. She leaned over and skimmed her fingertips across his lips.

He snatched her wrist, jerked her forward, a blade now pressing along her ribs. "*Sweet Jesu,*" he whispered, dropping her hand, easing his dagger back under the fur. "I could have killed you."

"Why did you not?" She crept forward so her knees rested on his pallet.

"The scent of lavender."

She waited. He said no more. She wished to read his eyes, know his thoughts, but the shadows enveloped him.

She put her hand on his chest, and knew he felt as she did by the rapid beat of his heart that surely matched her own. She pressed her lips there as she eased his lacings open and followed the parting linen with her fingertips and lips. When she exposed one of his nipples, she skimmed it with her tongue.

He made a feral growl in his throat, dug his fingers into her hair, and held her. He took a deep shuddering breath. She licked a path up his chest, along his throat and his chin, rough with the day's growth of beard. When she reached his mouth, his hard, arrogant mouth, he took control.

He rolled her beneath him, crushed her mouth with his, a warrior conquering. And she wanted to be vanquished, taken, ravished. The heavy throb between her thighs grew almost painful in its intensity, and she knew, as he lifted her hem, that he would touch her *there*.

Aye, she craved that touch. And equally must lay her hands on him.

She gripped his shirt, pulling it up to feel the muscles cording his back. She reveled in the feel of him under her hands, the hard, the smooth. She swept her hands down to his hard buttocks then over his hips.

Heat and need stabbed into her, ran like a wild fire through her blood. She gulped in the taste of his mouth, the feel of his tongue. Every muscle of her body went taut in anticipation of what he would do—what he *must* do or she might scream.

Guy caressed her hip. The calluses on his hand were more enticing than ever costly silk might feel sliding across her skin.

She held her breath. He skimmed her stomach. Her muscles quivered beneath his touch. She dug her nails into his hip. The beat of her heart filled her every sense. He slid his hand between her thighs.

She went rigid beneath him, buried her face against his throat, and gasped as wave after wave of sensation roiled from his touch.

Guy held Joia close as her body shook. He bent his head to kiss her, but she tore from his grasp and fled, cold air rushing in to take her place. When the door whispered closed, Guy sat up and pulled down his shirt. He took deep breaths to slow his heart's hammering beat.

Had he dreamt it? Dreamt her?

Nay. Lavender filled his head, and his fingers were slick with her passions.

His body ached from need unfulfilled. Why had he not barred the door? Had he been expecting her? *Inviting* her?

He fell back on his pallet and pulled the fur up and over his head. He was lost. Completely and undeniably lost.

EIGHTEEN

Martin yawned and watched Avis stretch. Dawn was only a few hours away. He wanted her gone. "Should you not get back to the keep?"

She sat up and quickly plaited her hair. "Aye, I must see to Walter, though he's like a flower picked but left in the sun these days."

Martin grinned. "Ah . . . wilted." He shrugged. "He's a glutton. He's likely just suffering of belly troubles."

"Nay, 'tis that witch, Joia." Avis drew on her clothing.

"If it is, then when I'm wed to her, the man will be back to plying his sword twice nightly."

Avis smiled. "Please, I beg you, not twice nightly. Such play is for you younger men." She bent and kissed him on the mouth. "What if she'll not wed you?"

He pushed her away. "She *will* wed me. Of that, you may be certain. I shall garb her in silks and drape her in jewels."

Avis shook her head. "You men never learn. She has enough of jewels and gowns. Joia—and every other woman—wants to be loved. Woo her with soft words. Tell her what she wants to hear."

She doused the candle, and lifted the curtain that separated Martin from the rest of the men. She disappeared into the dark.

Woo her. Avis's words lingered in Martin's mind. He should not have to woo, Joia. She should give his offer the due respect it deserved.

He stacked his hands behind his head. Soon, everyone would give him their respect. He knew his scheme to be brilliant in its simplicity. It had come to him one night when Walter bragged of his high stature, so high the king would come to Edmund's wedding.

Martin had hatched his plan that very moment. And all had been in readiness when Edmund's betrothed had died. For several long months, Martin had been twisted with anger at the smashing of his dreams. Then Joia had returned home from Canterbury, her husband dead. One glimpse of her had aroused all Martin's early longing for her, and he'd realized if King Stephen would come to Edmund's wedding, the king would also come to hers.

Martin imagined the shock when he abducted the king at the wedding feast. Martin imagined the gratitude of Empress Maude and the chagrin of Gloucester, that damnable brother of hers when he, Martin Hursley, just a humble knight, delivered up the means of placing the crown permanently on Maude's head.

The Empress would reward him as King Stephen never had. Stephen would know his mistake when he found himself shackled and given over to his enemies. Martin looked about the meager quarters that were his until the wedding. He would demand Stonewold along with Robin de Tille's manors.

When all was finished, Martin thought, Joia could not complain as the wife of an earl. Had she accepted him when first he'd proposed, her brother wouldn't be languishing in a dank cell. It was her fault that Baldric had captured Edmund. Her fault if Edmund took ill and died. Her fault.

And once wed, she'd finally shut her lips and obey. Aye, Martin thought, I'll have her twice a night. He laughed out loud. Aye, such sport *was* for younger men.

NINETEEN

Joia forced herself to listen to Father Ilbert as he droned through the service. Her mind felt clogged with feathers. Her heart kept beating as if she'd run from one end of the keep to the other. She now understood the elusive references Edith made to a woman's pleasure.

Yet, Joia also admitted, she'd fled from that pleasure, from Guy, sure that he'd take her—and she would have let him.

She must not lie to herself. She'd gone to him with that intent.

Her insides were still in turmoil, hours later. Every part of her ached, her head, her breasts, her center.

Edith poked her attention back to the service with a sharp elbow. Edith. Sneaking off so many nights to a lover.

Was Guy now *her* lover? Nay, Joia, thought, she'd not taken him into her body. She shivered, clasped her hands tightly in prayer. An idea bloomed. All these aches were a chill from the fall in the river. That was it. How simple. She'd caught a chill in all those hidden places. She'd order a hot bath and soak out the cold. It had naught to do with Guy.

Joia renewed her vow to leave Stonewold. Sweet Crispin had agreed to lend her his pennies, and he had several pounds worth. Her throat tightened that the coins were bribes from her father. It was a sad thing that old pot of coins. Could she leave Crispin? Would he suffer without her? She'd miss him dreadfully, but a boy his age would soon be immersed in learning what it meant to be a man and would give up his mother and sister for male pursuits. Had Edmund not done the same at Crispin's age?

Her mind skittered away from the man who would have the teaching of Crispin. If she were cloistered she'd have none of these desires. Another thought nudged away the convent.

Might Guy take her away? She could be his mistress. Her quarry could keep them quite well.

What was she thinking? Martin and her father would hunt them down and kill Guy. Nay, a poor priory must be her fate, their strict routine the means of scouring away her longings.

She added Crispin's pennies to her tally of goods purchased with Owen's help. She could use Crispin's coin to hire a few pack horses and the men needed to take her to Winchester so she could sell her goods. Portsmouth was too intimidating. Then she'd have enough to travel north until she found a priory in need of her quarry.

If she avoided inns, the source of much gossip, she might need more pack horses. How would such a parade of men and horses escape her father's notice? What was to stop her escort from selling her whereabouts to Martin or her father the moment the priory doors closed?

Her gaze fell on a pair of jugglers her father intended should perform for the king. There would be more entertainers arriving. Many would not pass her father's scrutiny. Mayhap those her father rejected would take her away for a price. She could simply join a company of minstrels. She could call herself . . . Mistress Meadowlark. She sang well. She could even compose a verse if pressed.

Beltane was now only a fortnight away.

The convent or a life with minstrels?

How could she put her father and Martin off? Make them see it was too soon, dreadfully too soon.

Her mind kept returning to Guy and the feel of his hands on her. Each time, she pushed the thoughts away with rapid mental calculations of men, horses, and bribes.

Crispin leaned his fair head against Guy's arm. He was such a sharp contrast to Martin. Both men were well-favored, strong men, Guy taller, longer of arm. Then she chastised herself. It was

sinful to think of Guy in chapel just as it was to think of escape.
The two, Guy and escape, kept twining through her mind.

Her father frowned at her. Were her thoughts written on her
face?

But as Father Ilbert quoted from Pope Gregory's *Moralia*, it
occurred to Joia that regardless of how well-favored the two men
were, Martin and Guy, no matter how *in favor* with her father
Martin might be, it was how Guy and Martin treated those about
them from the lowest of servants to herself, that made Joia
suspect only one of them had morals.

Still, her mind strayed to the feel of Guy's bare skin beneath
her hands. Never, when she'd seen him in the stone circle had
she thought that she would one day run her hand over . . . she
must stop.

Her skin flushed at thoughts of what he'd wrought with just
the stroke of *his* hand. She gripped her fingers together and
begged for mercy to wipe the vision of Guy in the stone circle
from her mind.

She shifted her sinful thoughts to the more venial ones of
money and remedying her poverty. Coin hunting at the river
would take too long. She'd try the burial barrow. She said a
prayer that the barrow was rich in treasure and that she might be
free at last.

Guy left the chapel behind Walter and Joia, not feeling very
cleansed of his sins. In the cold light of day, he admitted he owed
Joia a great measure of thanks or those sins would be grievous
indeed. In truth, if she'd not run off, he'd have possessed her with
no thought to the consequences. Only disaster would have
followed the act. And on the heels of disaster—regret.

No matter what had happened between them in the night, it
couldn't happen again. He must see it did not. He must not
forget his reason for being at Stonewold. He needed to finish his

mission and head for Winchester to face the king and whatever royal wrath awaited him.

Guy gave Crispin a scant breakfast of bread and milk in the hall. He'd ask Joia to show him the Tavest Battle records.

The image of her face as she found pleasure in his arms made him clench his hand on the hilt of his dagger. Indeed, he must go before he could not go.

TWENTY

Baldric smelled his sister's musky perfume before she smoothed the hair from his brow. It mingled ill with the rest of the scents of the physician's chamber.

"I'm awake," he said. "I'd prefer to be asleep."

"Ah, temper. You must be healing." Avis took a seat by his side.

"Why are you not at chapel?"

"'Tis almost noon, Baldric." She bit her lip. "I need your advice."

He grinned. "When have you ever taken it?" She smiled back, but he saw she was distracted.

"I'm with child."

He shrugged. "If you play the game, you pay the consequences. Is it Martin's or Walter's?"

"Walter's," she snapped.

"You mean you wish it to be Walter's." Baldric steeled himself for one of Avis's rants.

"'Twas conceived whilst Martin was in Winchester. There's no doubt in the matter. If I were *not* with child, I would never take a chance and—"

"Fuck Martin?" Baldric finished for her. He yawned. "What do you want of me? You do want something, do you not?"

She lifted a finger to her lips, tiptoed to the door and peered outside to be sure there was no one about seeking the physician who was likely drunk in the hall.

"I want you to kill Crispin for me."

He stared at her. He'd oft thought her mad, her thoughts not always following the path that made the most sense. Now he was sure of it. Anger surged through him. She'd ruin everything.

He sat up and snatched her wrist. He jerked her close so he could speak in her ear. "You're mad! What the devil will that accomplish?"

She tried to wrench away, but he held her captive. "Was Robert of Gloucester not honored by the old king? Walter's a great man, and I want my child to be honored as Gloucester is."

Baldric forced himself to be calm. He lowered his voice to a whisper. "So, it was you who caused the accidents to the child, and put every damned soldier in Stonewold on alert and seen to the hiring of that damned man of Chelten's."

Her face flooded with color but she kept her voice low. "Edmund's dead and if Crispin were as well, Walter would honor my child."

"Unless it proves a female. Unless Walter simply passes you on to one of his friend's at court. Unless he simply weds you to a pig keeper who'll be happy for a few extra pennies for raising his lordship's bastard."

She burst into tears.

"Be silent."

She gulped and gasped, clapping her hands over her mouth.

Baldric took a grip of his anger. She knew not that Edmund still lived. He might not survive much longer, and Baldric knew he'd not hesitate to kill the man if it served them better that he were dead, but Crispin was another story.

Baldric studied his sister. Edmund's supposed death must have given Avis ideas above her station—twisted ideas.

Baldric's chest wound throbbed. He rubbed it as he swung his legs over the side of the physician's bed and faced her. "You never understood your place. You're Walter's *whore*. Whores birth babes all the time. Few can reach for what Gloucester has. He's the bastard son of a *king*. Do you think Lady Blanche will simply welcome your child? She'll be shamed by your presence here, and if Walter cannot part with you, be sure our lady will. You'll count yourself fortunate to be simply passed on to one of

Walter's friends."

She threw her arms around his neck. "You'll see to me, will you not?"

He pulled her arms away. "What have I to offer you? Think you Lady Joia will welcome you to Fairoaks when she's wed to Martin? For that's where I'll be." He would *not* tell Avis their plans. She'd an idle tongue and a malicious heart.

She dropped her face into her hands. Her shoulders shook with silent sobs. He waited until she was done. "You'll do naught without my permission. We'll have no mourning to halt Martin's wedding, do you understand?"

"Who are you to order *me*?" She hissed the words through clenched teeth.

He slapped her. She fell to her knees.

He crouched in front of her. "Martin and I have plans. You interfere in those plans, do you understand? Now, this is what you *will* do. You'll cease fucking Martin lest Lord Walter or Lady Blanche get wind of it. You'll forget Crispin exists. Do you understand?"

She nodded. Tears ran down her cheeks.

He slapped her again. "Say you understand."

She struggled to her feet. "I understand."

"And will obey?"

"And will obey."

He wrapped his arms around her and pulled her against his chest. "I have plans, Avis. I cannot let you ruin them. I will promise you when Lady Joia and Martin are wed, I'll go with you to Walter, and we'll bargain with him over the child. 'Tis the best I can offer you."

She nodded, but he wasn't sure whether she was agreeing or appeasing him. He must keep a sharp eye on her until Beltane. He was about to repeat his orders when he heard footsteps— Martin's footsteps—outside.

Baldric stretched out on the bed.

When Martin entered, Avis bent over him and drew back his bandages to inspect the stitching of his wound. "Are you eating

147

well?"

Martin grinned and rolled his eyes. "He eats like my destrier."

"Edith sees to my meals," Baldric said. "She visits me thrice a day."

Martin exchanged a grin with Avis.

"She's good to be so devoted," Avis said. She patted her brother's covers into place.

"And are you well? Your cheeks are flushed." Martin asked her.

"I'm well. 'Tis just that Walter's always seems angry these days. He's so tormented by Joia. She'll kill him as surely as if she wielded a knife. Why can she not do as she is bid?

"Says one who never followed anyone's advice," said Baldric. He didn't like her tone.

She ignored his barb. "We must get you better. Did you know Walter has invited the king to the Beltane festivities? There will be a feast like none other if he comes. There will be roasted swans and mayhap even peacock tongues. Wine's being sent from Walter's vineyards in France. There will be almond cakes and dates and candied orange peel." Then she stamped her foot. "Why should she be so honored? Forgive me, Martin, but she doesn't even want to wed you!"

Baldric let her rant. Mayhap her goads would force Martin to act.

Avis put her nose in the air and left them. Baldric sought to wipe the frown from Martin's face. "I'd rather be at the bedding than the wedding. Whilst you secure the king and transport him down river, I shall tie Lady Joia to the bedpost so she cannot escape you." He grinned at Martin. "Mayhap, if you're not pleased with the lady I could have the use of her."

"I didn't realize you lusted after her."

Baldric caught the edge in Martin's voice. "I was jesting. And likely your lady love is still a virgin. I've no patience for virgins."

"Robin de Tille was old as the hills and sickly, likely could not stiffen up." Martin sat on the stool Avis had vacated and leaned forward, elbows on knees. He whispered. "Avis gave the news ere I could, but a messenger arrived and the king is coming for the wedding. The moment he's left alone or his guards are unwary, we'll take him."

"Aye. I've asked Walter if I might see to the wine stores for him. I'll see that the king's guard get more than their fair share. But if you cannot secure Joia's agreement to the wedding, all our plans are for naught."

"Walter says she only needs time to prepare herself as she still mourns Edmund. Walter will command her and she will obey."

Baldric had no confidence in Walter's power to command his daughter. He stretched and winced. "If the lady doesn't see sense in a day or two, we should use our threat."

"Aye. I agree. A day or two. I'll wait no more. After all, a threat is simply that, is it not?

"Lady Joia will never endanger Edmund, and after the wedding, after our plans are fulfilled, and you are honored by the Empress, your lady will forgive and forget."

Martin nodded. "Aye. She'll forgive and forget."

"I think we should get rid of Crispin's guard before the wedding."

"Why?"

Baldric gave Martin a long stare. "He makes a formidable opponent."

"Is that your way of saying you might not be able to best him if he interferes in some way?"

Baldric shrugged. The barb hit too close to home.

"Killing such a man would raise many questions."

"Mayhap we need not kill him right away," Baldric said. "He was in Chelten's service. We simply sow a few seeds of doubt about his loyalty to King Stephen. A word here, a word there. Walter won't want the man loose for the wedding lest he be a spy. If nothing else, if we do it right, Walter will lock him up as a precaution against treachery, and we can kill him afterward."

"How?"

"We shall simply ask Avis for her help."

"Avis? What do you intend her to do? Fuck him to death?"

Baldric threw back his head and laughed. "Nay, I meant she can begin to whisper in Walter's ear of Chelten's treachery and Guy's connection to the man."

Martin grinned. "I'll ask her to start working on Walter the first chance she gets." He stood up. "I'm off to the hall. I intend to take Joia riding. I shall woo her with soft words, promises, and words of love. When do you think *you* can ride?"

Baldric rose and mimed hefting an ax and swinging it. "I can ride any time, if I have something for the pain." He looked at the shelves of dishes, the hanging herbs and bubbling simples. "Surely the physician has a potion that will do the trick."

"Aye, ask the man, but rest my friend; I cannot do aught without you."

From his place in the practice yard, Guy watched Joia ride in with Martin Hursley, watched the man help her from the saddle, hands at her waist. Moments later Guy realized his fists were clenched as well as every muscle of his body, even his teeth. The reaction chilled him. It smacked of jealousy, and worse, *need.*

Had he not just convinced himself he had no need of any woman? Women were twelve a dozen. 'Twas just a simple concern for a lady under pressure to wed a man she didn't want.

And here he was, lying to himself.

Crispin tugged his tunic. "Guy, I'm tired of wooden swords and stones."

Guy went down on one knee by Crispin. "You did so well with both, we'll put the weapons aside." Walter was holding a small manorial court, and Guy knew Owen must be in attendance. "I'll ask Owen to see the manor records—"

"I saw how much the king gets," Crispin interrupted with a scowl.

Guy had decided he would not ask Joia's help to see the battle records. The less he spoke to her the better. "I want you to understand how much the other families gave up to have their sons back. The better you fight, the less likely you'll end up watching your father turn over a cart of ransom for you. And a lord should always know his steward's work." Guy was not sure they were good arguments for seeing the castle records, but they were the only ones he had.

The boy set one foot on Guy's thigh and climbed to his shoulder. He sighed. "I think I'd prefer to learn the baker's duties, but if it must be Owen's, it must." He tugged Guy's hair. "But you must promise me——"

"A juggling lesson," Guy said, before the boy mentioned his other weakness—pears and honey.

Guy found Owen in the hall, noting down fines and punishments as Walter listened to the complaints and entreaties of the villagers. Before approaching Owen, Guy sat down and watched a few of the petitions. Walter meted out harsh fines for petty matters which Guy decided should not surprise him. A man who could publicly whip his daughter would be no less merciful to a man who might be unable to pay his rent. Guy wanted to intervene twice when Walter showed no compassion to those who couldn't afford the seed to replant after the Stonewold forces had trampled their fields.

But it was Joia's entrance that surprised Guy. The mood within the hall suddenly lightened. She took a seat beside her father. Guy noticed that without obviously contradicting him, she softened several of his penalties and offered counsel instead of fines. She respectfully greeted the petitioners and knew their names.

After one whispered comment at her father's ear, he suddenly grinned, rose, called his hounds, and hastened from the hall. She slid over to her father's chair and took up the judging without protest from Owen or those who awaited judgement which told Guy she'd likely been doing so since she'd returned to Stonewold or, at least, since Edmund's death.

He couldn't tear his eyes from her. There was not another

Joia. She was like no other woman he'd ever met. She was as regal as the queen. Guy knew King Stephen's Matilda had stepped in for him on occasion, wielding his power with the same simple courtesy and gentleness Guy saw in Joia.

Guy admired the subtle way she'd turned the proceedings from a tension-filled procedure to one of practical problem solving. He thought with regret that if Joia had been a man, she might have held Stonewold for Crispin. Guy wanted to remain in place and hear her judgement of each case, but Crispin wriggled with impatience beside him.

He made his way down the side of the hall and waited. When Joia shifted her attentions to the shaky progress of an elderly man and woman who approached the dais, Guy spoke in Owen's ear. "I'd use this time to show Crispin how much a man might cost in ransom." He shifted Crispin before him. "Such records will——"

"Go. Go. The key's under my mattress," Owen whispered, scratching numbers on a sheet of parchment.

It wasn't quite a lie Guy had offered Owen. Guy intended to examine the records with Crispin in attendance, but if Crispin should curl up on Owen's bed like a lazy cat, so much the better. Guy also hoped Owen wouldn't mention to anyone that Guy had examined the records, for to do so, Guy would have to read, not a usual skill in a simple soldier.

Owen's small chamber in the men's quarters, carved out of a space against the bakehouse wall, was warm and snug. Guy scratched his head over a teetering heap of what must be Joia's market purchases, or *gifts*, that filled one corner. The two saddles he'd seen her purchase were ridden by a bolt of green linen, several skins, as well as baskets and small casks.

Owen had a huge bed, with a goose feather mattress and with Joia's goods, there was little room to move about. Crispin did indeed curl up like a cat in the furs and pillows and promptly fall asleep. Guy dug under the mattress for Owen's key, shaking his head at how easily anyone might do the same, and then looked under the bed and saw a row of chests.

He hauled them out, flipping them open until he found the

one containing the most recent castle tallies. He sat on the floor and sorted through the rolled parchments, and skimming them, noting that those who stood in Stonewold's courts this day were likely grateful 'twas Joia who heard them and not Walter who charged excessively high fines. He'd also charged high ransoms for the Empress Maude's men, de Lorien's being among the least of what Walter had gathered in from the Battle of Tavest.

The light was poor and Owen's writing crabbed and shaky. Still, one item from the Tavest records sent a chill through Guy.

Brown Gelding ~ Bald knee right fore ~To Fairoaks 13 March ~ Two Marks

Alan's horse.

TWENTY-ONE

Avis kept her hood low as she walked through the bailey. She found the hordes of mummers, jugglers, and tumblers especially annoying as they persisted in readying themselves for the king's visit by performing for whoever was about, somersaulting everywhere, singing and dancing, prancing and mincing.

She almost screamed when a group of men encircled her, joined their hands, and sang of the beauty and grace of a Beltane bride.

Not *her* beauty, not *her* grace.

Avis broke through their arms and scuttled along at the side of a cart loaded with wood destined for the ovens. She saw Blanche in the distance, arm in arm with the idiot of a priest. The man's black robes were green with age at the hem. How could Blanche tolerate so much time in his company? But Avis knew that few listened to Blanche with such interest and patience.

Avis should not complain about Blanche. She never spoke an ill word, and Avis knew in her heart Blanche was grateful to hand her conjugal duties to another.

Avis hastened to the women's solar lest she draw Walter's attentions, although it seemed he, too, wished to slip responsibility this day as it was Joia who presided at the judgements. Here, too, Joia took on much and all seemed to defer to her. Envy knotted in Avis's belly.

The solar stood empty, despite a blazing fire on the hearth. She dropped her mantle over a bench then opened one of her chests. She carefully shifted aside her precious gowns and pulled out a wooden cask carved with vines and leaves. She drew out a key she kept hidden on a chain about her neck. Inside the cask were linen pouches any wife might possess to heal the sick. She glanced about, but who'd be watching? The mice? A few spiders? She shook off her fears. One pouch was older and more worn than the others, one she'd had from her mother, God rest her.

Avis opened the soft linen sack. Inside was a yellowish powder. It would rid her of the child she carried. She kneaded the soft linen between her hands as she sat by the fire.

Baldric's anger shamed her. He'd looked after her all the years since their mother had died. He'd helped her secure a place with Lady Blanche, had he not? Baldric was the most excellent of brothers. Her eyes welled with tears. But Baldric didn't understand what it was to be a woman. She rose and went to the window that looked out toward the Tavest River. It lay like a brown skein of wool on a green cloth.

A few years before, she'd thought Martin might wed her, but he'd chosen Isabel, that ugly mouse instead. Then when Isabel died, Avis had thought her time had come with Martin. Instead, Lady Joia returned, ending Avis's hopes yet again. Martin might want what lay between her thighs but that was all.

She dashed her tears away. Nay, Baldric was wrong. Walter loved her. He would do more than hand her off to some other man. He cherished his time with her.

Avis stared down at the linen pouch in her hand. Why should she destroy this child?

She looked over Walter's domain as anger filled her. It was wrong that one child should have so much and another so little. And what of the mother? Her gaze fell on Lady Blanche's discarded stitchery.

If Blanche were gone, Walter would wed her. Blanche was long past breeding, and if aught happened to Crispin, she could not give him another heir.

Avis touched her belly. Soon no amount of stitchery would conceal the truth.

She thought on Baldric's words. He was most often right, but mayhap this time he was wrong. He might be right about Crispin, but he'd not thought of the Lady Blanche.

There would be plenty of time for Crispin later. Much could happen to a boy betwixt childhood and manhood. She could obey Baldric and still have her way.

Avis searched deeper in her cask and found a dirty linen pouch, a twin to the one she held in her hand. Inside was a coarse gray powder, fine for killing rats. She'd made it up, long before she'd been favored in Walter's bed, for the rats had bedeviled her when she'd been naught but a seamstress, simply a sister to one of Walter's knights. She stroked her fingertips over the silky threads of Blanche's embroidery. She knew she couldn't be that lowly woman again, her fingers sore from hours of plying a needle. She put the yellow powder away.

Edmund dug about in the dark, found his trencher, and broke off a morsel of bread and sour drippings. He'd give the rest to Alan when he woke. He couldn't let the boy die. They were both here because *he* was the poorest swordsman in Christendom. If he'd been quicker, abler, stronger, Alan would be free.

When they escaped, and Edmund was determined to somehow save this young man, he'd see Alan was well rewarded for saving his life. Edmund stretched his limbs. In truth, he should serve *Alan*. It was obvious from Alan's conversation, he'd been taught all manner of tactics, knew the use of most weapons, and could wield them. His sainted father had seen to it by fostering him to a knight who knew his business.

Edmund sighed. His father had handed him off to old Godric who preferred to tell stories of his time with King Henry, rather than actually teach Edmund how to survive on the battlefield.

That stupidity had cost Alan his freedom and possibly his life.

"My kingdom for a light," Alan said.

"You might not like the view," Edmund said.

"The rats are getting bolder. I hate rats."

"I'm not so fond of them myself."

"Rats are the only thing my indomitable father fears. I remember well a time a rat jumped onto the table. My father was ten feet away, behind a serving wench, before the creature reached the end of the planks."

Edmund laughed. "My father would probably ask the cook to sauce the thing in red wine and honey. He'll eat anything."

They spent the next few moments regaling each other with tales of their finest meals. Then Edmund said, "Did you not say your father could kill a man eight ways with just his bare hands?"

Alan sighed. "Aye."

"Tell me how; it might pass the time."

Alan shifted to a new position, his chains rattling. "First—"

But Alan broke off when they heard the sound of someone lifting the bar to their prison. They were blinded a moment when Father Ilbert waved his torch about to look them over. He set the torch in a bracket outside the door. He stood there in the entry, looking down at Edmund.

This was the first time Father Ilbert had come twice in one day. There was no food sack in his hand.

"I must ask you again, Lord Edmund, if you will write to your sister and ask her to do whatever she is bid?"

Edmund shook his head.

"I beg of you, my lord," the priest said. There was a quiver in his voice, but it was the man who stepped past the priest and into the cell that made Edmund's heart begin to pound.

Baldric pointed to the door and the priest scuttled away like one of Alan's rats.

Confusion swept through Edmund. "What're you doing here?"

"You've been asked to perform a simple task. Write to your sister."

"Why should I?"

Baldric ignored his question. "If you don't write to your sister, saying you're alive, well cared for, and wish that she do as she's asked, I'll take her a token of your liveliness. A finger."

Baldric hefted his ax. Saliva flooded Edmund's mouth. "You wouldn't."

"I would," Baldric said. It was the lack of emotion in his tone that made Edmund's insides clench.

Then Baldric smiled. "But one finger is much like another. 'Tis your companion's finger I'll take."

"Don't give in, Edmund. There's some evil he wants of your sister. Don't give in." There was no fear in the hard look on Alan's face.

Edmund's mind raced. Baldric was one of his father's knights. He was also Martin's good friend. And Martin wanted Joia. Was Martin somehow involved in his capture?

Edmund swallowed, his throat painfully dry. It could not be. Martin and he had known each other since childhood, hunting the forest together, fishing for eels. Martin could *not* cut off anyone's finger.

But Baldric was different. He licked his lips and smiled as he idly swung his ax. Edmund knew without doubt that Baldric would enjoy the business.

"Bring me pen and ink," he said.

TWENTY-TWO

Guy leaned his elbows on a table in the hall and watched the minstrels practicing for their entertainment of the king, but a brown gelding occupied all his thoughts. A brown gelding with a bald knee.

Edith sat beside him. "Lady Joia's a sore trouble to manage."

Guy almost smiled. Edith sounded as if she were Joia's mother not her maid.

"Sir Martin will not like her acting the servant."

He watched Joia and a pair of women who were scattering fresh rushes. She had a basket and she followed after them, casting something nearly invisible as if casting seed in a field. Some fragrant herb, he supposed. Lavender?

He imagined her in a field of lavender, then shook off the thought and tried to concentrate on Joia's perfidious maid. He interrupted her assessment of the jugglers now tumbling about before Walter. "Edith, who's your lover?"

"Not you." She tossed her head.

"Aye, not me, but you led Lady Joia to think it was, did you not?"

Her voice was very soft, her cheeks flushed, when she finally answered. "Aye. I didn't think she'd approve. He were Edmund's man, but now, he's Martin's." She ran her hand up and down Guy's arm. A sultry expression replaced that of contrition. "She'll think he—or we—spy for Martin. You'll not tell on us, will you?" She batted her eyelashes.

Guy was conscious that Joia moved closer, although she seemed to be distracted by the singing and dancing. He shook off

Edith's wandering hand.

"That depends. *If* you tell Lady Joia on your own, then I'll not. Simply be honest. But if I find that you've not told your lady you have a lover—and it is *not* me—then I'll tell her for you. And if a few thoughts of spying were to accompany my telling . . . ." He let the thought drift.

"But how will it differ if I tell her?" Edith twisted her hands in her lap. "She'll still think we spy for Martin."

He took a long, steadying breath. He wanted to shake Edith, but it was very important to him that when he left Stonewold Joia knew he'd not lain with Edith.

"Tell Lady Joia two things. One, I was never your lover, and two, you love one of Martin's men. If you then ask her help, beg that she assist the two of you in some way, you'll not find yourself scrubbing those tables." He stood up. "I fear you're carrying on in a manner that ensures you'll soon be doing so, if not worse, mayhap even stirring laundry pots—"

He broke off as Crispin spun into the hall, tripping over his feet. He grabbed Guy's hand.

"Come, come. Tink needs you. He said there's a horse as cannot be ridden. Tink's scared."

Guy followed the running child to the stable yard. He bowed to Walter whose hounds milled about his feet as he awaited his hunting party. Tink held a destrier by the reins, standing as far as the leather leads would allow.

"Thank the saints," Tink whispered. "'Is lordship said to learn 'im. I'll not get on this beast and neither will any o' these lads if they value their lives."

Guy looked the great destrier over. The warhorse, as were they all, was uncut. It served the horse well, that aggression in battle, but could also make the horse dangerous if not properly trained. He took the reins from Tink, hesitated one moment, aware what he was going to do was not the action of a simple soldier. He looked about the yard. No one seemed to be paying attention to them, intent instead on Walter and his hounds. Guy vaulted into the saddle. Without mail and weaponry, it was easily done.

The horse sidled, danced, pawed the ground. Then it sat back on its haunches. Moments later, the horse was careening from the stable yard. Guy gained control just as the horse reached the open castle gates. He used his knees, hands, and heels and several ripe commands to send the beast the signals he should know. This must be de Lorien's horse the grooms complained about. In truth, the beast was poorly trained, but after a long struggle, settled down and did as bid. An hour later, Guy trotted the beast back into the stable yard, heavily lathered, but obedient. Walter still loitered at the stables, so Guy led the destrier to a far door to avoid the hounds lest they agitate the horse anew. He stepped down from the saddle.

Walter approached, fists on hips, but had the sense to keep his dogs away. "Well, Guy? Sell him? Eat him? Keep him?"

Guy patted the huge horse's neck. "He needs patient retraining. He acknowledges orders, but when it suits him. But, I like him. If he were mine, I'd keep him."

Walter slapped Guy on the back. "*If* I can find someone to ride him with such boldness. Mayhap you'll give him some time?"

Guy bowed without answering.

"Bring my hunter," Walter ordered a groom. "We're wasting a fine day."

Guy watched Lord Walter wander among his hounds, stroking their heads, teasing one or two, a wide grin on his face. What an unpredictable man, angry one moment, smiling the next.

Tink edged toward the destrier, but Guy waved him off. "I'll tend him." He went into the stables as quickly as he could to forestall any further talk of training the animal. He'd not be here to train de Lorien's horse, and he wanted to avoid an outright lie. He cleaned out the huge hooves, whilst Tink finally crept near with a rag and bucket to deal with the lathered coat.

"I've read the ransom lists from Tavest," Guy said.

Tink washed down the destrier who stood as if he'd not an

hour before tried to kill every man who neared him. "And?"

"Alan's horse is on the list."

"The devil ye say!"

"Aye. The devil has it. Bought from Lord Walter by Hursley."

"Hursley." Tink spat in the straw and plied his rag with extra vigor. "Alan's 'orse 'as never been stabled 'ere, not whilst I been 'ere. And where's our boy, then?"

"I could find no trace of Alan or his weapons in Walter's records, just of his horse. I've examined every building of Stonewold, the storerooms, the dungeons, the gatehouse cells. I've been through the village as well. I swear I've seen every dagger, sword, lance, and bow and *rat*. I've spoken to the remaining prisoners and one was a groom who knew Sir Edward's squires. No one knows aught of Alan. I want you to leave with the leather merchants at the next market, and I'll follow in a few days."

"Why not hie to Fairoaks and see if ye can find aught of our boy there? Mayhap a groom or two might know some gossip. If Hursley 'as him, 'e may ransom 'im yet."

"I've heard nothing of Hursley holding any Tavest men."

"Ye 'ave to look."

"Alan might have simply been unhorsed, run off, and made his way somehow back to the Empress's allies."

Tink touched Guy on the shoulder. "Ye don't believe that or ye'd not 'ave come for 'im, nor taken a chance wiv the king's temper. Ye know ye may find yerself a prisoner yerself fer leaving court."

Guy had nothing to say. And what he thought in his head, he could not say to this man who cared so much for Alan. What if the reason for Alan's disappearance was simple desertion?

"Guy. Did Chelten not say Alan disappeared? Ye know the rule. Yer the one as reminded me o' the rule when first ye came 'ere. Send word. 'E would a sent word if 'e were back wiv Chelten or Sir Edward."

Guy ran the brush over the horse's coat in long sweeps.

Desertion, the dishonor of it, would affect every member of the de Maci family.

"If Hursley knows Alan be a de Maci, 'e may 'ave some plan to cheat Walter o' 'is ransom. 'E 'as only to wait upon the wedding and then do as 'e pleases. Keep the spoils for 'imself. Walter would ne'er gainsay 'is son-by-marriage."

"It seems unlikely, Tink."

"I'll see to it on me way to Winchester." The old man turned a stubborn shoulder to Guy. "I won't believe our lad is gone. I'll not give up on 'im. I know what yer *not* sayin' and I'll no believe it. Alan would *not* desert." Tink's voice rose and broke, tears glittering in his eyes. "Alan's at Fairoaks. I know it."

"You'll not set one foot on Fairoaks, do you hear me?"

Tink ducked his head. "Who'll stop me?"

Guy sighed. He couldn't allow anything to happen to Tink. "If I can contrive an excuse, I'll go." Guy put his hand on Tink's shoulder. "I'll not give up on Alan, Tink. I just know he's not here at Stonewold."

"Mayhap Crispin could be an excuse," Tink finally said. "To see 'is sister's manor. 'Twill be 'ers at Beltane. Guy? Guy?"

But Guy didn't answer. Joia stood on the steps to the keep. Her hair was unbound, blowing about her shoulders. He thought only of how her hair felt like silk, sliding over his hands, and how when she was mistress of Fairoaks, he'd be in Winchester with the king.

Joia saw her father by the stable, his favorite hunter saddled, his hounds at his feet. She lingered in the doorway to the hall as Martin and Baldric stood a few steps down. She was loathe to draw Martin's attentions. He'd forgotten her the moment she'd suggested he hunt with her father.

So, Baldric was on his feet again. The thought didn't sit well with her. Why didn't they go? She contemplated pushing Baldric down the stairs, then crossed herself, and muttered a prayer for forgiveness.

"What did you see there, my friend?" Martin asked Baldric, pointing toward the stables.

"A man on a horse."

"A *knight* on a horse."

"A knight?"

"Aye. Only a knight can ride like that."

Martin and Baldric strolled slowly down the steps. Joia kept her distance, but followed for they could only be talking about Guy. He'd been the only man mounted in the bailey.

"Yet, my friend," Martin said, "he does not call himself a knight. Why is that?"

"I asked a few men if they knew where he was trained. He claimed some German master."

Joia bit her lip and stayed out of sight until her father and Martin led their hunting party over the drawbridge. She thought of what they'd said. She, too, thought Guy more than he claimed to be. Not for his ability to ride a horse, but from the deference men offered him. Was he a knight who had a grievous sin on his soul and did the menial task of guarding a child to atone in some way?

It bothered her to hear Martin and Baldric speaking of Guy. It bothered her almost as much as Baldric healed from his injuries.

She entered the stable and sat on a bale of hay and watched Guy help the old man, Tink. Most of the grooms had gone off with the hunt to care for the horses. She quickly plaited her hair, tying off the end with a length of silk from her purse. The two men worked companionably on the great destrier. One moment Guy was leading men in warrior training, the next brushing down a recalcitrant horse.

She watched his hands. Strong hands. Gentle hands. Heat flushed her body. She wished to know what he thought of her coming to him in the night. Should she, could she, tell him how overwhelmed she'd been? How frightened by the intensity of his touch?

Nay, she'd not been frightened. She'd been enthralled, beguiled. In love.

Love? She bit her lip. Did she love this man? One couldn't love so quickly. So intensely.

It must be simple lust. Just a spell he wrought with his hands. Or mayhap it was all that warm skin over hard muscles. How did one tell where lust ended and love began? Robin had loved her. She'd loved him, but it had grown slowly from friendship and respect. She'd never before felt the sensations that flared through her like a disease. Even now, watching Guy's hands, a heaviness had settled deep within her and made her ache. She had no woman to ask. No friend. No one.

The old man had much to say, but she couldn't hear the conversation, sitting by the door. Guy washed his hands in a bucket near her, but ignored her.

"Guy. I want to take a ride to a barrow near the river."

"Barrow?" He shook the water from his hands, then wiped them on a cloth Tink handed him. "Ah, buried treasure." He shrugged. "I'll find Crispin and we'll go."

"Crispin's with my mother. I don't want him along. He'll tell my father everything we say and do."

Guy finally looked at her. Looked? Nay, his gaze bore into her, saw through her as if she'd been thinking aloud, been stripped naked now, here in the stable before him. Then the moment passed as he turned toward the old man who took brushes and cloths to stow away. Guy shrugged. "If you want to see the barrow, you will need to accept a guard."

She imitated his shrug with what she hoped was an equal indifference. "So be it. Gather whomever you wish. But now. I want to go now whilst my father hunts."

TWENTY~THREE

The barrow lay in a clearing. One could smell the river, although it was hidden by the forest. The barrow's entrance faced east, and Joia imagined it had once been alone in solitary splendor before the trees had grown to embrace it. It was one of hundreds across England, burial places of ancients.

A great slab of stone stood as a doorway. She imagined even a man as tall as Guy or Tom could walk upright inside. She dismounted, tethered her mare, and waited for Guy and the six men he'd brought as escort. He set a perimeter about the barrow entrance, close, but still, far enough away she was satisfied they'd not be overhearing any conversation and gossiping of it later in the hall.

"Is this your barrow?" Guy asked when at last he joined her.

Where had the man who'd touched her so intimately gone? He demonstrated none of the discomfort she felt. Did he have so many women, he didn't need to feel uncomfortable with them the next time they met? She decided to pretend she'd had dozens of lovers, and he was but one of them.

"Certainly the barrow's not mine," she said. "But I intend to claim all that's within."

He nodded. "Let us get this over with." He was standing, hands on hips, looking at the stone doorway.

"You're very amiable."

"Hmm. I assume you expect me to move this stone?" He looked down his nose at her.

"It should be child's play for such as you."

"First, a bargain."

"I'll not give you my coins." His eyes looked darker here in the woods. He looked taller. She took a step back.

"It's not your money I want." He dropped one hand to the hilt of the long dagger on his hip.

The air heated with his words. Her insides felt heavy. Liquid. She glanced toward the guards. They had their backs to the barrow. What bargain would he demand? She looked at his mouth.

"Your thoughts are on your face, do you know that?"

She became aware of the utter silence of the glade. It had the same unearthly quality as she'd found in the stone circle. Mayhap they'd do more than kiss in this silent, dark place. She shivered. "What am I thinking?"

"You're thinking of last night."

"You flatter yourself. I was simply wondering what you wanted to move a paltry door." One that weighed as much as Tom's anvil.

"As you wish." He said it as if he thought her lying.

"Well, what do you want?" She felt her cheeks heat at the double meaning of her words. He didn't react, nor lift his arrogant brows.

"I want you to contrive an invitation to Fairoaks. I want to accompany you there."

Her mouth dropped open. It was the last earthly thing she could have guessed. "Why?"

"The why's not important. There are two other parts to this bargain. One, you don't ask me why I'm striking it. Two, I want your agreement to make it seem your desire."

Desire.

She threw off her mantle, took it to her mare, and strapped it on the back of the saddle. She used the chore to think. Why did he want to visit Fairoaks? It was the last possible place *she* wished to be.

He was down on one knee, examining the portal stone, running his hands over a spiral marking.

"Spirals are a symbol of the passage of life," she said, going to his side. "Did Martin pay you to carry me off? Make me a prisoner there?"

He examined the door from the side, running his fingertips along the space between it and its stone surround. "If I wanted to carry you off, I'd simply do so. I'm sure these men would help me." He sighed. "If I was asked to carry you off, I'd not need to contrive an excuse to get to Fairoaks, would I? So what's it to be? A door opened or not?"

He rose, stood blocking the doorway, his arms crossed over his chest.

"I must know why you want to go there."

"Let's say, I have my reasons that have naught to do with you. It's part of the bargain that you not ask."

She stroked the creases from her gown. "I cannot think of any reason I might visit Martin's manor. I despise the man."

"You could say you wish to see the bridal chamber and test the mattress for softness."

"Never." She folded her own arms and struck his attitude— stubborn and cold. How could he speak of Martin's bed when she'd been in his the night before? Guy was a man like any other. She'd offered herself, and he'd simply done what men do. If it had been Edith, he likely would have lain just as easily with her.

"Never," she repeated, anger chasing all sense of discomfort away.

He shrugged and headed to the horses, taking an ax from his saddle pack.

"Wait. Wait!" She ran after him, but he passed their mounts and continued into the thick stand of oak that bordered the glade. She made to go after him, but he hefted his ax in a gesture to one of the guards who then stepped in front of her. She frowned and went back to the barrow door.

Guy disappeared into the woods, but returned in a moment, dragging the branch of an oak. He hacked it into six lengths, shaped them into wedges, and ignoring her avid interest, forced his wedges into the spaces between the door and its frame, two on a side, two at the lintel, using the head of the ax as a hammer.

He stopped and faced her. He crossed his arms on his chest again, this time with the ax in his hand. She felt menaced. "Why did you stop?"

"We haven't yet struck a bargain, so I'll not lay one more strike on these levers until you've agreed."

"I'll simply do the same as you. It doesn't look so hard."

He bowed and held out his ax. It was very heavy in her hands. She swung it at one wedge and missed, striking the rock, sending a jolt up her arm to her shoulder. She bit her lip on a yelp and determined she must open the door herself.

After what seemed an hour, she stopped. Her body was bathed in sweat, her plait undone, her hair a snarled mess down her back. She had blisters on her palms; one was bleeding. Guy, on the other hand was lying back against a log, legs crossed at the ankle, hands behind his head.

"So, you win. I've made not one impression on these damnable wedges. I agree."

He was up in an instant, hand raised for silence. She glanced over at the guards who found her efforts amusing.

He lowered his voice as he neared. "And never ask why, or admit I've anything to do with the journey there."

"Agreed. Now time is slipping by. You'll need to get back to Crispin, and I'll not get into my barrow."

He plucked the ax from her hand. "Crispin's to learn to play a song on the rebec after his writing lesson with the priest in order to impress the king. Your mother is supervising the musical effort. We have hours."

"I sometimes hate you." But she couldn't help smiling as she said it. He gave a few taps to his wedges, and she almost lost her toes as the stone slab that served as a door fell with a thud before her. "I loosened it for you."

Guy grinned. "Did you?" His bow was courtly as he swept out an arm that she might precede him into the barrow.

She took a deep breath. "I must fetch a torch." She fetched the torch she'd taken from the stable along with a bundle containing her flints and a small tool with which to dig. In a moment, she had the torch burning. At least she wasn't completely incompetent.

She peered into the silent barrow. Webs hung thickly by the doorway, but she smelled only damp earth, alleviating her fears of dead things moldering inside. If the barrow held treasures, she hoped they were valuable and not just old bones. She wasn't afraid of bones. Or not much.

"Do you want me to go first?" he asked, taking the torch and holding it aloft. "Are there rats in these places?"

"Rats? Nonsense. And if there are, just wave your torch at them." She swept aside the webs. "It's said these doors faced east, mayhap to admit the dawn light at solstice. It may be when they buried their dead or held ceremonies."

"Who are they?"

"No one knows and that's why 'tis now *my* barrow." She swore beneath her breath. Although only a few feet from the entrance of the barrow was a circular side chamber of almost perfect proportions, the way forward was filled with stones of all sizes from floor to ceiling.

Guy lifted the torch to light the way as she stepped into the side chamber. Something sharp pierced her shoe. She cried out in pain. Guy planted the torch in the dirt and went down on one knee. He didn't beg her permission when he gripped her ankle, lifted her foot, slid off her slipper, and set her foot on his thigh.

She tried to be dispassionate about the hard muscles beneath her foot but failed utterly, and had to grab his shoulder lest she overbalance. He drew his fingertip along the rent in her hose, and she shivered at the sensation. He examined her, touching, stroking. She almost gasped at the pleasure of it, the desire she had to throw herself into his arms and beg him to do more than just touch her. She wanted more—so much more—all she'd found in his arms the night before and more. More. More. More.

She jerked her foot from his hands.

He handed her the damaged shoe. "You'll live. But you've ruined your hose along with this slipper. Next time you examine a barrow, wear something less delicate."

170

"Thank you," she managed. Her face felt hot.

Guy used her little tool to dig up the offending shard of pottery that had cut her foot. He dropped it into her hand.

"Just the handle of a jug," she said. She slipped her shoe on and limped about. "I want jewels and coins, not jugs." All she saw was bare earth and broken crockery in the corner. "Let's see if we can shift those stones. Surely, someone filled the barrow to conceal a treasure."

"It must wait for another day."

"Will I have to agree to yet another bargain to have you bring me here again?" She stood in the circle of light cast by his torch. She tilted her head up to see his face—an expressionless mask.

"It will take a team of men to shift that stone, or a week of work by one man."

"We've six men."

"They're soldiers, not laborers."

She bit her lip and couldn't prevent a pout. He was right. Her chance of gathering a team of men was slim at best. "I must think about it."

He was very close. She touched his sleeve.

He snatched her into his arms. She wrapped her arms about his neck, her legs about his waist. She devoured him, took in his very breath, kissed him with all the ardor she felt inside. He hugged her tightly to his chest, his phallus a hard ridge pressing her center. She moaned and bore down on him.

His arms held her so tightly she could barely breathe. There was nothing cold or uncaring in his embrace. She closed her eyes and savored the heat of his body and the heat of his tongue sliding over hers.

He pulled his lips from hers. "Why did you leave me last night?"

"I was afraid." The words were out before she could stop them.

"I would never hurt you," he whispered.

She looked into his eyes and knew that she believed him. He touched his lips to her forehead, her cheeks, her mouth.

"I slept not at all for thinking of you, your taste, and how you rose to my touch," he murmured against her lips.

She wanted to feel those same lush sensations again. He shifted his erection against the smoldering heat between her thighs. It was as if the torch had penetrated her clothing.

"There are men waiting outside," he said.

A spasm of desire almost made her cry aloud. She wanted to lie on the floor and know this man completely. He eased her away so she could put her feet back on the ground, breaking the heated moment. She fussed with her hair whilst he turned away, to collect himself, she thought, but he was ever sensible, and for that she must be grateful, though 'twas a trait she could grow to hate.

They left the barrow. He extinguished the torch. He froze when she brushed a few webs from his shoulder. "What bargain will you ask for shifting the stone yourself?"

He grinned at her. "I'm not going to shift that mountain of stone, so don't try to bribe me. I just want the one time at Fairoaks."

"What're you going to steal?"

Surprise crossed his face. "I'm not going to steal anything."

"Would you if I asked you to?"

His grin disappeared. She saw and felt his withdrawal. The glade was suddenly cold.

"You think me capable of theft?"

Heedless of the guards and the frost in the air, she stepped closer to him. "It would not be theft if I gave you permission to take back the valuables my mother gave Martin as surety I'd wed him. They're *my* jewels, *my* coins, and I want them back."

Guy watched Joia stalk to the horses. He'd not thought her so enamored of gems, could not reconcile it with what else he knew of her. He gave her a leg up on the mare.

Blue hose. Something more to torment him in the night.

He slid her foot into the stirrup. He felt the weight of her insult that he might condescend to theft.

Mon Dieu, he was a knight, but . . . she didn't know that. She knew him only as a man willing to seduce his lord's daughter, a woman promised to another man. Why should she not think him capable of theft?

The stone slab door was harder to put back than it had been to remove. He tossed the wedges behind a rotting log, then handed the ax off to one of the men.

He followed Joia at a leisurely pace, two men in front of them, two behind, the others at Joia's sides. He thought he'd like to hunt with her. He imagined she flew a bird with a skill equal to that of her riding. But that would never happen.

How soon would she ask Hursley to take her to Fairoaks?

Guy couldn't think of any reason Alan would be important to Hursley beyond ransom. And why, if he held Alan, had Hursley not demanded a ransom by this time? Was Tink correct that the man merely waited for his marriage to ransom a wealthy grandson whose price should by rights go to Walter?

Guy knew what he'd pay for Alan and where he'd like to put the sword as he handed it over.

Through Hursley's chest.

But as Stonewold's towers appeared over the treetops, Guy faced the fact he was not only making the bargain to visit Fairoaks to appease Tink, he also made it to garner a few more hours with Joia.

TWENTY-FOUR

Joia waited impatiently as Edith wrapped a long cord of green silk about her waist. She decided to leave off her head cloth. She slid her feet into the narrow shoes that had been dyed to match the gown. Even the ribbons that bound her hose were dyed green.

It had been five days since she'd made her bargain with Guy, and she'd yet to fulfill it as Martin had not been at Stonewold for those five long days. Before she'd plucked up the courage to speak to Martin, he'd been sent by her father to the land on the Solent—to examine the site for a castle. Her father had spent *his* five days, alternately rubbing his hands and crowing over another castle in his control or ranting in a drunken rage that he'd draw and quarter the men who'd killed Edmund.

But Martin was back now and she must speak to him.

There was another to whom she must speak as well. Each time she'd sought Guy, he was either off with Crispin or training her father's men, leaving her to be guarded by others. At first she thought it happenstance, but now, she felt he was avoiding her. She'd not gone to him in the night, no matter how many times she'd been tempted.

He'd not come to her, so she'd not go to him. He gave her no sign he cared for her or wanted her as he had in the barrow. And, in truth, she'd never go to Crispin's chamber again whilst her brother was there. To have done so was folly. Mayhap it was all a dream.

She shivered as Edith wound ribbons through her hair.

"You look like a forest faerie, my lady. You just need wings and you could fly away."

Joia frowned at the image Edith painted. Joia imagined faeries dancing about her barrow. She loved her mother's tales of the forest folk and worked them into every cushion she stitched. Soon, when she escaped this place, she'd put aside such fancies. She imagined nuns thought ill of the little forest folk—another reason to leave with disgruntled mummers of which there were at least three parties still in the village. Could she contrive an excuse to speak with them? "Edith, where do you sleep at night? Not in the solar, I'll wager." Before she could stop herself, she said, "Do you lie with Guy?"

Edith's cheeks flushed red.

"Tell me the truth, Edith."

Edith fell to her knees and burst into a wailing weeping. Joia felt her insides churn as fear of the answer filled her.

"I love him so. Sir Martin would never approve me as his match—my father was a thief, my lady." She burst into a fresh round of wails.

"Ah, so 'tis one of Martin's men, is it? Not Guy, not Tom either," Joia pressed her hands to her chest in relief.

Edith hung her head. "Nay. I've never been bedded by Guy."

Joia noticed Edith didn't make the same denial about Tom. The man must never sleep.

"Forgive me, my lady, I thought you knew 'twas Harald I meant."

"Edmund's man, the one you pointed out to me who has red hair?"

"Aye, now Sir Martin's squire. I thought you'd object, or think we spied on you for him."

"So, your father was a thief," Joia said. She felt a touch of sympathy for Edith whose father's worth also hampered any possibility of a match she might want for herself. "And what makes you think this Harald is *not* using you to spy on me for Martin?"

"Never, my lady." Edith clasped her hands as if in prayer. "He was Edmund's man, and I swear we meet only as we love each other. He never asks about you. We don't . . . talk so much."

Joia went to her table and took up a small book of prayers. "I want you to swear on this holy book that you hold no intent to spy on me with your lover for Sir Martin or any other, my father included. If 'tis proved otherwise, you offer yourself for whatever punishment I deem fit at the time, including devoting yourself to the church, mayhap as a nun."

Edith swore with a shaking hand. "There's no place more horrid than a nunnery."

"'Tis a place of refuge as well."

Edith studied Joia. "Is that what you intend? To run off?"

Joia ignored her lest she be spying for Martin.

Edith touched Joia's hand. "I'm such a fool, forgive me."

Had Edith made protests, excuses, Joia knew she'd always wonder if the woman was spying with her lover, but Joia thought it was genuine contrition she read in Edith's eyes. Joia hoped she wasn't making a mistake.

"Guy said I should tell you of Harald, but I was afraid."

"He did, did he?" Joia thought on that for a moment, not sure why Guy was caring of Edith and Harald's love affaire.

Edith fussed at Joia's hair, her hem, and Joia finally sent her away. She couldn't put off her promise to Guy, was only delaying with the lengthy dressing.

Her legs felt unsteady as she took her place between her mother and Martin in the hall. Guy sat on his usual bench, but she knew he was very much on guard by the sword on his hip. How had she found herself in this coil? The last place she ever wished to be was Fairoaks. What if Martin imprisoned her there? With his men about him, his word law in his own manor, how would she escape? She toyed with the bones of the quail she shared with Martin. She'd no appetite for the quince poached in wine either.

She took a deep breath. "I'm in a wretched coil about this marriage. I don't want to wed. I have no need to wed." Martin opened his mouth, but she lifted a hand. "If I saw your manor, it might help me make a decision. After all, I know little of your home. Certainly, I've not been to Fairoaks since we were children together. I could meet your servants. Take their measure."

"I'm glad to see you soften. My home's not so grand as Stonewold, but it's very comfortable. There hasn't been a woman in residence in many a month, so I beg you would not be too harsh in your judgement."

"Could we start out after chapel tomorrow?"

"With all pleasure, my lady." Martin took her hand and kissed it, then leaned close, his breath a winey warmth at her ear. "You'll find the bed curtains pleasing, but 'tis the mattress you'll most enjoy. You'll find much gratification in its soft depths once you're naked there."

As Hursley kissed Joia's hand, Guy's jealousy bubbled up like a stew did when left too long over the fire.

She rose and gathered Crispin into her arms and, ignoring his squeals of protest, carried him into her father's bedchamber. Before she ducked behind the tapestry she looked across the hall to him.

The child still howled and thrashed about when Guy entered the little alcove off Walter's bedchamber that housed his bathing tub. Joia was having as much success in dousing Crispin as she would if she tried to put a live pig in a caldron. Guy took the child and dropped him into the steaming water. Joia knelt at the side of the small tub and dipped a cloth into a pot of soft thyme-scented soap.

"Martin has invited me to see over his manor house. I said I wanted to take his servants' measure."

Guy studied Joia's face, but couldn't read her expression. The last five days had been torture, wondering if he was simply indulging Tink, or if he really should see Alan's horse for himself.

Now, the matter was out of his hands.

"Might Crispin and I accompany you? You'd like to see Fairoaks, would you not, Cris?"

Crispin slapped at Joia's hand when she tried to wash his hair.

"Guy, order this child to be still." The front of her gown was soaking wet, clinging to her breasts.

"Cris, be done. The faster she bathes you, the faster 'twill be over."

A moment later, Crispin surged from the tub and shook like a dog who'd come in from the rain, but before he could escape, Guy snatched him up and wrapped him in a length of linen. He gave the boy a brisk rub, then lifted the curtain separating the alcove from his parents' chamber, and shoved him out and into the arms of Ivo and Peter, who grinned as they carried him away.

"Thank you for keeping to our bargain," Guy said.

Joia dabbed at her gown with a dry cloth. "He's an imp— Cris that is, not Martin. I hope you'll get what you want."

❧

An unintended meaning of her words heated the space between them. She dropped her voice to a whisper, though no one was about, her mother and father in the hall, being entertained by a group of jugglers who'd arrived that morning with recommendations from the Earl of Surrey. "These past five days I've wanted . . . to speak to you."

All her doubts of Guy fled when he enfolded her in his arms. He kissed her, his mouth hungry on hers as if he, too, had felt starved for this these past five days.

She ran her hands up and down his tunic. She wanted to devour him. She kneaded his chest with her fingers, wished to feel his skin, feel the beat of his heart. His arms tightened about her.

"Not here." His words were warm against her temple.

"Aye. Not here." She wouldn't ask him where—or when, but she would ask the questions that also kept her awake at night. "Why do you want to go to Martin's manor? What if he imprisons me? What if a priest is brought, and I'm forced to wed him there whilst everyone here knows naught of the matter."

"I'll not let any harm come to you. You'll ride in with me, stay with me, leave with me."

Would that she could leave with him—really leave. "Still, I'm afraid."

He drew his sword from its sheath. "Look me in the eye. I'm not lying to you. No harm will come to you. None. I swear it on my sword." He took up her hand and wrapped her fingers around the sword's hilt, then curled his fingers over hers. She gripped the cold hilt, but it was the warmth of his palm against her hand that really felt like a promise she could believe.

Joia drew away from him, her color high. "If Martin saw us, my father might kill you. It angered you at first, the thought that I endangered you with my careless actions. What's different now?"

Guy stroked a tendril of hair from her brow. She truly was an innocent if she didn't understand that coming to his bed had changed everything. He pulled her toward the tub, where he sat on the edge. "I think you kissed me too many times."

He kissed her now—not on her lips, but instead, he leaned forward and touched his mouth to her breast. He ran his hands down her back to cup her buttocks and bring her closer into the V of his thighs.

Her body quivered against him—sent a bolt of heat straight to his cock. He was on fire. He moaned. When could they be truly alone? When could they talk to each other that he might prove to her he was a man of honor? That thought stopped him cold. He set her away from him. He saw the disappointment in her eyes. If he had any honor he wouldn't be alone with this woman—ever. "Joia, what is it you want of me?"

She plucked the wash rag from the tub and busied herself wiping the wet floor, not meeting his eyes.

"You want something. What is it?" he asked again.

She shot to her feet and threw the rag into the tub. "Freedom, Guy, freedom from the demands of men. But no one can give me that." She tore open the curtain to her father's chamber and darted through it.

Guy scrubbed his hands over his face and thought long and hard on Joia . . . and Martin Hursley. Guy wondered if Joia was including him in her wish to be shot of men.

She was a puzzle he could never solve, a woman he could never have. Guy had desired women before, had them with little effort, but Joia tied him in knots. He felt as if he'd gone mad when he was with her. Was her passionate response to him simply that of a woman who was newly learning her own desires? If so, Hursley could satisfy those desires as easily as he.

Jealousy made Guy want to rip something apart. Yet, he knew Joia and he had no future. If they became lovers, it would end badly.

When asked, she'd not said she wanted him. Nay, what she wanted was freedom from men like him. And, in truth, it mattered not. After he'd inspected Fairoaks, he would leave her.

TWENTY~FIVE

Joia smiled sweetly at Martin who stood in the bailey, hands on hips, complete confusion on his face. "What the devil?"

He surveyed the two carts of men and women gathered in the bailey. "Who're these people? What're they doing?"

She walked past him, pulling on her gloves. "They're seamstresses, carpenters, other worthies."

"But why are they coming with us?" Martin followed her to her horse.

She'd invited every person she could think of, from the woman who hemmed bed linens to the baker who would create confections to please the king.

"I must have opinions, Martin. I must have them!" She climbed the mounting block and nodded to Guy and Crispin.

The boy sat in front of Guy on a huge warhorse her father said was in training. Crispin whooped with delight to be so high.

"Is Crispin safe there?" she asked Guy who, for the first time since she'd met him, wore a hauberk under his tunic. The mail shirt was visible as he settled Crispin before him. He wore a short sword, a long dagger, and had a long sword sheathed on his saddle.

"He's a good boy," Crispin said and leaned forward to hug the horse's neck. Guy fisted his hand in Crispin's mantle and grinned. "Set your mind at ease. I ran the fight out of him an hour ago."

"Crispin or the horse?"

Guy grinned. "Both."

Joia smiled back, but the presence of the destrier and Guy's many weapons sent a shiver of unease through her. The weather did naught to raise her spirits, the early morning sky low and dark with clouds. A mist filled the air, entwining tree trunks, and muffling the horses' hooves.

"We should have waited for the morrow; 'twill rain by noon," Martin complained.

"The rain is good for crops," she said.

Martin's manor, Fairoaks, lay south of Stonewold on the banks of the Tavest, at a wide ford. It took two hours for their party to reach the manor house. It was a rambling stone building of one level, surrounded by outbuildings built recently, as Joia did not remember so many from her last visit here. She must admit the neatly sown fields through which they rode spoke of Martin's prosperity as did the manor's forecourt. The house, itself, stood within high palisades, and was in good repair, the servants clean and well-garbed. Most women would be pleased with the situation, but Joia felt as if a dungeon door had closed with the closing of Martin's gates behind them.

"I shall wait with the horses," Guy said. He set Crispin before her.

"Nay. Nay. You promised. You promised you'd ride in with me, stay with me, and leave with me." She hated the quiver of fear in her voice.

"I did. And I will. But the horse . . . I would not want him to harry a groom."

"Joia!" Martin's call was sharp, brooked no disobedience before these many people.

"Come with me." Joia thought Guy meant to say more, but didn't. He took Crispin's hand and walked close on her heels as she followed Martin into the manor house. Both Martin and his shadow, Baldric, gave Guy a look, but Joia forestalled their protests at his presence, by taking Crispin's other hand. It would not do to have a quarrel over Guy's presence.

They entered the manor's hall. It spanned almost the whole of the house. It did not have a hearth as did Stonewold. Instead, it had a central fire pit, with a louver in the ceiling for smoke to escape. The ceiling overhead was black with soot. Chairs surrounded the fire, now damped down, but steaming lightly from the soft rain that had begun to fall.

Joia frowned as she circled the chairs. "How long is this room? Is the floor oak? When were the walls last white-washed? Who'll clean this ceiling for me? Where's the solar?"

Joia rapped out questions in an endless stream, forestalling all other conversation. Guy smiled at her when once she caught his eye. She also hauled Crispin close which allowed him to follow closely as well. If there was a plot afoot to keep her here, she must depend upon Guy to see her safe.

She pressed her hand to her breast. Never had she trusted a man as she now trusted Guy. Was not trust a foundation of love? And here she stood with one man who wanted her, inspecting his home, whilst inside, she wanted another.

She forced herself not to jerk her arm away when Martin took it.

"Come," he said and led her to a small room. "This is the bedchamber."

Joia called the seamstresses forward and waved them into the chamber. They huddled in a corner looking quite out of place, whereas Martin looked enraged.

"I must have your opinion on these draperies," she said to no one in particular. In truth, she fairly shoved two women forward to examine the lovely red and yellow cloth, dyed, Joia thought, in Lincoln. The bed took up most of the space. A great deal of money had been spent in this small room. The walls were painted with scenes of the hunt, but with a romantic taste Joia assumed was that of Martin's late wife.

"I'll want to paint these out," Joia said sweeping her hands out to encompass the walls. "I cannot sleep with red anywhere about."

She lowered her head and pretended to speak to the top of Crispin's head though her question was for Guy. "Where else should I see?"

Martin, who'd become trapped in a corner by a seamstress of

large girth, couldn't hear them.

"Storerooms. Stables. Outbuildings. Every inch."

Guy also spoke whilst looking down at Crispin, but he radiated a tension that made her afraid again.

"My lady," Martin called. "Shall we have some refreshment? I ordered wine and spiced capon—"

"I must see *everything* else how can I make a list of improvements? You're keeping the list of my wishes in your head, are you not, Guy?"

"Oh, aye, my lady."

"I'm hungry," Crispin said.

"You're not," Guy said absently.

To Joia's amazement, her brother merely nodded.

Martin edged in her direction so she urged her servants from the crowded room, then knelt and peered beneath the bed. His boots paused by her hands.

"I see old rushes here, Martin. See they are swept out and replaced. And I much enjoy lavender. It aids sleep and keeps down the fleas."

Martin hauled her to her feet. She quickly pulled her hands away and grabbed Crispin.

"Did you hear that?" Martin asked Guy with a touch of a sneer in his voice.

"I have noted it. Lavender. Fleas," Guy said. Crispin giggled, and Joia tugged him along as she sailed from the room, her nose in the air, sniffing for scents not fresh or flowery.

They wandered toward the only other two rooms in the manor house. One was a solar, the air there stale with disuse and dust. There, in a corner, sat her two chests. She ran to them and flipped up the lids. "My lovely things."

Martin leaned on the doorjamb. She looked up and realized he was waiting for her to beg for her belongings. She would not beg anything of this man. To her surprise, it was he who broke the icy silence.

"You may take a token, nay two tokens, if you wish."

"Tokens?"

"Aye, of my love."

She stared down at the folded gowns, stitched with gems, the cask with her jewelry. Her throat tightened. Although they might help her escape to a convent, there were two things she didn't want to leave behind when she headed there. She reached inside and drew out two linen-wrapped bundles.

Martin pushed off the jamb and took them from her hands. "These?"

She watched him unwrap the bundles aware also of the many, Guy among them, who stood at the door witnessing their exchange.

"A book?" Martin's tone was contemptuous. "A sword?" He bellowed a laugh and thrust them into her arms. "With my pleasure, my lady. Take your prizes."

Joia handed them off to Edith and left the solar for the last room, an armory, Martin's amusement causing heat to sear her cheeks. He looked bored, and Guy pleased when she examined every dagger, scabbard, and lance in the weapon cache. Guy noted the ones she thought dull, although all the weapons were well honed and ready for combat to her eyes. Martin stood in the doorway and as she made her rounds, his look of disdain dissolved quickly to annoyance.

"Surely, you don't care who hones my blades?" he asked. Baldric joined Martin, and Joia felt a shiver as the man's gaze swept over her with a lazy insolence.

She returned Baldric's bold stare. When he looked away, she turned to Martin. "If a manor is to be well managed, its mistress must see to every detail, for when you men are off to your wars, it will be the mistress who sees to these matters in your absence."

Myriad expressions crossed Martin's face, but he said nothing more. As they left the weaponry, she gave it a final look. There were far more weapons than she would expect for the number of Martin's men.

As they crossed the yard to the stables, Crispin yelped. "Guy, my hand, you're squeezing too tight."

Guy met her eyes over the child. "Forgive me."

Joia realized every line of Guy's body was taut. What did he fear here? Or was he just more alert with Baldric and Martin following on their heels?

Her heart began to beat more quickly. She drew Crispin closer and lagged a step so Guy took the lead. Rain plopped in huge drops as they entered the stable. She ordered Guy to inspect each horse from teeth to legs. She had her hands full, controlling Crispin who wished to hug each horse whilst Guy did as bidden. When finally they left the stable she knew why Guy had come.

The look on his face when he'd examined one unremarkable brown gelding had made her heart clutch. The horse had tossed its head and bumped Guy in the chest, and she'd met Guy's eyes. For just that brief instant his impenetrable guard was down, his self-possession in shreds. She'd seen the inner man. It was grief she'd read on his face.

She led Crispin away to give Guy a few moments alone. When he joined them, his armor was back in place.

They continued with their retinue into every outbuilding, the rain coming harder now. Finally, they perched on Martin's many cushioned chairs around a huge table. Dozens of beeswax candles lighted the space. Capons dressed with chestnuts filled the center of the table. The fire had been built high, warming the hall, though she thought of the poor servants she'd dragged on this visit who were likely shivering and damp in the stables, awaiting her pleasure.

She couldn't hasten the meal. Guy leaned close and whispered, "Ask what he does with thieves and the like."

"Does Fairoaks please you?" Martin skimmed her cheek with his knuckles.

She nibbled a bone. "It needs much work. I'll send my a list to your steward, shall I? I'd like it perfect." She spoke the next words loud enough that Guy could hear, "And have you any dungeons?"

"Dungeons?" Martin stared at her. "What the devil? Nay, I have no dungeons."

Baldric and Martin exchanged a look she couldn't fathom.

"Then what shall I do with recalcitrant servants or thieves?" she asked.

Martin threw back his head and laughed. "You'll tell me of their sins, and I'll see them punished. Thieves I hang, my love. As to servants . . . a few lashes, a few kicks, and most matters are solved."

"Of course." Joia imagined some of those kicks or lashes might be directed at her. She hoped Guy was satisfied. She wanted desperately to take him aside and ask him about the horse. Since visiting the stable, he'd been more distant and cold than usual and eaten nothing, ignoring Crispin's gluttony as well. "Would you have my party assembled, Martin? I've seen enough."

Guy said, "I'll take Crispin to the privy."

She smiled. That was one place they'd not yet inspected.

Martin thumped his goblet to the table. "Does this mean you're finally willing to wed me?"

Joia gripped his wrist lest he leap to his feet. "I need time. I beg of you to give me time."

"Your father said you feel you haven't had time to properly honor your brother, yet your father also agrees with me that the greatest honor would be to name our firstborn son Edmund. So, take a grip of your grief, Joia, for we'll be wed ere the king arrives. Stonewold demands it of you." Martin put his mouth near her ear. "I love you." He squeezed her fingers, raised them, and licked the tips.

She felt a sudden chill as if an icy wind had blown down through the louvers. She rose. "We must go; the rain will only worsen."

As her servants milled about choosing places in the wagons, and Baldric and Martin organized their respective men, she used the confusion to amble her mare to where Guy was settling Crispin in the saddle. "Did you hear Martin say there are no dungeons?"

Guy mounted, the rain now falling in sheets. He enclosed

Crispin within his cloak and nodded to her.

"Is there aught more I may do for you?"

He shook his head. "The bargain is made. I thank you."

She examined him. His hood cast a shadow over his face and hid his expression. "What did you want here? Nay, don't answer, I know I promised not to ask."

Flora nipped at Guy's destrier, so she jerked her sharply away lest they have a battle on their hands. Joia led the way as she had before, flanked again by Martin and Baldric. They rode into the darkening afternoon. The forest that lined the road seemed to hem her in as did the two men who rode at her sides.

Their mantles were soaked, legs splashed muddy, but she paid little heed to the discomfort as Martin's words had tied a knot in her stomach. *They'd wed ere the king arrived.* But other words he'd said, along with guilt, had twisted that knot tight.

Stonewold demands it of you.

Was she selfish to refuse Martin who could hold Stonewold? She gripped her reins and wished to be a man that she might hold Stonewold for Crispin—she and she alone.

One moment she was contemplating her fate, the next, lying on her back, Flora struggling to rise beside her.

Screams filled the air, screams of women and horses.

She saw the chain across the road, strung between two trees, the links now broken by the force of three horses meeting it dead-on.

A blur of men ran at them, grabbed their downed horses' reins, and scrambled into their saddles.

Brigands.

She rolled to her knees. More men burst from the trees. They ran for the carts. The women and men there swarmed over the sides and headed for the woods in the opposite direction from the thieves.

The air rang with shrieks and shouts.

She turned, frantic, then saw Guy who was still mounted. The brigand who'd captured Baldric's horse rode toward Guy. "Cris," she screamed.

Guy didn't turn away. To her horror, he rode straight at the brigand, drawing his sword from the saddle's sheath. Just as the man neared, Guy's horse sat back on its haunches and raised its front legs, pawing Baldric's horse. The horse screamed and fell to its knees, its rider falling with it.

With a swing of his sword, Guy took off the man's arm.

Joia ran for Guy. Ran back. Dropped to her knees and gagged.

"Cris," she cried again, rising and heading for where Guy circled the dying man. He rode away. Away from her.

"Guy." She darted past Martin, her boots sinking into the churned mud. He captured and swung up onto her Flora and engaged another brigand who'd mounted his horse.

Where was Guy going?

She tripped and rolled into a ditch, stones bruising her knees. She saw Guy stop beneath a tree, pull Crispin from the shelter of his mantle, and toss him toward a lower branch. She gasped as Crispin grabbed for the limb and clung a moment, feet dangling, before he boosted himself into the shelter of the foliage.

Guy handed Cris one of his daggers, and then wheeled his horse. He pounded toward her. She threw herself flat. The horse leaped over the ditch and her, raining clots of mud down on her.

She ran for Crispin.

"Up, up," he called to her, his face pale, but his voice quivering with excitement. "I'll protect us." He brandished Guy's dagger.

She scrambled up the trunk as she had years before when playing with Edmund and Martin. She hugged the trunk and Crispin and gasped for breath. As much as she wanted to hide her face from the screaming and clash of men and weapons, she couldn't. She must know Guy's fate.

He rode straight at Martin's mount. The outlaw saw him coming, but hesitated, Martin on his one side, Guy coming on the other. The thief turned the horse and slashed at Martin's sword.

Guy dropped his reins. He tore off his cloak and flung it at the horse. The horse shied. The rider raised his arm.

Guy thrust his sword into the man's armpit.

Guy didn't wait for the thief to fall, turning his horse again.

One brigand ran for the trees—for them—sword raised.

"Guy," Cris screamed. This time, Joia turned her face from the sight of Guy's horse running the man down.

Martin jumped off Flora, and with Baldric, ran for their own horses, now loose, reins hanging. Baldric's horse limped badly, great gashes from Guy's destrier streaming blood down its breast. Martin and Baldric mounted, and despite the horse's injuries, headed for the dozen or so brigands who were raiding the cart. Her Flora, loose, ran into the woods.

The thieves saw Martin and Baldric and broke for the woods as well. A few of her men who'd armed themselves with branches as cudgels, chased after them.

Guy didn't follow Martin and Baldric. He headed for their tree. He held out his arms and caught her brother when he leapt down. Guy wrapped his arm about the boy's waist, then he held out his hand. "Come. This horse can bear the weight of three."

She shook her head, hand to her chest, could barely speak, suddenly afraid to leave the shelter of the branches.

"The blood." It was all she could manage. Blood drenched the gauntlet he wore. Blood had sprayed across his mantle, his horse, his legs.

"Stay there, my lady, I'll fetch your Flora."

He rode toward her mare, who quivered at the edge of the woods, reins dragging. Joia shinnied down the tree trunk and waited in the ditch. Bodies lay in pools of blood, sightless eyes to the heavens. She swallowed hard to keep from vomiting.

Guy reined in several yards away from Flora and just sat. In a few moments, Flora stumbled toward the destrier. Guy turned and at a slow pace, headed to where Joia stood, Flora following a few yards behind.

Joia saw blood on Flora's mane. Hands at her sides lest she frighten the mare, Joia approached. She put her face on the Flora's neck. Tears burned her eyes. She slowly stroked Flora's neck until she felt she could reach for the reins. She wrapped them tightly about her fist and led the horse to where Martin and Baldric assessed the harnessing of the carts, stopping only to pluck Guy's trampled cloak from the mud.

"Is anyone hurt?" Joia asked the men and women who crept from the shelter of the forest. A seamstress wailed and buried her face in a carpenter's chest, but he assured Joia they were just frightened. Joia wrapped the woman in Guy's cloak.

The cart, filled only with sacks of grain to make the ride tolerable for the party, was empty, the sacks thrown over the sides, split by knives, their contents spilled across the muddy ground when the thieves had found naught of value there.

They would need that grain, Joia thought. It was a terrible waste.

This was her fault.

"This is my fault." Guy spoke her thoughts aloud.

She shook her head, looking up at him. The rain came down in sheets. It ran down his face, dripped from his chin, caused the blood on his gloves and clothes to run in rivulets down his legs. Guy had Crispin hidden in his mantle, sheltered from the weather and the carnage in the road.

"Nay, Guy, I'll not allow you to share this burden. I'm the one at fault. I brought these folk—Crispin—with us, afraid to be alone with Martin. I found it all amusing, to toy with him, to try his patience. For mockery, I caused this."

Once home, Joia inspected each person of the party, sending some to the physician for the bumps and bruises they'd received chasing the fleeing thieves, and others to the kitchens or the bakehouse as a warm place to dry themselves. She ordered a hot pottage and extra ale, and instructed Owen to distribute a reward to everyone no matter their station.

Joia stood in the stable and watched Tink inspect Flora and

then Baldric's mount. Baldric's horse was gravely injured, but as his limbs weren't broken, Tink said he'd see what he could do. Her Flora stood with her head down, and Joia wondered if her poor girl had lost her spirit in the melee.

Crispin tugged her skirt. "Papa wants everyone in the hall."

Her footsteps dragged. Her father stood on the dais, his hands on his hips. "Martin. I've been waiting. What happened?"

"Forgive our delay. Baldric and I tried to hunt the thieves, but his horse was too weak, and we learned little. But we do know at least two of the thieves knew how to fight on horseback and four had swords. Mayhap they were unhorsed at Tavest and have hidden in the woods these many days."

He stepped onto the dais and addressed not just her father, but also the household gathered in the hall.

"This is a lawless time, thanks to this war," Martin said. "If this war were ended, there would be time to hunt those bastards and hang them. We'd not waste our time and resources in the battlefield. We'd not see soldiers riding through fields, devastating crops, killing each other for a monarch who . . . forgive me. My blood is up."

Walter clapped his hand on Martin's shoulder. "We all feel as you do. 'Tis a lawless time. Were any of the thieves killed?"

"Guy killed them all," Crispin said.

"Only three," Baldric said.

"Where is he?" Walter asked, kneeling by Crispin and drawing him into his arms.

"Seeing to his horse," Crispin said. "He's covered in blood. You should've seen him. He kicked Baldric's horse and that was it."

"Guy kicked Baldric's horse?"

"Nay. Guy's horse kicked the horse!" Crispin grinned.

"So, the horse did well?" Walter ruffled Crispin's hair, still wet and dirty from the day.

"You should give it to Guy! He can ride with no hands."

"As can any *knight*," Martin said.

"Fetch the man, I'll see him rewarded, but Baldric, I hear

your mount may need to be destroyed."

Baldric bowed his head.

"Have the destrier in its place, my man. I thank you for your defense of my daughter and son. You, too, Martin."

Her father sat heavily in his chair. He put a hand down to one of his hounds who licked it. "Now, please. Leave me."

Joia stared at him. He looked as if it had been he, not them, in a melee. She realized her father had grown old. For the first time, she appreciated how he must feel the loss of Edmund and want another he trusted to stand in her brother's place to protect not only Crispin, but Stonewold's people.

Her knots of guilt grew more knots.

She turned and looked for Guy. He could protect them all. He could stand in Edmund's place.

A log settled in the fire, sending a cascade of sparks across the floor. Just as the sparks extinguished themselves on the wood, damp and muddy from the many boots that had crossed there this day, so she felt the spark extinguish itself within her.

Guy was but a man-at-arms, no matter how much she suspected he'd been more at one time, no matter how his horsemanship proved it. What mattered was that Guy had no land on the Solent to offer her father. With lagging steps, every muscle in her body sore from the day's trials, she climbed to her chamber. She wanted to bathe away the day's chills and memories.

After the bath, she sat before the fire in her father's chamber and dried her hair. Her mother laid aside her stitching and took the comb. "What did you think of Fairoaks?" Lady Blanche asked, tugging at a snarl.

"Well kept." Joia's hands still shook from the attack.

"So you'll stop this nonsense?"

Joia jerked her hair from her mother's hand and stood up. "I'll not marry him." But she found she could not utter the words so vehemently as she might have this morn.

"Joia, I love you, but you don't understand marriage. You've a duty to obey your father and wed where he directs you for

Crispin's sake."

"I cannot do it. 'Tis said Martin beat his wife to death for taking a lover."

"First, get your head from the clouds. If Isabel had a lover, he'd a right to beat her. But I don't believe Martin could do such a thing. We've known him since he was a small boy, and if he were capable of such a thing, I'd sense it. I firmly believe she took a chill as he says. Why would he lie?"

"Because to do otherwise would make him a cuckold." But a thought occurred to her. Mayhap Martin didn't have the guts to do it, but his friend, Baldric, might.

"Don't believe all the gossip you hear. Martin was Edmund's friend. Edmund would never have spoken for the match if he thought Martin had done such a thing. Did not the man defend you today?"

"When Edmund left, he said I should make my own decision."

"Nonsense!" Her mother resumed her seat and took up her needlework. "If Edmund could speak to you now, he'd say you should obey your parents. 'Tis a grievous sin to do otherwise, and in truth, my love, by visiting Fairoaks, you gave Martin hope for his suit that he didn't have before. 'Tis folly to raise a man's hopes and then dash them. Your father's patience is near its end. He gave you a few weeks and you've had them. To take any more time is wickedness on your part. You'll wed Martin; Crispin's welfare demands it."

Joia tossed her hair over her shoulders. She had no answer for her mother. She found it hard to breathe in the close, warm chamber. She needed air. She needed to escape.

Guy watched Joia leave her parent's bedchamber and then the hall. She slid past the guard without a backward glance. With no will to stop himself, he followed her. She passed the bakehouse and entered the chapel. He found her, not in the chapel itself, but in the garden bent over a row of plants, plucking leaves.

"Joia."

She started and sat back on her heels. "Where's Cris?"

"With the Rogers and the jugglers who are teaching him all they know."

She knelt just outside a pool of light cast by a torch. He assumed she'd placed it in the wall bracket to guide her efforts. Her hem was wet from the puddles on the pebbly path. All around him, the scent of herbs filled the air along with that of wet earth. He couldn't see her face nor read her thoughts.

"Is this not a poor time to gather herbs?"

"What do you want?" she snapped, turning from him and plucking more leaves which she dropped into her lap.

He had no answer to her question.

"I'll not allow you to blame yourself for what happened today."

He went down on one knee by her side. "And yet, it is I who suggested the journey."

"Don't play the martyr; it ill becomes you."

"Or you." Guy thought he heard a hint of humor in her voice, but still, she didn't face him.

"No one suffered any lasting injuries." She sighed. "And most are making merry as I instructed Owen to give them both a barrel of ale and a purse to share."

Indeed he could hear laughing and singing in the bailey. "You surprised me."

She turned her face to him and into the torch's light. "I did? When? When I ran from the thieves like a coward—"

"You ran *to* your brother; that's not cowardice." He plucked one of the leaves from her lap and crushed it between his fingers. Mint. "Nay, I meant . . . when Hursley allowed you to choose from your coffers. You chose a book and an old Roman sword."

"I suppose after asking you to steal my jewels back, you'd expect it of me, but I realized when I saw the chests that there were only two true treasures within. Edmund gave me the book—verses he wrote. The sword I found with my husband. I know 'tis likely brittle and useless, but I thought 'twould be a fine gift for Cris one day."

He cupped her upturned face in his hands. "Two gifts . . . from the dead."

She licked her lips. "May I ask you a question?"

"You promised not to ask me—"

"You knew that horse did you not? The gelding with the bald knee?"

He jerked his hands away. He rose and turned to the shadows that she might not see his face. *Aye, he'd known Alan's horse.*

"Don't lie to me." She came after him, stood so close he could smell lavender under the mint and sage she held in her hand. "You knew that horse, and he knew you, greeted you, so to speak."

He'd never felt so alone. It tempted him to touch her, feel her arms around him. It tempted him to spill out his reason for coming to Stonewold. "You promised not to ask me why I wanted to visit Fairoaks. I can only say to answer you would be to answer the other."

She pulled on his arm, dragging at him to face her. "I'll not settle for a riddle as an answer. Who owns that horse? And how would Martin come by a horse that knows *you*, Guy of Chelten?"

He heard compassion in her voice, but he fisted his hands to keep them off her. She mustn't know his grief was for a lost son, one he'd failed. Even if Alan were alive and well somewhere, they'd not meet again, or not whilst two monarchs both claimed the same crown. Alan might have worked his way back to the Empress Maude's forces on foot, or mounted behind a fellow soldier. He may have deserted and joined a band of brigands like those who'd attacked today. It mattered not.

Alan was gone.

And under it all, in the hot stew of Guy's emotions, was another kind of grief, grief that he had no reason to remain at Stonewold. He'd leave and never see this woman again, either.

As Guy watched the flicker of torchlight lay a net of gold on her hair, he had a sudden vision of her, kneeling before the king, with Hursley, saying vows only God could break.

Joia ran her hand up and down his arm as she might to soothe Crispin. She dropped her voice to a whisper. "I want to help you. If aught brings you sorrow—"

"It is nothing. Nothing." He jerked from her grip. "Nothing."

She backed away, hands up as if warding off some violence. He saw that his sharp retort had sliced her as if he'd used one of his blades. He fisted his hand and slowly lowered it, tried, and failed, to find words to apologize for treating her ill when she offered only kindness.

She picked up the herbs she'd dropped. "Martin says we'll wed ere the king arrives."

Jesu. "Wait."

She remained where she was, a few feet away, but yet, it was an impossible distance.

"I have something for you." He dug in his purse and pulled out the sack of buttons that had once been his silver buckle. He'd been carrying them since they'd returned from Fairoaks. He took her hand and curled her fingers around it. "Take this."

She plucked one of the buttons out, turned it about in the torchlight. She dropped it into the sack, and then looked up at him. "I cannot take something so valuable."

He shrugged. "And yet, if you don't, I'll be insulted. You could use them as coins for bribes, for . . . whatever you need . . . if you are still intent on the convent."

She set the gift on her little pile of herbs, then put her hands on his waist, stroked her fingers along his heavy leather belt, curling her fingers over the common iron buckle there. She pulled him closer, and he knew she understood where the buttons had come from.

His heart thudded so hard he thought she might be able to see it despite the layers of shirt and tunic.

He meant to thrust her away, but couldn't do it. He kissed her with all the hunger he had inside, ravaged her mouth. She arched against him, met his ardor, her tongue sliding against his. Her body fit so tightly against him, he felt every soft curve as if she were made of wax and melted to him.

"Not here," he said.

"Not here," she answered.

He swept her into his arms and carried her under the pear trees. He set her on her feet, then settled his mouth on hers again. She jerked his belt open and cast it aside. She tore off the pin that held his mantle. As the mantle fell to the ground, he bore her down on top if it.

She sealed her mouth to his and all the hunger he felt for her flared through him. She tugged up his tunic and shirt, unlaced his braies and freed him.

He'd never wanted so much—never wanted a woman's hands on him as he wanted hers. He cupped her breasts, stroked the taut tips, groaning as she caressed the swollen length of him to the point of madness. He was mad.

He pulled her hand away and pressed her to her back.

"Now, Guy."

He fought her skirts. She was hot and wet. Slick and ready.

She moaned as he sheathed himself within her.

He pushed deep, catching her breath with another hard kiss. Her hips rose, driving him deeper. He wanted deeper.

She gripped his hips and threw back her head, arching beneath him. He watched her face as he drew himself out, reveled in her throaty gasp when he plunged back in. Her nails dug into his skin. He wanted to remember every expression on her face.

He braced himself on one arm. "Joia. Look at me."

She opened her eyes. She brought her hands up to cup his face. Her blue eyes looked black in the shadows, but were so intent on his he thought she might be able to see inside his mind. They widened as he pushed deeper, then deeper still. Then it was he who moaned when she arched her hips to him again and again.

She whispered his name as she found release. A moment later he pulled out of her. With regret. With sorrow.

TWENTY~SIX

Joia lay beneath Guy's heavy weight, aware only that she never wanted to move. She tangled her fingers in his hair and kissed the point where his blood hammered in his throat. There were words that needed saying, but she was afraid of them.

"I'll see you safely to your priory," he said at her ear.

He'd just made love to her, and he wanted to take her to a convent? And was it making love if a man didn't spill his seed inside the woman?

She shoved at his shoulder, and he lifted off her but only so far that she could see his face. And yet, here beneath the tree, there was not enough light to tell what he was thinking.

When had she ever known what this man thought?

He smoothed his fingertips along her cheek. The gesture was unutterably tender. Surely, his hands and mouth had said all his words for him. She would hold onto that.

In truth, his words were simply a statement of what she already knew. They could not be together.

"I'll not have you involved. Papa would make assumptions . . . he might have you killed. But men I hire, well, they are just hired men, not possible lovers."

She'd said the word. *Lovers.*

She could not have Guy take her anywhere. To do so would endanger his life.

He stroked his hands over her, frowning. "Do you remember when we met in the stone circle?"

She felt heat rush up her face. She covered his hand and drew it to her breast. "How could I forget the sight of you?" Her throat felt tight. "You moved in the moonlight . . . and I was lost."

And she realized she had probably fallen for him in that first moment.

She thought she detected a dark flush rise on his cheeks to match her own.

"I think I was changed that night," he said.

"How?" She found it hard to concentrate as his fingertips gently stroked across her breast.

"I found some value in disobedient daughters."

She laughed. He smothered the sound with his mouth.

He was hungry. Again.

She felt it in the tautness of his muscles beneath her hands and the press of his manhood between her thighs.

She was hungry, too. For several long moments she kissed him, took in the very air he breathed, felt as if she were part of him.

He smoothed her hair from her face and drew the edge of his mantle over her. "At least, in a priory, you would be safe from marriage, although the practical part of me says you should marry Hursley for he can hold this place. The impractical part of me—the jealous part—says I hope he falls in the Solent—weighted down by several long swords."

She ducked her head and pressed her lips to Guy's throat. "I feel the beat of your blood here. And here." She picked up his hand and turned it so she could kiss the blood coursing through the veins that lay on his wrist. "I'll not wed him.

He hugged her so fiercely she thought her bones might crack.

"You must understand, Joia, I saw the ransom paid by de Lorien to have his son back. If your father took only that to a convent they'd turn you over with no regrets."

She looked away to the towers looming overhead. Every arrow loop showed its outline as servants prepared for the king's arrival. "You forget, I've a quarry to offer." She would try to be as hard as that stone when the door closed behind her.

"Joia." He took her chin and forced her to meet his eyes.

"You'll make a wretched nun."

"I'll make a wretched wife for Martin."

Guy rolled to his back and scrubbed at his face with his hands. She knew he must be regretting the joining. She pushed away from him. She wouldn't regret it.

"Mayhap I won't need to seek a convent. I could join a minstrel band, travel with them, earn my bread and the quarry be damned."

"You'll do no such thing."

"You cannot stop me. You'll see to Crispin, and if Stonewold is ever lost because I didn't wed Martin, I believe Crispin will forgive me. You'll teach him to stand on his own two feet and have no need of castles."

"You make too much of what I can do for him." His words were sharp. He took her hand again. "I cannot stay here with Crispin."

She felt her heart begin to pound. Her skin flushed hot but her hands felt cold. "What are you saying? You're leaving? You made love to me because you're leaving?"

"I had no plan to make love with you when I followed you here." He lifted her fingers to his mouth.

She pulled her hand away and combed her fingers through his hair, brushing it back off his brow that she could see his eyes. She sighed and tried to keep a quiver from her voice that would show him the depth of her emotion. He must not know the depths of her feelings for him—ever. "I cannot be angry. I made love to you knowing I was leaving for the convent. Who am I to judge you? So, do we regret this or let it pass?"

"I have another gift for you. You can add it to your quarry as dowry for your convent, but it still won't be sufficient if your father hunts you down."

"A gift?"

"I buried a sword in the stone circle at the foot of that flat stone, the one lying on its side." He covered her mouth with his hand when she tried to speak. "Just listen. I had a valuable sword that might raise questions here, so I buried it. There's no mystery to it. It was my grandfather's, nothing more. Dig it up and make use of it with my blessing."

"Who are you that you have belts and boots and a sword that mark you as wealthy and yet, you have no horse, no lord."

"Chelten was my lord."

"Not an answer, Guy. It tells me not who you are. Or why you're leaving."

He kissed her breathless, pulling her against him. She closed her eyes and ran her hands over his shoulders, down his arms, linked fingers with him and felt the strength of him.

He kissed her silent. He was not staying at Stonewold with Crispin either, so she could not, in her lonely nights in her poor priory, imagine him here, moving through his duties.

She could not have him. No matter what happened when the sun rose on the morrow, she'd still be the daughter of a baron and he a mere soldier. Nay, there was nothing ordinary about him. She gave him a gentle shove, and he lay back on the mantle.

She climbed astride him, guiding the hard length of him to her center. She settled on him, reveling in the feel of him deep inside her and in the capacity she had to make him moan.

He cupped her breasts. She watched his haunting eyes. Her need for him built inside her like a storm. And all around them another storm rose, wind whipping at her hair to sting her cheeks and howl past the castle towers looming overhead.

And was it she who howled when her release punched through her middle? Or was it he when he withdrew at the moment he gave up his seed?

TWENTY~SEVEN

The next day, Guy made sure others served as Joia's escorts that he might set a distance betwixt them. He didn't look for her, nor place himself where she could easily find him. As the evening meal drew close, he took advantage of Crispin's absence whilst the child perfected his juggling in the hall, to gather his weapons and roll them into his pack.

He'd crossed a line with Joia. Whether she went to a convent or remained and accepted the match with Hursley, he must put her from his mind. He must leave whether the rain stopped and whether the roads were passable or not. He could find shelter in the forest and might even relish meeting a few brigands. He had no fear of traveling alone. He did fear remaining here one moment more than necessary lest he do something incredibly foolish like challenge Hursley for Joia.

Guy stood still a moment, the ties of his pack biting into his palms as he thought of leaving her. Of never seeing her again. Never touching her. He felt as if someone had thrust a blade deep into his chest.

There were terrible truths he'd found here at Stonewold. The truth that he'd failed his son. The truth that he loved a woman he could never have.

The door opened behind him, and he knew without turning who it was. Would he ever smell lavender again without thinking of her?

"What are you doing?"

He continued to tie up his weapons.

She touched his sleeve. "You're leaving? So soon? Without a

word?" she said softly.

"You and I both know it's the best thing I can do."

"Crispin will miss you dreadfully."

She'd not said she would miss him. Just as she'd not named him when saying all she wanted was her freedom. But he hoped 'twas just that they were alike. Neither of them could voice aloud something that was so ripe for disaster.

Guy turned and leaned his hip on the table. He crossed his arms lest he reach for her. He needed her to understand. "What we've done is against every precept of honor—"

"You'd leave without word?" she interrupted. "Had I not come here to find you, you might have been gone, even in this rain?" She put her hand on his heavy cloak, draped over the foot of Crispin's bed.

"I thought we'd said all that needed saying in the garden."

"Crispin will feel betrayed."

This barb struck deep. He felt the heat rush into his face. "I intended speaking to Crispin ere I left; I'm not completely devoid of feeling."

"You're a stone. Nay, a blade. With all the capacity of one to cut, but remember, Guy, a blade that will not bend eventually breaks."

He had her by the arms ere he could stop himself. "Am I unbending? Is that truly how you see me?"

"Unbending and hard to leave me without a word."

Her eyes were huge in the dim light, and glittered enough he thought she might be on the verge of tears. She must not cry, or he'd be undone.

"I'm not who you think I am, someone to save you."

A tear made its slow way down her cheek. He reached out to wipe it away, but she pulled from his grasp. At the door she turned back.

"I know who you are. Once a knight—you ride like one. Once used to command—the men all defer to you with respect. Once a man of wealth, with buckles and belts and swords to display it. Once the owner of a brown gelding. Who are you this day, Guy? This night? In that, you're right, I don't know you, and yet I fear I love you. But what would I know about love? 'Twas probably just lust, and that can be found over and over if one but looks for it."

Her hand was on the latch.

Every word she spoke hammered at him. "Joia, don't go."

She stood there, waiting, her eyes downcast.

"I took the task of guarding your brother that I might seek my son, missing at Tavest."

She looked up, tipped her head, but her face was expressionless. Had she learned to wear a mask from him? She went to the arrow loop and stood there, her back to him. "You'll need to say more than that."

He took a deep breath, and knew he should have unburdened himself to her at the barrow, before traveling to Fairoaks. "When Chelten went renegade, my son, squire to one of the earl's knights, went with him. He wasn't ransomed. Chelten said he disappeared."

She looked over her shoulder. "Why the secrecy?"

He shrugged. "Two reasons. I didn't want to be taken for spying, and I don't have the king's permission to search for my son."

"Why did you not simply ask after him?"

"Tink thought Walter and his men too incensed over your brother's death for me to be so bold. The king is also incensed with Chelten and may not have seen me freed if your father locked me up. I did serve the earl."

She swung around. Her cheeks were flushed.

"So, you, and *Tink*, who I must suppose is your man in some way, come here, you take on the position of guard, and seek your son. That's why you wanted to see the dungeons and the gatehouse. What did you find?"

"Nothing."

"That doesn't explain why you wanted to go to Fairoaks. Ah, it does. That horse. Your *son's* horse?"

"Aye. A gift when he was made squire. Your father sold the

horse to Hursley, and I thought if the horse was there, Alan might be as well."

She rubbed her hands over her face. "I cannot say you were wrong to be silent on why you came here. My father's grief was raw and he may have imprisoned you, on that I will agree. But he'd have ransomed you."

"My father made it clear he'd not pay any ransom for me or my son."

"Ah, another father dictating the fate of his children—grown or not. So, I imagine you'd not relish tending my father's sheep in the Marches, either." She walked around the foot of the bed. "So. Who do you serve now?"

"My family serves the king."

"You think him a better ruler for England than Maude?"

"Are we going to discuss the merits of both? King Stephen is an able warrior, a poor king. Empress Maude, if she listened to Gloucester, might be an able queen, but no man wants to serve a woman."

"Indeed?"

He tried for patience. "My family has served Stephen's family for four generations; my father believes that if Stephen offers a suitable bribe, Chelten will return to the fold. Why play on a swinging gate?"

"Would the king have ransomed you?"

"It depends on the state of his anger with Chelten. The day I left court, nay."

"You've not found your son. Where do you think he is?"

"Here," he touched his chest. "I no longer know. I thought I'd feel it if he were dead. But here," he touched his temple, "here, I can only assume he was unhorsed and ran into the woods, mayhap into the very stand of oak where an archer might have taken you the other day."

"And made his way to the earl?"

Guy shook his head. "He never returned. The earl, or my son, would have sent word if that were true. My father knows where I am. He may have disowned me for this effort, but he'd still send word if aught had arrived after I left. Sending word . . . it is a rule we live by."

"Your son may have joined some of those who live in the forest, owing no one. I'll pray for him, and that he not feel a need to join any outlaws. I shall pray he sends word that you might be at ease."

"The king is coming. I cannot be here when he arrives. He'll likely be enraged with me when I return to court, and I don't want the further sins of angering your father over you on my soul." He went to the door. "You must go. Whatever happened between us must be forgotten."

"So easily?"

He heard a quiver in her voice. He didn't trust his own, but must speak to make amends for all his silences. "Never easily. I think you'll dwell on my mind for—"

"Don't go. Stay for the king's arrival. I'll tell him I gave you permission to seek your son. In the stone circle. That first night. I'll tell him I suggested you guard Crispin."

"I'll not let you lie for me."

She threw herself against him. He stumbled back against the door, and he found himself pinned there. She rained kisses across his face. Every soft curve of her pressed to him.

"If you won't stay, then will you seek me in the convent one day if ever you want me."

"Want you?" It was all he could choke out.

He wrapped her tightly to his chest. He buried his face in her hair as she jerked his tunic up. Then they tangled hands as she pulled it off and unlaced his shirt. He tore it off. When she spread her hands over his chest he knew he'd lost a battle somehow.

He hoisted her into his arms, set her on the bed and shook off her searching hands. She knelt on the bed and drew off her gown, her linen underdress. It was just as he'd imagined her, kneeling splendidly naked on the furs, her eyes as deep a blue as the sapphire in his grandfather's sword.

This was a mistake.

One he and she would likely rue for many a day.

He dropped the bar on the door.

Twenty-Eight

Joia watched Guy peel off the rest of his garments, revealing his long, hard-muscled thighs and taut abdomen.

"Don't move," she whispered. "I want to look at you."

If he felt any shyness at being openly examined, he didn't show it. He stood still and she took her time, drinking in all the lean lines, the scars, the way the sun had bronzed his face and arms, how the hair grew in a narrow line from his navel to point to his swollen manhood. She wanted him to turn around, but, instead she beckoned him near.

He knelt before her. She stifled a cry when he pressed his mouth to her breasts. She ran her hands and her lips over his shoulders, his throat, his hair, reveled that she could finally touch all of him and taste him.

She arched and moaned as he captured one nipple, sucking it, sending a shock of sensation from his lips to her belly. He moved to her other breast. She cradled his head and whispered how much she wanted him . . . and to herself, how much she loved him.

He knotted his fist in her hair and dragged her head back, and swept her tongue with his.

Then he stopped and held her shoulders. His agate eyes, gone dark in the dim light, searched her face. Need swamped her, roiled through her, breached all her defenses as surely as the river outside the castle was breaching its banks. Her insides ached and throbbed, and she craved what was to come. She reached between them and encircled his manhood in her fist. "Now," she whispered. "I need you now."

"I need you as well," he said softly, covering her hand, and gently peeling it away. "But I cannot simply plant my seed and on the morrow—"

"I want you."

"I understand." He kissed her palm, then laid her back against the bedding and bent his head. He touched his lips to her knee and then her thigh. She fisted her hands in his hair when his fingertips found her, stroking her, opening her to him. Everywhere he touched felt swollen, heavy. His lips trailed her inner thigh, his breath so warm.

Then he set his mouth on her *there.*

He feasted on her, held her hips so she was a prisoner to his kiss. Heat ran from his lips and tongue. She felt devoured.

Her insides wept, hot and slick, as he slid his fingers deep inside her.

The shimmering, shattering moment was so close. She wanted it so badly, was burning from the inside out. She whispered his name again and again like a chant. The golden thing was so near, almost upon her.

She moaned, twisted in his grip, and rode the crest of that shining, lovely wave. It flooded through her, racing from where his mouth caressed her. It stole her breath.

She lost all sense of time, of place, just arched and arched to him until she fell back in the furs, her arms limp, her thighs quivering.

He soothed her with his lips and fingertips, stroking the insides of her thighs, following the path of his hand with his lips. It was heavenly.

He rose before her and put out his hand. She let him pull her up to sitting, but felt so languid, she thought her bones might not support her if she tried to stand. She wasn't ready to leave him. His body wasn't ready to separate from her, either.

She encircled his waist and pressed her cheek to his hard abdomen, ran her hands up and down his hips, over his hard buttocks, then took him into her hand. "You give me pleasure, but I give you naught in return."

He made a feral sound deep in his throat as if some wild thing clawed at him. She wanted him to let that wild thing out of its cage. She licked the length of him, skimmed him with her fingertips. He crushed her against him, but she leaned away, to see him as well as touch. She felt an urgent need to give to him that ecstatic release he'd given her. And when he closed his eyes and threw back his head, she knew he wanted it as well.

She learned the taste and shape of him, learned how to make him gasp, how to make him moan. She licked the path of his veins to the swollen head of him. She cupped his stones and marveled at how different his body was from hers. She caressed every inch of him from base to tip.

She used her nails and teeth to make him hiss and her tongue to soothe. Then she drew him in deeply and held on as he lost his battle against her and poured himself out with a gasp that was her name.

With the final pulse of his coming, he snatched her up against his chest and kissed her hard, mingling the tastes and scents of them together. His heart thudded against her breast. Then he gentled the kiss to one that was achingly tender as he eased her to the furs. He took her hand and kissed the length of each finger, then smiled.

I love you, she said, but only to herself.

Then a burst of clapping and stomping from the hall below brought the world back to tear apart what had happened between them.

"I'll tell Crispin this night, that I must go, and go I will at dawn."

She would not weep. "You know where I'll be, Guy of Chelten, if you ever feel a need for me. Look for a poor priory as far from Stonewold as one can go." She felt as if something inside her had cracked, and if she didn't preserve her dignity, she'd shatter to pieces.

He gathered her close, but he didn't kiss her. Instead, he ran his fingertips along her cheeks, her brows, her lips as if committing her face to his memory for when he was gone.

She eased from his embrace and with shaking hands, pulled on her clothing. He did the same beside her, wordlessly sheathing a long dagger at his waist. When she went to lift the bar, he drew her back.

"Joia." He smoothed his hands over her head, lifted her chin so she couldn't avoid his eyes.

She didn't want any hollow words to remember when he was gone, so she touched his lips with her fingertips to silence him.

"Shh." She turned her head and kissed his callused palm. "Wait a moment or two so we're not seen together."

But when she opened the door and moved into the dark stairway, shrill screams erupted from below.

TWENTY~NINE

"Stay." Guy thrust Joia behind him. He ran down the stairs. Chaos met his eyes. A cluster of women ran about the high table screaming. Jugglers huddled, arms about each other. Walter shouted for the physician. Guy pushed through the crowd, parting women and men with little heed to who they were or what their status.

He saw Avis holding Lady Blanche's head as she knelt and vomited into the rushes. Red wine. Pears. Other unidentifiable foods.

Then he saw Crispin. The child knelt behind his mother's chair, his face as white as hers, his lips stained as red. Guy thought of a deer slain in snow, the blood the only color splashed across a blanket of white. He went down on one knee. The child toppled forward into his arms.

Joia grabbed for Crispin, but Guy elbowed her away. "See to your mother. I'll take Crispin to her chamber." The crowd fell still as he turned with the child in his arms. No one showed signs of aught but dismay. The crowd parted silently, for Crispin lay as limp as the dead.

In the warm chamber that belonged to Walter and Blanche, Guy placed the child on the bed. Joia burst into the room, supporting her mother whose gown was stained red on the breast. He helped Joia get her mother to the bed.

"Bring the physician, a large jug of water, and a basin." He took Lady Blanche's hand. "What did you eat that the boy ate as well?"

"Pears," she whispered. "Is he dead?"

"Nay. How many?"

"Not so many as I, one . . . mayhap . . . two?"

The physician bustled into the room. "What ails them?"

"Poison, I think. I ordered water and a basin. Have you something to make them vomit?"

"I'm sure they've *not* been poisoned," the small man said. He reeked of ale and robes not washed for many a day.

Guy grabbed the noisome tunic. "I know they ate the same thing and no others are ill, are they?"

The physician shook his head. "Just these two."

"Then we'll assume 'twas poison. Even if it's just tainted fruit, you'd want them rid of it, would you not?"

"Aye. Although I do believe a good bleeding——"

"No bleeding. Fetch a purge. Now." He thrust the man away and put his hand on the hilt of his dagger.

The man's eyes followed Guy's hand. He swallowed. "Of course. I'll be but a moment."

"If the child dies because you dawdled, I'll have your stones."

The man flitted from the chamber.

Joia went to her mother, but Guy saw her eyes were on her brother, who lay so silent and pale.

"Don't let him bleed us," Lady Blanche gasped. "I've a good purge in my——" She waved her hand.

"I know where it is." Joia ran to a chest that served as a seat, threw the cushion atop it aside, and rummaged about, drawing out several linen pouches, sniffing and, at last, finding the one she needed.

"Mustard," Joia said, bring the pouch to the bed.

"All of it . . . jug," Lady Blanche managed to whisper. "As much down Crispin . . . I . . . can wait."

"Do as she says," Guy ordered, for Joia looked stricken with indecision. "She's emptied her belly a number of times and can likely withstand a greater measure of whatever they were given." He prayed he was right.

Joia dumped the contents the pouch into a jug. The physician arrived as she stirred the mixture. He sniffed and nodded. "I, too, have mustard."

Guy supported the child and watched the man pour a small amount of the purge down the child's throat. Crispin's throat worked, and Guy thanked God most of it went down. For all his evil smell and dirty hands, the physician did well administering the purge.

Joia held a basin and at long last, Crispin spewed his guts into it. "Another dose of mustard and then we soothe his belly with goat's milk." The physician looked at her with kindness in his eyes. "I think we should get some of this mustard into your mother now."

Walter burst into the bedchamber. "Is he going to live?" he asked the physician.

Lady Blanche's hands fluttered on her breast where they lay folded. "Walter?"

The man ignored her. "Well? Will he?"

The physician shrugged. "We don't know what they ate. We don't know how much poison——"

"Poison?" Walter reeled from the bedside. He sat down heavily in his cushioned chair. He gripped the armrests, his knuckles white. "God's punishing me."

Guy wanted to say that God didn't put poison in wine-poached pears, but kept the words behind his lips. Joia helped her mother drink the mustard infused water. It worked quickly.

Guy felt the child stir in his arms.

"Guy?" Crispin's eyes opened for the first time since he'd been carried from the hall. "Mama?" He began to struggle, so Guy set him in his mother's arms.

Joia looked from him to the physician. Her gown was wet from waist to hem, splotched with the remnants of pears. "That was the last." She clutched the empty jug. "What if it wasn't enough?"

"I have more mustard," the physician answered. "I'll fetch it.

Walter looked up at Guy, his face ashen, his hands twitching in his lap. "I cannot thank you enough. All those women screaming." Walter shook his head, then went to the bed and sat at Blanche's side. He stroked a hand over Crispin's head where it lay on his mother's breast.

"Is there aught I may do?" Avis stood in the doorway.

Joia's voice was as cold as the winter wind. "I think we've no need of your services." She walked to the door and shut it in the woman's face.

"I think you can do without mine as well," Guy said.

"Nay. Have your weapons brought. I want you on guard. Someone tried to kill my son, and if you'd been on guard instead of those other men, this never would have happened."

Guy felt the full weight of Walter's words. He couldn't look at Joia, although he felt her gaze like the touch of a hand.

He also felt a surge of anger and guilt entwined. For all the training he'd done of Edmund's men, he'd not saved the child from harm. Or the mother. He'd thought of direct attack because of the falls, thought of abduction as Walter's son would command a fine ransom, but Guy realized he'd forgotten Owen's words that first night at Stonewold.

He has also twice sickened who is never sick.

THIRTY

Joia dropped into her father's chair. Guy put a hand on her bent head, but she shook him off. Her eyes were bright with tears as she whispered, "I kept you from your duties."

Before Guy could say she must not blame herself, one of Walter's soldiers entered with his weapons. He belted on a sword and changed his dagger. "I'm going to stand watch outside so your mother has some privacy."

He wanted to embrace Joia and comfort her, but drew away. He went to Walter's fine glass window. Fog obscured the world below. He felt as if the castle were floating somewhere near heaven but was thankful neither Lady Blanche nor Crispin would be in that paradise today. His head ached, filled with the stench of the sickroom.

Guilt hammered him. What had he been doing whilst someone had been poisoning his charge? Satisfying his baser urges with a woman who was another man's promised wife, no matter her insistence she was entering a convent.

It mattered not which men had the care of Crispin whilst he'd been making love to Joia. He was responsible, and he alone.

Never before in Guy's life had he failed in his service to another—failed to do his duty. Never until this day.

He pulled open Walter's door. The man standing guard there was Edith's Harald. He tried to peer into Walter's chamber, but Guy settled the tapestry firmly over the doorway.

"Has anyone tried to enter?" Guy surveyed the hall.

"No one. Lord Walter insists the cooks are each to take a bite of his or the child's food from now on."

Guy frowned. And what of Lady Blanche's or Joia's food? "What gossip do you hear?"

Harald shrugged. "The men think 'twas simply carelessness in the kitchen. Did not three men die last summer of tainted meat prepared there? Oh, you were not about then."

"Who were the men?"

"Simply soldiers."

"Could it have been poison?"

Harald shrugged. "Poison's a coward's weapon."

"So a coward poisoned those men as well?"

"Tainted meat, more like, though we all ate much the same that night. I remember it more because they were brought before Walter earlier that week for taunting the women in the marketplace. Called Lady Blanche's women whores." Harald lowered his voice. "Now, had Lady Blanche poisoned the women, well, one could understand it as they all shared Walter's bed at one time or another." Harald winked. "But likely 'twas just carelessness in the kitchen."

He said it with a finality that told Guy there would be the devil to pay for the kitchen folk for many a long day, especially with the king's imminent visit.

He dismissed Harald and took up the post. The two Rogers approached, looking as if they expected to be tossed into the dungeons. They explained they'd been standing near the child and had seen no one put anything in Lady Blanche's food. They also admitted they'd enjoyed the jugglers, laughing as Crispin had begged for their wooden balls and performed nearly as well as the performers themselves.

Guy chastised them for watching the jugglers instead of their charge. But as he stood guard by the tapestry, he thought he couldn't fault the men for they were new to such duties. His mind returned again and again to the fact he'd been lying abed with Joia.

Guilt smote him as if someone had taken a mace to his head. But he forced himself to do his duty. He examined every person in the hall. It was filled to capacity with every seat taken. There were many strangers here from mummers to the highborn with their own retainers, all come in anticipation of the king's visit.

When the weather cleared, merchants would come as well, twice that as for a normal market. Was there one among these strangers who wished Blanche and Crispin ill?

Harald thought poison a coward's weapon, but it was also the weapon of those who wish to observe their handiwork from a distance and savor the results. As Guy stood at his post, he looked over the many who gossiped in small groups, their tones hushed as befit the gravity of the situation.

Who benefited if Lady Blanche or Crispin died? Guy doubted a stranger had a hand in the poisoning. It was one of those in this hall, a man or woman he knew by name.

THIRTY~ONE

Joia shifted uncomfortably in her father's chair. She got up every few moments to wipe both Crispin's and her mother's faces. Guy opened the door just before the noon hour to admit her father. Guy stood as straight as any guard and shut the door without acknowledging her. She knew why. Guilt. It sat as heavily on him, she imagined, as it did on her.

Her father combed his fingers through Crispin's hair. "This is why you must wed Martin. I'm too old for this. Just too old."

Her father's eyes were threaded with red, his shoulders bowed. "I want you to make your acceptance of Martin clear this night. I want you to sing for him. Play for him. Honor him. And mayhap, then, whoever plots against me will see that they'll have Martin to deal with as well if any more ill falls on my house."

"I can hold Stonewold, Papa. I can. I ran Robin's manors whilst he was sick, not his sons. The people here respect me. They'll heed me if I have a strong man to command your garrison, a man such as Guy."

Her father stared up at her, his eyes unblinking as if he were one of his old hawks who'd suddenly had his hood removed and was seeing for the first time in days.

"Martin has land on the Solent." He looked at her as if she were one of the servants who had suddenly spoken out of turn.

"That's the true reason for this marriage, not holding Stonewold for Crispin."

Her father surged to his feet. He took her arm and flung her to her knees by the bed. Her mother reached out and gripped her hand.

219

"She'll do as bid. Please, Joia, you will, will you not?" Her mother's voice was a hoarse whisper.

Joia looked at Crispin curled in her mother's arms, his face pale, the skin about his eyes almost blue.

In her heart, Joia knew that if Martin had not the land on the Solent, she could hold Stonewold with Guy's help. She felt the well of tears, but fought them. She would not weep before her father.

"Aye. I'll do as you bid."

Edmund waited until Father Ilbert had handed off the sack containing bread and cheese before he attacked the man. "So, you a good Christian would have allowed Baldric to cut off this man's hand?"

Ilbert hunched his shoulders.

"I've thought long and hard over what's happening here. Why are you a party to this? Come, Father, tell me. Since you keep feeding me, I can only assume I'm meant to live. I'll know all as soon as I'm set free. Why not tell me now?"

Father Ilbert peered around the door, then glanced toward Alan. Alan was snoring heavily and hadn't wakened with the arrival of supper. It worried Edmund.

The priest dropped his voice to a whisper. "He promised me a bishopric." He nodded several times as if convincing himself. "It's promised. I had only to feed you. I can come and go from the church without question, you see."

"Ah, clever. You deserve such an honor." He imbued his voice with admiration.

An expression of avarice wiped all holiness from the man's lean face. "Surely, you must remember two winters past when the archbishop passed me over for his nephew?"

Edmund nodded. Father Ilbert had been in tears for days.

"I, whose father was a baron, whose mother was cousin to our old queen, I was passed over for a mewling boy. As long as I feed you, Martin says I'll have my bishopric." He dropped his gaze. He licked his lips. "And if I don't obey, Baldric says he'll kill me."

"Then glad I am you have this chance," Edmund said.

For one brief moment, Edmund thought the priest would come close enough to be overpowered, but after nodding several times, the man tucked his hands up his sleeves and departed, dropping them back into Stygian darkness with the dropping of the bar.

As Edmund listened to Alan's snores, he understood one thing, but not another. He now knew for a certainty that Martin had a hand in his imprisonment. But how could Martin and Baldric, who were naught but knights, secure a bishopric for Father Ilbert?

Joia sat with her embroidery in her hands but hadn't taken a single stitch. The rebec lay on her bed, a simple reminder that she was to fete Martin after declaring her intentions. Her mind shied again and again from what was to be. No matter her resistance, she was going to wed him. Crispin would be as safe as she could make him without taking up a sword herself and that must be her comfort.

She'd not think of Guy nor play the game of what might have been. If she couldn't have Guy, she wanted no man, and thus, it mattered not who she wed, did it?

Guy could leave without guilt. She and Crispin would be safe in Martin's care, if not happy there.

Joia stroked her fingertips over her stitches. Nay, Guy wouldn't leave without guilt. He was not that kind of man. He may say he was returning to court, but although he might do that first, she knew he'd find a way to continue his search for his son. He *was* that kind of man.

There was a light tapping at the door. She cast her stitchery aside and lifted the bar. Martin stood in the deep shadows of the stairwell.

She curtsied.

"May I come within?" He didn't wait upon an answer, but swept past her.

"Did father send you?"

"Your father? Nay, I've not seen him. Does he want me? I've just returned from inspecting the roads. I'm worried the king may grow restless awaiting the ebb of the Tavest and return to Winchester."

"So, the king is on his way." Joia perched on one of her stools and watched Martin wander the small space, kicking once against the bucket that captured the water trickling in the arrow loop. She must remember, no matter what ill she suffered at this man's hands, Cris would be safe.

Martin's pacing allowed her to compose herself for which she was grateful. He finally came to stand before her. She saw what her father saw. Martin was a warrior who'd captured the king's favor. He'd build on the Solent and please her father. This night he wore a fine surcoat of red, lined in fur. Her stomach did a little dance. She tried to appear calm.

"I've waited long enough for you to accept me. Every day— every moment—you delay makes a mock of me." Before she could speak, he lifted his hand to silence her. "I'll not stand for it. You *will* wed me. Edmund's life depends on it."

"You mean Crispin's.

"Nay. Edmund's."

Joia stared at Martin. For a moment, the chamber spun. "Edmund? Edmund's dead."

Martin slapped his hands on the table and leaned in. She shrank back. "Nay, Edmund is alive and well." He abruptly drew back, dug in his purse, and brought out a small square of parchment. He held it out.

She took the parchment and unfolded it. The words there jittered before her eyes. She needed to press one hand to her heart, it pounded so rapidly in her chest. She knew Edmund's hand well.

My dearest Joia,

I ask that you lose no time in doing as you are bid. Do not delay as my liberty depends upon your acquiescence. I am well, and well cared for this twenty-seventh day of April.

Your loving brother,
Edmund

She looked up. "I don't understand."

Martin snatched the letter from her hand. "He's well and well-treated. If you wish him to remain so, you'll do your duty and wed me the moment the king arrives."

For a moment, she felt as if 'twere she who'd eaten the tainted pears. She dropped her head into her hands as Martin paced and rambled on. A few words finally penetrated her shock. "Baldric? What of Baldric?"

"I said, 'twas Baldric's idea. He was sure you'd been ruined by Robin de Tille. He indulged you, gave you freedoms no woman should have."

She rose unsteadily. "Why do you want me so much?"

He opened his mouth, then closed it. After several moments of silence, he said, "I love you."

She stared at him. His face flushed.

"As I said before, I've loved you for years."

She pointed to the letter he held in his hand. "And that's how you show it? By making a prisoner of my brother? By making threats?"

His eyes widened. He looked at her as if she were a fool.

"'Tis not my fault. 'Tis Baldric's misguided plan. But 'tis done and can be quickly undone with your agreement."

"And you condone this?"

He came to her and lifted her chin with his fingertips. She forced herself not to rip away.

"Look at me. Would it be so very terrible to wed me? I've told you, I'll treat you well, you'll want for nothing and have not one moment of regret."

If he'd not seen her father, he didn't know she'd already agreed to the marriage. "I'll agree only if you release Edmund this very day. Bring him to me, and I'll wed you whenever you so desire."

"I'll only release Edmund when you and I stand before the king and say our vows."

Her voice quivered with fear. "Why wait upon the king? It might be days before he arrives with this weather. What if he never comes? Why not let Edmund go now? I agree. I agree." She knew she was begging, but couldn't stop herself.

"You don't understand. I wish to rise in this world, and having a king at my wedding will give me stature. Who knows what gifts the king might bestow during a wedding feast if he's in his cups? Edmund remains where he is until the king is seated in the chapel."

"Where is he? Fairoaks? If you won't release him, at least take me to him. Allow me to see him and assure myself he's well. Please, I beg of you."

"It's so lovely to see you beg. You'll see your brother when you say your vows. Now, have we an understanding?" He released her chin and made much of folding up Edmund's letter and returning it to his purse.

So, 'twas ambition, man's ambition, that drove these men. Baldric must also be discontent with this life as one of her father's knights, and meant to rise at Martin's side as well. She drew in a deep breath. "Be sure Edmund is waiting at the altar to hear the vows."

Martin's next words were harshly spoken as if he ordered his men. "Be sure to smile as you say the vows. And, Joia? Seal these luscious lips. Tell no one that Edmund lives. Not your father, the priest, your maid, no one. Edmund will die if you do. I'll deny your outrageous accusations, convince your father you're mad— after all you run about after druids." He picked up a cushion.

"You dwell with the fairies." He threw the cushion aside. "I'll deny your charges, and then I shall forget where I put Edmund. Who'll feed him if I cannot remember where he resides?"

"You cannot mean this." She clasped her hands to keep from attacking him.

"And Baldric, well, his memory is even shorter than mine. So seal your lips if you wish Edmund to live, and lest you think to hunt your brother's abode, know that Baldric will be watching you. Now, swear that you'll hold your tongue, my love."

"I swear it." The words were dust in her mouth.

His countenance shifted from stern to smiling. "See, you'll make an obedient wife." He took her arm and led her to the door, opening it as he said, "You'll curb your tongue now, and I'll teach you the proper use of it when you're in our bed at Fairoaks."

He drew her arm through his and escorted her down to the hall. She sat beside him at the high table, and shared his trencher, though she couldn't force the eel stew past her lips. She avoided Guy's gaze, shivered as the men around her speculated on how soon the king would arrive. It couldn't be soon enough. The sooner, the better for Edmund.

Edmund was alive. The joy of it, mingled with the fear for him, made her almost dizzy, but she forced herself to behave as if naught concerned her. It wouldn't do to have anyone question her behavior, lest Martin think to punish her—or Edmund—in some way.

Her father rose at the end of the meal. He held the attention of everyone in the hall. "We've had too much of pain and sorrow at Stonewold these last few months. Let us lift our cups to celebrate the fine news that my daughter is to wed Sir Martin on the day of the king's arrival for our Beltane celebrations."

The hall rang with shouts of approval, Martin's men stomping their feet and whistling. Joia couldn't prevent a glance in Guy's direction. His position, guarding her father's bedchamber door, reminded her that more than Edmund's life was at stake. She read nothing in his impassive gaze. He might be raging inside, he might be relieved, but she knew deep inside one thing he would never be was indifferent. She wished she could run to him and beg his help.

Martin rose and held out his hand. She took it and allowed him to draw her to her feet. She smiled though she wanted to cry out to these people that Edmund was alive, and they should rise up against Martin, not laud him. Instead, she lifted her cup and drank along with the cheering crowd, then she took the rebec Edith handed her and sang for him.

THIRTY~TWO

Guy stood guard before Lord Walter's chamber door from dawn to the noon meal. At that time he took a seat in the hall. Crispin sat beside him, picking at the bread softened in broth that was all the physician would allow. He seemed remarkably recovered from his ordeal, although he had shadows about his eyes. Guy urged him to eat, but absently, as his mind was still on Lord Walter's declaration the night before.

One moment Joia was claiming she wanted to be off to a convent, asking him to find her there if circumstances changed for him, and the next, she was agreeing with seeming contentment to wed a man she claimed to despise. Guy knew the decision must have been made whilst he stood guard. It must have been then she'd given in.

He needed to understand her change of heart. He'd never before wanted to know the workings of a woman's mind. This sudden need to know was torture. Love was torture.

Crispin tugged on Guy's hem. "I won't go with the priest. He smells. He pinches my ear."

"You must do as your father wills, Cris. I've no say in the matter."

He leaned on Guy's side, wrapped his arms around his waist. "I want my mother."

Guy smoothed his hand over Crispin's head, and realized he also loved this child. Two men, the able brothers, Elwin and Peter, stood patiently by. Father Ilbert came and took the boy and his shadows away, so Guy headed for the stables. He needed to see Tink.

Two grooms sat outside, drinking from a jug. They rose hastily as he approached, but he waved them back to their seats.

Tink beckoned him near. "Alan's 'orse is 'ere."

"The devil you say!" Guy followed Tink deep into the stables to the stalls relegated to road horses. Alan's horse whickered a greeting when Guy ran his hand down his neck.

"It were rid by one o' Sir Martin's men who brought a message from Fairoaks."

"I intend to leave on the morrow, and I want you gone, Tink, no more arguments. Find the first merchants heading for Winchester and be off." Guy drew open his purse and handed Tink what he needed for the journey. "And if something troubles you ere you go, see Lady Joia. I've told her you're my man." The horse butted Guy's shoulder. "I might take Alan's horse with me. I'm sure I can make a claim on it with the king."

"What does the lady know?"

"I told her why I was here." He wouldn't say more. He embraced the old man. "I'll see you in Winchester. It's where the king will expect to see me next."

"Aye. It wouldna do fer the king to see ye 'ere. A messenger came this morn fer Walter. Only thing betwixt King Stephen and 'ere is a ford 'e canna cross."

"And thank God for that."

"Aye. I were shocked to 'ear Lady Joia agreed to wed Sir Martin. I wonder what changed 'er mind?"

Guy didn't answer. Thinking about it meant examining all that had passed between them, and he wasn't ready for that. He gave Tink a final embrace. He'd little to do save wait for nightfall. He'd secure his weapons in the stables so they were at hand when he took Alan's horse.

He was done here.

He gave Alan's horse a last pat on the rump, then the commotion of the grooms leaping again to their feet drew his attention. Joia stood in the stable door.

She took a seat on a low stool at her Flora's stall. The horse still lacked spirit, and Guy feared he saw the same lack of spirit in

Joia's eyes as she met his.

He went to her as a moth to a flame, and touched her lightly on the head as he might Crispin. "I'm sorry she's not better."

"Tink said she ate well for the first time yesterday. Mayhap all will be well."

He saw the grooms were busy harnessing the lesser horses to be taken to a field outside the castle walls. The king would need these places for his mounts.

He crouched in front of Joia, took her hands, stroking his thumbs over her soft skin. "I'm responsible for her sorry state as well."

"You cannot make yourself responsible for everything." She dropped her voice to a whisper. "I must speak to you." She bent her head and hastily pressed a kiss to the backs of his hands. "When I see your hands, I imagine them on me." She looked up and met his gaze. "Should I be ashamed of that?"

Guy had no answer for her. "I failed Crispin by making love to you."

"Oh, Guy, what nonsense. Is this why you look so grave all the time? Your warrior honor has been tarnished? Crispin was with my mother *and* father in the hall. Why would anyone think him in danger?"

"Still. If I'd been there, I might have noticed something amiss."

She didn't speak, just traced her fingertips over his hand. It was just another kind of torture. Finally, she broke the heated silence. "I must admit, I think the same, myself. We've that to share."

She brushed a few errant blades of straw from her gown. It was as blue as the sky overhead. A gold chain, studded with pearls, graced her waist. Tiny pearls trimmed her head cloth.

"I saw men carrying your trunks to your bedchamber."

Her cheeks flushed, and she glanced around, then drew him deeper into Flora's stall out of the sight of gossiping grooms. "I've something to tell you but must have your promise what I say will be kept as solemnly secret as if your life depended on it. I beg you, please."

Before he could open his mouth, she threw herself against him. She laid her cheek on his chest and encircled his waist. "I need your help. I know you care for me, so you must help me."

He couldn't deny her. He folded her into his arms. "Oh, Joia. What could possibly make you shift from hating Hursley to wedding him?"

"You must promise you'll repeat not one word I say, nor act upon it no matter how much you feel you must."

"What ails you?"

"I cannot tell you if you won't promise."

Guy pulled her away so he could see her face. "What madness is this?"

Her eyes were huge in the dim light of Flora's stall. "Your promise first. I must have it. I must."

"I promise. Whatever you need, I promise it."

He felt some of the tension ease from her body. She stepped away and began to plait the horse's mane, an idle way to justify her presence.

"I needed your promise as I fear you're a man who'll rush in with sword drawn, and I need someone who thinks, not someone who fights."

He gave a small laugh as he watched her nimble fingers plait the mane. "Crispin's always complaining I ask him to think too much. Now tell me what made you agree to wed the devil."

"Martin asked me to marry him three times. As you know, I refused him each time, then, after the Battle of Tavest, where Edmund . . . ." She faltered, pressing a hand to her breast.

He knew the pain that filled her words; he felt it for his missing son.

She took a steadying breath. "Then Papa became so insistent on the wedding. Rabid. He wants land on the Solent, but that matters not. Martin thought my father could persuade me, but I refused Martin again and again."

She looked as if she might weep. She must not weep or he would be undone.

"Oh, Guy, Martin said Baldric took Edmund hostage at the Battle of Tavest. They hold Edmund to my acceptance of the troth."

Guy grabbed Joia by the shoulders and held her away from him. "Your brother's alive?" It was the last possible thing he'd expected her to say.

"Martin made Edmund write to me, assuring me of his good health and urging me to do as bidden. It's truly in Edmund's hand and bears yesterday's date. Martin has promised to set Edmund free at the wedding if I promise, in turn, to say the vows."

Guy stared at her. "One of us is mad."

"Martin. He must be."

"Shall I kill them for you?"

"Oh, Guy!" She set her hand on his fist that gripped his dagger. "I don't need your sword. I've thought of a marvelous scheme to save Edmund and myself but it cannot work without you."

Guy hoisted her into his arms, kissed her breathless, then set her aside. "I want to hear the scheme, ere I agree to it."

"You promised. Do you not trust me?"

He smoothed the loose tendrils of hair about her brow. "I trust you. I also believe I'll agree to any scheme if it means you'll not be Hursley's wife in two days time." He glanced overhead. "One day and a few hours."

She outlined her plan. "It's so simple. First, on the morning of the wedding, Edith will make sure Baldric is completely distracted. She's very charming, is she not?"

Guy knew not to answer that question.

"Secondly, you'll be at Crispin's side, and I shall insist he be at *my* side for the ceremony so he can have the best view of the king. Third, at the very moment when I'm to say my vows, you'll draw your sword and accuse Martin before all the company of taking Edmund hostage. I'll support you. Edmund, I'm sure, though he knows you not, will support you. Martin shall be arrested. All will be well."

Her breath came as if she'd run a great distance. "It's a perfect scheme, Guy, is it not?"

"And you think no one will remark Edmund's sudden appearance in the chapel?"

She frowned. "I'd not thought . . . Martin must intend concealing him from the company in some way. He may keep him in the antechamber. Or disguise him. It matters not. When Edmund appears, you step forward with your sword."

"I would imagine no weapons will be permitted at the wedding."

She smiled. "You don't need a sword. You'll think of something. An iron candle stand can crush a skull. I'll have one placed at hand."

She was so beautiful, so fanciful. "And if Hursley doesn't produce your brother?"

"You'll demand he produce him. You could command a king to do your bidding if you wished it."

The thought of commanding the king was laughable. Instead, Guy thought of King Stephen's reaction if he saw him in the chapel—far from his duties in Winchester. That alone might cause unwanted commotion at the wedding. Were the king angry enough, he might find himself in chains unable to help Joia or her brother. The thought that Edmund lived seemed nigh impossible. The fact Hursley wanted Joia enough to take Edmund, was very believeable. She was a beautiful and desirable woman, and lamentably, a beautiful and desirable woman with a powerful father and a wealthy quarry.

"Why not go to your father and reveal Martin's treachery now?"

"Martin said he'll deny it. And," her voice quivered. "He said he won't reveal where Edmund's hidden. He said Edmund shall eventually starve."

"You don't think your father would use torture to discover Edmund's whereabouts."

She dropped to the little stool. "Nay, if he couldn't torture strangers to reveal who'd burned his son's body, he'll not be able to do such a thing to Martin or Baldric who've been knights in his service for years."

Guy didn't think Walter so unable as Joia thought, but he needed time to think about all she'd revealed, and time to think of a better plan for rescuing her brother.

He crouched before her and took her hands in his. As he kissed her ragged fingertips, he saw she'd bitten her nails to the quick. "You're so trusting in my abilities."

"I know you, Guy of Chelten, you'll save my brother."

He wished he felt as confident in the outcome, but he'd give his sword arm to help her. Yet, it made no sense that Hursley would suddenly produce Edmund before such a company.

He said the only thing he could. "I shall not fail you."

"We have this night. Would you spend every moment of it with me?"

Guy looked away to the east, to Winchester where he belonged. "It would be impossible."

"Why? Because you've left us already? You intend to take that brown gelding. I'll wager you're only here to arrange it. Can you not sleep in Crispin's chamber as you always do for one more night? Cris will sleep with my father and mother, your able men at hand. And he'll not be allowed to trespass there again as the room's prepared for Prince Eustace. My mother won't countenance Crispin muddying the bedding." When he hesitated, she rushed on. "We can be alone. Alone, Guy, and . . . I'm afraid. Martin said Baldric will be watching me."

Her words were like a hot ember in Guy's belly. He thrust her aside, drew his dagger, and stepped from Flora's stall. He saw only a few grooms mucking out the stalls for the king's horses.

He sheathed his dagger and returned to Joia.

"I evaded him," she said. "I, too, learned from your lessons."

"I am your guard from this moment." He cupped her face in his hands. "I was leaving," he admitted "I couldn't watch you do it. I couldn't watch you wed him."

THIRTY-THREE

Moments after entering Crispin's bedchamber, Guy heard a light knock on the door. Joia? He'd just left her with her mother and the Rogers.

Harald stuck his head in the door. "May I speak to you ere I take up the watch on Lady Joia?"

"I thought Baldric had that duty."

"He's been called away. Hursley's to gather a party and escort the king to Stonewold. Merchants arrived and said they're but a day ahead of the king, and Lord Walter wants to make a good impression, I suppose. Besides me, there will also be two of Sir Martin's men guarding the tower, top and bottom o' the stairs."

"Hursley thinks the lady needs guarding?"

Harald grinned. "He's not taking any chances she'll run off with the king so near. He'll set his tents on the morrow according to them merchants. About sunset.

Guy washed his face. As he dried it he thought on Hursley and Baldric being gone. "But this isn't why you want to talk to me, is it?"

Harald's cheeks flamed as red as his hair. "I, well, that is, I used it as my excuse to . . . well, to ask if you might put a word in with the lady."

Guy realized this was likely Edith's lover. The man confirmed it with his next words."

"I wish that you ask Lady Joia to sanction my marriage to her maid. Sir Martin would never agree, but if Lady Joia asked him during the joyous moments of her wedding, he'd acquiesce, I just know it."

Joyous moments of her wedding.

The words smote Guy as if someone had thrust a lance through his breast. He might try to stop the wedding, might try to rescue her brother, but in truth, Joia had but to say the vows to save her brother.

Guy put his hand on Harald's shoulder. "I'll do as you ask. In turn, I may have need of you come the wedding, and I ask that you look to me in the chapel."

Harald bowed as if Guy were the lord of Stonewold. "Command me any time. Would that I served a man such as you and not *him*."

"And Harald," Guy said as the man went to the door, "I'll take the guard of Lady Joia this night. Find your Edith and make her happy."

After Harald left, Guy considered the news that Hursley was gone from Stonewold. That meant there would be no chance of following the man and mayhap discovering the location of Edmund.

Was Edmund secreted someplace at Fairoaks? Guy pondered the idea. He'd inspected every corner of the manor but only within the manor walls themselves. There could be a dozen huts scattered about outside the walls or in the surrounding forest. There was no time to visit Fairoaks again.

He made a last circuit of the hall ere everyone took to their beds. The place was heaped with baskets of greenery. Ribbons and fresh nosegays of bluebells and violets would grace the chairs at the high table. Snow white linens were folded and ready to drape the tables for the wedding feast.

Every step he took in the hall hammered home the idea that Joia might be lost to him within hours. He forced his thoughts to Hursley, questioning the men who took their ease there. All agreed that Baldric had ridden out with Hursley after Walter's command they escort the king. The earliest they all might arrive, now the river fords were passable, would be the noon meal on the following day, but many thought sunset more likely.

Guy studied Walter as he regaled everyone on the new painting in his bedchamber, soon to be occupied by the king. Walter's behavior told Guy that the man knew naught of the anguish of his daughter or the resurrection of his heir.

He wondered if he should take Walter aside and tell him of Hursley's perfidy. What would be the result?

Walter might launch an immediate attack on Hursley. Could Walter reach Hursley before Hursley reached the king? As Joia feared, Hursley would likely deny the accusations, or simply refuse to speak and leave Edmund to languish and die in some hidden location.

It was, unfortunately, done far too often. Guy knew of two men who'd been left in pits to starve when their fathers had not paid their ransoms. The memory of those bodies reminded Guy that he must not do anything to imperil Edmund's life. Guy felt an impotent rage that he could do little save await Hursley's return. Then he might risk speaking to Walter.

On the other hand, Edmund must be retrieved at some point. It might be a better time to act. No matter, Guy knew he must not risk harm to Edmund. He must find an excuse to stop the wedding.

THIRTY~FOUR

Guy climbed the tower stairs. He assured himself Joia was in her chamber, then went to Crispin's. The bed was drastically different from the tumbled twist of linens in which Crispin usually slept. Guy pulled back the bedcovers. They were the finest of linen. He realized the mattress was freshly stuffed with feathers, the rushes on the floor were fresh as well. No wicks in oil dishes here. A brace of wax candles stood ready on a new table, draped with embroidered linen. He recognized both the table and the linen from the solar. A large chair with a soft blue cushion awaited the princely rump.

As Guy folded his clothes he smiled at the thought of sleeping in a princely bed—with Joia—if she could make her way here. His conscience wouldn't trouble him. If he rescued Edmund, the king might grant him leave to petition for Joia's hand.

Would Joia be happy with someone so low as a mere guard to the king, knight or not?

He was hopelessly entangled with an undisciplined woman. Somehow, he couldn't desire those tangles unknotted. What a glory it had proved to lie with a woman who made love with such passion.

He stretched out on the soft mattress. Joia's scheme was as womanly as her plot to run away to a convent. Her plan was fraught with problems, could go awry within a heartbeat. But Joia trusted him, and he must prove himself worthy of that trust.

Guy groaned. He didn't like complications, especially complications conceived by someone else. He tried to make his mind rest. He tried to let it drift. Ofttimes he found that sleeping on a weighty matter made it seem clearer in the morning.

If Edmund was alive, he was as well hidden as Alan.

Guy sat bolt upright. He gasped and pressed his fist to his chest. Pain ran through him. He gasped again, could not catch his breath.

He suddenly knew where Alan was.

Buried in Edmund Fortranne's grave.

A man who'd not been ransomed. A man who'd disappeared. A body needed and burned beyond any possibility of recognition.

Guy fell back on the pillows, pressed the heels of his hands to his eyes, and wept.

Thirty-five

Edith agreed to sleep in the woman's solar, deserted this night, leaving Joia alone. Those who usually slept in the solar had been banished to the hall or the storerooms below as the space was needed to provide private quarters to the royal retainers. Joia imagined Edith's quick agreement meant she'd not spend the night alone either.

Joia peeked in the solar. The space had been divided with a pale yellow cloth that seemed to glow as if the sun were captured within. She checked on the guards on the ramparts and hall entrances to the stairs. She asked if they had need of anything and when they'd be relieved that they might seek their own beds. She used her questions to gauge how much time she had with Guy.

She slipped into Crispin's bedchamber. There was a small possibility they'd be discovered, she and Guy, but Joia was sure providence shined on them as even Martin and Baldric were gone from Stonewold.

Crispin's chamber was no longer scented with child or Guy's weapons. It was fragrant with sage and rosemary. Moonlight crossed the room to stripe the bed. It was piled with pillows for she had seen it so. She wanted to lie in clean linens with Guy, had ordered the bedding with him in mind, not the prince. The bedding was finer than that on her father's bed where the king would sleep.

She set the bar and then waited by the door for her eyes to adjust to the flickering light of one candle. Guy lay on his back, face in shadow, one hand behind his head. She went to his side, dropped her girtle, her head cloth, stripped out of her gown, her linen underdress, rolled down her hose. She shivered—with anticipation.

She touched his cheek. He turned his head to kiss her palm. She pulled down the bed covers to look at him. Her insides contracted as if a small climax had rippled through her. He was fully erect, ready for her.

She felt the liquid heat of the changes within that would ease his way. She took a long steadying breath and tried to memorize the planes of muscle, the pattern of hair and scar, and when he shifted under her scrutiny, the supple play of shadow and moonlight across his skin.

Kneeling beside him, she ran her hand over him, his shoulder, his arm. She ran her fingertips along his ribs, traced an old scar, and the taut muscles of his belly. She leaned over and pressed her lips to his chest, encircling his erection with her hand.

He tangled his hands in her hair. Again and again, he ran his fingers through her hair whilst she caressed up and down his length, her cheek against his heart.

"I love you, Guy."

Guy hoped she read naught of grief in his eyes, that she saw only the desire that rampaged through his body. It was stronger than he liked, fueled by his hatred for Martin Hursley who might dare to touch her.

Every ounce of Guy's being was filled with anger. He had no room for love in his heart. Only hatred.

He would be silent.

He shifted her hair and saw in the moonlight the marks of her father's whipping.

For this, too, he owed Hursley, and Guy knew he must make the man pay. Guy feared his need for revenge might spill over on her, twist the desire that gripped his body. He leashed that hatred ruthlessly lest it run out of control.

"I'll free your brother," he whispered. "I swear it." It was all he could offer her, and all he could manage without choking.

He pulled her up, claimed her mouth as if Martin Hursley stood at the foot of the bed, watching.

She met his ardor, though her kisses were still innocent, the hand on his cock still learning the differences between a man and a woman. He pulled her hand away and gasped for air whilst he fought for restraint.

"You're so beautiful." She kissed his palm. "I have only to see your hands and I want them on me."

She ran her tongue along the veins of his wrist, feeling the throb of blood beneath her lips. She sensed something amiss. He held himself from her. She sat back on her heels and studied him. "Should I leave?"

He leaned on one elbow and brushed the hair from her brow. "Forgive me. I was thinking of your brother and it made me angry. I don't want that anger to hurt you in anyway."

"You could never hurt me." Her insides ached for him. She was on fire and frantic to know every inch of him. She whispered, "I want you now."

He bore her to her back, rising over her. She encircled his neck and lifted her hips. "Now, now."

He plunged into her. She stifled a cry against his shoulder, thrusting back. Sensations streamed through her, a desperate ache expanding as he filled her. She pulled her thighs higher on his hips to drive him deeper.

Every inch of him was molten hot. She clung to him. She thought she might need to scream. He looked down at her, his face a fierce collection of shadows she couldn't read. She gripped his sides and moaned aloud. The gathering sensations inside her coalesced into a hot flame of need, yet she arched to meet it. It came like a searing bolt when he leaned down and covered her mouth. She heaved against him.

Guy rode the wave of her climax, her sheath pulsing around

him. It pushed him over his own precipice. He slammed into her without control.

Again and again.

He was mad with a need to possess her.

"You're mine," he said against her lips, plunging into her one last time and emptying himself.

He fell away from her, to his back. Spent. Still angry, his hands in fists.

She curled against his side, her body shuddering. He forced himself to wrap his arms around her, forced his fingers to caress, not bruise. She drew up the bedcovers. He kissed her forehead in an attempt to soothe; he'd taken her too quickly, too roughly.

She cupped his face and looked into his eyes. He feared what she might see there, so he kissed her with his tongue, his breath.

"I never knew it was so devastating. I didn't know a man could feel so perfectly, perfect."

Perfect? He'd been a rutting beast. He closed his eyes, rubbed them. "It will be better next time," he whispered.

"Better? It could be even better? When do you think we could do this again?" She pulled on him so they lay nose-to-nose.

He stared at her blue eyes, so wide, so curious. "When I catch my breath." This time he vowed, he'd not play the savage.

"So soon?" She stroked her hand along his hip.

"Sooner than I had thought possible," he said softly.

Joia pressed her face into his throat as he slid his fingers inside her. He used the slickness of his seed to tease that one, so very sensitive spot that still throbbed from their joining. She shackled his wrist and tried to catch her breath.

Need and want entwined in her body, threatening to flame out of control again. She whispered his name as he tantalized and conjured sensations she couldn't endure. All her imaginings hadn't come close to how he could make her feel. She pushed against his fingertips, rocking on the sensations flooding through her. She felt the storm gathering again as his caressing fingertips circled, delved, slicked over her—in her. She groped for his mouth and came apart.

She rolled to her back and flung her arms out, sure she'd been among the stars somehow, the ones she saw through the arrow loop.

He propped himself on his elbow. "You're the most beautiful woman I've ever seen." He ran his hand over her breasts.

She closed her eyes and savored the words. And the caress.

"If one of us is perfect, 'tis you. Your breasts. Your hips." He cupped her. "Here. Perfect."

"Is it always thus? I feel as if I were a goblet of glass and you flung me on the hearth and shattered me into a thousand pieces." She wanted to tell him again how much she loved him, but he'd not said the words in return.

"Touch me as I'm touching you."

She stroked his manhood, watched it filling, swelling. "Can I hurt you?"

"There are many ways you could hurt me, but your hand, on me thusly, never."

She stroked her thumb across the tip with its drop of seed that gleamed like a pearl in the moonlight.

He gasped.

"I want you inside me, Guy. Nay, I *need* you inside me."

She shoved him onto his back, climbed astride him, and guided him into her. She gripped his shoulders and shifted.

He stifled a moan as he rolled her nipples between his fingertips.

"I feel what you are doing with your hands as if it were connected down here." She touched where they joined.

He watched her face. The moonlight gilded her hair and painted her shoulders and breasts as white as the purest alabaster, and he thought that this was how he would remember her, with her eyes intent on his, a small smile on her lips, the tips of her full breasts taut from his touch.

She rocked on him, moving as he suspected pleased her. He forced himself to lie still for her, to allow her to set her own pace. Her hot, slick sheath slipped and slid on his cock. Her long hot thighs embraced him, and her silky hair skimmed his skin with the exquisite lightness of a feather. She covered his hands on her breasts . . . rocked, rocked, drove him mad.

Then she forced his hands back against the pillows, linking her fingers with his, and leaned over him. Her eyes drifted closed as she rode him. Her breathing turned to urgent pants and then she gasped.

The pulses of her climax rippled along his length. He couldn't wait another moment. He drove himself up into her, ending in a violent rush of sensation, draining himself.

She lay on him, her legs tangled with his, and slept.

He couldn't.

He lay there for half the night. His mind dwelt on what they'd done. The consequences. He thought of Hursley and Baldric. Of Joia's brother and his own son. Grief helped him keep watch over her.

The moon moved on its path, casting the chamber into darkness.

As dawn neared, Guy realized several things. Taking Edmund was too drastic a way to secure a bride. The killing of Alan to take his place made little sense either. Hursley and Baldric's careful execution of Walter's battle plans at Tavest did not speak of men who acted rashly. Something was amiss.

If Stonewold were a placid pool, there was a snarl of snakes seething beneath the surface.

And how were the accidents to Crispin, the poisoning of Lady Blanche and the child, connected to Hursley's plans?

Guy wanted vengeance for Alan's death, but would hold back until Edmund was secured.

He stroked his fingertips along her brow. Too many men to secure a bride, he thought. He kissed her sleep-soft lips.

He knew he must rouse her. He wanted to look over the chapel and then take Alan's horse and find a place to await

Hursley and Baldric's return. Mayhap he could follow them and be led to Edmund.

He caressed Joia awake, learned every lovely inch of her, the valley of her spine, each bone, the soft globes of her buttocks, the down on her thighs. He stroked and soothed, and when he sensed she was completely at his mercy, he learned the shape of her breasts with his mouth, moved lower, opened her to him, tasted and savored her, drenched as she was in his seed.

He urged her to another climax, felt the fist of need grip him again as she said his name in a breathy sigh. He urged her up again, took her to the precipice and made sure she came again. Only then did he join himself to her, but gently, slowly this time, and realized she'd somehow purged him of some of his pain.

She fell almost instantly asleep. He kissed her brow and whispered words he'd thought himself incapable of saying, "I love you."

THIRTY~SIX

Guy went to the arrow loop. Joia was gone. It was four in the morning, but the sky was beginning to stain with dawn. By noon, the king's tents might fill the hills. He wanted to look for Hursley and Baldric, see where they went upon their return.

Guy had assured Joia he'd somehow rescue her brother, so if Hursley had Edmund, Guy wanted to know where—must know where.

Could he find Edmund before the wedding?

He belted on his sword and dagger and made his way to the bailey, filled as if 'twere mid-day. As he wove through the frantic last minute preparations for the royal arrival, carts of baked goods being delivered, squealing pigs and squawking fowl meeting their ends, he found he was watching with different eyes.

Too many men from Fairoaks lingered in the bailey, though their knight was gone to fetch the king.

Guy entered the chapel. Candles burned in iron candle stands next to the altar placed there by Joia, Guy was sure, but the garlands of greens and bluebells tied with ribbons that draped the altar and the chairs for the king and queen's party reminded him most vividly that a wedding was to take place at the king's pleasure. Would it be immediately upon his arrival, or would the king want a day of rest? Guy hoped for the latter. It would give him more time to search for Edmund.

Even the air was scented for a wedding. He stood at the garden door and surveyed the ground, looking for ways to take Edmund away from Hursley if his search for the man failed.

He would need help. He mentally chose men from those he'd

trained to guard Crispin and would ask Harald to gather them and station them at hand.

The doors of the chapel opened as did the garden door behind Guy. Lord Walter stood in the chapel entrance.

Guy felt the press of a dagger in his side. He knew instantly he'd made a terrible mistake, not watching his back, but didn't turn to see who held the dagger or how many men came from that direction. The shadows cast on the floor indicated at least three.

Anger and a sense of grief swept through him, but he must not let it take control of him. He watched Walter march forward, eight men flanking him, men Guy had trained and who now knew many of his tricks. Whether they'd recognize them when used against them or could use them themselves was another matter. He moved his feet, but kept his gaze on Walter's face.

"Guy of Chelten." Walter said.

"My lord." Guy bowed.

Walter held out his hands. Guy looked from the shackles to Walter's face, forcing himself to control the emotions roiling through him.

"I know you've done naught but see to my son's safety, and this seems a poor reward, but there've been questions raised of your loyalty. I know you can take ten of my men, so that's why I've brought twelve. These men know your methods, and they'll not be such easy bait as in the stone circle.

Guy held out his hands ere anyone thought to have him place his hands behind him. Walter gave the shackles to Ivo whose expression told Guy the man regretted his duty. As Ivo placed the chains, one of the men behind Guy plucked his dagger and sword.

"What's this about, my lord?" He tested the chains and measured their length, his anger twisting into something darker and deeper.

"Spying."

The dagger slid into Guy's flesh, along a rib, and he stifled a grunt of pain. Blood trickled down his side. "I've never spied, my lord."

"I'm inclined to believe you, but still, you were Chelten's man. We'll discuss the matter when the king and his company are gone. If I've wronged you, I'll gladly set you free and compensate you for your troubles."

For Joia's sake—for Edmund's sake—Guy must free himself. There'd be a way out of this coil, and he'd take it the instant it presented itself. He opened his mouth to spill Joia's secret to Walter, but something held him back. Instead he said in what he hoped were calm and rational tones, "You've but to take me before the king, and he'll vouch for me."

Lord Walter grinned. "And if you're a spy—or worse—I'd be putting you within arm's reach of him. Never.

Guy shifted his hands and the chains rattled. The man behind him spoke at his ear. "I would dearly love to thrust this home and pay you for the cut."

So Baldric was *not* escorting the king at Hursley's side.

Guy ignored the taunt. "My lord, who accuses me of spying?"

"Take him to the gate cells," Walter said, ignoring Guy's question.

THIRTY~SEVEN

"Leave us," Baldric said to the other guards when they reached one of the gatehouse cells.

Guy contemplated his fate. He thought it wouldn't be long ere someone informed Joia that he'd been marched through the bailey and into the gatehouse. The time alone with Baldric might be unpleasant, but Guy also knew that with a little luck, and a few inches of chain, he could kill Baldric.

Nay, *needed* to kill Baldric, for surely, this was the man who'd killed Alan and burned his body.

"I'm unarmed and bound," Guy said mildly.

"Aye. I was surprised you acquiesced."

Guy shrugged. "If Lord Walter's to believe I'm not a spy, it wouldn't do to disobey him."

Baldric grinned and drew a long dagger, then swore as Guy ducked his swipe. Guy knew he'd but a moment or two left to act. He charged Baldric, smashing him against the door, tangling his chains around Baldric's blade. They crashed to the floor. He drew on the chains, lifting Baldric's blade to slice the man's throat.

The door flew open. "Cease! Immediately!" Walter shouted.

Guy rolled to his feet. Baldric did as well. Blood dripped from Baldric's nose to splatter on the dirt floor.

"Hand over that dagger," Walter snapped at Baldric.

He did as bid. "My lord, he attacked me. He broke my nose."

"And you're not some mewling babe to complain. The man's chained. Had you simply locked him in here and not sought revenge, you'd be with Martin and the king who have crossed

249

the Tavest as we speak. I came to fetch you, but you cannot see a king covered in blood. I'll make your excuses."

They stood in silence. Walter sighed. "Down on your knees, Guy, can you not see the man won't pass you without fear of what you'll do. Kneel."

Guy slowly sank to his knees and braced for what was to come.

Baldric moved to stand before him. He made Walter a deep bow and then turned. Guy's world went black.

Guy groaned as someone peeled up his eyelid. Light dazzled. His head throbbed.

"Guy. Guy, wake up!" Crispin lifted his eyelid again.

"Leave 'im to sort 'isself out, lad."

Tink.

Guy shifted and stifled a groan. Lord Walter must have allowed Baldric more than just a kick to the head.

Tink helped him sit up. The room spun.

Crispin cupped his face. "Joia said Ivo said you were here, but Tink didn't believe me."

Guy struggled to his feet. "Where's Baldric?"

"In the hall, standing wiv Sir Martin who's fawning o'er the king and queen."

Crispin unlocked Guy's chains. "Hugh gave me the key. He won't be punished will he?" Crispin bit his lip, his faced pinched with anxiety.

"I'll see he doesn't suffer for this," Guy said, setting his hand on Crispin's curls. He was garbed in a fine blue tunic, and his yellow and blue striped hose were, for once, clean and rent free. The implications of his garb hit Guy as if Baldric had kicked his head again.

"Is she wed?"

"Nay. Now, put this on, yer a bloody mess. And hurry." Tink

held out a priest's robe.

"I have to get to the wedding."

"Ye need to let me see to yer wounds first. Ye'll never get in the chapel lookin' as if ye just fought the Battle of Tavest. And the wedding's postponed. Lady Joia delayed the matter. It were 'er as sent us the moment she 'eard what become o' ye and suggested to her father the king should eat first after such a journey."

Guy donned the priest's robe. His side screamed with every shift of muscle.

There might be time. Precious little, but still, some time. As he walked behind Tink, Crispin patted his arm. "You can lean on me."

And Guy did place his hand on the boy's shoulder to steady his steps. His head throbbed with pain and his left side felt caked with blood. Fresh blood welled from the wound there, and he knew not where else he might be injured. In truth, he ached head to toe. Why hadn't he killed Baldric in the cell? He couldn't remember very clearly what happened there.

Lord Walter. Walter had called a halt.

Guy couldn't think straight, his head not only throbbing but feeling as if it were stuffed with rags.

He thanked God for Tink and leaned against the wall whilst his man and Hugh planned how Guy would escape his cell and not cause the guard to be blamed. In the end, Tink shackled Hugh, smeared some of Guy's blood on the man's face and tunic, and locked him in a far cell. Hopefully, the wedding would prevent anyone from looking in the cell and when they did, it would appear as if Guy had overpowered the man.

Why had Baldric not set more guards? Then it occurred to Guy that Baldric might not want any witnesses if he intended coming back later and killing him.

Tink went down on one knee to Crispin. "I'll see 'im to the village church. No one will question a priest goin' in a church. When 'e's fit to be seen, I'll bring 'im to the chapel. "

Crispin wrapped his arms around Tink's neck, then around

Guy's waist, hugging him hard. Then he was gone.

Guy pulled the hood up, hunched his shoulders, and tucked his hands into the sleeves as he'd seen Father Ilbert do on many an occasion. He needed Tink's sure hand several times as black dots swirled in his vision and nausea cramped his stomach.

The village seemed deserted of all save the bakers, with everyone in the castle grounds for a glimpse of the king.

He stumbled on the steps of St. Cedric's, where Tink dumped him on a bench before the altar. "My father and brothers, Tink?"

"I've no seen 'em. Mayhap the king dinna want any o' Chelten's men wiv 'im though the number o' tents is legion. They could be there, and I'd be no the wiser. Walter'll be poor as a church mouse after feeding that army."

Guy struggled out of the priest's robe.

"God's blood. Yer black and blue and ye need this stitched," Tink said, examining the knife wound in Guy's side as he laid a pile of clean clothes on the bench. "Tom willna like getting 'is clothes back bloody."

"There's not time. Lady Joia expects me to stop this wedding. Did you see her brother anywhere?"

"Crispin were just 'ere."

"Nay. Lord Edmund."

Tink placed his hand on Guy's forehead. "Ye must be feverish. Edmund's dead these past weeks."

"That's the point, Tink, he's not dead. Hursley holds him hostage to Joia's saying of the vows. He promised her Edmund would be in the chapel and that he'd be freed at the saying of the vows." Guy knew he was repeating himself and must sound mad to Tink. "She expects me to stop it . . . there's more to it." Guy took a deep breath to fight the tilting of the chapel. "There's more to it. I like it not the king is here. And Alan. I have to kill Hursley. And Baldric. I know 'tis Alan in Edmund's grave and they're responsible."

Tink gasped. Guy watched the old man's face crumple and tears well and run in the deep wrinkles of his face. He let them drip unheeded as he bound a strip from the priest's robe around Guy's middle and helped him with Tom's shirt and tunic.

"They musta flayed . . ." Tink's voice broke again, "to conceal who—"

"Tink, we haven't much time." Guy couldn't tolerate the images Tink's words conjured.

"I were in the chapel looking fer ye, Guy. Hursley and Baldric were in and out, fussin' o'er the preparations there wiv the priest, but there's no man about as I don't know. Crispin would be full o' it if Edmund were about. Everone would be. Are ye sure yer not just damaged in the 'ead?"

"Where is he? Edmund? Where could Hursley have him?"

"Yer no fit to do aught about this. Yer barely able to stand. I'll try to find yer brothers, shall I?"

"And Harald. Harald will help you fetch them. I want—"

The church went dim. Guy fought to remain upright. "Nay, just fetch Harald here with a sword."

Tink ran from the church, banging the door behind him, leaving Guy in the gloom.

The side of his head was swelling. The taste of blood filled his mouth. He pressed his hand to his side as he hid his bloody garments behind the altar.

He was having trouble concentrating. He moved to the altar and got gingerly to his knees. He dropped his head to his folded hands.

He was going to fail Joia.

He felt it in his bones.

And when he failed her, he would also fail Edmund.

Just as he had failed Alan.

Thirty~Eight

Joia stood in the the priest's private chamber just off the chapel. The wedding would begin in but a moment. She shook with rage. There was no Edmund in the chapel.

"You said Edmund would be here."

Martin reached for her, but she backed away. He shrugged and smiled. He wore his best blue tunic, trimmed in gold, a sword and a long dagger at his waist.

Too many weapons for a wedding.

Her insides clenched with fear for Edmund—and herself. "I said I wouldn't wed you if Edmund was not present to hear the vows. How could you lie to me?"

Martin lifted one brow. "The king and queen are in their seats. I'm sure they—and your father—are chafing to get the ceremony done. Would you anger a king? I promised you that you'd see Edmund, and I shall honor that promise when the vows are said. Baldric has his orders."

"Baldric?" She feared she'd been played for a fool.

"Baldric." Martin moved close to her, leaned his lips by her ear. "I told Baldric that should you not say your vows loud enough so all can hear them, he should kill Edmund."

The door opened and her father poked his head inside. Joia opened her mouth but Martin's fingers gripped her so hard she almost screamed.

"The king and queen are impatient to begin." Her father slammed the door, leaving her alone with Martin again.

"Edmund is safe. The longer you linger, the longer until you are reunited." Martin adjusted the circlet of pearls that held her head cloth. "You've never looked more beautiful."

"I want a moment for prayer." She went to a *prie dieu* and knelt. She bent her head over her hands. She prayed Edmund was still alive and would be returned in a few moments, safe to his family. Tears ran between her fingertips. Would Tink be successful in freeing Guy?

When Guy arrived, would he notice Edmund was not present for the ceremony?

Of course he would.

Guy saw everything. Had he not said many things could go wrong? He'd be prepared for every eventuality as only a man such as he could be. He'd stop the wedding and demand Edmund be freed. With a quick thank you to God that He had already answered her prayers by sending Guy to Stonewold, she rose.

Her knees shook as she followed Martin into the chapel. It was so crowded with the king's men she had to hunt for her mother who sat on a side bench as if she were of no importance. She searched the crowd for Guy as well, but so many filled the space, king's men, folk from both Stonewold and Fairoaks, that she saw only a blur of faces.

The king and his queen sat near the altar in carved oak chairs carried in from the hall for their comfort. Neither smiled as she took her place, the king especially looking ill pleased. She didn't care if the king was pleased. She cared only that her delaying of the wedding had helped Guy escape.

Her father took her arm.

Guy will save me.

THIRTY~NINE

The sun shone through the oiled skins that covered the church windows. A dozen or more candles burned on the altar. It was still and peaceful, the sounds of the village muted by the thick stone walls. Nay, he couldn't hear the village because the villagers were all at the wedding.

Joia's wedding.

Guy pressed his fingertips to his bloody brow.

Tink and Harald must hurry or he'd miss the wedding. The church spun, bile rose in his throat.

He bowed his head again. He'd not yet prayed for Alan's soul. He tried and failed to banish revenge from his heart.

A wave of dizziness assailed him again. He drew in a deep breath to steady himself.

He realized the church didn't smell of the wax candles burning on the altar. Nor did it smell of the herb strewn rushes crushed beneath his knees.

He staggered to his feet, and took another deep breath. He recognized this scent, faint though it was and entwined with the herbs, the beeswax, and smoke.

He flung open a door at the rear of the chapel. It led to a chamber where he imagined the priest might sleep when not at the castle. It held a pallet and a table. The table was littered with scraps of parchment and crusts of bread. The scent was stronger here. He looked about and saw the trap in the floor partially covered by the pallet. He shoved the pallet aside, pulled at the recessed ring, and lay the door back, exposing a short, steep flight of stone steps. The stink of the dungeon assaulted him.

He held his bloody side as he ran to the altar and snatched up a candle, and then forced himself to slow his steps and shelter the flame. As he entered the priest's chamber he heard a sound that made him lift his head and pause.

Horns. Horns that could only signal a procession.

The candle wavered in his hand. He desperately wanted to go to the castle and disrupt the wedding, but he'd promised Joia he'd save her brother, and as Guy stood at the head of the steps, he knew somewhere below was Edmund. As the sound of horns rose again from the castle, Guy knew he couldn't do both.

He walked slowly down the steep flight of steps that could only lead to the church crypt. The space below was broken by low arches supporting the church above. The walls were lined with niches and held what he assumed must be the remains of past priests and village worthies. He lifted the candle and saw the red eyes of a rat crouched on ancient bones. It scuttled down the wall. He leapt aside as the rat ran up the steps and into the priest's room.

Guy forced himself to ignore the other rustlings among the bones. With a silent prayer to the patron saint of whoever protected men against beasts, he bent beneath the low ceiling, lifted the candle, and walked deeper into the crypt. The floor was littered with muddy footprints. He followed them and saw two doors in the distance. One was barred. No man stood on guard here either. Guy shook his head over Hursley's arrogance, but again, no guards meant no witnesses if the prisoner wasn't meant to live.

Guy lifted the bar, set it aside, and took a step into complete darkness. The stench was overpowering. He raised the candle and stared. A figure scrambled away from him, into the murky shadows. With shock, Guy saw the figure was that of Prince Eustace.

The young man cowered, his chains chiming on the stone floor when Guy stepped toward him. It was then Guy saw the other two men. Or creatures. They were filthy, bearded, and shackled hand and foot.

The chamber spun.

Disbelief, elation, then fear swept through him. Guy put out his hand to the wall, gathered his much vaunted control—control about to slip from his grasp.

He desperately wanted to kneel before these two and look into their faces, to confirm what his instincts told him was true. This was not only Joia's brother, Edmund, but also Alan.

The prince whimpered. Guy realized duty must come first. He turned away and went down on one knee. "My prince. I'm Sir Guy, of your father's guard." He examined the young man's manacles. "Have you any knowledge of the keys to these?"

The man that must be Edmund rasped out, "I think they're hanging out there somewhere. The priest who brings us food used them a time or two to treat his wounds." The shackles rattled as he gestured to Alan.

Guy nodded to the shadowy figure and went back into the outer crypt, taking a deep cleansing breath. He saw no keys. He forced himself to remain calm, forced his thoughts from the implications of the prince in this crypt, forced himself not to ignore the noble son for his own.

His belly tightened as he skimmed his fingers among the shelves of the dead. Their tattered garments disintegrated as he examined them. Rats stared and shifted, ran down the walls and over his boots as he moved along the niches near the prison cell. As the rats scampered away, his stomach clenched.

No keys.

He began shoving the bones aside, scattering generations of the pious. He took another long shuddering breath. He must control himself. He wasn't thinking.

Then he saw it. The same trail of muddy foot prints that had led him to this cell led to a corner niche. Guy saw a small reliquary thrust into the chest cavity of one corpse. Two rats guarded the box. He castigated himself for a coward. He thrust his candle toward the creatures and they scurried off. He flipped back the lid of the reliquary and drew out a single shiny key.

He unlocked the prince's shackles. "Wait by the steps, my

lord," Guy said to the prince who shook with fear and looked far younger than his ten and three. "Don't go any farther. I don't know if we're alone and would not see you recaptured." The prince struggled to his feet, then stumbled out the door. Guy hoped he'd obey the simple order. The prince was not known for obedience or cooperation.

Guy turned to the other two residents of the hell hole, knelt and setting the candle between them, kept his eyes on the business of unlocking the closest man's shackles, the one who must be Edmund.

The man said softly, "I think I cannot walk."

Guy cast the shackles away with such violence they bounced off the wall. He scooped Edmund into his arms and carried him from the crypt. He tore a hole in the oiled window cloth and inspected the empty village, and then went out into the misty day.

Guy strode into a copse of trees, aware the prince was loping along behind them. He set Edmund down gently on the carpet of rotting leaves behind a deadfall.

The prince struggled to pull off a dirty priest's robe.

"Stay here with this man, my prince. Do *not* reveal yourself to any passersby, villagers, soldiers. *Anyone.* I'm not sure who to trust. I intend to hide you, and go for your father's guards, ones I know I can trust."

"How do I know I can trust *you?*" Prince Eustace had a haughty look on his dirty face. His costly tunic and hose were filthy after what could only be a few hours in the crypt.

Guy fought for patience. "I'm Guy de Maci; my family has served yours for four generations. Your grandfather knighted me."

The prince seemed to shrink. He slumped to the ground. "Can we not go now? Come back for him later? Surely another few hours will mean nothing to that man."

"That man is Lord Walter's son."

Guy went down on one knee to Joia's brother. "Before I fetch Alan, is there aught you need?"

"Nothing. Go to your son."

Guy touched Edmund on the shoulder. "I'll be back." He grinned. "Don't run off."

The young man gave him an answering grin, his teeth showing white against the dirty face and matted beard.

Guy cautiously approached the crypt again, hoping the prince would remain silent. He didn't expect Hursley to leave his wedding or the feast to come here, but would Baldric be sent to fetch Edmund? Or the prince?

Guy had no time to worry about the prince. He entered the church, ran down the steps, and through the crypt, heedless of the blood that now soaked his side. He set the candle on the floor of the cell.

He knelt and snatched Alan into his arms, holding him hard against his chest. He couldn't speak; his eyes burned as he hugged his son in the dark corner of the crypt. He put all he had never said and wanted to say into the embrace. Then he set him aside, fumbled the key into the shackles, and freed him.

Alan said nothing as Guy carried him from the crypt and into the copse. He was glad to see the prince hadn't wandered off, but sat by Edmund, plucking at his tunic with dirty fingers. Guy gently set Alan down. His son was filthy, almost unrecognizable, even in the light of day.

A roar of sound came from the castle, sending a bolt of pain through Guy's middle as if Baldric stood there and stabbed him.

"What was that?" Edmund whispered.

"Your sister has wed Martin Hursley."

FORTY

"Sweet *Jesu*—" Edmund broke off as they heard the sound of a horse.

Guy saw panic on the prince's face and thought him likely to bolt into the forest. He knelt behind the deadfall and clapped a hand on Eustace's shoulder and whispered. "Hold, my prince, it's only those who would aid us in rescuing you." Guy hoped he was right and it wasn't Baldric.

Tink came through the clearing before the church leading Alan's gelding. Behind him, on foot, came Harald.

Guy stood up. "These men will take you to a safe place until I can return with men I trust."

The moment Tink saw Alan, he ran and embraced the boy, tears streaming down his face.

"Your son needs food and drink," Edmund said, watching the two.

"As do you. I'll see to it—"

"I should have the horse," Prince Eustace interrupted. "You can send servants for these two."

"I beg to differ with you, my lord," Guy said. "I'm not sure who took you—"

"Sir Martin." The prince rubbed the side of his head.

Guy found himself doing the same, although he knew his bodily pains would soon be swamped by others. Others that couldn't be mended.

"Sir Martin asked me to come to the chapel," the prince continued, "to see that all was in readiness for my father. I woke up here."

"Still, my lord, your life is in grave danger. I can think of no reason for your presence here save that Hursley is plotting against your father."

Edmund gasped. "That would be treason. And Joia wed him?"

"Indeed," Guy said. "Now, we must hurry from here. We don't know how many men are involved in Hursley's scheme or how many would rally to him given the offer of enough rewards."

"Nonsense," Prince Eustace said. "Give me this horse, and I'll return to the keep and kill this Hursley. Have you no sword?"

Guy bowed low. "I'm sure you can ably defend yourself, my lord, but I'm equally sure that to enter in haste might put your father in danger. Please give me leave to serve you." He forced himself to put servility into his voice as he knew the prince preferred a fawning servant over a bold one.

Guy didn't, however, wait for the prince to speak. He lifted Alan into the saddle. The horse looked over his shoulder and lifted his head twice as if acknowledging his master.

"My old friend," Alan said softly, rubbing the horse's neck. Guy placed his hand over his son's and smiled that the two were reunited.

Tink slapped the saddle bags. "There's bread and cheese, wine 'ere." He lowered his voice so the prince couldn't hear. "A dagger or two as well. I couldn't find yer brothers, though they's there as I saw their tent." He drew Guy a quick map in the dirt, indicating the de Maci tent in the king's camp.

Guy rubbed out the drawing, and then slung Edmund up behind Alan and without ceremony put his hands together for the prince to mount.

"I'll not ride pillion with these men!" the prince cried. "It would be an indignity."

Guy prayed silently for patience. "Death's an indignity. They cannot walk. You should not. Please mount."

They heard voices—men's voices. The prince stepped onto Guy's hands and leapt up behind Edmund.

Guy handed the reins to Tink. "I suspect the villagers tasked with serving the king are returning. I know you'll look after Alan. Take these men to the barrow. You'll find wedges near the entrance, behind a log. Use them to open the barrow door." He instructed Harald on obliterating their tracks and hiding Alan's horse whilst remaining on guard there, well hidden, until he came for them.

"I want clean clothes," the prince said, though his eyes were wide with fear as Guy walked the horse deeper into the woods, away from the voices.

Guy realized Alan remained in the saddle only because Edmund held him in place. "Look to their care, Tink, Harald. I may be a few hours."

Guy went to his son and placed his hand on his arm. They studied each other for a moment. "Alan, I have—"

"I didn't think you'd look for me," Alan interrupted.

Guy swallowed the lump in his throat. "I was looking for your horse. I spent a pretty penny for him."

Alan grinned and Guy found himself able to smile back. He slapped the horse's rump and watched them disappear into the shadows of the forest, the prince bouncing along on the saddle bags, the two young men so thin, they hardly made one man.

He turned toward the king's encampment. He needed a sword.

FORTY-ONE

Joia stood in her father's chamber and watched Martin pace and spew words, excited words about the wedding, the king, the queen. Lethargy crept over her. When Edmund hadn't been waiting in the chapel, nor Guy, her will had trickled away as if 'twere sand in a broken hourglass.

Her only hope was that Guy would burst through the door at any moment and take her away. And if life were kind, Edmund would be with him.

Tears stung her eyes. She choked them back as she had in the chapel, refusing to do aught but hold her head high and do as she must.

Cris had told her Guy was free, but she'd had no chance to speak to her brother since then. So much time had passed. Where was he?

What if Guy were dead?

Nay and nay, Guy was *not* dead! She would know it.

She placed her hand on her belly. Even now, his child might be growing within her. At the first possible moment she must slip away and speak to Cris. She would ask to use the privy.

Martin froze in his circuit of the bedchamber. "Are you listening?"

Before she could answer, he gripped her arm in a bruising hold and shook her. "Are you not listening to me?" he asked. "When I speak, you'll listen."

She bowed her head.

"When we go back to the table, you'll smile. You'll tell the king how happy you are."

"What of Edmund?"

He shook her again. "This isn't about your brother. And he'll need to choose when he learns how this wedding enabled me to end a war with nary a drop of blood shed—unless we count yours. For you'll be bloody if you don't obey."

A glimmer of hope rose in her breast. Martin spoke as if Edmund was alive. Then Martin's words penetrated her concern.

"End this war? What are you saying?" She searched the room for a weapon, realized she had naught to defend herself save her swan dagger. She faced Martin, who stood before her, legs spread, arms crossed over his chest.

"You're mad." The words were out before she could stop them.

His eyes glittered with anger, then his mouth twisted into a smile. "Am I? I've contrived to end this war between King Stephen and Empress Maude with the simple—and brilliant— expediency of a wedding."

"How does our wedding end a war?"

"I've taken the prince."

She backed away. He was mad. She must get away from him.

"Aye. Your brother's enjoying the company of Prince Eustace in his little cell."

Joia had been too sunk in her own misery to notice the prince was missing. Before she could draw her dagger, Martin grabbed her arms. He forced her back against the wall, pressed his body to hers. He whispered in her ear. "I intended taking the king. Baldric was to do it, but I saw just as fine an opportunity, an easier way, so I took the prince instead."

So that was the reason for the king's harsh looks at the wedding.

My plan works with the prince as well as with the king." Martin encircled her throat with fingers that were icy cold. "Eustace is arrogant and stupid. I had but to ask him to step into the chapel and approve the arrangements there—as if I cared one jot for his opinion—and he did it. I took him out with one blow to the head. I put him in one of the priest's robes and hauled him away. Anyone would think I was helping a drunken Father Ilbert."

"Why, Martin? Why?"

"Simple." He thrust away from her as she jerked her knee up. "Ah, a sweet move, that one. Baldric!"

Joia's stomach knotted when Baldric stepped into the room. He drew his dagger. "Is she troubling you?"

Martin snorted in derision. He pointed a finger at her. "If you make trouble for me, lift your knee or your hand to me, I'll send Baldric to take a slice out of your precious brother."

"You were friends with him, Martin. You grew up together."

"And he has what I want. It's time I got what *I* deserve. I served your father for years, took the crumbs. And what do I have for those years? Land on the Solent, and a directive I build a castle there. Do you know what I said to the king a few hours ago when he was instructing me as if I were one of his masons?"

Joia shook her head. The man before her was not the same one who'd run and played at Edmund's side. That man was lost in this one's madness.

"I told the king I had his son. I said I'd kill the prince if Stephen didn't do as I said, nay *ordered*. And it seems the king is fond of Eustace and has agreed to trade himself for the boy. He agreed to say the prince was ill and would rest during the wedding.

"The king will meet with me—alone—at midnight at the ford of the Tavest. I'll have a boat there ready to take him away. When I give the signal we're clear, Baldric will release the prince—and your brother."

"Martin, you cannot do this. It makes you a traitor."

He smirked. "A traitor fights for the *losing* side. I've a seagoing vessel at my new manor on the Solent, and I can have the king in the Empress Maude's hands in the turn of a tide."

"Maude will ransom Stephen back," Joia said, hating the quaver in her voice when Martin took her hand and raised it to his lips.

He grinned. "That's why I'll give Stephen to Maude's husband. Geoffrey of Anjou knows how to win a war. He'll have learned from Maude's mistakes, and I'll accept no paltry land on the Solent as my reward. I'll settle for no less than an earldom. I'll demand your father's lands and your precious Robin's as well." He pulled her around and ran a hand over her breast. "Will it not please you to be the wife of an earl?"

The mist had spread, had become a dense fog. Guy took comfort that as it slowed his progress through the woods, it would also slow a search by anyone who might visit the crypt and discover the captives gone.

Guy's first thought was that he should have lain in wait in the crypt but as he reached the edge of the king's encampment, he knew he hadn't the strength to take Baldric, even if the man were alone. His tunic was soaked with blood. His head pounded.

He knew none of the guards on duty at the camp's perimeter, but he joined a group of servants who dragged sledges of firewood to the king's camp. They knew him and accepted his presence without a word. They must not have heard of his imprisonment and were grateful when he offered help. He kept to the left of the men so they'd not see his bloody tunic and ask questions. When the wood was delivered, he melted away between tents and found his father's.

Every moment's delay chafed and the music and sounds of revelry from the castle stoked his anger and need for revenge.

For Joia. For Alan. For Edmund.

And what of Crispin and Lady Blanche's pain and misery?

The day waned, the light almost gone. Inside his father's tent he knew what he'd find. Pallets neatly rolled. Traveling chests in a line, weaponry ready, armor likewise. No father, no brothers. Guy wondered if they'd been in the chapel, if they might be in the hall if he needed them. Would they do as he asked—

instantly—without question or comment?

Never.

Guy threw up the lid of one coffer, that of the older of his two brothers who was like him in size, and drew out what he needed. His mind was finally clear as he stripped from his bloody garments. He made a pad of cloth and bound it over his wound and then garbed himself as he'd done a hundred times albeit more easily with the help of a squire or page. He donned gambeson, hauberk, and tunic. When he was done, he was once again what he had always been—a knight.

He belted on a sword and long dagger and drew on a helm to conceal his identity. To the guards outside, he looked like one of them.

He was one of them.

He strode through the tents, the fog swirling away from his feet, through the castle gates unchallenged. Servants rushed about like wraiths in the foggy, torchlit twilight burdened down with platters of steaming meats and towering sweet cakes, great jugs of wine and ale.

He should have no trouble entering the hall. What he would do when he got there was not in doubt. He would kill Martin Hursley.

FORTY~TWO

Joia sat between Martin and Baldric. She now saw what Martin said must be true. The king didn't eat, no matter what her father pressed upon him. King Stephen's cheeks were pale and Queen Mathilda's likewise.

Martin leaned near her. "You look around this hall as if you expect someone. You know I've secured Crispin's guard in the gatehouse, don't you?"

"Why would Crispin's guard be of interest to me?"

She tried to rise, but Martin clamped his hand on her thigh.

"I must use the privy."

"Then Baldric will take you there."

She seethed inside as Baldric dogged her footsteps. As they returned to the high table, Joia turned on him. "I'll speak to Crispin and you'll stand aside." The man backed off but only a pace, but she thought it enough. Crispin stood by the hall doors, peering out into the fog. She knelt by him and put her arm about his waist, hugging him close. "What do you watch for, my love."

Crispin gave Baldric a fearful look and leaned his head against her shoulder and whispered. "Guy. Tink and I set him free, Joia, but he was very bloody."

Bloody. "When? When, Cris? When did you set him free?"

"In time. Before you married Martin."

So long ago. Hours. And Guy was bloody. All her fears for Guy, fear he might be dead rushed in. Her hands trembled as she smoothed Crispin's curls. "Keep watch, Cris. For me."

Baldric took her arm and almost dragged her back to Martin's side. She picked at the nuts and sweetmeats. She gripped her little swan dagger and wondered how she could use it against these men, but each time she looked over at the queen, she reminded herself that any action she took might have dire consequences. Could she not just rise and shout to the assembly that Martin had kidnapped the prince? Demand her father's men take action?

Would the king deny her words for fear of his son's life?

What of Guy? Set free before the wedding and yet he'd not come. And bloody, Crispin said.

Each time the far doors opened, she looked there in hopes it was Guy come to save her. She watched Crispin dallying at the doors. Eudo and Godwin strolled the hall, singing a song written especially for her and Martin whilst other men, garbed in red and gold in honor of the king, danced in the aisles.

Baldric and Martin cheered a tumbler who performed in front of Stephen. She wished she'd bought the ugly dagger that day Guy had lectured her on a blade's purpose. She much desired to kill Martin for his treachery, giving him one jab for every drop of blood Guy might have shed, and when Martin was dead, she'd deal with Baldric.

Guy entered the hall unchallenged just as he'd passed through the castle gates. He looked about. Jugglers and mummers tumbled and danced among the tables. Eudo and Godwin sang. The king, at the head table beside Walter, was milk-pale.

Next to Walter sat Hursley, smiling broadly and whispering in Joia's ear. On her other side sat Baldric. She wore a gown of brilliant blue. Around her neck were chains of gold, entwined with magnificent cabochones of amber. More amber shone in the gold circlet in her hair. She looked like a pagan princess.

Until he'd entered the hall, he'd thought of only one plan. Kill Hursley. But too many of the man's company were interspersed with the king's and Walter's. They weren't attending to the entertainment but on alert.

Guy felt a tug on his tunic. He looked down and saw Crispin. Before the boy could speak, Guy hauled him away from the door and put a finger to his lips.

Crispin nodded as if part of a great secret and whispered, "I knew it was you! I knew it the instant you walked in. Why are you wearing that tunic?"

Who else had noticed him, Guy wondered, but as he glanced about, he thought no one paid him any heed. He'd thought the helm and tunic enough of a disguise. Now, he wasn't so sure. Then an idea struck him. He crouched by the boy. "You've proved a good soldier today. You set me free. But I don't want anyone to notice me yet—"

"You're evading notice."

Guy touched Crispin's curls. "Aye."

"Joia's worried. She told me to look for you."

Ah, Joia, he thought, Am I too late to help you?

He lifted Crispin's chin. "If I ask you to do something for me, would you do it even if your father might be angry later?"

"I'll do whatever you ask."

"I want to walk through the hall, to the high table. I want to walk right up to Sir Martin and challenge him."

Crispin's eyes went wide. "Everyone will see you."

"Aye. That's why I need you. I want them watching you."

"They're watching the jugglers."

"Not really. See, the king and Martin are pretending to watch."

Crispin craned his neck, went up on his toes to see where Guy indicated. Then he nodded.

"So, do you remember pitching stones?"

Crispin grinned. "I can do it quite well now, can I not?"

"You learn quickly and now, you must put your lesson into practice."

Crispin put his arm around Guy's neck and put his lips near his ear. "Where would I find a rock? And can I hit Martin in the head?"

Guy squeezed the boy. "I think his chest is a bigger target. Could you not borrow a juggler's ball for a few moments? You're not to injure Sir Martin, just make him angry enough to look at *you*, long enough for me to walk from here to there."

"And you will kill him?"

Guy did not answer. His very being cried out to kill the man for taking Alan, but as Guy examined the high table, he knew Hursley's death wouldn't please the king. Guy was sure the king would want Hursley's death for himself. The king carried a sword and dagger and knew how to use them—enjoyed using them.

Guy stood, put out his hand and clasped Crispin's small one in his. "Go, Crispin, show me all you have learned."

The child skipped through the crowd, spoke a moment to one of the jugglers who grinned and patted Crispin's head. A moment later, Crispin stood on a low stool before the high table. He began to juggle. Hursley and the others watched.

Guy gripped his sword hilt, wanted to charge, but waited on the boy. Crispin tossed the colored balls about in the air as deftly as the jugglers who watched and laughed, many around them joining in. Then Crispin turned and threw hard at Hursley, hitting him on the shoulder with one wooden ball and in the arm with the second. The ball bounced into a tower of cakes, dripping with honey. They cascaded across the table.

Guy strode through the hall as Hursley and Lord Walter leapt to their feet and screamed. Crispin lobbed another wooden ball. It hit Hursley squarely in the chest.

Joia rose with her father, shocked by Crispin's attack. She put out a hand to ward off the splattering honey.

Then she saw him.

Guy strode through the hall—straight toward them. Her

heart leapt into her throat. She knew him despite the helm, the tunic, knew no other man who moved as he did or held his head so high.

She watched him come, watched his sword clear its sheath. She took up her swan dagger.

Guy reached the head table. He took Crispin by the back of his tunic, handed him off to a nearby servant, stepped onto Crispin's stool, then onto the table. He stepped across the carcass of a swan, and set his boot on Martin's chest.

Before anyone could speak or react, Guy stamped down, tipping Martin over onto his back. He pressed his sword to Martin's throat.

Behind him the hall fell silent.

"I arrest you in the name of the king," Guy said with a snarl. "I arrest you in the name of the king for the taking of Prince Eustace."

A gasp ran the hall. Baldric, still seated, shifted. Joia thrust her dagger deep into his hand, pinning it to the table. He shrieked, and with the sound, the hall erupted into pandemonium.

King Stephen rose as if he were suddenly ancient. "My son?"

Guy pressed the sword tip deeper into Martin's throat. Joia watched blood well around the wound and wanted Guy to thrust the blade home.

"Prince Eustace is well, sire," Guy said.

The king sank into his seat. "Thank God. Thank God. Men, my men. Seize him."

Joia sank into her seat as the king had. Baldric ripped her dagger free and raised it. Guy shifted his sword. "Do it, Baldric. Make a move. This time, I will not stay my hand."

Guy watched Baldric drop Joia's little dagger and stumble back into the arms of the king's men.

The rest happened in an ordered flurry. Hursley was dragged away, screaming protests. Guy remained where he was on the table, legs spread, and looked down on Joia. Her cheeks were flushed. She stared at the sword in his hand. He sheathed it and pulled off his helm, eyes only for her.

"Sir Guy," the king said. "I should've known 'twas you." He turned to Walter. "There's none so faithful as this man."

Walter's hand shook as he lifted his goblet of wine to his lips. "*Sir* Guy?"

"Of Chelten," Guy snapped at the baron. "I serve the king. I found your son and the king's imprisoned in the crypt of St. Cedric's church. Edmund is alive, though half-starved."

"Edmund? Edmund!" Walter's goblet fell from his hand and rolled across the table, spilling what looked like blood across the white linen cloth. Lady Blanche's lips went white; she burst into tears. Walter wrapped his arms around her and buried his face in her hair.

Joia ran around the table and put out her hand.

Guy stepped down from the table and took it, lifted it to his lips. "Forgive me my tardiness."

She gripped his hand, her eyes swimming with tears. "Thank you, for Edmund. When may we see him?"

Before Guy could answer, the king pulled him away, asking the same question of Eustace.

The crowds parted for them. Guy accepted the touches of congratulations and slaps on his back though he knew the crowd didn't comprehend anything that had transpired save Hursley was under arrest and the king pleased, especially pleased with Guy, and many wished to be a friend to one who pleased a king.

Guy saw his father and brothers waiting at the door. They all looked much alike, tall and dark, though his father's hair was threaded with gray. Guy threw up a staying hand lest they say anything to him. They'd said enough when he'd vowed to find Alan.

Guy told the king he'd muster men and bring in the prince. He felt the return of every ache and bruise, knew his side was seeping blood. He cared only to see his son and think about the consequences of Joia's marriage.

He ordered a group of men of Walter's garrison to round up Hursley's men ere they disappeared into the forest. He then picked the party to bring home Edmund, sent a servant to fetch clean clothes for the prince, and accepted the boy's dresser as one of the party.

He ignored everyone who wanted to speak to him as he made his way to the stables. He ordered horses saddled and a cart prepared with two well-stuffed pallets. He ordered a groom to gather food and watered ale, another to gather some decent garments from the laundry for Edmund and Alan.

With an entourage of ten mounted men, three grooms, and the dresser, Guy left the castle grounds for the burial barrow. There, he first brought out the prince, chafing at the many moments the royal servant took to ready the prince to return to Stonewold. 'Twas almost midnight ere the prince was finally mounted and escorted away. Guy kept only the Rogers to help with Edmund and Alan.

Guy assisted Edmund to his feet and stood off when the young man insisted he'd not be carried this time. He helped him strip and garb himself in clean linen and wool, gave him a wet cloth to wipe his face and hands, and settled him on a pallet in the cart.

Then Guy went back into the burial barrow, setting the torch to the side. He went down on one knee and looked at his son. Alan had tracks from tears in the grime on his face.

"I'm come to take you to Stonewold Castle. I guarantee you'll not be treated as a prisoner, but as a guest." Guy prayed the king would agree. "When you're strong enough, I'll see to your safe conduct—wherever you choose to go."

Alan nodded, swallowed, and bowed his head. He didn't speak.

Guy placed his hand gently on his son's head, smoothed over the filthy curls matted to his scalp, as he might have Crispin, then he gathered Alan into his arms and carried him from the barrow.

FORTY-THREE

Joia knotted and twisted her hands in her skirt. Queen Mathilda had kept her sequestered in the solar since Martin had been dragged away. She felt like a prisoner in the room now divided into so many cell-like spaces.

What was wrong? What was happening below? She desperately wanted to see Guy and Edmund. She'd been listening to the raucous sounds of revelry filtering up from the hall for what seemed hours.

The door opened. She stood and then sank into a deep curtsey to the king and queen. Behind them were her father, Edmund, and Guy.

The king came forward to embrace her. "Forgive the long wait. Your father wished to fete your brother's return."

Joia wondered why she'd not been invited to take part as well. Stephen patted her back as if she were a child. She tried to keep her eyes on him, could barely restrain herself from running to Edmund, who leaned heavily on their father—or to Guy who stood still as a Sentinel in the stone circle. The king linked his arm with hers and drew her to a padded bench. "I fear I have sad news for you."

She realized her mother was not here. She pressed her hand to her lips. "My mother?"

"Your mother?" The king looked puzzled. "Nay. This news is of your husband."

"My husband?" She looked around the solar.

"Sir Martin. Your husband."

Queen Mathilda sat beside her and took her hands. "Sir

Martin will be hanged for conspiring against the king."

Joia could only nod.

"As his wife, you'll likely be much troubled with this shameful matter. The king and I believe you should be sheltered from his misdeeds. Your father suggested, and I agree, a convent will be a most peaceful place to await Sir Martin's fate. I've ordered our faithful servant, Sir Guy, to escort you to St. Mary's ere he returns to his duties."

Sir Guy. Our faithful servant.

Joia felt the heat rise on her face. She controlled her panic. "But sire, it was not a true marriage. Martin's threats to Edmund forced me into this wedding. Surely, 'tis not valid without . . . without the consummation of the vows."

The solar was silent save for the crackling of the fire in the hearth. Joia looked from the king to the queen. The king looked away. Mathilda cleared her throat. "My dear, Sir Martin has been examined at great length, and he assures us you consummated the vows."

Joia leapt to her feet, went to the king, and dropped to her knees. "Sire, I protest. Martin—I'll not call him Sir, for he has displayed none of those qualities one ascribes to such—Martin has *never* touched me." She bowed her head and folded her hands in prayer. "I swear it. I swear on my mother's head, Martin never touched me."

Her skin crawled from the intent scrutiny she knew was on her. It was only the king's presence that prevented her from running to Edmund, to Guy, to beg their help. They stood in silent attention beside her father, who wouldn't meet her eyes.

"Sadly, my dear," the king said. "There's no way to prove who speaks the truth here. Martin assures our queen he consummated the vows in the hour you spent alone with him after the ceremony."

Joia felt anger and grief roiling up inside her. "Sire—"

The queen lifted her to her feet. "Fret not. Sir Martin will be duly hanged for his treason, and then you'll be free. Meanwhile, go gently to your fate. Our good knight will see you to the convent, and we suggest you go immediately. Pray for Sir Martin's soul."

Her father stepped forward, but Edmund placed a hand on his arm. "Father, I wish a moment alone with Joia."

Joia looked at Guy. He stared ahead as if he were any soldier of the king's company who had no interest in the matters before him, his gaze on the wall opposite. No flush colored his cheeks, no emotion seemed to choke him as it choked her.

Sir Guy. Faithful servant.

Guy followed her father and the king and queen from the solar. Joia waited with hands folded until they were gone, her head respectfully down, then threw herself into Edmund's arms. She couldn't stem her tears. "Oh, Edmund, I thought you were dead. We grieved for you." She kissed his cheeks. "You need a bath. And soon."

He laughed and she delighted in the smile on his face. He leaned on her arm and hobbled to the bench where she wrapped her arms around him.

"Martin's mad, Joia. He'll hang and you'll be freed. It won't be long. In the meantime, you're safer in a convent."

"Why? Why can I not stay here with you?"

"I've proved myself rather poor as a protector."

She laid her head on his shoulder. "Oh, Edmund. You're all I need."

"Indeed, I'd have said yon knight is more what you need."

She broke from Edmund's embrace. She paced the small space of the divided solar and hammered her fist into her palm. "Why did he not speak? Wretched man! What held his tongue? And why did he not save me from this fate? Why did he not speak? Wretched, wretched man!"

Tears ran down her cheeks. How could she gainsay a king?

Edmund cleared his throat. "Ah, Joia, I simply meant Sir Guy is likely able with that sword on his hip and can *protect* you better than I."

Heat flushed her face. She sank down beside her brother and dashed away the tears. "Oh, he's more than able with that sword."

"Do you have feelings for this man?"

Joia shrugged. "Feelings? That's too mild a word for what I have." Her head ached; her eyes burned. She leapt to her feet again, paced the solar, then sank back down beside her brother again. "How can the king believe I was bedded by Martin? Do you think Guy believes it? What am I going to do? Take me to a convent? He knows how wretched I'll be there. Why does he not contradict the king?"

Edmund stroked her hair. "I imagine no one contradicts the king."

Joia bit her lip. She was on the verge of tears again. She pressed her fingertips to her lips. "Of course, I must call him *Sir* Guy. I love him. Love him! I'm not ashamed to admit it to you. I told him of Martin's plan to present you in the chapel if I agreed to say the vows. Guy promised—nay, swore—he'd step in before the vows were said then guard you so Martin couldn't hurt you. But he ended up in the gatehouse. How? How? Wretched man. What did he do to be sent there? Something with that sword, I'll wager." She took a shuddering breath. "He let me marry! How dare he fail me! It was a perfect scheme. My own scheme. Mine!"

"As I recall not all your schemes were so perfect."

She sighed. "I had to agree to the marriage. Martin threatened your life if I didn't, but I thought it unlikely Martin would keep his end of the bargain, and so I asked Guy to help me. It was so simple. I walk to the altar, Guy stops the proceedings, demands you be released. If naught else, questions would be raised. Martin must produce you then. But father locked Guy in the gatehouse. Why?"

Edmund took her hands. "You're babbling. Father said it was some confusion about spying. No matter. It matters only that all is well now. We find that Martin only insisted on the wedding to draw the king here. It appears he intended taking the king, himself, but found easier pickings in the prince. Had Guy not rescued us, the king would've traded himself for Eustace at midnight. Martin's plan almost worked."

Joia swept her hand through the air as if swatting a fly. "He was late. Late, Edmund."

"And as for being late for the wedding, I believe Sir Guy was rescuing me as you wished. Did you know his son was imprisoned with me?"

Joia nodded, but Edmund was wrong—all was not well. She was wed to Martin, going to a convent by the king's order. "Guy said he was in search of his son, and Crispin said he was found with you. What is he like, this errant son?"

"I like him very much. He saved my life and was taken in the process."

"Oh, poor man."

"He's not much more than a boy, but still he saved me. Alan was squire to one of the Earl of Chelten's knights. When the earl gave his allegiance to the empress, Alan went along. I think he regrets the effort. I know he was greatly distressed by how his family, his father, must view him."

"Guy said his father cast him off for searching for Alan."

Edmund sighed. "What trouble we sons cause our fathers. I spoke to the king, and he agreed to let Alan recover here as thanks for saving my life. When Alan is well, the king will give him safe passage to Gloucester or Chelten, or should Alan wish, he may serve the king without penalty."

She heard movement and voices in the partitioned chambers of the solar and bit off what else she wanted to say. Some had tired of the revelry below and sought their beds. She signaled Edmund to lower his voice. "I would meet this son of Guy's."

"Mayhap you can meet all of them one day."

"*All* of them?"

"Ah. Alan has two brothers younger. Albert and Adam. And a sister, Adela, a year older and much like you in that she's not happy with her father's choice of husband for her."

Joia stared at Edmund. "More secrets. The man has too many secrets." She counted on her fingers as she spoke. "Alan. Adela. Albert. Adam. Has the man no knowledge of the rest of the letters?"

Suddenly, she realized that although Guy had told her his reason for being at Stonewold, he'd not done so willingly. He'd never mentioned this unhappy daughter. He'd had so many opportunities to tell her of himself and yet, he'd held himself apart whilst she'd poured our her fears and desires and told him she loved him.

Had she been building castles in the air?

She felt the rush of heat to her face. "How could he not trust me? How could I know nothing of him? What must he think of me?"

"I'll speak to the man for you, if you like. He's rather a formidable looking person, but if you managed to fall in love with him, well, he must be approachable . . . somehow."

Joia gripped his hands. "Never! Edmund, never! Say nothing. If *Sir* Guy didn't trust me with the simple information that he has four children. *Mon Dieu*, four. Four! Then I want nothing to do with him. Nothing."

There had been so many opportunities for him to speak. It was a rejection of her on the most simple level. That rejection was worse than Martin's assertion they'd consummated the wedding vows. She forced herself to be calm, not to allow her brother to see the pain that threatened to destroy her.

"Well." Edmund coughed into his hand. "Shall we change the subject from the formidable Sir Guy to our mother? What of mother, Joia, she looks quite frail and ill."

"Father has treated her most miserably by flaunting Avis, but she and Crispin were terribly ill, mayhap poisoned—"

"Poisoned?"

Joia quickly explained how things had gone since the eating of the pears. They speculated on how the poisoning tied to the taking of Prince Eustace. "At least their illness seems to have brought Mama and Papa together. Whether it will keep them together is another matter. As long as Avis is here, she'll divide them."

Edmund squeezed Joia's hand, anger in his voice. "I'll see to

Avis."

"I'm so glad you're well." She stroked his hair from his face. "How could Martin have done this terrible thing?"

"Juvenal once said that no man became extremely wicked all at one time. He's not the man I grew up with. He seems consumed with greed and even more so since Isabel's death. Mayhap his friendship with Baldric contributed. Baldric was always contemptuous of Sir Godric's authority, though father could never see it. But you must not fret whilst you're at St. Mary's. Martin will pay for his crimes but I, I shall mourn the friend he once was."

They sat in silence, Joia's head on Edmund's shoulder. More of the king's retainers entered the solar, and Edmund stood up, groaning as he stretched sore muscles. "Now, you must gird your loins and see Sir Guy." Edmund embraced her. "He's a hard man, according to his son, a man who gives no quarter, has no heart. Mayhap you were misled in your understanding of his intentions. At least ask him about his children."

"I cannot. I will not." Joia felt cold. She must think about how Guy had held so much of himself separate from her even at their most intimate moments, and she must find a way to persuade the king, or mayhap the queen, that she should remain at Stonewold.

Reluctantly, she accompanied Edmund to the hall and chafed at the many who rushed to bid him welcome. Crispin crawled into Edmund's lap. A stark realization hit her like a blow.

Crispin was now safe. They'd no more need of Guy's services. It was likely any of the men he'd trained could take on Crispin's lessons and do a satisfactory job of the task. It wouldn't be the job Guy could do; there was no finer man with a sword, but, in truth, even if Crispin needed Guy, the man would return to what he once was.

Crispin laughed. He wouldn't laugh when Guy left. And when the king left, Guy would leave. *Forever.*

Tears welled in her eyes. She hastily dashed them away lest anyone in the hall see her misery, and assume it had aught to do with Martin.

If Guy accompanied her to the convent, it would be a torture. She'd ask the king for some other escort if she couldn't remain at Stonewold.

She leapt to her feet and found herself at Crispin's chamber where Alan de Maci had been placed ere she could stop herself. She opened the door and saw Guy sitting on a stool by the bed. Alan was asleep. He was gaunt, a scraggly beard all that laid dispute to the young man in the bed not being a child. She knelt by the bed and inspected the bandages on Alan's wrists. "What did the physician say?"

"He'll recover."

"Don't let the physician bleed him."

"Of course." Guy folded his arms over his chest.

"Why did you not tell me this young man is but one of your many children?" She whispered lest she wake Alan.

Guy raised his gaze from his son to meet hers. He blinked as if startled. The silence stretched and before he answered, he looked down on his son again. "I have no answer. I'm . . . used to keeping my own counsel. I . . . I have no answer."

She couldn't prevent her voice from rising with her distress that he'd no reason to explain himself. "You didn't trust me."

Color suffused his cheeks. "Of course I trusted you."

"You told me the least of all you are. And worse, you told me when you really had no other choice. Had I not seen you with Alan's horse and taxed you with it, you'd never have told me aught."

Guy's eyes were in deep shadow. With only one candle burning behind him, she couldn't read his expression, but she could interpret his silence.

"Thank you for saving Edmund. I'll see my father rewards you."

She rose and, with what she hoped was dignity, she left him.

FORTY-FOUR

Prince Eustace, having celebrated for many hours, wanted his bed. Guy settled Alan on a pallet in one of the small spaces carved out in the solar. He'd have another pallet brought and sleep beside his son as he'd slept beside Crispin.

The small cell barely held enough room for two pallets and felt like a rat's nest. Guy stirred up the brazier and thought of Joia's words. He couldn't dispute any of them. He could make no amends, couldn't go back in time and speak. The moment was lost. As was she.

The thought was a vicious pain. He wanted to feel only joy that Alan was alive, but instead, felt as he might if given a fine sword only to find its edges pitted and dull. He felt bruised, her every word a blow to his composure.

The solar was like a rabbit warren now, every corner filled with the jabbering retainers of the king. They woke Alan, so Guy helped his son sit, offered him a cup of broth kept warming in the brazier. "This was made by a cook who has a special fondness for Crispin," Guy said. "He saw to the order himself. He's becoming quite a little tyrant."

"I must thank him. I feel as weak as a newborn colt." Alan sipped the broth then fell back into the pillows. "So, Lady Joia . . . what's between you two?"

Guy felt heat rush up his face when Alan arched a brow. *Sweet Jesu* how much had Alan heard of Joia's words?

"The two of you are more entertaining than a dozen of jugglers." Alan's voice was hoarse, dark shadows ringing his eyes. He looked haggard, his hand trembling on the fur that covered his knees.

Guy held out a basket. "Crispin sent you honey cakes."

"Better than that gruel." Alan dipped into the basket. "Lady Joia's very beautiful, and I must assume she loves you."

"It's not your business." Guy saw an unexpected grin light his son's face.

"All my life, I've watched everyone instantly obey you, give you complete respect. Suddenly, here's a woman who's not afraid to shout at you. I'd find a way to make her happy if I were you. Aye. It's not likely there are *two* women in the kingdom who would—or could—stand up to you."

Guy stared at his son. Then he grinned back. "She wasn't shouting. So, you learned more than sword play in service to the Empress."

Crispin peeked around the thin partition and threw himself into Guy's lap when he saw Alan was awake. He reached out for the basket of cakes with both hands. Alan grinned and extended it to the boy.

"Are these not the finest cakes in all of Christendom?" Crispin took one of the sticky cakes.

"Indeed." Alan smiled at the child, and Guy saw the man Alan would become. The ordeal had aged him in more than one way, made Guy realize just how far apart they were as father and son.

"In truth, I learned one shouldn't always blindly follow where led," Alan said, "I was so caught up in being squire to an earl's knight, a knight who never had an independent thought, I discover. Now, Chelten and Sir Edward rue the loss of their lands, and I the loss of my family, and," Alan took a deep audible breath, "I think part of me was pleased to anger Grandfather."

"And me, I imagine." Guy shifted Crispin so he could set his hand on Alan's arm. "I owe you a deep apology. I don't think I listened much to what you had to say. In having the care of this child, I've learned how little I influenced your growing up. How can I now chastise you for going your own way when I never forged any of your paths?"

Alan shook his head in denial. "You believed fostering me to Sir Edward's house would help me along in the world. If Chelten had remained loyal to King Stephen, you'd not be sitting here, would not have endangered your life, been rejected by Grandfather or my uncles. I've much to answer for. Edmund and I had many long talks during our imprisonment. I told him you were perfect, had never made a poor decision in your life, whereas I, I seem to trip over my own good intentions."

Guy stared. *Perfect?* Joia had also called him perfect. He'd never felt so far from that state in his life than at this moment. "Edmund explained how you risked your life to save him, a stranger. There's no finer offer a man can make."

"Aye, and I followed it by bragging of Grandfather, his wealth, and his connections to the king. At least it kept me alive for you to find."

"So, Grandfather came in handy, did he?"

"Aye. That man, Baldric I think his name is, said he would trade me for a goodly sum, though, in truth, I had to admit to the king, I never saw his face until he threatened Edmund. And I never saw Hursley at any time. Only the priest."

Guy shook his head. "Baldric's greed is also Hursley's greed. The man has a fine manor, was given an even finer one on the Solent, but still, he wasn't content. We've all called him mad, but mayhap all he was is greedy. He wanted to be a lord."

Crispin stirred in Guy's lap. "Edith says Guy is lord of the—"

Guy clapped a hand over Crispin's mouth. "I think 'tis time you sought your bed."

Crispin slipped off Guy's lap.

Alan grinned. "Who is this Edith and what does she say about you?"

"Nothing fit for your ears."

FORTY-FIVE

The next day, Guy went to the chapel to be sure that the king's guards were vigilant in their duties guarding Hursley who was locked in the priest's quarters. Guy thought Hursley and Baldric belonged in Stonewold's dungeon, in chains as Alan had been, but there was status to taking a king's son, and the royal lawyers and scribes, who must question Hursley, couldn't be expected to visit a dungeon and write in the light of a torch amid the rats and stink.

Guy paused before the chapel doors. The iron candle stands by the altar reminded him that he'd failed Joia. Would that he might have used one and brought Hursley down ere the vows were said.

A woman knelt on a *prie dieu*. Avis. Guy wondered if she prayed for Hursley's soul. She rose to her feet. He nodded. She didn't curtsey or acknowledge his nod, but swept past him, nose in the air. In that brief moment, when she turned, he saw something that gave him pause. He went in search of Edmund.

He ran Edmund to ground in Owen's chamber in the men's quarters. "Where's Owen?"

Edmund grinned. "Bedded down in the village. I think he'll never forgive me usurping his space. I'd have been happy in with the men, but my father wouldn't have it, and I'll not put Joia out, so I'm reacquainting myself with the castle records." He kicked his heel against one of the chests beneath Owen's bed. "I understand the king intends visiting the Solent castle site on the morrow and then returning for the Beltane festival." Edmund poured Guy a tankard of ale. "By-the-by, it appears the body in my grave was likely a poacher. I'm seeing he gets a decent burial no matter who he is."

Guy nodded, thankful it hadn't been Alan, but sorry for the hapless victim as well.

"I want to lay something before you," Guy began. "I just saw Avis in the chapel. When she rose from her knees, I realized she has a certain roundness to her figure." He laid out the issue of the poisoning of Blanche and Crispin. "We assume Hursley had something to do with the poisoning, but now, I'm having second thoughts. I cannot leave without its resolution. If Avis is with child—"

Edmund interrupted. "She may want to replace my mother and see my father acknowledges her babe."

Guy nodded. "If your father wed her before the birth of the child, and Crispin were gone, her child might inherit Stonewold."

"What of me?" Edmund gave a wry smile.

"Baldric claims Avis knew naught of their plot and thought you dead."

"He may be lying to spare her." Edmund rubbed the angry sores from his sojourn in St. Cedric's crypt that encircled his wrist. "I think I know how to handle Avis."

Guy saw much of Joia in her brother now he was scrubbed and clean-shaven. They shared the same fine features, deep blue eyes, fair hair, and determined natures. "Shall I play Baldric to your Hursley?"

Edmund grinned. "If you would. And if Avis insists she's with child by my father, well, he must see to its care. He owes his child, if not the mother. He can have her sent somewhere to await the birth. Then, if she's responsible for the poisoning, he can decide her fate. Even if only gone from here, well, my mother and Crispin will be safe."

Guy decided he'd kept enough secrets. "I believe there is something between Avis and Hursley."

"Hmm. *That* won't please my father." Edmund stood up and groaned. "I think my back is ruined forever. If Edith were not so enamored of that Harald, I'd ask her to rub it for me." He wagged his eyebrows at Guy.

Guy could find no humor in the matter.

"Come, you're far too serious, dour even. How did Joia ever fall in love with you?" Edmund shook his head.

Did every benighted soul in the castle know about them? "And what of Harald?" Guy turned the conversation.

"He wishes to wed Edith. I've no time to think about them. You've given me enough to worry about, and I think I'll not add matchmaking to my burden. I think ere I call for Avis, I'll take a quick look through her things. I find a woman's coffer a fascinating window to their minds."

FORTY~SIX

Edmund had Avis fetched to Owen's chamber. When she took a stool, Guy stepped from behind the curtain. Her face paled almost as white as the pearl-trimmed gown she wore. Her hair was bound up in a net stitched with pearls as well. She was more finely gowned than Joia.

"Avis, you're plump as a goose," Edmund said, leaning his elbow on the table as if he had naught to concern him, his manner pleasant, his tone friendly.

Her eyes widened.

"A goose, Avis. You look as plump as a goose. Are you increasing?"

Guy watched her face. Her eyes slid around the room, avoiding both Edmund and him.

"I don't think that's quite a question for the present company."

"Would you rather answer it with my father present? Or my mother?" Edmund stood. "Answer the question. You've no champion here; he's in chains."

Guy admired the way Edmund changed from pleasant son of a baron to the haughty heir to one.

Avis slipped off the stool, going to her knees. She dropped her face into her hands and wept—or feigned the weeping. Guy couldn't tell from where he stood. Had he ever had the skill to read a woman's intent?

"Enough," Edmund said. "Guy, take her to the dungeons. A few weeks in a cell will tell the matter. She'll either bleed or she won't."

Avis gasped. Color rushed up her face. "Nay, my lord, I beg of you. 'Tis as you say."

"My father's or Hursley's?"

She swayed on her knees. Her eyes closed, and her lips moved as if in prayer. They waited in silence. She crossed herself, opened her eyes, and met theirs. "Your father's."

"I'll ask you to offer some proof of that answer," Edmund said.

Avis babbled a jumble of words that, when stripped of entreaties and begging, revealed Hursley had been in Winchester being rewarded with land on the Solent when the child had been conceived.

Edmund watched her for several long moments, absorbing her words. "So, what do you hope for? My father's acknowledgement of the babe? A rich husband to raise a baron's by-blow? Marriage if my mother were dead?" Edmund stalked across the chamber and snatched Avis from her knees. "You bitch. You poisoned her, did you not? You tried to take her place."

"Nay, nay," she screamed, clawing at Edmund's hand, breaking open his scabs, smearing her fingers with blood. Guy didn't step in. The man deserved this moment.

Edmund cast her aside and threw a small, dirty pouch on the floor by her hand. She scrabbled away from it as if it might burn her fingers. Guy assumed it must have come from her coffer and must have held some form of poison that Edmund recognized.

"I want you to confess your sins, beg God's pity and forgiveness, for you'll have none from any with the name of Fortranne." He dragged her from Owen's chamber, to the keep, then down to one of the storerooms where Father Ilbert was on his knees at an altar he'd made in his confinement among the barrels of wine.

Edmund ordered Ilbert to hear the woman's confession. The priest nodded and put his arm about Avis's shoulders. She clasped her hands together and began a whispered torrent of words.

Edmund turned to Guy. "When she's done, lock her in one of the other storerooms. I don't want to kill her child, but I want her imprisoned in some way until my father decides her fate." Edmund watched the pair for a moment. "And I must decide Father Ilbert's fate as well." He sighed. "He's begged my forgiveness for not freeing me and your son. Had he only been afraid of his own fate at Baldric or Martin's hands, I could do it, but he wanted a bishopric. He's as greedy and sinful as they."

"Juvenal says, 'No man becomes—'"

"Completely evil all at once.' We read the same philosophers," Edmund said. "And I remember Ilbert's teachings and the many hours he spent with me—good hours. I read and write well—mayhap even think well—because of him."

Edmund leaned against the wall, and Guy felt the young man's indecision. "Mayhap you could have him sent to the archbishop. Let the church decide his fate."

Edmund left Guy. He listened to Avis's weeping voice droning, punctuated by Ilbert's soothing murmur of what Guy assumed was forgiveness. He looked away as Avis pressed the priest's hand to her cheek. Guy wondered if he'd have found some measure of peace if he'd confessed his overwhelming desire for vengeance to a priest?

Had Guy taken his vengeance in the hall and killed Hursley, the king might have been displeased. King Stephen had yet to discuss Guy's abandonment of his duties. Yet, king's pleasure or not, that vengeance would have freed Joia from Hursley. Now, one of King Stephen's closest men said the king wanted a lengthy, public trial to discourage his barons from attempting similar crimes against the crown. The bigger the trial, the more lawyers, the more words. It could be months. Guy thought of what Edmund had said. In a few weeks Avis would bleed or not.

And what of Joia? Was she increasing? Would his child bear the name of Hursley?

Joia took a candle from the small table by the steps to the south tower, lit it, and then wearily began the climb to the solar. She'd remained in the bailey as long as necessary for her to become exhausted. She'd inspected every flower garland, tucked fresh blooms where needed, ordered the rushes replaced, scattered herbs. She wanted no dreams of Guy to disturb her.

She yelped when a shadow coalesced into a man. His hand was over her mouth before she made another sound. His breath was warm against her cheek. "Do you never sleep?"

She relaxed against Guy's hard body. He encircled her waist. "Tom? We cannot meet this way."

She felt Guy's body stiffen, then he laughed and released her.

"Oh, 'tis not Tom. A pity."

Guy reached for her hand, but she moved down a few steps. "Nay, you cannot do this. I hate you."

He followed her down and cupped her face. "You don't hate me. You're simply angry—"

"There's nothing simple about my anger."

He continued as if she'd not interrupted him. "You feel I wasn't honest with you." He plucked the ribbons that held her plait. "I love your hair. I want to feel it against my skin."

"I'll not let you seduce me."

He sighed. "We need a place to speak of this trouble between us."

"The solar?"

"We cannot talk there. Your chamber?"

She shrugged. "Edith and Crispin are there." She felt a heaviness, a lethargy that she feared had no cure.

"I know a place where lovers sometimes meet."

"We're no longer lovers, Guy."

He gripped her arms and pulled her against him. "You're mine. I don't care if the king pardons Hursley or if he hangs him. You're mine."

She struggled against his grip. "Men. You think to make

claims, but you don't earn the right. Well, you've only earned an empty bed for your silence."

He held her tightly to his chest, and she knew she was powerless to break his grip. She sagged against him. "I must set this candle down, or we'll go up in flames."

He instantly released her. She tipped the candle, spilling wax on the step and then planted it in the puddle. She sat, her back against the wall. He stood over her a moment, then unbuckled his sword belt and set it aside. He sat on the step below her.

"You had many opportunities to speak, *Sir* Guy, and now you must listen."

He looped his arms round one knee, leaned back, and looked unconcerned in the flickering light. It angered her as much as his statement that she was his. "You could have spoken at the river." He nodded. "Or in the barrow when you asked to go to Fairoaks. Or when I taxed you over Alan's horse. The only answer is that you don't trust me."

"I trust you."

She wished he weren't in deep shadow that she might see him more clearly. Nay, she'd never seen him clearly.

"Four children, Guy? A daughter my brother says is in conflict with you over whom she'll wed? And no wonder you can make Crispin behave. You've had four children to practice on."

"I beg to differ—"

"I'm not finished. You've been silent so long, be silent for a few more moments. And what of their mother? Is she the wife you lost? Or were there *mothers*? Or a bevy of mistresses? Or mayhap a company of mistresses, an army of them for all I may know? You might also have spoken when . . . when we were together in the garden. When I asked you who you were with your wealthy man's buckles and boots." She'd bared her soul to him. She thought she must do it one more time ere she left. "You promised you'd never hurt me. You lied."

He leaned forward and took her hands. He raised them and kissed the backs. "I'll tell you who I am. I'm the veriest fool in Christendom for not telling you everything at once. I can only say, as I did before, that I've always kept my own counsel. Gossip is deadly, Joia, court gossip especially so, and with this turnabout of Stephen's barons, I've found myself even less likely to speak. And yet, that's still no excuse."

He shrugged and leaned back, distancing himself again. "I came believing Alan had been imprisoned here, that despite your father being King Stephen's man, he was my enemy for taking my son. I thought only to find Alan and go. And then I found myself entangled and trapped."

"Well, you're free now. Take your son and go."

He shook his head. "I berated myself over why Alan would choose a path different from mine. I never really listened to him. I can order men and they obey, but 'tis not enough. I can wield a sword, but *that* is not enough. The night before your wedding, I thought I'd figured out Hursley's plot, that he'd taken Edmund to force you to the altar, and if Edmund was alive, who was the man in his grave? I thought 'twas Alan. I've been wrong in every way."

She took Guy's hand. She'd sensed something wrong that night, but not pushed him to speak. If he had, could she have offered him any comfort for a son's death?

His fingers curled around hers. "If I hurt you, it was never my intention. I cannot leave you at St. Mary's. I will not."

"Will not?" It was an arrogant statement and yet, she found her eyes filling.

"I'll ask the king if I may remain there with you in some capacity."

"You could offer to spy on the nuns for him."

"At least you'd be a boarder, not a nun. I failed you."

"Nay," she said softly. "You saved Edmund. Never think I'm angry you missed the wedding, never that."

"But you're tied to Hursley."

"You saved Edmund. That's all that matters."

The candle flickered in the centers of his eyes. Eyes that she would never forget.

"My children all have the same mother, who died birthing

my youngest, Adam. I keep no mistresses. I've never loved a woman until you, not even my wife, although I held her in great esteem. I've no excuse for my silence and cannot promise I'll not disappoint you again in the future."

"Oh, Guy."

She bowed her head, but he lifted her chin and kissed her lightly on the lips.

"I must know of your daughter and her betrothed."

He stood up and raked his fingers through his hair. "Enough of betrothals. I surrender. I shall write to her on the morrow and tell her to pick her own damned husband, beggar, pig keeper, or thief!"

Joia smiled. "I wish to meet your children. I already like Alan—" She leapt to her feet. "Guy! You're bleeding."

He put his hand to his side, but she pushed it away. "Come. Let me see to this." She snatched up the candle and ran down the steps, glancing over her shoulder to see if he followed.

She led the way to the small chamber among the storerooms where the physician plied his trade. He was not in the chamber, and when Guy ducked his head and entered, she barred the door. "He's probably drunk in the village somewhere. Take off your tunic and shirt." She lit every candle and then searched among the physician's shelves until she found needle and thread. When she finally turned, she gasped. He was black and blue, the pad of bandages about him dark and crusted with dried blood. Baldric had enjoyed his few moments alone with Guy.

"I should've bought that other dagger and planted it in Baldric's chest for this," she said as she untied Guy's bandages. His wound was angry along the edges, seeping blood from stitches poorly done. "Can you not feel this?"

"I've had worse."

"Nonsense. You've barely a mark on you. Lie down. Stop! Remain where you are. There could be fleas—and worse—in that bed. Just lean on the table." She prepared a poultice of goose grease and herbs and heated them over a brazier.

When the mixture was ready, she set the warm dish by him

where he stood, arms propped on the table, the muscles in his arms taut.

He was a feast for the eyes. One she must ignore.

She quickly snipped away the physician's stitches, cleaned the wound with hot wine, and then stitched it anew. He made not one sound as she worked, though the wound was deep and ugly. The man was stone.

Finally, she packed it with new cobwebs that abounded in the physician's space and then smoothed on the poultice. "I'll bind this, and we're finished."

She padded the wound and wrapped clean linen about his middle, trying to ignore his hard chest and abdomen. When she knotted the linen, she stepped away and washed her hands in a basin of clean water.

"Are we finished?"

Before she could answer, he took her into his arms, and she knew he wasn't speaking of his wound. She ran her hands over his hard-muscled arms, then laid her cheek against his heart that beat so quickly.

"I cannot promise I'll not hurt you in the future, but I cannot let you go."

She reached up and pulled his head down, kissed him silent. His manhood pressed thick and hard against his braies as she undid his laces.

Moments later she stood in his embrace, skin to skin. "I'm afraid to touch you," she whispered. "You're so bruised."

He drew her hand to his phallus, saying, "One place unbruised."

He groaned as she encircled him and stroked him to even greater tumescence.

He kissed her breathless, then backed into a chair. She climbed astride his lap and sheathed him. She pressed down, slowly taking every inch of him, relishing how perfectly he fit inside her. "Don't move. Not yet. I want to . . . feel you inside me."

He moaned. His manhood pulsed. She pressed her forehead

to his and savored the still silence around them, the heavy scent of herbs, the thud of his heart, the hard length of his shaft filling her.

She combed his hair from his brow and stared into his beautiful eyes.

He cupped her bottom in his palms and smiled. "You want me to tell you again that I love you."

She couldn't help smiling back. "Will I always have need to pull every fact from you as the physician pulls rotten teeth?"

"That's not what I want in my head at this moment." He kissed her, gently. "I love you, Joia. You're as important to me . . . as my sword."

She shrieked and slapped his shoulder, but doing so drove him even deeper within her and she lost her ability to speak. She pressed her face into his throat and reveled in the feel of his hard thighs flexing beneath her and the hard length of him sliding in and out of her as he lifted her on his shaft.

His eyes closed as he lost himself, but she remained outside herself, watching. She wanted to remember the thousand shades of brown that mingled in his hair. She wanted to remember how his skin felt beneath her fingertips and lips.

She kissed up his throat to his jaw, his cheek, rough with the day's growth of beard. She wanted to remember the taste of his mouth, how his tongue moved on hers, stoking the fires within her, and how his hands felt gripping her buttocks.

She planted her feet and rode him.

She reveled in his groans each time she lifted nearly off him, then plunged down to take him deep.

His muscles jumped taut. He sealed his mouth to hers. They breathed the same air. His fingers dug into her and he came, moaning through the climax.

When he was gone—and she was sure he would need to go—she'd remember every nuance of this moment, how the pulse in his throat throbbed beneath her lips. Her insides clenched as she felt his final thrusts and the heat of his seed pouring into her.

He wrapped her tightly against his chest, his breath rasping by her ear. Every part of him, every texture, scent, and taste were hers, if only in this moment, she thought, as she met her own exquisite end.

FORTY-SEVEN

Joia surveyed her small chamber, soon to be returned to Edmund. Her coffers were now on a cart ready for transport to St. Mary's. Her dun-brown traveling gown lay across a stool. Her cushions would remain here, no faeries allowed in the convent according to her mother.

She had no polished steel to see herself, but she hoped she looked her best in her sky blue gown embroidered with gold thread. She slid her little eating dagger into her gold-embroidered purse. Edith had polished her hair with a silk cloth until it shone. She'd wear no head cloth this last night, for she knew hair was a vanity in a convent to be concealed at all times. Finally, although she knew 'twas foolish, she tucked a few bluebells into her garters.

Men moved up and down the steps to the ramparts, changing the guard. She heard every scrape of a boot, every whisper of mouse and man. She was intensely aware that Guy had slept only a few steps away in the solar after they'd parted the night before. She'd dreamt she could feel the press of his weight on her. The soreness of her nipples and that special place at her core were not dreams. Nor was the slick, slippery feel of his seed. She tortured herself with the memory of his calloused hands on her.

Guy had said he loved her, but had also followed it with a jest. Did that diminish his declaration? At least they'd have some time on the journey to speak of his intentions for when . . . nay, she'd not think of Martin. She pressed her hands to her face.

What if Guy's jest meant he didn't really love her?

Lust was simply not enough. She'd forget the lust, would she not? The nuns would scour it away with prayers and penance. And she'd be grateful to them if Guy hadn't meant the words.

Her father had pledged a year's board to St. Mary's with many words composed by Owen of what her father would expect returned upon Martin's death.

How coldly her father had written of that distant day. She'd thought she wanted Martin dead, but when she'd seen it written, she'd realized she pitied him as much as she hated him. She just wanted to be free. She must pray that when he was taxed by the king's lawyers, he'd confess to lying about the consummation.

She stepped into the stairs. There were so many torches in the hall, it looked as if 'twere filled with sunlight. The hall had been finely decorated for the wedding and now, it was even more so, laden with greenery and the blooms of pear trees, cowslips and bluebells in honor of Beltane.

Joia found herself seated between her mother and the queen. Her father sat beside the king, her brother next, and to her consternation, Guy sat next to Edmund. The two spent most of the meal deep in conversation. She strained to hear their words, but the hall was a babel of voices. Eudo and Godwin performed a round in honor of Prince Eustace. They, and other singers, repeated it endlessly to the prince's delight and to her desire to break the rebec over Godwin's head.

She couldn't stomach the peacock in wine sauce, nor the delicately poached quail stuffed with sweetmeats, although it would be the last of such fare for many a long day.

The king rose and lifted his goblet. The hall fell instantly silent. "I give you Lord Walter's health."

They all drank to her father, whose men stamped their feet in accord with the king. The king continued. "I also want to express my gratitude to one man, the man who rescued my son." The king grinned. "Words are well enough, but accolades are better."

The king was very handsome, Joia thought, his charm evident. No wonder so many barons followed him in preference to Maude who had a haughty, disagreeable manner, but King Stephen had his own faults, Joia knew, just as all men did.

"I am this night," the king continued, "awarding our most faithful servant with all Martin Hursley's lands, coin, men and weapons, horses, pasturage; I need not enumerate it all. Let the lawyers do that!" The hall burst into a cacophony of cheers and stamping feet.

Joia watched surprise run over Guy's face. He rose, went to the king and went down on his knee. The king urged him up, and Guy returned to his seat, high color on his cheeks.

"See," the king said to the company, when they finally fell quiet, "the man is speechless. Another trait I much admire."

And the one trait that gives me much pain, Joia thought.

"On the morrow, I intend leading a party to Sir Guy's manor to inspect a castle site. I hope Sir Guy won't mind resting his sword until Solent Castle is raised."

The king lifted his cup and for the next few minutes, man after man called out toasts for Guy, who must, by tradition, lift his cup and drink.

He'll need to be carried out on his shield, she thought. And now, now when I cannot have him, he's suddenly a landed knight with all the properties my father much covets married to the king's admiration and indebtedness. That Guy would be so close, just hours away from St. Mary's, would be a torture.

Queen Mathilda touched her hand. "We'll take you with us on the morrow and leave you at St. Mary's. I told Stephen I want to see you settled myself."

I will survive this.

As the evening waned, as the many gathered were felled like trees from a surfeit of wine and ale, she gathered her courage and went to Guy. He immediately rose and bowed. She curtsied. "Pleased I am at your good fortune, Sir Guy. I wish you all the best, with all my heart."

He took her extended hand and raised it to his lips. "I wish you all the best as well, my lady." He said no more, nothing of his heart, and she slid her hand from his.

As she headed for the solar, one of her father's men bowed before her. "My lady, Father Ilbert begs a few moments of your time ere you leave for St. Mary's."

With a sigh, Joia followed the man from the hall down to the storerooms. The light of the many candles on Father Ilbert's altar bathed the vaulted chamber in gold. "How may I serve you, Father?" she asked.

Ilbert snatched at her hand, pressing kisses to the back. "I beg of you, please take me to hear Martin's confession and his apology to you for all you've suffered."

She jerked her hand away. "I cannot forgive him what he did to Edmund."

"He asks only that you listen, that you hear his apology for the injuries he has done you. Just listen, I beg your mercy on his behalf."

"And what of you? Have *you* made your confession?"

Tears ran down the priest's cheeks. "Aye. I'm so ashamed, but I know 'twould be most saintly of you to hear what Martin has to say."

The old man's tears didn't touch her, but she wondered if Martin would confess his lies about the consummation of their wedding vows. "I'll do as you ask—listen—but I'll not promise to forgive."

FORTY-EIGHT

A page summoned Guy to Lord Walter's chamber. He groaned. More ale or wine to be drunk, he imagined. He only wanted his bed. Nay, he wanted to find Joia, find a quiet corner and make love to her as many times as he could ere they left on the morrow. He'd not yet told her he'd see to any child she'd conceived, and do so with joy.

He'd not told her enough how much he loved her. He wanted there to be no question that she was his when the doors of St. Mary's closed behind her. She needed to know he'd be standing at the convent doors the moment she was freed.

When a servant opened Walter's door, and Guy saw the row of men assembled there, he stiffened. He made the requisite bows to the king and ignored his father and brothers.

The king frowned. "I understand there are hard feelings amongst the de Macis, and I'd have them done with."

Guy didn't speak.

His brothers looked to their father as they always did. His father's mouth was a thin line of displeasure. "I believe I may satisfy you, sire," his father said. "Guy has chosen to take the side of a son who followed the Empress Maude. There's nothing else to say." He bowed to the king.

"What say you, Guy?" The king leaned back in Walter's chair and rapped his fingers on the arm. It was a sign of his displeasure. A small hint to his mood.

"You ever have my loyalty, my sword, sire. Alan has asked to make an oath of fealty to you, so 'tis for you to decide if you'll accept it or not."

The king waved his hand. "What's one simpleton squire? He begged my forgiveness for following that ass Sir Edward, so I've forgiven him, as I likely will Sir Edward should he come to his senses. Now, I want to see some forgiveness amongst you men or my patience will be sorely tried."

Guy's father bowed stiffly to the king. "If you've seen fit to forgive my grandson, then I must as well."

"Embrace," the king ordered.

Guy knew the king wanted only a public mending and cared little how they might behave behind closed doors from now on. The king had made his point. He wanted no more trouble from the de Maci family. Guy decided one of them should move. He went to his father and embraced him, moved down the line and gave each of his brothers the same. Their faces ranged from stoic compliance to a rueful grin from his oldest brother who was more tolerant and thoughtful than the others.

Guy made his escape ere the king decided to bring up the matter of Guy's abandonment of his duties at court. He looked about the hall, but Joia was gone. He inquired in the solar, but Edith said she'd not sought her bed, and in truth, the maid had only noticed Harald's place among the throngs of people still celebrating.

He stood at the keep's door and surveyed the crowded bailey. He no longer cared if anyone questioned his interest in Joia. "Has Lady Joia passed this way?" he asked the soldier there.

"Aye. She accompanied Father Ilbert's guard over an hour ago. I saw them head for the chapel."

Guy frowned. "Father Ilbert? The chapel?" A feeling of unease seized Guy. He ran down the steps and pushed through the crowd. As he neared the chapel, he broke into a run.

"Is Lady Joia within?" he asked the guard who stood before the chapel doors.

"Aye, she and Father Ilbert."

Guy threw open the door to the chapel. It was well-lighted with candles on the altar and in Joia's great iron candle stands. He saw no guards at the door leading to the priest's quarters where Hursley and Baldric were housed.

He drew his dagger and eased open the door, then threw it wide. The stink of blood and bowels filled the antechamber. He ran past the two guards who lay in a pool of blood, their swords and daggers missing, and threw open first the priest's bedchamber door and then the other. The table was littered with a prisoner's meal, a chair on its side. Guy dropped onto one knee by Ilbert. The priest's eyes flickered open as Guy pressed a hand to his throat. Whereas the guards' throats were cut, this man had been gutted.

"Joia. Where is she?"

The priest coughed blood. Guy leaned low as Ilbert tried to speak. "Garden. Martin. I told him . . . the king . . . inspect—" The priest coughed more blood, his lips stained black. "To inspect castle site. He intends taking him."

Guy cushioned the old man's head with an altar cloth. "Where's Joia?"

The man groaned. His hands fluttered over his eviscerated belly. "She. Martin." The priest shook, gasped, and coughed a final gout of blood. Guy closed the priest's staring eyes.

He leapt to his feet and flung open the door to the garden. The two guards who had the duty there lay naked, stripped of their garb—the king's garb—their throats slit, eyes staring at the heavens.

The benches had been stacked up against one wall. Guy didn't need to see the bloody hand print there to know the way the men had gone—over the wall, through the deserted practice yard, and likely through the gates with the many who flowed in and out for Beltane, secure in the king's colors. But how had they secured Joia's cooperation? He went ice cold as he envisioned Joia in Baldric's hands.

He searched the ground and saw among the men's footprints, the signs of a woman being dragged, her toes digging furrows in the dirt.

Guy ran through the chapel and sent the guard to raise the hue and cry, then ran toward the stable, heard his name, turned and saw Edmund and Alan. Guy kept running, calling over his shoulder, "Joia's taken. Hursley and Baldric killed their guards, stripped them."

"You'll want your weapons," Alan called. He ran in a loping limp toward the men's quarters.

"I'm coming with you," Edmund said as Guy reached the stable.

"I cannot wait for you," Guy said, throwing a saddle on de Lorien's destrier. "If Hursley gets to France, he's lost."

And so is Joia. Lost. Wed to Hursley. Forever.

As he tightened the girth, Alan limped in, half-dragging Guy's weapon pack. Guy tore the pack open and pulled out two short swords and a long dagger. "I'll not need that," Guy said of the shield Edmund brought forward, and "I've no time for those," when Edmund offered a mail shirt and spurs.

Wordlessly, knowing it was important to his son, Guy submitted only to Alan, who helped Guy belt on the sword and dagger. He vaulted into the saddle as Alan slid the second sword in the saddle's sheath.

Alan stepped back, but Edmund clung to Guy's saddle. "You'll not find them. They could be anywhere. You must wait. My father's assembling a company."

Guy shook his head. "I'll not wait. Ilbert said Hursley thinks to see his plan through, taking the king when he inspects the castle site on the morrow. That tells me Hursley has men waiting. Enough men he thinks he can challenge however large a party might appear. I intend overtaking them ere they reach those men."

"Madness."

Guy shook his head. "I cannot let them reach the Solent. With this moonlight, I can move quickly. Tell Walter to look to his maps." Maps Guy could still see clearly in his mind with roads to the Solent and waterways deep enough for ships. Guy was also sure Hursley and Baldric knew every path well by now. How many of their trips to the castle site involved the plan to take the king?

As Guy urged the horse forward the people in the bailey scattered. He heard men shouting, running, orders called. He kicked the horse to move.

Hursley and Baldric were on foot. But for how long? He must trust Joia to hinder their every step. And Guy knew, when he found them, he would kill them. No mercy, this time.

FORTY~NINE

Joia did all she could to slow Martin and Baldric. They dragged her into the woods where they were met by a band of disreputable men who had a few horses. Cold fear ran through her. She understood what Martin had done with his hours searching the forest for the brigands after their attack. He'd not been hunting them, nay, he'd been enrolling them to his cause.

Baldric threw her down in the heavy roots of a tree. Her stomach rolled; she fought the urge to vomit against the noisome gag fashioned from a strip of Father Ilbert's robe. Baldric's blood-stained tunic sickened her. It had been Martin who'd killed the guards with the daggers Ilbert had brought hidden beneath his robes. And foolish, foolish, Ilbert had stared in disbelief when Baldric had turned one of the blades on him.

Trust no man, Guy had warned. Now, she must pay for that error.

It had been child's play for the men to climb the garden wall and disappear through the practice yard. Her one chance to cry out when they reached the bailey, for they must pass through the gates, had come to naught when Baldric struck her. She'd woken in the woods, bound and garbed in one of Father Ilbert's robes, being dragged between the men who now wore the dead guards' tunics. Who else had they killed?

Her head throbbed. She looked about for some way to escape, but Martin glanced over to her every few moments. She heard only scraps of conversation among the men, though most of what she heard concerned payment for some task Martin set before them, or, more accurately, lack of payment if one judged by the rising tones of the men's voices, the snarling as if they were a pack of wild dogs.

She muttered a prayer when she saw one of the brigands, a man she recognized from the attack on the road from Fairoaks, hand Baldric an ax.

Martin approached her. She scrabbled back against the tree roots, her heart in her throat. He lifted a curl of her hair and brought it to his lips. "I love your hair. I want to see it spread across my pillow." He drew a dagger and sliced the lock off, tucking it into his tunic, then lowered her gag. "Come, wife, no need to shrink from these fine men; they know you belong to me, and they'll soon be gone. I'm sending them to warn the others."

"What others?"

"All those I have awaiting my arrival. This time, we'll need to take the king on the road."

"Martin, this is madness. Why not just hie to France?"

"Nay, I *must* take the king. And likely it will be a simple matter for he is arrogant. He'll want to hunt me himself, and that will be his undoing. Now, up." He grabbed her arm and jerked her to her feet.

"You're a traitor, Martin."

He grinned. "Only if I lose. I'm free at the moment, so I'm just another man who fights for the Empress. And these men," Martin gestured to the brigands, "they care not a jot for whom I fight."

The party of brigands melted into the forest, all save Baldric who idly hefted his familiar ax.

"Gag her," Baldric ordered.

Martin ignored Baldric, ran his dagger tip along her lips. "Do I need to gag, you, wife, or will you be silent?"

"Silent," she whispered, hating the quiver in her voice as Martin lifted her into the saddle and mounted behind her. She barely kept her balance with her hands bound.

The men argued a moment over her gag, Martin winning, but Joia imagined it wouldn't be for long, as Baldric seemed to hold sway over Martin. How much of Martin's actions were at

Baldric's prompting?

They followed a deer path. She tried to get her bearings, and realized they were circling, likely to see if anyone was following. She noted the position of the moon, tried to guess how long they'd been on this road. Not long.

Baldric kept his voice low. "Martin, how will you pay the men?"

"I'll see to them," Martin whispered back.

"We must go to Fairoaks. We've enough there to pay them."

"If we take the time to go to there, we'll miss the king and worse, the tides."

"If we don't go there we'll have no men to take the king."

An idea bloomed in Joia's mind. "I can help you."

"Be silent," Martin said with a hiss.

"I can help you. I swear it," she said hastily when Martin grabbed the rag still looped about her neck and made to shove it into her mouth.

"You can help me by stopping your mouth."

"I know of buried treasure in the stone circle."

Martin pulled up his horse and gripped her chin. "Treasure? What treasure?"

Baldric drew beside them. "We must to Fairoaks or the Solent. Now. Whilst the moon is up. She's simply delaying us. Let me see to her."

Joia jerked away from Martin's grip. She thought to simply fall from the horse, but to do so might break her neck or mayhap worse, bring down Baldric's wrath. She forced herself to straighten her spine and shrug. She kept her voice pitched to a whisper. If she could delay these men, surely someone might track them. "There's a sword with a sapphire the size of a goose egg buried in the stone circle."

Baldric and Martin exchanged glances.

"Where?" Martin asked.

"At the base of one of the stones."

Martin pulled her close. His breath, scented with stale wine, bathed her face. "How do you know of this sword?"

"I saw Guy de Maci bury it the night he came to Stonewold," she lied.

"I told you he was up to something," Baldric hissed.

He circled his horse and Joia feared he'd ride off, causing Martin to follow.

"Had you not insisted on keeping his son, we'd be free of the man. I'm cursed by him."

Joia thought 'twas a good thing, this anger between friends.

But suddenly Baldric smiled and said, "Then let us relieve the man of his treasure."

They rode in silence through the woods, finally gaining the road that led to the henge. Once there, Martin tied the horses behind the same deadfall where she'd concealed Flora the night Guy had come to Stonewold.

Baldric pulled her from the saddle. He jerked her against his bloody tunic. She felt the swelling of his excitement at having her in his power, but forced herself to pretend no reaction, lest it encourage him

Martin snatched her out of Baldric's arms. "She's mine. Remember that."

She felt like a child's toy, being pulled back and forth between the men.

She allowed Martin to lead her through the trees. She wondered if anyone had found the dead guards. She pitched her voice for only Martin's ear. "I'll not run away, Martin. Please, my hands are numb. Untie me."

Martin turned and slapped her, driving her to her knees. "You'll not order me, wife."

A surge of anger swept through her. "Wife? I'm *not* your wife. I don't recognize the vows we said." Another idea prompted her to say, "Nor do I recognize the church in which we said them."

"What?" He froze, his hand raised. Then he dropped it and laughed softly. The sound rippled along her skin. She shivered.

"We must move," Baldric said, jerking her to her feet. This time, Martin didn't object as Baldric pushed her along, falling into step behind his friend. When they reached the edge of the woods, they halted.

The stones looked as they had one month before, gleaming in solitary splendor on the rolling heathland. To the south, the road to the Solent was a ribbon of white. Joia imagined if the king were not at Stonewold, the villagers would be here. Dancing. Worshiping. Making love.

Her throat ached. It was here she'd first seen Guy. Would he come after her?

"This is nonsense," Martin said, his gaze sweeping the empty circle of stone.

"The men won't challenge the king if there's not some surety they'll be paid. We've nothing, Martin. *Nothing.* Why should they do aught for us? They're mercenaries. They only fight if paid." Baldric impaled Joia with a hard look. "If she's lying, we'll simply bury her in the stone circle next to the non-existent sword."

"They'll be after us, may already be on our trail."

"They won't know we're gone for hours, and you know Walter's ways—he'll send a company after us. They'll have torches. We'll see them—and hear them—ere they see us."

Joia sensed Martin weakening. She imagined he oft gave in to Baldric's plans. She also sensed they'd lost interest in any danger she might present. She wanted them to think her harmless. "Martin, we should wed whilst in the circle."

The men turned and stared at her. She shrugged. "I practice the old ways. What do you think I was doing in the circle on the last full moon? I said I don't recognize this marriage. Mayhap a druid can be found. He could wed us. 'Tis Beltane after all." She looked hopefully about as if searching the shadows for signs of druids.

"Druids? You're the one who's mad." Martin barked a short laugh, took her arm, and led her across the dry moat to the embankment and up. He hesitated before passing between two of the stones.

Did he feel it? The eerie silence? The thickness of the air? The holiness of the place?

He stepped in, pulling her to the altar stone.

"I'll not consider this a true marriage if we don't say our vows in the circle." Joia dropped to the ground, leaning back against the stone.

"Oh, 'twill be a true marriage if I take you here in the dirt."

She couldn't conceal a shiver at his words.

Baldric drew his dagger. "Which stone?"

She hesitated. "It looks so different from this position."

Baldric drew his blade down her bodice, slicing her gown open. "If you cannot remember, you're of no use, are you?"

She froze, Baldric's blade cold against her skin, a warm trickle of blood tracing her breast. Martin made no move to interfere, just crossed his arms and watched.

"Let me think. Please." She lifted her bound hands and pointed to one of the smaller perimeter stones. "I think . . . seventh from the entrance. There. At the base. The other side."

The men ran to the stone, attacking the turf with their daggers. She worked at her waist, contorting her hands, straining against her bonds to reach her purse and the swan dagger inside, then stopped when Martin glanced over at her. She seethed with anger she couldn't quite reach the little dagger. She inched around the altar stone, inspecting the grass. She saw naught to tell her where Guy had buried his sword. As she felt around, she knew she couldn't let them take her beyond this place.

She should have bought the killing dagger.

She tried to remember some of the tactics Guy had taught the men. She could, at least, kick one of them in the bollocks. Her nails broke as she scraped at the rough grasses, the ropes cutting into her wrists. She must get to her dagger or Guy's sword. Her purse swung against her thigh, dislodged by her efforts to dig in the turf. She used her thumbs to spread open the purse and grip the swan dagger, almost crying aloud in frustration as it slid from her fingertips. Then she hastily threw her skirt across it when Baldric came and crouched before her. "The sword's not there. Now, where is it, you lying bitch?"

She licked her lips and wondered how far she could push him. Not far. "Mayhap I counted wrong. I told you, it looks so different sitting down here. Let me think."

He hauled her to her feet, his dagger against her throat this time. "Find it. Now. Or I'll kill you." Then Baldric lifted his head.

A horse.

The sound was muffled here in the circle, its hooves sounding an unearthly drumming on the heath.

"*Merde*," Baldric muttered, thrusting her aside. She scrabbled for her dagger and turned it inward, cringing at the pain in her wrists as she sawed at the ropes. Martin remained crouched at the base of one of the stones, blade stabbing the earth, unheeding of the horseman who approached.

Guy rode into the stone circle.

Just as the rope parted about her wrists, Baldric pulled her before him, much as Guy had done a few weeks before. Martin ran to where they stood, drawing his sword.

Guy contemplated them in silence. She felt his scrutiny almost as if it were his hand he skimmed across the men, her gaping bodice, the blade at her throat. He stepped down from his horse, pulling his sword from its sheath. Blood trickled down her neck, across her chest.

"We *will* kill her," Martin said.

Guy stood there, legs spread, the sword in his right hand. He fisted his left hand and slammed it into his chest. "She is *mine*."

Baldric thew her aside, and in concert the men rushed Guy. In one smooth motion, Guy pulled his long dagger from his waist.

Joia swallowed a scream as metal clashed with metal. Baldric circled to Guy's left and Martin to Guy's right. They hammered his blades with frantic blows. She dropped to her knees by the altar stone and hacked at the turf with her little blade. The men drove Guy toward the tallest Sentinel stone.

Or was it he who drew them away from her?

Frantically, she scrabbled about in the dirt for Guy's sword. He parried their blows, never attacking. They turned and twisted, moving quickly.

She almost cried aloud with relief when her fingertips encountered leather. She hauled the rolled bundle from the dirt and did cry with frustration at the knots securing the pack. Finally, they parted.

She flung the oiled leather aside and stood, dragging the heavy sword with her as she moved toward the center of the circle.

Blood ran down Guy's arm. Blood soaked his tunic from his old wound. Moments later, Baldric swung his ax, backing Guy into a stone, hammering again and again at Guy's sword until it spun from his hand.

Guy whistled. The huge war horse charged. Baldric stumbled back, momentarily separated from Guy. When the horse continued on, crossing the circle, not breaking stride, she saw why Guy had called the beast. He held another sword. Martin and Baldric attacked him again, this time it was definitely them who drove Guy toward the center of the circle.

She backed away. Her stomach rolled.

Why did Guy not just order the horse to kill them, run them down? But the destrier now stood on the opposite side of the circle, breathing heavily, snorting down his nose, lathered from his long run from Stonewold.

She heard more horses coming from the north.

Her father's men? Or more brigands?

She held the heavy sword before her, darting glances between Guy and Martin and Baldric.

A company of men and horses, Edmund leading them, coalesced from the night. She heaved a sigh of relief. The heavy sword trembled in her hands.

Edmund leapt from his horse, climbed the embankment, limping badly. She screamed as he drew his sword.

He ran to her side and hauled her so her back was against a stone, his eyes locked on the center of the circle. "*Jesu*, they'll kill him."

More men, armed men with torches, crowded into the circle, but none approached those who fought there. Instead, they formed a circle, a grave, silent circle.

Baldric worked with steady intensity, but Martin was in a frenzy, smashing his sword again and again against Guy's as if half-mad. Guy's intent expression never changed.

The men in the circle began to chant Guy's name and hammer their shields with their sword hilts. The rhythmic, clashing sounds seemed to echo and bounce about the circle. Her heart slammed in her chest, faster and faster with the noise.

And then she did scream, for the two men pressed Guy at the same time. Blood ran down his arm, dripping from his hand.

Joia ripped from Edmund's grip and ran at Baldric, raising Guy's jeweled sword. She swung it in a circle and smashed Baldric in the back of the knee as she'd seen Guy do. Baldric didn't fall, instead he turned to her, murder in his eyes.

The instant Baldric turned, Guy dropped to one knee, and thrust his bloody dagger up into Baldric's exposed armpit. He fell like a toppled tree. Martin stumbled over his friend, looked down, and Guy ran his sword through Martin's side.

Martin dropped his sword. The men shouted, hammering even louder on their shields. Martin fell to his knees.

Edmund limped to where Martin knelt. A hush swept around the circle until every man stood in complete silence.

Joia ran to Guy's side. He cast aside his dagger and took the jeweled sword from her hand. He clutched his bloody side and went to Edmund who stood over his friend. The circle of men edged closer. Only Martin's whimpers broke the utter silence.

"You held me prisoner," Edmund said, a tremor in his voice. "You threatened the life of an innocent man. You killed innocent men." Edmund raised his sword.

She knew what he would do.

Martin looked up from where he knelt. "I beg your mercy! Edmund! Edmund, 'tis me. Your friend." Martin's voice was a hoarse whisper. A black stain spread across his tunic from Guy's thrust. "Help me."

Edmund hesitated, his sword raised.

Joia saw Martin reach toward his boot.

"Edmund!" she screamed just as Martin lunged at her brother, a dagger in his hand.

Guy stepped between them, taking the blow against his sword. He tore the blade from Martin's hand and swept it across his throat. Martin looked up at Guy, surprise on his face. He toppled over, silent, eyes staring at the heavens.

Edmund discarded his sword and fell to his knees beside his friend. When Joia tried to run to her brother, Guy stepped in her way, wrapping his arm around her. "Leave him," he said softly.

She allowed Guy to lead her away, and knew Edmund would be plagued forever by his hesitation as it might have cost his life.

And she, she would never forget Guy stepping into Martin's blade.

FIFTY

"I want to kill them again for this blood," Guy said, running his fingertips over her skin. He tucked the edges of her gown together and sent her to stand by the entrance stones.

He distracted Edmund from his misery, urging him to direct the men who'd need to be led to the castle site on the Solent. Edmund only faltered once, when giving the directive to carry Hursley's body to Stonewold.

Alan arrived in a company of men, King Stephen at their head. To Guy's annoyance, the king considered him too injured to join the party.

Within moments of the king's arrival, the circle was empty and silent in the moonlight, the king's men a distant string of torches heading to do battle with Hursley's forces on the Solent.

Nay, it was not being left that made him angry.

He paced from stone to stone, sometimes pounding his fist on the lichened surface. Finally, he found himself before Joia, hands on hips. "What do you think you were doing attacking Baldric?" he shouted.

"Saving your life," she shouted back. "I watched many of your lessons. 'Tis not so hard, what you do."

He broke into a grin. "They were almost weary of their efforts, tired of chasing me about the circle. I needed no help."

She shrugged and walked to the altar stone, dragging his jeweled sword along behind her. He cringed thinking of what she was doing to the blade's edge.

He groaned aloud as she dropped it on the turf, then disappeared behind the stone. "A sword should be handled reverently," he said.

Her head popped up. "I suggested they use the sword to pay their men. I told them it had a jewel the size of a goose egg." She disappeared behind the stone again.

"Mayhap a quail's egg."

He heard a ripping sound and assumed Joia was slicing off the front of her hem with her little swan dagger, making strips destined to be his bandages. "You were cutting up your gown the last time we were here," he said when she came to his side.

She wore the blue hose. His whole body clenched.

She touched his arm. "This needs stitching, and you've opened up the other wound."

She helped him pull off his tunic and shirt. Her hands were none too gentle as she wiped the blood from his arm and side then bound up his wounds. She knotted a strip of blue linen at his side. "I'll stitch these when we return." She touched the arm wound. "One of them got you here. Careless of you."

He shrugged. "'Tis nothing. And I was not careless, I was allowing them——"

"I know, to exhaust themselves. And was the *chest* pounding a strategy as well?"

"Indeed. Angry men are careless."

"Careless?" She lifted her brows and looked at his arm. "Indeed."

She sacrificed more of her hem, and he allowed her to wrap the soft blue cloth around his arm as well. An awkward, heavy silence filled the air between them.

He couldn't stand still. He paced before the altar, watching her as she cut another strip from her gown, exposing even more of her lovely legs. She wiped the blood from his grandfather's sword, running her hand up and down the jeweled hilt. He felt each stroke as if 'twas on his manhood.

He was already hard. He grew harder still.

She met his gaze. "You saved Edmund's life—again. A magnificent sword for a magnificent man."

He took the sword and placed it gently on its oiled leather

wrap. "It was my grandfather's. I'll give it to Alan."

The moon was dipping behind the trees and the stones cast long shadows. It must be the first of May. "If we went back to the castle, I imagine we could enjoy the Beltane bonfires," he said.

"Or we could drink of my mother's special May Day mead," she answered.

"Or you could join the jugglers."

"Or you could Morris dance."

"I think not." He lifted her into his arms and kissed her hard, feasting.

He was hungry. Hungry in a frantic way and knew some of it was blood lust.

He set her on the altar stone. He threw up her skirts, standing one moment in reverent silence as he studied her blue hose. He plucked a wilted bluebell from her garter. "Do you always have flowers under here?"

"Oh, Guy." She dashed a tear from her cheek. "I was so afraid."

"It's over now. There's nothing left to fear." He knelt between her thighs and kissed the bare skin above her garter, and then licked up her thigh to her center, drew in the scent and taste of her. He found the swollen nub within the soft, warm folds and used his tongue and teeth to tease it, to stir her passions to match those that raged within him. He reveled in the slick heat that surely meant she wanted him as much as he wanted her. She fisted her hands in his hair and bucked against his mouth, crying his name.

He rose, lowered his braies, and thrust himself inside her, riding the lust that threatened to consume him.

She gripped his arms, gasping, dislodging the bindings there, but he cared not a whit. He moved within her in long, deep strokes. She met his pace, her eyes on his, her thighs so warm they almost burned him where they gripped his hips. Her hair flowed in a golden river over the altar stone, and it felt like silk when he cupped her head.

He claimed her lips. Her body.

He drove her to her peak, pushed her over, used his hands, mouth, and manhood to take her up again. As her sheath clenched around him like a hot silken fist, he emptied himself into her.

And knew complete peace for the first time.

FIFTY~ONE

The sun shone in a deep blue sky. The grass within the stone circle sparkled with morning dew. Joia rose and left the circle to pick a few bluebells among the trees.

She walked back to him, slowly, plaiting the bluebells into a garland for her hair. His eyes never left her. He lay on their clothes, his hands behind his head. He was very intent on her every move, she noted. Very intent.

He was black and blue, bandaged, beautiful and naked.

She sighed and knelt on her gown. "'Tis said a child conceived on the first of May is truly blessed. And should that child be conceived in the fields, it blesses them as well."

Guy absently rubbed his hand over his chest swathed in bandages. "There are no crops to bless here," he said, rising and kneeling before her.

She set her hands on his shoulders. "Then we shall bless these flowers instead." She checked his bandages to be sure they were secure. She ran her hands down his arms—slowly—to savor the warrior strength of him, then entwined her fingers with his, raised them and kissed them. She pressed her lips to his palms, first the right and then the left.

His hands had touched her both gently and roughly the night before. She craved both.

"I washed my face in dew this dawn whilst you slept," she said. 'Tis said to offer one long life."

His eyes were the palest of blue in the morning sun. She brought his hands to her breasts. She wanted to make him groan and gasp and moan.

323

She combed her fingers through his thick, dark hair. "If we were in the keep, I would bathe in lavender-scented water. For your pleasure," she finished in a whisper.

He moaned as he bent his head and kissed her. He ran his fingers over her nipples, raising an intolerable ache there. He kissed her throat, her shoulder, and her heart almost stopped beating when he moved his mouth to her breast. He gently kissed her wounds.

She arched under the warmth of his lips, his tongue, moaned herself as he scraped his teeth across her nipple.

She took his hand and drew it to her center. "Touch me here."

It was all she could manage. He did as bidden and slipped his fingers between her thighs. He caressed all the swollen, hot places that craved his touch.

He moved his mouth back to hers whilst his fingers aroused her to an unmerciful peak. She couldn't stand it. 'Twas torture. She broke apart, crying his name.

He took her hand and folded it around his manhood.

"Now?" he asked softly.

She guided him to her center. He slid into her. She clung to him, rode the tide of emotion she sensed rising within him. He braced himself up on his hands and watched her. She cupped his face, stared back at him, and willed him to speak.

But he was silent.

He moved with agonizing slowness, drawing out then pressing in on her. She cried his name again as another climax struck like a clap of thunder, stealing her breath.

He went with her.

Joia sat astride Guy's hips and studied him. He looked very complacent. "Do you think it terrible we made love within these stones?" He used the tip of her plait to tease her breast. She slapped his hand away. "Answer."

"Nay. I wasn't troubled about it last night, nor this morn. I think in some small way, we chased away any troubles that may linger here."

She waited, resisting the urge to fill the silence.

He grinned and kissed her fingertips. "I love you, Joia," he said, arching up and capturing her mouth, pulling her down over him.

She felt the warmth spread through her at his words.

"I love your skin. The way you smell. The taste of you. Here," he kissed her lips, "and here," he touched her between her thighs. "This love . . . it leaves me feeling utterly defenseless. You have left me with no weapons. I surrender all to you."

Her throat felt tight at hearing those precious words. She nuzzled his neck. "I love you, too, and I hope your children will come to love me, as well."

"I want to have my sons fetched from their fostering. My time with Crispin showed me how little I knew of Alan's needs. I'll not say the same of Albert and Adam."

"They must miss you very much. Will you fetch your daughter as well?"

"Only if she wishes it. She hates me."

Joia stared at him. "Oh, Guy."

"Mayhap when I've written to tell her to wed whomever she pleases, she'll soften to me."

Joia hugged him. "We'll invite her here. Curiosity to meet me will bring her close, and over time she'll see that you're a changed man."

"Am I?"

"Well, I hope not so changed. I liked the original from that first moment I saw you here." She swept out her hand to the stones.

His generous mouth curved into a wide smile. She wove a few bluebells into his hair. "*My* father shall likely see you as a suitable match now you've become a landed knight."

"I'll not ask your father for your hand."

Heat flushed up her cheeks. She slapped her hands on his chest. "So, you have your man's pleasure—several times—and then you think to abandon me?

"I didn't say that. I said I'd not ask your father for your hand. You want complete honesty, and I'm determined to fulfill my promise that every thought that goes through my head will come out of my mouth."

"So, what are you thinking now?"

"I'm thinking that if you continue to wriggle about on me, I'll have need to flip you to your back and have again—as you say— my man's pleasure."

She frowned down at him. "I shan't wriggle if you'll explain yourself."

"I simply meant that you need to tell your father your wishes. You are right that too long has he commanded you against your will. You're free now. Whenever I asked what you wanted, you always said freedom. It is the only gift I can give you."

His voice grew rough with emotion. "I'll wait as long as you want me to." He stroked her hair from her face. "I cannot say I'll wait patiently, but wait I will."

Her heart lurched that he offered her freedom and the time to enjoy it. "I can think of only one thing I want more than freedom and that's you. I cannot imagine you would ever make me feel like chattel. I want you, Guy. For my husband. Forever."

She crushed her mouth to his. He clasped her tightly to his chest. The heat that always seemed to shimmer between them flared anew. She smiled and wriggled her hips, trailing her fingers down his hard stomach and over him.

"If you touch me there I'll need to make love to you again."

"If you are capable of making love so soon after that last round, my fine knight, then you truly are, the lord of swords."

The End

AUTHOR'S NOTE

I wrestled with the Empress Maude's name. She's also correctly known as Mathilda. I chose Maude to differentiate her from King Stephen's queen who was also a Mathilda. In addition, I've taken a few historical liberties to suit my tale, but none that should make a scholar scream. Anachronistic words and phrases are my choice to ease the flow of the story.

ABOUT THE AUTHOR

***USA Today* Bestselling and award winning author, Ann Lawrence** writes both historical and paranormal romance. Her books take you from the pageantry of medieval England to the world of a fantasy war game with a stop off in an idyllic village in the Cotswolds. When not reading, writing, and researching romance, Ann's living the real thing with her husband in the Philadelphia suburbs. She loves to hear from her readers and answers every email personally, so drop her a line to tell her how you like her books!

You can find excerpts of all Ann's books as well as contests and news at Ann's website. If you want to know what's on Ann's mind, visit her blog and Facebook fan page. Truly passionate readers who will help spread the word are invited to join Ann Lawrence's Street Team.

AnnLawrence.com

MORE BOOKS BY
ANN LAWRENCE

*Ann Lawrence invites you to enter the time of Richard the Lionheart and meet
a trio of powerful warriors and the indomitable women who tame them.*

LORD OF THE KEEP

Gilles d'Argent is a powerful baron used to getting what he
wants, when he wants it—until he meets **Emma**, a humble
weaver. From the instant he passes judgment on her in his manor
court, he's as captivated as if she has woven a magic spell around
him. Is it merely lust? Or has he finally found love?

Emma is bound to protect her daughter, but her weaving
barely keeps them alive. Should she accept Gilles d'Argent's
protection, although it means placing herself within reach of a
man she fears? And will Gilles defend her once he discovers who
fathered her child?

LORD OF THE MIST

Durand de Marle rode out of the mist and Cristina's life
was never the same. Wife of a perfidious merchant, **Cristina**
fashions soaps, perfumes, and love potions for the ladies of Lord
Durand's manor. Can Cristina make a potion for herself...one
strong enough to resist the captivating power of Durand de

Marle?

Durand is a warrior lord who prides himself on his honor. Can he discover who has betrayed him? Is it his brother? A friend? Or yet another? And can Durand claim he's honorable if he can't resist the love and desire he feels for another man's wife?

LORD OF THE HUNT

Adam Quintin (from LORD OF THE MIST) is on the hunt for a traitor to the English crown. To find the traitor, Adam must join the many suitors of England's most desirable heiress. But no sooner does Adam arrive at Ravenswood Castle to begin his mission and his courtship, than his life is saved by Joan, the seductive daughter to the keeper of the hunting hounds.

Joan Swan has her own secret mission—preserve her father's livelihood as master of the hunt. Her task becomes nearly impossible as suitors flock to court the lady of Ravenswood. Can Joan protect her ailing father? Can she protect her heart once she falls in love with Adam Quintin, a man destined for her lady?

Ann Lawrence's Paranormal Romances

You don't have to believe in fantasy or magic to be captivated by Ann's "Perfect Heroes" series, they're virtually heavenly!

VIRTUAL HEAVEN

Nothing extraordinary has ever happened to **Maggie O'Brien** until the day she plays a fantasy game for the first time. When something goes awry, Maggie finds herself a slave in a frightening world engulfed in war.

Kered is a warrior tired of war. When he seeks the advice of a wise man, he finds a woman who can't remember who she is or where she comes from. His warrior code will not allow him to abandon her. And when he falls in love, he knows only one reality . . . he can't let her go.

VIRTUAL DESIRE

Tolemac warrior **Vad**, has only one desire—regain his sword and the warrior honor it represents. He's willing to do anything—even cross the forbidding ice fields into the unknown. When a beautiful and alluring woman appears to him, he's sure she's been sent to help him.

Gwen Marlowe desires only peace and quiet, something hard to find at her game shop in Ocean City, New Jersey. When a gorgeous war-gamer insists she "enter" a game and help him complete his quest, she thinks he's crazy. But soon, crazy or not, Gwen discovers she'll follow this captivating and sexy man anywhere.

VIRTUAL WARRIOR

Ardra needs a strong warrior to defend her fortress from the enemies amassing on her borders. When a stranger arrives, he suits all her requirements, but he's also devastating to her senses.

Neil needs a place to lick his wounds and thinks he knows just the place, a place of mystery and magic. When he arrives in Tolemac he's dismayed to discover Ardra thinks he's the solution to her problems. Neil's not so sure he wants to wage a war, but he is sure he won't fight too hard if—*and when*—Ardra decides to seduce him.

If you think evil can't reside in a picturesque English village, don't believe it!

DO YOU BELIEVE?

Rose Early earns her living photographing happy family groups. She views her world through a camera lens, and with her computer, can "fix" what she doesn't like. When Rose goes to England in search of her missing sister she meets **Vic Drummond**, horror novelist. Vic is fascinated by Rose's view of the world. She doesn't believe in love . . . or evil. Soon, Vic realizes he must change her mind about both!

To learn more about Ann Lawrence and her books,
visit her website.

AnnLawrence.com

CPSIA information can be obtained at www.ICGtesting.com
Printed in the USA
LVOW13s1503181013

357591LV00002B/339/P